FIVE STRANGERS

FIVE STRANGERS

E.V. ADAMSON

SCARLET
NEW YORK

FIVE STRANGERS

Scarlet
An Imprint of Penzler Publishers
58 Warren Street
New York, N.Y. 10007

Copyright © 2021 by Andrew Wilson Media Ltd.

First published in Great Britain by HarperCollins Publishers Ltd., 2021

First Scarlet edition

Interior design by Maria Fernandez

Library of Congress Control Number: 2021914484

Cloth ISBN: 978-1-61316-242-2
eBook ISBN: 978-1-61316-243-9

10 9 8 7 6 5 4 3 2 1

Printed in the United States of America
Distributed by W. W. Norton & Company

For Clare Alexander

1

JEN

From a distance it looks as though all of us are trapped in a spell. We are standing at the top of Kite Hill, on Parliament Hill Fields, gazing down at the city. Not many people speak, apart from the occasional brief comment about the changing nature of the London skyline.

It is an impossibly bright day, one of those afternoons when you can almost smell the optimism in the air. The sky is cloudless and blue, and the light is of such quality that everything seems precise and well-defined. But it is the unreality of the view, rather than its beauty, that has rendered us speechless.

There is a dreamy quality, too, in those strangers' eyes, as if all of us have willingly allowed ourselves to be drawn into a make-believe world. The city seems as though it is showing its best side. We are viewing it from afar, away from the ugliness of buildings seen at close quarters.

The spell will soon be broken by an event so horrific it will also seem like it could only exist within the realms of fiction. But for that moment—or rather, those long, lazy minutes before the incident on that day, 14 February—many of the spectators exist in a balmy glow of contentment.

It's Valentine's Day, after all. Couples have taken the day off work, or perhaps escaped their normal routine of a sandwich at their desks, to sneak away from their offices in order to climb this hill to admire the view. A dark-haired man in his twenties and his beautiful girlfriend, sitting on one of the benches, are sharing a bottle of fizz and some chocolates. An elderly couple stand hand in hand, eyes closed and heads tilted back to capture the full rays of the sun on their pale faces, before slowly moving on. A middle-aged man, who despite his age has the perfect skin and glossy hair of the rich, and his younger boyfriend sit at one of the other benches, stroking their sleek Weimaraner, their fingers occasionally brushing against each other's across the dog's elegant back. The younger one pulls out his phone and starts to take a selfie with their dog. As he presses the button even the dog seems to grin.

As I watch the other couples, drunk with love, I hardly dare let myself dream about tomorrow, about Laurence. Apart from the occasional text or email, I've had little contact with him since that awful night last year, but the next day we're due to meet up for lunch. I feel what I can only describe as a giddy fluttering of the heart, a delicious sensation of excitement and anticipation. Do we still have a future together? Is he ready to take me back? As soon as these thoughts enter my mind I push them away again. I can't allow myself to think like this. I've talked about my hopes with Bex, and she listened patiently to my fantasies of getting back together with him, before telling me that I was delusional. "Who'd want to go out with a mad bitch like you?" she said. Although I knew she was joking, there was an element of truth to this. I'm not the easiest person to love. I've driven some men away. But as I've often said to Bex, I'd rather be single than trapped in a loveless, failing relationship.

I'm meeting Bex here, halfway between Hampstead Heath and Kentish Town, and although it was her idea, there's no sign of her. We're going to have a coffee and then get the bus into town to see a film and grab some food. I also promised to have a glass of pink champagne with Penelope back at the house later. Penelope has been without her last husband for thirty years—she'd kicked him out on Valentine's Day, 1989—and this morning she had suggested a celebratory drink.

In the distance, a reflection bounces off one of the glass towers. For a moment I get the feeling I'm standing in front of a mirror. The whole skyline seems to melt away and I'm faced with nothing but a shimmering surface where once the city had been. I see myself as a young teenager standing in front of my parents' full-length mirror. I know the glass is showing me something I don't like. And then, with a blink of the eye, the skyline defines itself once more. I take a deep breath and squint into the horizon, making out the Crystal Palace transmitter and the hills of the North Downs. This is the here and now, and it is beautiful. The past I don't have to think about.

What is it that first alerts me to the fact that something is wrong? Is it the sound of a bottle hitting the ground? Or is it the stifled cry of the woman? I turn my head to see the young couple on the bench. The man has raised his voice and his girlfriend has started to edge away from him. I catch the eye of the older gay guy with the dog—both of us are probably thinking the same thing: should we intervene in some way?—but then the man on the bench puts his arm around his girlfriend and starts to apologize. She smiles and nods her head. Whatever argument they've been having is now over. I turn away and check my phone. It is 1:17 P.M. Where the hell is Bex? She is nearly twenty minutes late.

As I finish scrolling through my emails—still no reply from any commissioning editors to the ideas I had sent out that morning—I take in the scene around me. There is a young Indian woman wearing nice, expensive clothes sitting on another bench with eyes closed, headphones on, perhaps asleep, certainly dead to the world. A teenage boy has stopped to look at the plan of the skyline, his eyes flitting between what has been mapped out on the plan in front of him and the vastly different reality in the distance. An overweight, late middle-aged white woman, with a vaguely familiar but very red face, dressed in gray sweat gear, stops for breath as she reaches the top of Kite Hill. A male jogger, with a black hoodie pulled over his head, is running up the hill, racing past her when, in that instant, all of our lives change.

I say in an instant, but it happens both so quickly—as if time has somehow sped up—and also so slowly, the very worst things being cruelly dragged out as if to prolong the agony of it all. I hear the smash of a bottle and then a cry.

I turn around to see the young man pulling his girlfriend to her feet. He holds the broken champagne bottle to her neck. The liquid pours down his arm onto the front of his girlfriend's white blouse, making the fabric translucent. My first instinct is to rush over and cover her up. She doesn't need the world to see the outline of her breasts.

"You bitch," the man says, spitting out his words as he bends his girlfriend's left arm behind her back. "You fucking whore." He presses the sharp edge of the shattered bottle down onto her neck, drawing blood. A drop falls onto the collar of her white blouse. Her eyes stretch wide with terror and with her right arm she grapples for something, anything, she can use to defend herself. But there is nothing around to grab hold of apart from the top edge of the bench. Her fingers start to claw at the wood.

"Of course I still love you," she says. "Dan, I'll always love you, but—"

Dan draws her closer to him and she cries out in pain. "I told you I'd kill you and you didn't listen," he says. His accent is from the East End or Essex. "You didn't fucking listen!"

The older guy with the dog, who I later learn is called Jamie, takes a step forward. I notice that he looks pretty strong and muscular. What is he thinking of doing?

"You need to step away from her," he says. "I'm sure we can sort this out, make sure nothing gets out of hand."

"And what the fuck do you know?" shouts Dan. "Do you know what she did?"

Jamie raises his right hand as if he is trying to calm a wild animal. "What's her name?" he asks. There is no response. "What's your name, love?"

The girl opens her mouth to speak, but Dan raises the bottle and smashes it into her mouth. "Don't you fucking talk. Don't you say another fucking word!"

The girl's scream splits the air. Blood splatters across the front of her blouse. Her mouth looks like a mass of red ribbons. Her free hand comes up to try to dislodge herself from Dan's grip, but as she tries to scratch his face he tears into her flesh with the sharp edge of the bottle.

4

As Jamie rushes toward her, his boyfriend screams at him not to get involved, and the Weimaraner barks its own terrible warning.

Dan points the broken bottle at Jamie's head. "Take another step and I'll cut your face into pieces too," he says. "Get away from me you fucking queer!"

Jamie looks around him in a desperate bid for help. His boyfriend is talking into his phone as he tries to explain to the police what is happening, holding onto their dog, which is straining at the leash, going mad with anxiety and fear. The teenager has frozen to the spot, panic paralyzing him. The woman in the gray track gear has been forced to steady herself by one of the benches and looks as though she might be sick. The young woman on the bench still has her eyes shut and remains oblivious to the scene that is unfolding before her.

"Hey you," Jamie shouts to the jogger, who has slowed his pace slightly. "We need some help here, mate."

But the jogger, instead of stopping, seems to quicken his pace and continues to run over the crest of the hill.

"Stop!" Jamie shouts after him. "For fuck's sake—someone, please help! Alex?"

Alex shakes his head. He is too scared to move. Jamie begins to walk back toward his boyfriend, but then in a move that surprises us all, maybe even Jamie himself, he turns and launches himself at Dan and tries to take him down.

Dan tries to withstand the assault, whipping the bottle around his head with a frightening ferocity. Jamie manages to push the girl out of the way and she falls back onto the ground, her face a bloody mass. I run toward her, to try to get her out of the way, but I feel a kick in my stomach, winding me with such force I can't breathe. The next couple of seconds remain a blank for me, but when I come round I see that Jamie has managed to wrench the bottle from Dan's hand. The fight has not been an easy one. Jamie's own hands are cut, and blood pours from his wounds, staining his skin and his clothes. Dan has suffered in the struggle—there is a cut on his cheek, his wrists and forearms have been gouged by the bottle—but it's difficult to have any sympathy for him. The attacker stands there, head bowed, hands on his knees, as he tries to recover.

5

"Are the police on their way?" shouts Jamie.

"Yes, yes, they are," says his boyfriend.

"Thank fuck," says Jamie, as he turns to address Dan. "What the hell were you thinking?"

There is no response.

"And we need an ambulance too," he adds. "Did you ask for an ambulance?" His boyfriend nods, temporarily struck dumb by the thought that Jamie has just risked his life for this young woman. Jamie bends down next to her, stares into her bloody face, asks her name again, tries to comfort her, but she remains silent. "He's done a lot of damage and she's losing blood, but he hasn't cut into any of the major arteries," he says. It seems that he must have had some kind of medical training. "I think she's in shock though—well, all of us probably are."

"Jamie, you're bleeding," says the younger man. "Does it hurt?"

"I'm fine, honestly," says Jamie. "You don't need to worry about me. It's the girl I'm worried about."

Our little group—one that will be bonded together in ways none of us can ever have predicted—stand there not knowing what to say. There is an interchange of "Are you okay?" and "How are you feeling?" and mutual assurances that although the woman has been savagely attacked, at least she's escaped with her life.

"Thank goodness you stepped in when you did," says the middle-aged woman in the gray exercise gear to Jamie. "What's your name?"

"Jamie, Jamie Blackwood," he says, wiping some blood from his face.

"Very brave of you." She speaks with the upper-class accent of the privileged and well-educated. I realize I know who she is: Julia Jones, the Labour MP. She turns to me and thanks me for my intervention too.

"And what's your name?" she asks.

"Jennifer—Jen Hunter," I reply.

"That name sounds familiar," she says. "Have we met before?"

"I don't think so," I say. "But I used to have a column in—" But before I can finish I hear a scuffle and then a scream. Dan has grabbed hold of his girlfriend again. In his right hand he has a knife. A split second later he presses it to her throat.

"Put the knife down!" shouts Jamie.

"Don't come anywhere near me!" says Dan. Tears stream down his face. There is a desolate, empty quality in his eyes, as if he knows the game is over.

"Listen, Dan, you need to stop this now," says Julia Jones.

"Who are you to tell me what I can and can't do?" Dan says. "The fucking Queen?" He turns to his girlfriend, who has her eyes closed and is shaking with fear. He starts to stroke her hair and for a moment, it looks as though he is going to let her go. He kisses her forehead, whispers something in her ear, and then, with a quick slash, whips his knife across the young woman's throat. The girl opens her eyes in shock, tries to break free from him, but he holds her close as the life begins to seep out of her. Blood spills from her, so much blood, flowing down her neck, staining her clothes, pooling by her feet.

"Help! We need the police!" shouts Jamie. "Where are the police? Where did he get that fucking knife from?"

"Oh my God," cries Julia. "Can't anyone help?"

"Shit, shit," says the teenager.

Dan lets go of his girlfriend and her body collapses in a heap by his feet. As she falls, a line of blood spurts from her neck and splashes across the cheek of the woman sitting on one of the benches. Her eyes take in what is happening; she whips the headphones from her ears and runs across to the body.

"I'm a doctor," she says, kneeling down as she quickly assesses the young woman's wounds. "Sir, you need to step away from her," she says to Dan, who is still clutching the knife.

But Dan does not move.

"Be careful," shouts Jamie. "He's dangerous."

It hardly needs to be said; the evidence of the man's capacity for violence lies at his feet.

"What happened here?" asks the doctor, as her fingers delicately examine the wounds.

A number of people start talking at once—me, Jamie, Julia, the teenager—and from these fragments the doctor pieces together a horrific sketch of the events of the last few minutes. "There's still a pulse," she says. "But it's weakening. I need to stem this bleeding. I need something to stop—"

But she is cut off by the teenager's cry. "Watch out—the knife!"

Dan raises the knife once more. What the fuck is he about to do? He has clearly gone insane. Anyone in his line of sight is at risk. We are all potential targets. Me. Julia. Jamie. The doctor, who is doing everything in her power to save the life of the woman who had once been Dan's girlfriend.

I reach out and, with shaking fingers, touch the doctor's shoulder. "Can we move her?" I whisper. "Get her away from here?"

Dan must hear me, or realize what I was asking, because he lurches forward, stabbing the air. Globs of spit bubble in the corners of his mouth and there is a fury in his eyes, a mania that gives him the look of a rabid animal.

"She's not going anywhere," he says. "Vicky's staying here, with me."

In the distance, I hear the sound of sirens. Thank God they've arrived. But will they be in time to save the life of the poor woman, Vicky, who is bleeding to death in front of us? The imminent arrival of the authorities makes the teenager panic, and he runs off in the opposite direction.

Now that the doctor knows the girl's name, she repeats it over and over again. "Stay with me, Vicky, stay with me," she says. The doctor's hands are smeared in blood, as is her face, as she attempts to stem the thick ooze flowing from Vicky's neck and breathe life back into her dying body.

"That's the police and the ambulance," I say. "How much time do you think . . ."

My voice trails off as I witness Dan raise the knife and bring it close to his own face. He smears the blade across his skin, the blood from his girlfriend staining his cheek. I hear the sound of footsteps running closer, the police fast approaching the scene. Surely the horror of it will all be over now.

But then Dan places the knife at his own throat and slashes deep into his skin. As he falls to the ground I see a bloody necklace, a mocking smile, as if Dan is insulting all of us even at the moment of his own death.

2

BEX

I t's normal for there to be a crowd of people up there. From a distance there's nothing remarkable about the semicircle gathered at the top of Parliament Hill Fields. It's only when I get nearer and I realize that the people are not looking out toward the glittering city that it becomes clear something might be wrong. The ragbag group of strangers, tourists, well-heeled residents, young lovers, and dog walkers are focusing on something on the ground. I quicken my pace. I hear cries of, "Oh my God," "I can't believe it," and "Just so tragic, so awful." A trickle of blood snakes its way down the incline. Faces are ashen.

This is where I'm supposed to be meeting Jen. But where is she? I look from person to person but can't see her.

Just then a police car and an ambulance speed up the hill, lights flashing, ripping up the grass verges with their tires. A moment later two police officers jump out of the car and push their way through the group.

"Out of the way, please, let us through!" shouts the policewoman.

"You need to stand back, all of you, please make some room," orders the policeman. "Over here!" he cries to the two paramedics. "A female and a male."

"Oh fuck," says one of the paramedics under his breath.

I take a step nearer and peer over someone's head. I see a pool of blood, flaps of skin gaping open, the blade of a knife glinting in the winter sunlight. There is a young woman whose hands are covered in blood. The paramedics speak to her quietly, thanking her for what she has done, and then try to work life back into the two bodies that lie on the ground. But still I can't see Jen.

"Do you know what happened here?" I ask an elderly, smartly dressed woman.

"Stabbing, that's what I heard," she replies.

"What? Not another teenager?"

"No, it's a man—apparently he killed his girlfriend and then himself."

"Did you see it for yourself?"

"No, thank goodness," she says. "But I think those people over there did."

She points a bony finger to a group of people sitting around one of the benches, whose figures have been hidden from me by the crowd. I walk around the cluster until I have a better view. There is a woman in her sixties in gray sweatpants who I think I recognize. A handsome man with auburn hair and fair skin whose hands look like they have been badly cut up. And there, sitting on the ground, is a blonde-haired woman who looks like Jen. I say looks like, because it is as if someone has taken her face and sucked all the life out of it.

"Oh my God, Jen!" I shout. I push my way through the crowd, past people who are reluctant to give up their ringside seats to this gory spectacle.

"Please, miss, I must ask you to stand back!" orders the policewoman. "This is a crime scene now and we're going to be sealing off the area."

"But that's my friend—there!" I say, pointing at Jen, who has dropped her head between her legs and still hasn't seen me. "I want to make sure she's okay." The thought that she might have been injured in some way spurs me forward and I try to make a run for her.

"I must ask you to step away from the area," says the policewoman, placing a firm hand on my shoulder.

"Jen! It's me. It's Bex." At this she looks up.

"Are you all right?" I shout.

Stupid question, I know. She is far from all right. She could really do without this. Everything seems to have gone wrong for her. First, that terrible thing with her cat. And her job: she lost her well-paid column, "Being Jen Hunter," her only source of income. Then she split up with Laurence, her boyfriend of five years, which meant that she had to move out of his house—although I've tried to convince her that she's better off without Laurence, it's clear she's still in love with him. I doubt they'll get back together though. After living with me in my tiny Kentish Town flat for a couple of months, she recently moved into a huge pile in Hampstead belonging to a dreadful old hack, Penelope Frasier. I shouldn't think that that arrangement will work out well either.

I watch as Jen pushes herself to her feet, steadies herself by the bench as she gazes down onto that scene of horror, and makes her way toward me. She is stopped by the policewoman, who says that she will need to provide a statement. Did she touch or come into contact with either of the victims?

"Yes, but I just need to talk to my friend for a moment," she says. Her voice is flat and lifeless. "Don't worry, I promise I won't go anywhere."

"Did you see anything?" the policewoman asks me.

"No, I just got here," I say. "I was due to meet my friend Jen, Jennifer here, but I got held up, and . . ."

More police have arrived now and the officer has to go and talk to them. She nods her head and tells me not to move any farther toward the crime scene. She also asks us not to touch each other as Jen's clothes will have to be taken away for forensic testing. The woman in gray sweat gear is now being sick into the grass.

"Oh my God, Jen, what the fuck happened?" I ask.

She shakes her head as if trying to make sense of it all. Her blonde hair falls across her pale face like a sun-bleached curtain. She raises a hand to her cheek and as she does so I notice that she is bleeding. She wipes her eyes and nose, leaving a trail of blood on her skin.

"Are you hurt?" I ask.

"Just a bit winded from a kick—and this is from a surface wound, I think," she says.

"What happened?"

"It was such a beautiful day," she says, as if the crime that has been committed here has turned the sky black. "We were all looking at the city, and I was waiting for you . . ."

"Oh, God, Jen, I'm so sorry," I say. "If I'd known you were going to have to witness something like this . . ."

". . . when this guy turned on his girlfriend. He had a bottle of champagne. They'd been drinking it. They seemed so happy. But then something happened between them, I don't know what . . ."

"When I heard it was a man who had attacked a woman, for a moment I thought it might have been you," I say. "I thought it might have been Laurence."

She doesn't respond. It's almost as if she hasn't heard me. Instead, she begins to talk more about what happened. "They started to argue and then he took her, held her. He smashed the bottle on the ground and threatened her. Someone, this guy, tried to stop him, but it was no use. She tried to speak, but the man rammed the bottle into the girl's mouth. Oh God, the blood. So much blood . . ." She is forced to stop as shock racks her body. She begins to shake and looks as though she might faint.

"We need to get you to a hospital," I say. "Doctor—please help! It's my friend and she—"

But Jen stops me. "I'll be fine, honestly."

"Can I help?" It is the young woman who I had seen kneeling over the bodies. "My name is Ayesha Ahmed; I'm a doctor."

"Yes, my friend here, I think she's in shock," I say.

"Not surprising after what happened here," says Ayesha.

She asks Jen some questions—how she is feeling? does she feel sick? how is her breathing?—before she looks in her eyes and takes her pulse. She goes and speaks to one of the paramedics who is treating the wounds on the hands of the handsome man with the auburn hair, and returns with a special blanket. She drapes it around Jen's shoulders and tells her that she will be fine.

"Is there no hope?" I ask, taking the doctor to one side so Jen can't hear.

"None, I'm afraid," says Ayesha. "I tried my best, and then the para-medics did too, but there was too much blood loss."

"Jen said the man used a champagne bottle," I say.

"He did to begin with apparently," she says. She lowers her head as she silently curses to herself. "If only I hadn't fallen asleep on that bench. I'd been up all night—I work at the Royal Free—and was due to start work again soon. I only intended to close my eyes for a minute or so. And because I had my headphones on, I didn't hear it. It was only when . . . well, when I felt something on my face. Blood. And by then the man had a knife and had used it to cut the young woman's throat. She was called Vicky."

"God, that's awful," I say. "But you mustn't blame yourself. You did everything you could, I'm sure."

"Thank you, that's kind," she says, trying to smile. "And don't worry, your friend will be okay."

"I hope so," I say. "It's just that she's had a tough time lately. I've been worried about her. I hope it doesn't trigger another . . ." My attention is drawn back to the late middle-aged woman in the gray sweat gear, whose face I thought I recognized. Something is niggling me. Where do I know her from? Then it comes to me: it's Julia Jones, the MP.

"Bex?" It's Jen. She needs me.

"Coming," I say.

When Jen asks for help, I drop everything. I always have. And I always will.

3

JEN

After I hand over my clothes to forensics and have various swabs taken from me, I give a detailed statement to the police. As I relate what happened on Kite Hill, I still can't believe it. It's all so unreal.

Finally, in a stranger's clothes, I return back to the house in Hampstead. Bex is an angel, refusing to leave my side, constantly asking if I need anything to make me feel better. But just having her there with me is enough. She offers to call Penelope to tell her what has happened, but there is no point in causing undue stress. It will be best to explain in person later.

"What a fuckup of a Valentine's Day," says Bex, as she takes my hand in the back of the police car. "I always thought it was toxic—all that love heart bollocks and romantic meals for two—but . . . *murder?*"

"I suppose you never know what's going on in any relationship," I say. "It may look nice enough on the surface, but . . ."

The thought of my own relationship with Laurence and its breakdown brings fresh tears to my eyes.

I feel Bex's gaze on me.

"Jen, I'm worried about the effect of all this on you. We don't want a repeat of . . ."

"You don't need to worry, I'm much better," I say.

Bex continues to hold my hand as she accompanies me up the long pathway through the brick-paved front garden. Penelope's house is one of a kind. It is a mad, mock-Gothic affair, huge and rambling with a grand stone staircase, and tucked down a side street in the heart of Hampstead village. Penelope had bought the detached house with her first husband, a publisher, in the sixties and, after various other husbands and lovers had come and gone, and her two sons had left home, she found herself in the position of living alone in a seven-bedroom property.

We've known each other for years, have judged various prizes together and sat on numerous panels, and have always admired and respected one another. Although we often disagreed about politics, I loved her tales of derring-do: dodging bullets in various hotspots around the world, her hilarious anecdotes of charming insane generals and flirting her way out of danger, and of course no one could deny she had been a first-rate reporter.

She seems fearless, a tigress with fuchsia-pink lipstick, long painted nails, and extravagant false eyelashes like fat caterpillars. I can't believe that she is nearly eighty. She lives at the very top of the house and, although friends had tried to persuade her to move down to the ground floor, she wouldn't have any of it. And despite her gung-ho attitude, Penelope is kind at heart. When she knew that I'd been forced out of Laurence's place and I was living with Bex in her cramped flat in Kentish Town, she offered me a place to stay. For as long as I wanted, and for a nominal rent.

I let us into the house and walk down the long hallway to the tiled kitchen at the back.

"Is that you, darling?" calls Penelope. "I've got a glass of pink fizz ready for—"

But the sight of me stops her words.

"Oh my, you look awful—what's happened?" she says, getting up from her chair at the head of the wooden kitchen table.

As I begin to tell her something of what I had just witnessed on the Heath, Penelope confines the bottle of champagne to the fridge and gets out the whisky instead. She listens like a true professional, nodding, mostly staying silent, while I complete the narrative.

"And how do you feel now?" she asks. "I mean, you were kicked in the stomach, you poor thing."

"I'm just a bit sore," I say, even though the pain is still quite bad.

"And did you see anything of this, Bex?" she asks.

"No, I was late, I'm afraid," she says. "Well, I say afraid, even though I'm pleased I didn't see it. It must have been horrific."

Bex could have said more about how worried she was for me, what with my history. But she knows that I haven't told Penelope much about my past. My landlady believes, as do most people, that I had been let go due to a round of cuts at the newspaper.

"And has the couple been identified yet?" asks Penelope, always keen to stay up to date with a developing story.

"No, I don't think so," I say. "I'm sure the police will be waiting to inform the parents or next of kin. All I know is that the man was called Dan and his girlfriend, Vicky."

"I suppose the motive must have been jealousy," says Penelope. "But it would be interesting to find out more." She looks at me, her eyes lighting up. "I've got an idea—why don't you write a news story about it?" She knows how hard it has been for me to get commissions since losing my column. There has been an interview with an actor, another with a writer, but they only pay a pittance at £300 or £400 each, nothing compared to my previous £150,000 a year contract.

"I'm not sure that would be good for her," says Bex.

"Why not?" replies Penelope. "It's exactly what she needs to do. Get it out of her system. I saw some horrors in my time, I'm sure you know that, and I found there was nothing better than writing about it. It was like a purging."

"I'm not so sure," says Bex.

"If you don't write it, you know someone else will," says Penelope. "That or one of the papers will interview the witnesses. You say Julia Jones was there too? How extraordinary. I'm sure someone is chasing her right now for an exclusive."

"But wouldn't it be upsetting for you, Jen?" asks Bex. "Wouldn't it be best to put it all behind you?" She looks distressed at the prospect. "And I'm sure Julia Jones would be far too busy to talk to you—what with everything that's going on with politics at the moment."

"Perhaps Penelope is right. I'm hardly flavor of the month at the moment. Beggars can't be choosers and all that."

"I thought the *News* didn't want anything more to do with you?" asks Bex. "After . . . well, after letting you go."

I fire a warning glance at Bex. But she's right. They will never commission me again. After the problems I had with them I know I was lucky to get away with the severance of my contract. At one point the managing editor said she could take legal action against me; she also threatened to make the whole sorry mess public.

"You could do it for a Saturday paper," says Penelope. "I know the editor of the *Mail*. He would love to run it. I could drop him a line, if you like."

"Would you?" I ask.

"Yes, and I'll do better than that," says Penelope. "I'll negotiate the fee for you myself. I'll be your agent, but without taking a cut. How about it?"

The deal is being done before Bex's eyes, and it's clear she's not pleased. As she frowns, a few lines crease their way across her forehead and cluster around her mouth, making her seem older than her forty-two years. Physically, she's in great shape—she's a keen runner—but if I were to be honest, I don't think her exercise regime has done her face any favors. Her cheeks look a little sunken, today she's not wearing any makeup, and she seems tired and stressed. She brushes a strand of her glossy brown hair off her face as she looks down and studies her whisky. I know she only has my best interests at heart. She's gotten me through some really difficult times. And I'll always be grateful for her. But she has to understand that I have to make a living somehow.

"Yes, I'll do it," I say. But then I realize about the deadline. "Shit, I forgot. I'm supposed to be meeting Laurence for lunch tomorrow."

"Can you put him off?" asks Penelope.

"I suppose so," I say. "I'll send him a text and explain."

Penelope bangs her liver-spotted hand on the table in a small act of triumph. "That's wonderful," she replies. "I'll get on to the editor right away.

And don't look so worried, Bex. Yes, Jen's had to witness a most terrible thing. She's seen it, lived through it, but by writing about it she can move on, and hopefully make some money along the way. What's the worst that can happen?"

4

BEX

The worst that can happen? Well, where do I start? An image of Jen slumped on my sofa, looking like the mere shell of a person, her blue eyes dead and empty, comes back to me. It was the morning after she'd heard the news that she was being let go by her newspaper. She'd insisted on drowning her sorrows with bottle after bottle of white wine, but the next day the hangover and the harsh reality of the situation had kicked in. Laurence knew she was going to stay the night at my place, but he didn't know the reason why Jen had got so drunk. She said she felt too ashamed to tell him.

She couldn't see a future for herself, she said. She was worthless. She hadn't been given a severance due to the nature of the dismissal, and she was worried sick about money. She felt so embarrassed that she said she would have to leave London and perhaps even go back up north. It was the end. She felt that she had shared so much in her column—she'd talked about so many intimate aspects of her life—and for what?

As she sat there, looking into the void that was her future, I felt seriously worried about her. I refused to let her out of my sight. I rang Laurence and told him that Jen was feeling the worse for wear after a particularly heavy night—he was used to her marathon drinking sessions—and that she would spend the day with me. He knew that I'd look after her. After all, I was her oldest friend.

I remember the first day we met in the autumn of 1995. We'd both arrived in London from the provinces—Jen from the north and me from Essex. That day, I was sitting in my room at the halls of residence feeling at a loss to know what to do with myself when I heard the sound of crying coming through the thin walls. I got up, peered into the corridor, listened again. There was a stifled sob drifting out of the room to the left. I knocked gently on the door and a moment later a girl with greasy, mousy hair, terrible acne, and thick glasses appeared. She looked like she was itching to get out of her own skin. It was obvious she was crying out to be helped by someone like me.

"Are you okay?" I asked.

The frightened-looking girl wiped the tears away and nodded her head.

"My mum and dad have gone and I'm feeling a bit low," I said. My words were more for her benefit than my own.

The mousy-haired girl looked nonplussed, but I continued. "I've got some cider if you want some?"

And with that the girl, who told me her name was Jennifer Hesmondalgh, smiled. She came back to my room and as the sweet cider took effect, she started to seem a bit happier.

"I'm so pleased you're here," I said. "Did your parents drop you off?"

Jennifer lowered her eyes. "I don't have any," she said.

"Sorry?" I asked.

"Parents—they're both dead," she said.

"Oh." I didn't know what else to say.

"But it's okay, I'm fine about it," she said in a way that suggested the opposite.

"What happened?" I asked.

"They died in a car accident when I was fourteen," she said. Her eyes blinked a little too quickly. Her fingers reached up nervously to her face. "I don't like to go on about it, but my life changed overnight."

"Who've you been living with since then?"

"My mum's sister," she said. It was obvious she didn't want to talk anymore about her past. She gulped down her cider and said, "I could get used to this. Any more?"

And with that we moved on to talk about where we'd grown up—she in Lancashire, me in the countryside just outside Colchester—our taste in music (she liked stuff like Take That and Celine Dion, while I couldn't get enough of the grungier Oasis, Blur, and Pulp), and our politics (we both agreed how much we hated the Tories and John Major). We discovered we had other things in common too: neither of us had any brothers and sisters, and both of us were doing English, but at different London colleges. By the end of the night she told me that I could call her Jen. Later, some of the cooler girls on the corridor asked me why I spent so much time with "that weird freak," as they called her. But I felt sorry for her, I guess. I'd always had a soft spot for the underdog. For the runt of the litter.

Jen seemed so vulnerable, so helpless. And she'd lost her parents when still so young. But gradually, as Jen learned to trust me, she opened up about her bulimia. Her low self-esteem. And so I made it my mission to try to bring her out of herself a little. I started by persuading her to ditch some of her frumpier clothes, and took her to Topshop. Then we addressed her diet, swapping junk food for healthier options. I persuaded her to get rid of the thick glasses and replace them with contact lenses. I took her to a nice hairdresser, who suggested she go blonde.

Jen got the bulimia under control, her acne began to melt away, and, with her new highlights, by the end of the second term she looked like a completely different girl. With her new appearance came a new personality, one that was funnier and more confident, able to engage with the world instead of retreating from it. The other students in the halls noticed it too. She started to get asked out by boys, some of them really quite good-looking too, and the bitches who'd been mean to her behind her back began to invite her for coffee and drinks.

And how did she repay me?

The trouble started soon after Jen began to work for the student newspaper and she fell in with a new crowd of people. Initially, she helped with production, checking copy and proofs, occasionally coming up with a witty headline. Then, at the beginning of our second year, the star writer of the paper, Samantha King, did not file her usual column. Guy Davies, the editor, was going mental, ringing Samantha repeatedly and, when he got no answer, he sent someone around to her house. But the news came back that Samantha wouldn't be filing her column. She'd taken too many drugs and was in a psychiatric unit after suffering a psychotic episode. There was a panic in the office—what was going to fill the empty space? Jen, there doing some subbing, offered to write the column.

I learned all this when we met up for coffee so she could explain what the fuck had happened.

"I thought you'd be pleased," she said.

"Pleased? How exactly would I be pleased?"

"Because you helped me so much," she said. "Without you I'd still be the tongue-tied, weird-looking girl that everyone avoided."

"But this, Jen. Seriously?" I said, holding up a copy of the newspaper. I looked down at her column and read out a sentence from the first paragraph. "'Bex came along and set about transforming me from an ugly duckling, if not into a swan then at least a passable cuckoo or magpie. She gave me the confidence to be me.' I mean, really?"

"I'm sorry, Bex, but I just panicked," she said. "It's just that when Guy told me to write about something that would appeal to freshers, the first thing that came into my mind was how unhappy I was when I arrived at uni. And it's all true, you know what you did for me."

"I don't care a fuck about the truth!" I said, my rising voice attracting the attention of strangers in Starbucks. "And why did you have to go and use my real name?"

"I honestly thought you wouldn't mind," she said. "And it's only your first name."

"And what's with *your* new name?" I asked.

The story carried not her own last name, that of Hesmondalgh, but Hunter; later, when she started work as a journalist, she changed her name by deed poll, a sign perhaps that she wanted to rid herself of the past.

"Guy said that they didn't have time to redesign the page and so I had to choose a new byline that was shorter and which would fit into the space."

I didn't say anything, knowing that my silence would hurt more than any words.

"Just looking at it now makes me feel sick," she said. "I wish I'd never written it. But Guy was looking over my head, asking me whether I'd finished, and when he read the first couple of paragraphs he told me that it was great, told me to keep going. Before I knew it he was sending it off to the printers."

"You should have asked me whether I wanted to be in it," I said. "Can't you see that?"

We fell into another horrible, moody silence before finally Jen began to speak. "What I did was unforgivable, and I can understand it if you don't want to be friends with me. I'll do anything—*anything*—to make it up to you."

I took one look at her quivering lip and the tears forming in her eyes. I couldn't be angry with her any longer.

"Never do anything like that again," I said. "Okay? Never write about me ever again. Promise?"

"I promise," she whispered.

5

JEN

SATURDAY, 16 FEBRUARY, 2019

VALENTINE'S DAY MASSACRE—
A DIFFERENT KIND OF KNIFE CRIME

Writer JEN HUNTER was one of the bystanders caught up in a horrific murder-suicide on Hampstead Heath on Thursday. Here she writes exclusively about the brutal crime.

It should have been a day like any other—no, better than any other. It was Valentine's Day, after all. Couples were holding hands, looking at the ever-expanding London skyline, planning their romantic dinners. The sunlight caressed our faces as we stood on Parliament Hill Fields, Hampstead Heath, London, enjoying the unseasonably warm weather. And then something happened, something that could have come straight out of a horror film.

The facts are these. A man—recently named as 28-year-old Daniel Oliver—threatened his girlfriend, Victoria Da Silva, 26—an interior designer and the daughter of the multimillionaire Portuguese businessman Pedro Da Silva—with a champagne bottle. He smashed the broken bottle into her mouth and then, when brave bystanders wrestled this off him, he pulled out a knife from his pocket and slashed the young woman's throat. Oliver then used the knife to slit his own throat. Both Oliver and Da Silva were pronounced dead at the scene.

Police have issued a statement saying they believe that the crime was a murder-suicide. Friends of Oliver, a city trader from a working-class family in Essex, say that they believe jealousy was behind the murder. According to one source, who did not want to be named, Oliver believed that Da Silva was having an affair. Yesterday, her father, who lives on The Bishops Avenue, one of London's most expensive streets, released a statement that said, "Victoria was the perfect daughter—beautiful, bright, artistic, and kind. She had the world at her feet. She was taken from us too early." He asked for privacy at this most difficult of times.

Oliver's family—his parents are divorced and still live in Essex—expressed astonishment and disbelief that their son could have stabbed his girlfriend to death. "Dan loved Vicky, we saw that with our own eyes," said his mother, Karen, 52. "I just don't believe he would do a thing like that."

Although Daniel Oliver's mother may not believe it, the truth of the matter is that he did do it.

I *saw* him do it.

I saw him smash that broken bottle of champagne into Victoria's mouth as she tried to speak. I saw the outpouring of blood, after he shouted at her, "Don't you f——ing talk. Don't you say another f——ing word!" I saw people, brave people, try to stop the attack. I saw it all with my own eyes, and I would give anything to wipe those images from my mind.

One of the other people standing at the top of Parliament Hill Fields that day was 42-year-old hedge fund manager Jamie Blackwood. He was out walking his dog with his boyfriend, Alex Hughes, 24. Blackwood suffered a series of minor injuries to his hands as he wrestled with Daniel Oliver in an attempt to take the broken bottle from him. And for a while, after Blackwood succeeded, we thought the whole horrible event was over. But then, as we waited for the police to come, Daniel Oliver took the knife from his pocket and slit Victoria's throat. The expression on the young woman's face—a mix of astonishment and horror—was one I will never forget.

A young doctor, Ayesha Ahmed, 25, who works at the Royal Free Hospital, Hampstead, and who was on her lunch break, did everything she could to save the life of Victoria Da Silva. She even tried to save the life of Victoria's attacker, too, after Oliver slit his own throat. But by the time the authorities arrived, the couple were both dead.

The scene looked like something from a slaughterhouse. There was blood everywhere. "I never saw anything like it, and witnessing it made me physically sick," says Julia Jones, the Labour MP, who was taking a run across the Heath. "And at this stage my sympathies go out to both families, who have been devastated by this horrific crime. There will, of course, be an inquest, and I'm helping the police piece together a picture of what happened on 14 February. But as this incident shows, it's important to remember that knife crime can affect any community—black or white, rich or poor. This epidemic of knife crime has to stop."

Police are keen to talk to a black teenager who was another witness, but who fled on foot just before the authorities arrived. They are also appealing to a male jogger who ran past the viewing spot of the famous Parliament Hill Fields just as the crime was unfolding. Anyone with information relating to the incident is urged to contact the police immediately, or call the Crimestoppers hotline.

Almost as soon as the piece goes online I get an email from Laurence. The sight of it pinging into my inbox lifts my spirits.

To: Jen@JenHunter.com
From: laurencejrobertson@gmail.com
Subject: You ok?

Hi Jen,

Just read your news story—God, how are you? What a horrible thing to have witnessed. Like you say, it sounds like a horror film. I can't imagine how you must be feeling. It seems as though the guy was driven crazy by jealousy. But what a thing to do.

Sorry we couldn't meet up yesterday. It would have been nice to see you. But as I said in my text I totally understand. I know we didn't part company on the best of terms. We both said some terrible things that night, some of which I regret. I'm sure you would say the same. But looking forward to seeing you soon. Let's make another date.

Laurence

It's obvious he still cares about me. I picture us holding hands in the cinema, cuddling on the sofa, enjoying a meal together. I don't allow myself to dwell on the idea of us in bed. But what do they say about clouds and silver linings? Perhaps the fact that he knows that I witnessed the attack will make him feel more sympathetic to me, and it might even serve as a way of bringing us back together.

The sudden frenzy on my Twitter feed disrupts my train of thought. I scroll through my notifications, bracing myself for the hate from the trolls. There's quite a lot of criticism about the headline, but also a few retweets and supportive comments too. Then comes a message from someone whose Twitter name freaks me out: @WatchingYouJenHunter.

@WatchingYouJenHunter Hello. You've got a pretty face.

I check the profile, created today, and I see that the person is now following me. There is no potted biography, neither are there any other tweets attached to the account. The image belonging to the Twitter handle is a picture of my byline photo. Then the messages come like a wave, one that unsteadies and unsettles me.

@WatchingYouJenHunter I think I recognize you from somewhere.

@WatchingYouJenHunter Have we met before?

@WatchingYouJenHunter Did you really see what you thought you saw?

I've endured my fair share of weirdos and social media trolls over the years—there is nothing like a personal column in which you share your vulnerabilities and weaknesses to bring out the world's nastiest people—and the best policy is to ignore them. For a moment I think about blocking or muting the account, but there is something about this last question that intrigues me. I've enjoyed a few glasses of wine with Penelope to celebrate the publication of the piece, and I'm now back in my room. And so I reply.

@onlyoneJenHunter What do you mean?

There is no response. And so I try again.

@onlyoneJenHunter Do you have any info about the Daniel Oliver–Victoria Da Silva case?

I stare at the screen of my phone. The app icons burn into my brain as I wait. Still nothing.

And then, just as I am about to put the phone down and get ready for bed, I receive another message.

@WatchingYouJenHunter Daniel Oliver didn't kill Victoria Da Silva.

6

BEX

Jen is behaving strangely. I suppose this isn't that surprising considering what she saw on Parliament Hill Fields. If I'd witnessed a brutal murder, followed by a suicide, I'm sure I'd be pretty warped in the head too.

I text her and arrange to meet at the Coffee Cup in Hampstead. As she comes into the cozy interior—with its wooden paneling and red carpet it looks like something from the fifties—she stares around her as if she's being followed. "Oh my God, Jen, are you okay?" I ask, even before she sits down.

"You won't believe this," she whispers, taking off her jacket. There is a crazed look about her eyes, as if she is being hunted.

"What's happened? You're really worrying me."

"Last night, about ten-ish, I got this," she says, thrusting her phone at me.

It's a series of messages — tweets — from an account called @WatchingYouJenHunter.

"Jen, that's so weird," I say. "Have you told the police?"

"No, not yet," she says, running a hand through her blonde hair.

"You do intend to, though? And you've blocked them, right?"

"Yes, at some point I will, but I think it might be worth doing a bit of digging first."

"Digging?"

"Just to see who's behind this—and also to find out whether there's any truth in it."

At that moment the waitress turns her attention to us. We order coffee and, after Jen checks out the other occupants of the café, we continue our conversation.

"What—that Daniel Oliver didn't kill his girlfriend?" I give her a sideways, skeptical look that usually brings her to her senses. "But you said you saw it with your own eyes. And what about those other witnesses? There was that MP there. And that gay guy, what's his name, the hedge fund manager. They saw it happen too."

"I know it sounds crazy, and perhaps it is, but I have a hunch there's something not right about this," she says. Her head swivels to the right, to the left, as she checks no one is listening to her. "Anyway, you know how tough it's been for me since I lost my column. I just thought if I managed to uncover something, then it could make for a good follow-up piece, perhaps even a book."

"Oh darling, I know how tough it's been for you, I really do," I say. "But I really don't think this would be a good thing for you, after—"

"What, after my breakdown, is that what you mean?"

"Well, yes, after your . . . breakdown. The doctor said you should try to avoid stressful situations. If you do need to work, why not try for some more lovely interviews with actors and writers? You do them so well."

"Interviews with actors and writers!" she says, spitting the words out. "I want to do some real work for a change."

"If you want to take your mind off things, I've always said you can start volunteering at the—"

"I know, and I will," she says, sounding guilty. "I really will come to the food bank and do my bit, I promise. I realize it sounds selfish, and it is . . . but I need to start making my own living again. It's the northern girl in me—you know me and my work ethic."

"But, seriously, what are you going to do about this?" I ask. "I don't like his Twitter handle, not one bit. Do you think it can be traced?"

"I've asked—well, insofar as I've searched on Google—and no, it's impossible, apparently," she says. "There's no way of getting someone's IP address—is that what it's called? But if the user becomes a threat, obviously you can inform Twitter."

"And we all know what constitutes a threat," I say. "When it's too late."

I see terror in her eyes.

"Oh no, I didn't mean it like that," I say. "Sorry, I'm sure you'll be fine. But you mustn't do anything rash. Or put yourself at risk—in any way."

Our drinks arrive—a black coffee for Jen, a skinny latte for me.

"Thank you," says Jen, taking a deep breath. "Just to change the subject for a second, you know I was supposed to meet Laurence but then had to cancel because of my deadline?"

"Yes, and?"

"I got a lovely email from him. He wanted to know whether I was okay. He seemed worried about me."

I feel there's no need to answer.

"He wants to make another date," she continues. "To meet up, for drinks or maybe even dinner. But I suppose he always was kind. Anyway, I thought you'd like to know."

"That was thoughtful of him and it's good that you can go forwards, as they say. You never know, at some point in time you could be friends again."

Jen's mouth twists into a grimace as though she is trying to stop her lips from quivering. Is there something she's not telling me?

She takes a sip of black coffee and tries to pull herself together. "I know—after this, why don't we take a stroll across the Heath?"

"Okay, that would be nice," I say.

"I could walk you back to your place."

◆

After the coffee we walk slowly down Flask Walk, past the little boutiques, artisanal bakeries, and gorgeous flower shops, and the charming but frighteningly expensive Georgian houses. When we pass the turning that leads down toward Penelope's ridiculously large house, I ask Jen whether she is happy with her living arrangements.

"In a funny sort of way I've become very fond of Penelope," she says. "Of course, she's very different to me, but I admire her achievements—and her spirit." She turns to me. "Why do you ask?"

"Just that you know you can always come back and crash at mine," I say. "The sofa is yours whenever you might need it."

"It's so nice of you," she says. "And in the fallout from . . . well, you were an absolute godsend. But—"

"But now that you've gone up in the world, living in Hampstead, you could never consider going back to a one-bedroom flat in Kentish Town," I joke. "Is that it?"

"Spot on," she says. Although she tries to laugh, the laughter is strained, artificial. "But seriously, I need to get my life back on track."

"I understand," I say.

We walk down Well Walk and onto the Heath, a place full of buds and the promise of life even though it's only mid-February. I make an effort to talk about things other than the case. Jen needs to take her mind off the Oliver–Da Silva thing. And so I rattle on about my job in the planning department of Camden Council, the cuts to local services, the problems with the bloody Tory government, the anxieties surrounding Brexit, until I realize that we are walking not down to the ponds but along the track that leads toward Parliament Hill Fields and Kite Hill.

"We're not going in this direction," I say, stopping in my tracks.

"What do you mean?"

"Jen, you know very well what I mean," I say. "Look, I realize what you witnessed was awful—truly awful—but going back over it all, raking it all up, returning to the scene of the crime. It's not going to help."

"Well, I'm sorry, but I think it may do," she says. "The person who sent that message said that I'd seen the whole thing wrongly. That I was missing something."

"If you had, I'm sure the police would have spotted it, but the truth is that they came to the same conclusion you did," I say. "You wrote it yourself, in a national newspaper: it was a case of murder-suicide. Daniel Oliver was driven by jealousy."

"But what if he didn't do it?"

"Jen, you're scaring me now."

"All I want to do is take a fresh look at the evidence. Perhaps there's something I overlooked."

"But what you're saying sounds . . . well, to be honest, it sounds mad. It sounds—you sound—completely fucking insane." I realize that my words are harsh, but I need to talk some sense into her. This cruel-to-be-kind approach has worked in the past, and I hope it will work now. "You *saw* him, everyone else there *saw* him. Who else could have done it?"

"You can either come with me, or I'm going alone," she says. "It's your choice."

I've learned from past experience that it is best not to indulge Jen when she is feeling like this. Even though it's painful, it's important for her to realize how irrational she is being. "Call or text me when you get back to Penelope's? Okay?"

Of course, I won't really desert her. I'll watch from a distance to make sure she doesn't come to any harm.

7

JEN

The area where it happened is still shrouded in a white forensic tent, contained within a larger circle of police tape. The specialist team employed to uncover the DNA evidence and the almost invisible traces of fibers have now disappeared, but there are still a couple of uniformed policemen standing guard. A group of Japanese tourists who know nothing of the attack look mystified as they come to rest by the viewing point. A crime scene is not on their list of must-see places in London. "What happened here?" asks one of the men in the group.

"A man killed his girlfriend and then himself," says a woman in a matter-of-fact manner.

That's the truth, surely? I run through the series of events again. I saw Daniel Oliver take that champagne bottle and smash it into Victoria Da Silva's face. I remember how he had a knife in his hand and how he slit Victoria's throat and then his own. The blood. Yes, so much blood. Ayesha Ahmed tried her best to save their lives, both of them. And then the paramedics and the police arrived. The couple was pronounced dead at the scene.

This is the reality of the situation, I tell myself again. A jealous man killed his girlfriend and then himself. The motive is as old as the hills. Perhaps Bex was right when she told me that I was "completely fucking insane." I've had my low moments before, lots of them. The doctor advised

me to avoid stress. My therapist, Annabelle, warned me about the importance of learning to distinguish fantasy from reality. And there are some
nutcases out there. It will be better, I know, to let the police get on with
their job, they will gather evidence, which they will present at the inquest,
and I can move on with my life.

But what life, exactly? I have no home, apart from a rented room. I have
no job, apart from the occasional freelance piece. And although I like to
think that the situation will change at some point in the future, the reality
is that I have no boyfriend. As I look around me I'm taken back to that
moment again.

I can't breathe, feeling as though an insect, a big one, is scuttling up my
windpipe, closing off my air supply. My heart is racing, almost as if I'm
having a cardiac arrest. I hold on to the bench, as I relive the slaughter.
The panicked breathing of Victoria. The look in her eyes when she realized what was happening. The sight of the broken bottle cutting into
her beautiful face. The screaming. The fight between Daniel and Jamie.
The horrible silence that followed, the sense of relief that the attack had
stopped. And then the glint of that blade in the sunlight. The skin flap-
ping open on the neck, the slow ooze of blood, soon followed by a quick
outpouring.

I have to stop this. I force myself to take some deeper breaths, pushing
the memories out of my brain. Were the other witnesses affected like this?
Perhaps I'm the only one. And it was stupid of me to come back here.
Bex was right, as usual. I should have listened to her. I will call her and
apologize.

It is important I think rationally. I have to get things straight in my
head. Perhaps I should contact Julia Jones? I hadn't needed to speak to
her for my news piece—the quote was emailed over by her office—but
she might be able to tell me more about what she witnessed. I won't
share with her the tweets that I received. But what reason can I give to
Julia Jones for her to meet me? She's a busy woman, she's already issued
a statement. Could I say that I'm doing a more in-depth piece about the
murder-suicide?

I sit on the bench, looking again at the mesmerizing skyline, until I feel strong enough to push myself upward and walk, slowly, away from the scene. I make my way back toward Hampstead and Penelope's house.

After a spot of lunch with Penelope, during which we discuss the possibilities of writing a more detailed feature, I go up to my room on the first floor and make a quick call to Bex.

I sit in front of my laptop and draft a carefully worded email to Julia Jones's office requesting an interview. I set about trying to find the other witnesses and send emails explaining the basis of the possible feature to Jamie Blackwood, the hedge fund manager, and Ayesha Ahmed, the doctor. I include the news story I wrote, as well as some links to a few of my old columns.

I had been there. With them. All of us were witnesses to the same crime. And I want to know what they saw.

8

BEX

Jen called me when she got back to Penelope's. She said she was sorry for snapping at me. She told me that I was right. She'd had a panic attack on the Heath. Now she is going to try to put everything behind her and forget that the murder ever happened. She will delete those tweets from that weird troll and confine them to the giant digital wastepaper basket in the sky. If this is the case then why do I spot her going into Julia Jones's house?

It's Monday morning and my plan is to turn up at Penelope's and surprise her with a box of almond croissants, her favorite. After all, she needs cheering up. But just as I'm turning the corner that leads down from FlaskWalk I catch a glimpse of her. I'm about to shout out, tell her to wait, but then I notice what she's wearing: a smart black suit, the kind of outfit she'd put on if she was about to do an interview. On her feet she's wearing training shoes. The mix is one I've seen plenty of times in town, busy executive women who wear comfortable trainers on the Tube, but then swap them for high heels in the office.

But I know Jen doesn't have a job.

What is she doing? Where is she going?

And given her past record she will most likely never have a job, not in the closed world of the London media. I wonder how many people know about her. Although the official line is that Jen Hunter has been laid off due to cuts, surely someone knows the truth.

I hope to God she isn't having another episode.

And so I follow her. I keep a good distance as she walks across the Heath, occasionally stopping behind the bulk of a tree or a long line of hedgerows in case she turns around and sees me. If she does, I have my excuse ready: I wanted to surprise her. Look—I have pastries!

But as she makes her way across the Heath, past the tumulus, and down toward the ponds—this time avoiding the place where it happened—she doesn't see me. She comes out onto Highgate Road opposite La Sainte Union school, walks past the Bull & Last, under renovation, and takes a turning down Woodsome Road. As I follow her down Boscastle Road through into Dartmouth Park Road I realize that I am stepping into a part of London that, although less than a mile from my flat, is a world away from Kentish Town.

Kentish Town is gentrified enough, but Dartmouth Park is on another level altogether. Not just in terms of the physical proportions of the houses, which are wider, grander, many of them with imposing steps up to the front doors, but in relation to the inhabitants too. This is the land of corporate lawyers, bankers, and film directors.

I kneel down behind a car and pretend to tie my laces. I watch as Jen bends down to take off her trainers, puts them in her bag, and slips on a pair of black heels. She climbs the stairs and presses the doorbell of one of the wedding-cake houses. Jen is a little nervous; I can tell by the way she shifts from side to side as she waits. A moment later the door opens to reveal a small, generously proportioned woman with a neat bob and a welcoming smile. It is Julia Jones, the Labour MP, who I saw that day on the Heath.

"So lovely to see you again," says Julia, stretching out her hand. "I'm sorry we couldn't meet under more pleasant circumstances. Anyway, do please come in."

"Thank you," says Jen.

I walk quickly away from the house, just in case anyone catches a glimpse of me. I go to the nearest shop, buy a *Guardian*, and take it with me into the pub opposite, the Dartmouth Arms. I pull out my phone to write a text to Jen, but then see a news alert to say that a group of MPs are abandoning Labour to form their own party. Fuck. Julia Jones is just the kind of woman who would do that, but I can't see her name among the list.

I punch out the text.

What are you up to? Fancy meeting for lunch? Xx

I know not to expect an answer soon. But the reply comes forty-five minutes later.

Sorry. Busy—in town today. Catch up later? Xx

I don't text back. I leave the pub, and as I do so I dump the box of almond croissants into the nearest bin.

9
JEN

"**W**asn't it awful?" says Julia, as she leads me through the hall to an enormous, book-lined sitting room. "I mean, I've never seen anything like it in my life. And you were so brave to try to stop him." She gestures to a large, bright orange velvet sofa. "Were you hurt?"

"Just a little bruising, nothing serious," I say.

"Well, that's good. Would you like a cup of tea? Coffee?"

"I'd love a coffee, thanks," I say, as I sit down.

"Louisa, darling!" she shouts. "That's my daughter," she says to me in a quieter voice. "Gap year between school and university. Going to Oxford."

A slim, dark-haired girl with a bright smile appears in the doorway. As she introduces herself I feel a wave of confidence oozing from her, but the self-belief is tempered by easy charm and a touch of humor. She is the polar opposite of myself at the same age.

"Your will shall be obeyed, ye mighty one," says Louisa, as she leaves the room to make the drinks.

Julia apologizes for not having more than twenty minutes to talk—despite the rumors, she's been taken by surprise by the formation of the new Independent Group ("what a fuckup, just what we need right now") before she returns to the matter in hand. She's read my news piece, she says, but she'd like me to explain why I want to write a more in-depth feature on the incident. What good will it do? And why do I need her help? It's obvious she's no pushover. Have I contacted the families of Daniel Oliver or Victoria Da Silva? I tell her that I have not, that I think it's too early, and that I believe they need time to grieve and that I respect their privacy. I tell her that their quotes came via a news agency.

"So you're one of the good ones, are you?" she asks.

"Excuse me?" I reply.

"That rare breed—a decent human being and a journalist," she says.

"I'm not sure about that," I say. "I'm uncertain whether I would even call myself a journalist anymore. You probably know that for the last ten years I wrote a column for the *News*?"

"Oh yes, 'Being Jen Hunter.' You developed quite a reputation for yourself. So brave to 'put yourself out there,' as my daughter would say."

"Well, for the most part I only ever wrote about myself and my . . . various problems. My disastrous attempts at dating to begin with, detailed accounts of my relationships. I've rather forgotten what it is like to do proper journalism."

"I heard that the *News* had to make some cuts. That must have been hard."

"Yes, yes it was," I say, as Louisa returns with a tray.

She places the drinks on the coffee table and, sensing the charged atmosphere of the room, leaves without saying a word.

"I'm not going to lie to you, Mrs. Jones," I say.

"Call me Julia, please."

I am conscious I have only one opportunity to convince her.

"Losing my column has been hard, not just psychologically, but financially too," I say, taking a deep breath. "Around the same time I also went through . . . a number of personal issues. So the truth is, this piece could help me get back on my feet. But I also feel that the feature would help raise awareness of what it's like to witness something as traumatic as this. I wouldn't want to lessen the impact of the crime on the families of those involved. It must be truly awful to lose someone you love in this way. But what I don't think has been explored is the impact this has on the unfortunate people who happened to see it. After all, none of us asked to be there that day." I take a sip of my coffee. "I don't know about you, but I can't get the horror of what I saw out of my mind. I keep seeing the incident unfold, in slow motion. I can see the bottle, that poor girl's face, the blood, the knife . . ."

Julia places her cup down on a side table. "Oh my God, you've taken the words out of my mouth," she says, almost in a whisper. "To be honest, I've been having nightmares about it. I'm waking up in the middle of the night in a hot sweat. Of course, I've been talking about it nonstop since it happened, but there's only so much poor Neil, that's my husband, and Louisa can take." She studies my face as she decides how much she can trust me. "This is off the record, of course, but my glass or two of wine with dinner has . . . well, let's just say it's turned into more like a bottle . . . or two. It's my way of coping. You see, witnessing all that horror stirred up some rather unpleasant memories." She takes out a tissue from her pocket and blows her nose. It looks as though she might be about to cry. "I lost a son. His name was Harry. He was only twenty."

"I'm so sorry."

She waves a hand in front of her face as if to brush away an invisible wave of grief. "It was a long time ago now, but of course it still feels like yesterday." She swallows and bites her upper lip. "It was nothing like what happened on the Heath—he died while trekking in India in the summer of 2000. He was from my first marriage. The grief tore me and my first husband apart. I met Neil as I was still grieving, and luckily we conceived—I think having that baby, Louisa, was the one thing that helped me survive. But . . ." Her voice trails off and for a moment it seems as though she might be stuck in the prison of her past. She takes a deep breath and tries to blink away the memories. "Anyway, you don't want to listen to me going on like this. As I said, I don't have much time. What do you want to do next? With the piece for the newspaper?"

"I hope to speak to the others, the others who saw it happen, so as to build up a picture of that awful day and its aftermath. I'm meeting with Jamie, Jamie Blackwood, later, but I haven't heard back from Ayesha Ahmed, the doctor."

"I'll never forget the sight of her hands covered in blood," Julia says. "They were so small, like a child's hands." Tears return to her eyes as the memory drags her back to Parliament Hill Fields. "And I'll never be able to go back there, you know? To that spot? It's where we took Louisa, as a girl, when she had her first kite for Christmas." She stops as she composes herself. "So, yes, I'll help. I'll help in whatever way I can." She coughs as she reinhabits the tough facade she has constructed to protect herself from the outside world. "But if you want to use anything from me, I'll ask for quote approval. Okay?"

I agree. She tells me again she can't do an interview today—she is due in Parliament soon—but she writes out her personal email for me.

"And what about the others?" she asks. "The teenager—why did he run away? And that jogger? I heard that the police are still looking for them?"

"I'm going to try to track them down, but I've come up with nothing as yet," I say.

"Well, let me know if I can help in any way," she says. "Now, I really must . . ." She stands up, a sign that our meeting is over, and as she leads me out toward the hall she makes a joke about how perhaps we should start our own support group. Witnesses for the execution. "Sorry, when times get dark I revert to black humor," she says, waving her hand in the air as if to try to erase her words. "It's a terrible habit. And please don't quote me on that."

"Of course not," I say.

As she shows me out I thank her for her time. Before I leave I turn to her and ask one last question.

"I wondered—have you received any odd messages, emails, or tweets, about it—about the incident?"

"Apart from the usual you mean?" She pauses as she selects a few choice examples. "'Die you bitch!' 'It should have been you, you commie cunt.' Or what about, 'I'm going to slash *your* throat and then fuck you in your dirty pipehole'? That sort of thing?"

The contrast between the foul language and her cut-glass accent could not be greater.

I smile sympathetically and say goodbye, feeling more than a little guilty. The tweets I received, alleging that the murder was not committed by Daniel Oliver, were nothing compared to these offensive messages. And Julia Jones has to deal with that level of abuse all the time. The tweets sent to me were just the outpourings of a lunatic or, more likely, a pathetic coward hiding behind the anonymity of a screen. There are a lot of freaks out there.

And one of them is watching me.

10
BEX

S upposing Jen was to have another breakdown, who would help? Was there anyone else I could call on? I run through the list of Jen's friends—Sarah, Lydia, David, Veronica, Laura—realizing that she'd alienated most of them by writing about them in her column. There is Penelope, of course, but she's the kind of person who would tell Jen that I was asking questions about her. Could I contact Laurence? Perhaps. And what was the name of her previous boyfriend, the one who dumped her just before they were due to be married? That was it, Chris. Or, as Jen called him in her column, Chris the Bastard. I'd heard that since that debacle he had actually married another woman, a solicitor called Steph, and that he was living very happily with her and their young son in Muswell Hill. Jen had told me Steph wouldn't let her husband have anything more to do with her—she didn't want Chris or herself to appear in "Being Jen Hunter."

Jen didn't have any family left. She had told me that her aunt, Kathleen, who had cared for her after the death of her parents, was herself dead now. So Jen really has no one to help her in times of crisis.

So for the time being, I will have to try to shoulder all the responsibility myself. Which is fine by me, as I enjoy looking after her and keeping her close. I was the one who held her head in my arms after she lost her job. I still remember the feel of her wet tears on my shoulder, the night she came round to my flat to tell me what had happened. After the wine-fueled bravado had melted away she started to sob, great big ugly sobs that sounded like the cries of a dying animal. At first, what she was saying didn't make sense. Her eyes were red from the constant stream of tears. Her voice cracked as she tried to spit out the words.

"I w-was only giving them what they w-wanted," she said, wiping a stream of snot away from her nose.

I stood up and went to get her some more loo roll. "Here, use this," I said, handing it to her. "You need to start from the beginning and tell me what happened."

She blew her nose, but instead of putting the damp paper to one side she gathered it together in her hands, using her fingers to pull apart the tissue into a pile of white shreds that fell by her feet. "I was in the office—Fridays are the days I go, well . . . used to go into the office," she said, trying to choke back another sob. "I was sitting at my desk; I'd just filed my column and was waiting for any queries to come back when my phone rang. It was Debbie, the editor's secretary—Jonathan wanted to see me. I stopped to say hello to her, but she was on another call, her head turned away from me. Of course, now I know she couldn't . . . she couldn't meet my eye."

Jen stopped as she tried to control her breathing. "Take your time," I said, squeezing her hand.

"I went into the office and saw Jonathan there, with the managing editor, Janice, and the head of HR. There was no small talk or funny banter. Instead, Jonathan told me to sit down and he held up a sheet of paper from his desk. He cleared his throat and told me that they'd received a letter from a reader, making a series of allegations about me. I asked what kind of allegations and he replied, 'That you've lied in your column. About something significant in your life.' I felt like I was going to be sick, but I had to try to control myself. I think I managed to laugh, say that it was absurd, but then I felt tears begin to well up in my eyes."

"Oh, Jen, I'm so sorry," I said.

"Jonathan said that the reader—the reader was a he, he said—had gone through my columns and picked up various anomalies. He thought these might have been genuine errors, at first. But then he started to check, and discovered there was something more . . . sinister going on."

"What kind of things?" I asked.

"Oh God, I feel so bad about it all," she said.

"What do you mean—you're saying that—"

"You know how hard it's been for me, you know the level of detail they wanted at the paper," she said. "The desperate need for me to tell the readers everything about my life, the more fucked-up the better. It started out with those dates, those evenings out that always ended in disaster. I'd told them all about my grim northern childhood. My bulimia. How I hated the way I looked. I wrote everything about my relationship with Chris, my love for him, the ecstatic buildup to the wedding, and then the humiliation of him dumping me. But no, that wasn't enough for them!" She snorted, a bubble of snot ballooning out of her nose. "Anyway, Jonathan said that they'd done their own investigation. He singled out a number of my columns and asked whether I could explain certain . . . discrepancies."

"Such as what?"

She looked absolutely broken.

11

JEN

I step out of Julia's house and check my phone. The first thing I see is a message.

@WatchingYouJenHunter Nice suit you're wearing today.

A second later there is another one.

@WatchingYouJenHunter And heels. Sexy.

I feel the light pressure of a stranger's eyes caressing the back of my neck. Although it is broad daylight, and the area is an affluent one, I still feel scared. I hear the sound of footsteps behind me. I stop and look over my shoulder, feeling my heart pound inside my chest. I freeze to the pavement. Someone is coming closer.

A pretty young mother with an expensive-looking pushchair stops and gives me a concerned glance. I smile apologetically and look down at my phone again.

In my years as a columnist, writing about the most intimate aspects of my life, I've encountered my fair share of weirdos. My postbag used to be vetted for me, but latterly, as communication shifted from paper to the digital format, this became harder to do. I mostly tried to ignore it, believing that a certain level of abuse was part and parcel of the job. But occasionally people could be cruel, hitting you exactly where it hurt. After doing a column about my bulimia, a female reader wrote to me to say that it's likely I had been sexually abused as a child. And God, the level of bile that came my way when I dared say that I'd had not one but two abortions.

Of course, sometimes the readers made valid points. Did I not see that there was a link between my column and my less than perfect life? Perhaps if I gave up writing about myself altogether then I might find that I'd be happier? And no wonder I didn't have any friends—that was another perennial observation. I could have told the readers about my close friendship with Bex, and how much she'd helped me over the years, but after an incident at my student newspaper when, in a panic, I'd mentioned her in a piece and she had gone absolutely mental, I vowed never to write about her again.

A text comes through from her asking to meet for lunch. I say I can't and leave it at that without going into detail. I don't want to tell her about Julia Jones and my subsequent meeting with Jamie Blackwood in case she gets worried.

I push the creepy tweets out of my mind and plot my route to Jamie's house. There is no point getting the Northern Line because I would have to get off at Camden and catch another branch, and so I decide to walk. I have time. And the exercise will do me good. I cross Highgate Road and make my way down Gordon House Road, but just as I am passing Gospel Park overground I see a figure on the pavement in front of me that stops me in my tracks. A man—tall, dark hair, handsome. Oh fuck. It's Laurence. Part of me wants to rush up to him. I feel like blurting out everything I've been unable to tell him. I could thank him for the sweet email he sent and apologize for the fact that I had to cancel our lunch.

Just as I make a dash to go and talk to him an image of his face—dark, cruel eyes, a vein throbbing with anger in his temple—flashes into my mind. He is telling me that he never wants to see me again. That what I did was unforgivable. That I am a monster. And he had meant every word. This was from the man who had told me that he would never let anything or anyone harm me. A man whose strong arms had enveloped me, whispering to me that he would never let me go. At one point, we'd been as close as two people could get. Now, we are like strangers, or worse. I slip into a doorway and watch him melt away into the crowd.

12

BEX

J en didn't respond and so I asked her again what her editor meant by "discrepancies."

"Oh God, I could do with a drink," she replied.

She looked around the flat for a bottle that still bore a trace of wine, but we'd knocked back everything.

"I think you've had enough," I said.

"Can you go out and get another bottle? Or have you got any whisky—or gin? What about gin? I'm sure you must have something."

"No, Jen, I'm not going anywhere until you tell me what happened."

Jen took a deep breath and swallowed, but the disgust on her face as she did so made it seem as though she was being forced to gulp down a mouthful of her own vomit.

"Okay," she said. "It started small. And it was reasonable, and professional too. I told lies to protect those around me. Anyone would do the same, swapping Sally for Sarah, Lucy for Lydia. So do you remember that column I did about orgasms? In that, I used stuff Sarah told me, about how she always had to go into the bathroom to masturbate after sex, but I gave her the name Sally. That's not bad, is it?"

I told her that I understood, and encouraged her to continue.

"But sometimes—well, sometimes there were weeks when I didn't have that much to say," she said, looking down. "I mean, how many times can you open up your soul and talk about your latest dating disaster, your terrible row with a good friend, that embarrassing period incident, or weird sexual fantasy, or whatever? Sometimes, life was, well, it wasn't always that interesting. And occasionally, well, occasionally I had to make the odd thing up."

"So, what is it you're saying, Jen?"

"They're saying I lied!" she said, spitting the words out.

"And did you?"

"I told them that I hadn't, apart from the occasional need to protect the privacy of some of my friends. Jonathan pressed on and asked, 'Apart from this, have you ever lied in your column?' He told me to think very carefully about how I answered. The readers of the newspaper expected only the highest standards of journalism. There was an unspoken bond between the reader and a columnist, he said. Hundreds of thousands of people, mostly women, bought the paper because of me, he added. It would do untold damage to the reputation of the newspaper if it came to light that I had lied about significant events in my life. And so he asked me again. 'Was I lying to him now?'

"I felt as though I was on trial. I couldn't bear it. And so I shook my head and said no, I hadn't lied. Jonathan looked away, as if he was disgusted with me. He said that he was disappointed and that he had evidence to show that I was lying. But how else was I supposed to keep up with that weekly deadline? It was punishing."

"So what are you saying? That you did lie? What kind of things did you lie about?"

"Some of the stuff that happened with early boyfriends, certain incidents and conversations," she said. "Things they couldn't check up on."

"That doesn't sound too bad," I said. "I don't understand what the editor's problem is. Surely it will blow over."

"I doubt it," she said. She went quiet again.

"He might be just trying to shake things up and will have changed his mind by Monday. You've always said how unpredictable he can—"

"I've been sacked, Bex, can't you understand that?" Her voice was full of anger.

"I'm only trying to get a clear picture of what happened, that's all," I said.

She took a deep breath and spat out the words, "What happened is that I lied about my parents!"

"What?"

"The death of my mum and dad, in that car accident," she said. She closed her eyes as if she were trying to protect herself from the horror of her disclosure. "They didn't die in that car crash. In fact, there wasn't a car crash at all."

"I don't understand. You told me that—that you were fourteen. Your life was turned upside down."

"My mum and dad died when I was in my early twenties, Mum first from cancer, Dad soon after from a heart attack," she said, reciting the words as if she were an automaton.

"But that's when we already knew each other," I said. "How could you lie like that?" I cast my mind back to the first conversation we'd had in halls. "I remember your words as clear as anything. How your parents had died in a car crash. I saw the pain on your face. I couldn't imagine how that must have been for you. I felt so sorry for you."

"I know, and it was wrong of me. Unforgivable."

"Unforgivable? Is that all you've got to say? For fuck's sake, Jen. But why?"

"I don't know, I suppose I thought you'd find me more interesting."

"So what happened? Did someone find out about your little secret?"

"Go ahead and hate me."

"I don't hate you," I said, even though I wasn't sure about the truth of those words at that moment. "I'm just trying to get my head around this."

"A reader sent a letter to the editor's office, outlining some of the things that he said I'd made up," she said. "For proof, the reader very helpfully enclosed copies of my mum and dad's death certificates. The managing editor checked it all out and it turned out she came to the same conclusion."

"Who was he? Was it someone you know? An ex-boyfriend?"

"I don't know, Jonathan wouldn't tell me," she said. "And he ordered me to clear my desk there and then. He told me that if I made a fuss or tried to fight him he'd make sure that the truth would come out. That I was a liar."

"Fuck."

"I know," she said. "Fuck." She put her head in her hands and started to sob again.

I didn't know what to say, how best to comfort her. Or whether she should be comforted at all.

13

JEN

Jamie Blackwood's house is like something you'd see in one of those glossy interior magazines. From a distance the four-story home appears like all the others in the terrace—tall, elegant, understated in a rich person's kind of way. There is a box hedge in the front garden that's so neat and manicured it looks like someone trims it every day. The window frames are painted a tasteful shade of gray. Is it Dove Tale or Charleston Gray? The idea that I can even recognize the possible shade makes me smile. After all, I grew up in a house with a swirly, patterned carpet and a radiant bar electric fire. As I press the button on the videocom I suddenly feel self-conscious and shabby, like an impostor. Who am I to think I can just turn up at the door of someone like Jamie Blackwood? Perhaps I should have listened to Bex after all. I'm on the point of turning away, but then I get buzzed in. I take a deep breath and step inside.

I assumed that the inside would be in a style I like to call traditional luxe—walls painted rich colors, gilt frames, huge mirrors, enormous squidgy sofas—and so I'm surprised to see everything so stripped back. Stepping into his house is like entering into a twenty-first-century monastery.

"Jen, how are you?" says Jamie, coming toward me and, as a matter of habit, extending his bandaged hand, before withdrawing it again. I notice that his forearms are strong and muscular, covered with the lightest dusting of freckles. "Sorry, still can't get used to the bandages."

"Will there be any long-term damage? Serious I mean?"

"I don't think so, but just as well I'm not a concert pianist or a bloody brain surgeon. Actually, funnily enough, before going into finance I did go to medical school. Luckily, I dropped out." He laughs. "Have you had lunch?"

"Yes," I say, lying. I can't face food at the moment.

"Tea? Coffee?" he asks, as he leads me down a concrete staircase to the lower-ground floor, an expanse of white that seems to stretch on forever. Personal possessions have either been confined to invisible cupboards or to the bin. There is nothing here that gives me a clue about the personality of Jamie Blackwood apart from the fact that he likes to keep things minimal.

"Just a glass of water would be great," I say. "God, your house is . . . well, it's amazing. I can't believe you live here with a dog."

"Why?" he says, laughing. "Because it's so clean?"

"Yes, and your dog—well, he's not a chihuahua."

"You can say that again, Freddie is definitely not a chihuahua." He walks over to a huge stainless steel fridge, the inside of which glows like an altarpiece. He pulls out a bottle of San Pellegrino and pours the sparkling water into two tall glasses.

"Alex is out with him at the moment, in Regent's Park," he says, passing me a glass. "He couldn't face Hampstead Heath after . . . after what happened."

"That's what I wanted to talk to you about," I say. "As I said, I'm thinking about writing a longer feature about the crime—what we saw, how it's affecting us all. And I wondered whether it was something you'd consider?"

"I've read all your columns, you know, I'm a fan," he says, smiling.

"Really?" I'm not sure how I feel about his praise.

"And it must have taken a lot of courage to write about some of the things you covered," he says.

"Yes, I suppose it did."

"Anyway, I don't want to embarrass you," he says, waving a bandaged finger across his face. "But you probably know you've got a huge gay following."

Why is he being so nice to me?

"Oh yes, the gays just *love* your pain," he says, in a mock-camp manner. "Anyway, despite all that, you're a damn fine writer. I bought the *News* just because of you."

What does he want?

"It's odd, though, I haven't seen your column recently." I feel a sliver of ice pierce my heart. "Have you been on holiday?"

The question seems innocent enough; after all, there hadn't been an announcement in the paper telling the readers that I was going to leave. What can I tell him? Certainly not the truth. I find my mouth opening and closing as I struggle to find the right words. I'm conscious of Jamie looking at me with a worried expression, and it's obvious that my reaction embarrasses him.

"Sorry, anyway, back to the here and now," he says. "Of course, I'm very willing to help you, that goes without saying." He takes a sip of water. He asks me about how I'm feeling after being kicked in the stomach, and I tell him I'm fine. "That's good." He hesitates before adding, "There's something I wanted to run past you."

Okay, here we go. This is why he is being nice.

I knew it wasn't just because he liked me. I've made that mistake before. I don't want to make it again.

"Yes, what is it?" I ask.

"I know how journalists work—one of my exes used to be one," he says. "He was a political commentator, very different kind of work, but he told me something that went on. And, of course, you'd only be doing your job."

What is he trying to say?

"The thing is that a few years back my boyfriend at the time, Sam, he died . . . from a drug overdose. I realize that this is something that might get dragged up, whether I agree to help you or not." He stops as he tries to think how best to proceed. "I know you'll have to mention it in your piece, but I'm just trying to think how best to manage it."

How best to manage me. That's what he really means.

"What I'm trying to say is that of course I'm happy to help with your piece, but I'd like some kind of assurance that you'd represent me . . . fairly."

"Yes, I see," I say. "It might be best if you told me what happened—with Sam."

He digs into his jeans pocket and pulls out his phone. "I've got a photo on here somewhere," he says, as he starts to scroll through his images.

I wonder if he was as young and as pretty as his current boyfriend, Alex.

"Here we are," he says, passing the phone over to me.

The boy was in his early twenties, blond, Scandinavian. He looked like a model.

"He was a wild card, that one," he says. "Loved to party, if you know what I mean. Well, I suppose both of us did."

After I pass the phone back to him Jamie gazes at the photo of this blond god with a look of yearning, sadness, and something else—a touch of guilt, perhaps? I stay silent, knowing that this is the best way to get someone to open up.

"It was a typical week. I worked crazy, and I mean really crazy, hours. Sam was a student, a medical student. What a fucking irony, heh? He should have known better. *I* should have known better. Anyway, we'd been to a club—a new one under the arches in Vauxhall. We'd been drinking, taking stuff—a bit of speed, some ketamine, booze, cocaine. Then we came back here with a couple of guys we'd met at the club. Everyone started to relax. Sam had taken crystal meth before—we'd done it together—but that night he must have taken too much. He paired off with one of the younger guys in one of the bedrooms. I said goodnight to him and I went off into my bedroom, alone. I woke the next morning to some shouting. The guys were going crazy, and then one of them ran out of the house; we never saw him again. I'm not even sure what his name was. Sam wasn't moving. I tried everything—I shook him, tried to give him coffee, threw some freezing cold water over him. But he wouldn't wake up. I dialed for an ambulance, but when the paramedics came, they . . . they couldn't do anything . . ."

"I'm so sorry," I say. "That must have been awful." I am conscious that my words sound feeble.

"There was something of a minor scandal after the inquest," he says. "Reports in the *Standard, Metro, Telegraph, Mail.* Work wasn't too much of a problem—I run my own hedge fund, you see—but even so the whole situation was pretty ghastly."

"I can imagine."

"Anyway, as I said, I'm keen to help you, but I'd hate it if what happened in the past was dragged up again. It's as much for Alex's sake as for mine. You see, Alex has persuaded me to ditch the whole scene thing. I've turned over a new leaf. Hence the dog. There's even an idea we might get married."

"Congratulations."

"We'll see how it goes," says Jamie, smiling weakly. "I know you may have to refer to . . . to Sam's death. But I don't want it to overshadow this incident. God knows, it's horrific enough in and of itself."

"Quite," I say. What we witnessed on Parliament Hill Fields had bonded us, all of us—Jamie Blackwood, Julia Jones, that doctor, Ayesha Ahmed, the teenager whose name I did not know—in a way that none of us could probably explain. But it means that my loyalties to Jamie are different to those I would feel toward any other interviewee. In a funny sort of way I feel protective of him now. "Although I can't be sure how the newspaper will handle it, I promise I won't go big on your friend's death or the inquest or what happened that night. It's what happened on Valentine's Day on Hampstead Heath that concerns me."

"Thank you, Jen, that means a lot," he says. But then a puzzled expression clouds his face. "I thought it was obvious what happened up there. You saw it. I saw it. There was a group of us that all witnessed the same godawful thing."

"Yes, you're right," I say.

"You don't look too convinced."

"I'm just being stupid, probably. It's nothing."

"What is it?"

"It's just that I got a message from someone, a stranger, to say . . . No, don't worry. It's too ridiculous to mention."

"What? What did it say?"

"Just that . . . that Daniel Oliver didn't kill Victoria Da Silva."

Jamie looks even more bewildered and confused. "But that's mad!" He speaks to me as a friend, not someone who is interviewing him.

I can't let my guard down too much and so I reach into my bag and pull out my tape recorder.

"Exactly, that's what I thought, anyway if I can just begin by asking whether you'd mind being recorded?"

"No, that's absolutely fine," he says. "And if you're in any doubt, you can always see the photos that Alex took. God, I wish he hadn't. But they're all there, shot after shot. He wanted to take some of Freddie, and of course the view too. But when it all . . . well, when it happened apparently Alex just carried on. We thought about deleting them, but I suppose we should show them to the police at some point."

I wonder why he hasn't offered them up already, but I don't say anything. Instead I ask, "So, he's got photographs of . . . of the incident?"

"Yes, dozens of them, it seems. And a short video I think. You're very welcome to see them, if you've a strong stomach that is. He won't be long, I shouldn't think."

He takes me through his experience of that early afternoon up on the Heath. He remembers the clarity of the light, the sense of an early spring in the air. He talks of a sense of happiness flooding over him, the promise of a new beginning after Sam. He'd endured a spell of depression after Sam's death, he said. With Alex he thinks he's found someone with whom he can share the rest of his life. He recalls the moment on the Heath when both of them were stroking their dog. The feel of its smooth fur against his skin. The touch of Alex's fingers on his own. The sunlight caressing his face. The goofy grin he pulled when doing that selfie.

He hadn't been that conscious of the other people around him. He'd vaguely noticed that there was a young couple nearby enjoying a bottle of champagne, but he hadn't paid much attention to the others—a young woman sitting on a bench wearing headphones, a middle-aged woman out exercising, a teenage boy, and me. If he'd known how we were all going to be joined together, fused in that moment, he would perhaps have paid more attention. But all this was on the periphery of his vision. He and Alex were talking about the plans they had made for later that day, when he heard the sound of raised voices. He turned his head to see the young couple arguing. What a shame, on Valentine's Day. But not entirely surprising. He recalls thinking about some of the disasters he'd endured on previous Valentine's Days, and then he heard a smash. There was glass, glinting in the sun. The man stood up, brandishing the broken edge of the bottle.

He takes me through the rest of the incident. The shouting. The way Daniel ground the broken bottle into Victoria's mouth. How he called out to that passing jogger, and how he tried to intervene to stop the attack. The relief that came knowing it was all over, shortly followed by the sickening feeling it had only just begun. The sight of the blood spilling out of Victoria's throat. The acidic aroma of vomit, mixed with the metallic smell of the blood. The hatred he had for the attacker, and the terrible surge of relief he felt when the man slit his own throat.

By the end of the account Jamie has tears in his eyes.

"I can't even bring myself to say his name—but that girl, that poor girl," he says. "There was nothing we . . . nothing anybody could do. We stood by as the life slipped out of her. But why? I kept asking myself that question, and I've been asking it ever since. Jesus knows, I've felt jealous, as I'm sure everyone has. I've even felt driven to the point where I've fantasized about doing something bad. Not seriously, you understand. But to actually go through with it, to actually kill someone like that? I don't understand it and perhaps I never will."

I am just about to say something when I hear the door open upstairs, soon followed by the barking and scuffle of a dog.

"It's Alex—and Freddie, of course!" says Jamie, standing up. "Alex, I'm down here—with Jen." He lowers his voice as he addresses me again. "Don't worry if Alex seems a little . . . off. He was dead against me talking to you. But I told him that it would be better if—"

At that moment the Weimaraner, as sleek and elegant as a racehorse, canters into the room and into Jamie's arms.

"Did you have a good walk? Did you?" says Jamie, talking to it like a clever baby. "Pleased to see Daddy?" He catches my eye and apologizes. "Sorry, as you can see, he's . . . well, Freddie's everything to us."

"No, I totally understand," I say. The feeling of loss hasn't gone away. Watching the exquisite bond between person and animal being played out before me brings back the searing pain. "I have, sorry, I had the same kind of thing with my cat, Henry." Saying the name always makes me smile, just because it seemed such a ridiculous name for a cat. Especially because Henry was a female cat. "Henrietta," I add.

"Oh yes, I remember now from one of your columns," he says. "Did she go missing?"

So he wasn't lying earlier; he was a fan, after all. "You've got a good memory," I say.

"I remember you said you were thinking of moving abroad—where was it? Switzerland?—with your boyfriend," he says. "And then you found that she'd been attacked by a fox. God, that must have been awful for you. But you decided against moving abroad in the end?"

He must have seen the expression on my face because he starts to apologize for being overly curious. "Sorry, I don't want to intrude—and you're the journalist here," he says.

"No, it's fine," I say. "That . . . that relationship didn't work out." I don't want to go into details, and luckily I hear Alex come down the stairs.

"Alex—you remember Jen, from . . ."

"Yes, of course," he says. The tall, dark-haired young man stretches out his hand and smiles politely, but there is a coldness to his gray eyes that betrays his true feelings. He doesn't want me here.

"Anyway, I don't want to take up any more of your time," I say. "But before I go, Jamie told me that you took some photographs that day."

"Yes, and I wish I hadn't," he says.

"I thought Jen might find them useful, to use as background," says Jamie, "I told you she's writing a feature about that day."

"Really?" asks Alex, his nose crinkling as if taking in a whiff of a bad smell.

"I'm sure I can look at them later, or you can always send a few over by email," I say.

Jamie puts his hand around Alex's neck and squeezes his shoulder slightly. The touch makes Alex relax and smile. "You can have a look, I don't mind," he says, taking his iPhone out of his pocket and unlocking it. He uses his thumb to navigate to the right page. "There you go. It starts here—with a photo of the skyline."

"Thanks," I say, taking hold of the phone. I'm instantly taken back to that afternoon.

Here is the expanse of the city. The glittering towers. St. Paul's in the distance. The Shard. The half complete blocks stretching into the sky. There is the photo of Jamie, Alex, and Freddie, their faces full of joy, just moments before everything changed. There is an image taken toward the ponds, down the path that travels eastward. I can make out Julia Jones. And the jogger, his face obscured by his black hoodie. There is a sleeve belonging to the teenager. I can see a fragment of a leg, which must belong to Ayesha Ahmed. I continue to scroll on, the photos documenting the horror of the incident frame by frame. The nasty scowl on the face of Daniel Oliver. His eyes full of anger. His hand raising the broken champagne bottle. The terror in the face of Victoria Da Silva. The muscles straining in her neck as she tries to scream. A spurt of blood. The cut in her face. There are some blurred shots of the ground, the grass, the corner of a bench, as Alex loses control of the camera.

"I think I must have switched on the video mode accidentally," says Alex. "It's pretty bad quality, I'm afraid."

"No, don't worry," I say, realizing that my focus is so intense that I don't want to look up from the screen.

I press the play button and watch the nightmare come to life.

I hear quickened breathing, a counterpoint to the screaming in the background. The image jumps, as if the phone itself is shaking with fear. I see Julia Jones, who looks as though she might faint. There is the peaceful face of Ayesha, wearing her headphones, enclosed in a state of blissful ignorance. I see myself, or at least a version of what looks like me, my eyes full of terror. And then I see the jogger, moving along the path toward Alex, toward the camera. The jogger's neck turns, his black hoodie falls back slightly. The camera goes out of focus for a moment, melting into a blur, before it restores itself. I can't take in what I'm seeing. I blink, trying to make my own eyes function again.

It's a face I know. A face I loved. Laurence.

14

BEX

Jen calls me in a panic.

"It was h-him, oh my God, Bex, it was him." She can hardly get her words out.

"Just calm down and tell me what's wrong."

"He was there, the other day, on the Heath," she says.

"Who? What are you talking about?"

"Laurence—he was the jogger."

"*What?*"

"I've just seen a video—Alex, that's Jamie's boyfriend, he took it on his phone."

"I thought you said you were going to drop this whole thing?"

"I know, I'm sorry," she says. "But there's something not right about this."

"You're scaring me now, Jen," I say. "You need to hold it together and tell me what's going on."

I hear her take a deep breath. "I know it sounds mad, but what was he doing there?" she asks. "And why didn't he come forward?"

"So you're saying that Laurence was there on the Heath, the day of the murder?"

"Yes, he had a black hoodie on—he ran straight past me . . . when it was all happening."

"And you're certain it was him?"

"Yes, I've just seen the footage," she says. "Alex, he sent it on to me. Oh Bex, what the fuck is going on?"

"I'm sure there must be some kind of logical explanation," I say. "I mean, look at it this way. Laurence lives—what?—a ten-minute jog from there? If he wanted somewhere to run then that place, Parliament Hill Fields, would be his nearest spot, wouldn't it?"

"Yes, but why didn't he stop when he saw what was going on?"

"I don't know, maybe he didn't realize until it was too late. Or perhaps he—"

"And why didn't he make himself known to the police? After all, he'd read my news story. It said that the police were looking for a jogger dressed in a black hoodie who was seen at the scene of the crime."

"Maybe he was scared, I don't know, Jen," I say. "Look—where are you?"

"I'm just outside Jamie's—Jamie Blackwood's house in Primrose Hill."

"Why don't you come over to mine and we can talk this through?"

The line goes silent. "Jen—are you there?"

"Yes, I'm here—I just thought I saw someone . . . someone watching me. What if it's that weirdo from Twitter?"

"Jen—what can you see? Who is it?"

I hear Jen's heavy breathing. I repeat her name several more times, but there is still no answer.

"Oh, it's okay," she says finally. "They've moved on, they've gone."

"So you don't think you're being watched?"

"I don't think so, I'm not sure," she says. "But I don't feel right." She starts to cry. "There's something wrong. Bex, I'm scared."

She is beginning to lose it. Again.

"Tell me where you are and I'll come and get you," I say. She gives me the address. "I'm going to jump in an Uber," I tell her. "And don't worry. I'll be there in fifteen minutes—twenty at the most."

I punch the address of Jamie's house into Uber and wait, thinking what to say to Jen. I rehearse some lines in my head, remembering how I've dealt with her in the past.

The journey passes in a blur as a series of images, all of them distressing, float through my mind. Jen, broken in pieces, after her confession to me. Jen, her makeup running down her cheeks as her face seems to melt away in a stream of tears. Jen, comatose from too much drink, a pile of vomit on the carpet by the sofa where she slept. Jen, a mess. A fuckup. But also my best friend.

Jen and Laurence seemed like the perfect couple. I remember the first time we met him. We were in the French House in Soho. It was a late Friday night in winter, and the space was packed with people. Jen and I had already had a few glasses of wine. I was coming back from the bar, trying to pass her a drink, reaching through and over the crowd, when someone nudged my shoulder by accident. The force of the impact pushed me forward, and I had to steady myself with my free hand, gripping the arm of a woman next to me. But I could do nothing to stop the contents of the glass flying out and splashing the faces of Jen and the man standing next to her. "What the fuck, Bex!" said Jen, blinking like a cartoon character.

"Indeed, what the fuck are you doing, Bex?" echoed the dark-haired man whose face dripped with white wine.

They turned to one another and laughed. He produced a clean handkerchief from his jacket—she joked what kind of man even carried a handkerchief nowadays—and the conversation was off. And didn't stop all night. He was called Laurence, an architect who lived in Tufnell Park. Mid- to late forties. Divorced. No children.

"And you're not gay?" she asked.

"No, what makes you say that?" he replied.

"Just that you seem nice. You're handsome. Funny and—" she said.

"So you don't think straight men can be nice or handsome or funny?" he replied.

The flirting continued in the same vein all night. Laurence introduced me to his friend, another architect called Peter, a slightly overweight man in glasses, and although we were polite, there was no spark between us. Peter and I had to stand by and watch as the electricity bounced back and forth between Jen and Laurence. I felt pleased that someone was taking an interest in her like this. It had only been a few months since Chris had jilted her, something that hit her hard but that at least gave her lots of material for "Being Jen Hunter." She wrote hundreds, thousands of words, about the humiliation of the split a few weeks before the big day, how she felt unworthy of love, how her low self-esteem held her back, how no man would ever find her attractive again. And here was someone who looked as though he was taking an interest in her.

Just before last orders we went to the loo together.

"I'm so pleased for you, Jen," I said. "He seems really nice."

"He does, doesn't he?" she said, her face lighting up with joy.

"Have you told him what you do?" I asked.

"Yep, he knows I'm a journalist. He's cool with that."

"But about what kind of journalism—the fact that you write a column about your life?"

"No, not yet. We've swapped numbers, but it's early days. We're just having a bit of a flirt, that's all."

At the end of the night we were really drunk, all apart from Peter, who left the bar early. Jen got a taxi back to her rented flat in south London, while Laurence and I agreed to share a black cab to Kentish Town/Tufnell Park. At some point as we drove up Camden High Street the cab driver swerved to avoid a cyclist, forcing Laurence's left leg to brush against me. Although he apologized, he didn't move it away. The sensation was electrifying. He turned toward me and placed his hand on my shoulder. I felt his lips touch my cheek. I had the chance, in that moment, to say something. But as I opened my mouth he slipped his tongue into it.

The cab pulled up outside my flat and he whispered in my ear about how beautiful I was and asked whether I wanted the night to end. I could come back to his house for another drink. That was another opportunity for me to step away. I could have said something as simple as Jen's name—one word that would serve as a sign that he should stop, a signifier that showed I valued my friendship with Jen more than a quick shag—but I didn't. After Laurence paid the driver we ran into his house, greedily feasting on one another, stripping off our clothes in the hallway, nearly fucking on the stairs, holding off with difficulty until we made it into his bedroom. By this time, any thoughts I'd had about Jen had disappeared from my mind. I'd become brainwashed by a combination of alcohol and desire. The sex when it came was like a little explosion that sent shockwaves through my core.

Just after dawn, my mouth sawdust dry, I blinked my way into a painful consciousness and spent a moment studying Laurence, who was still asleep. I'd had a few boyfriends, some I'd fallen for really badly. But was he the one? I'd thought that about other men in the past, but for one reason or another things hadn't worked out how I would have liked. Could I imagine spending if not necessarily the rest of my life with Laurence, then certainly a considerable stretch of time? Perhaps. He was certainly handsome and in good shape. No strings or baggage. With a great house. Oh and one helluva good fuck, which is what I intended to give him with when he woke up. As I got up to use the bathroom and rub some toothpaste around my mouth I ran through what I would say to Jen. Surely, she would understand. She'd want me to be happy. Yes, they'd liked one another, but they'd only had a drink. Nothing had happened between them. I would take her out for lunch and explain: how we'd started kissing in the taxi, and how one thing led to another. She would probably find the whole thing hilarious, something that perhaps she could write about in her column—the friend who stole a prospective boyfriend from under her nose!—just as long as she didn't use my real name. We'd laugh about it in years to come; perhaps she could even use it as a funny anecdote when she gave the best woman's speech at my wedding. But I realized I was running away with myself.

I slipped back into bed and pushed up against him. I felt him hard next to me. He groaned as I straddled him. The fuck was a quick one, and both of us came in a matter of minutes. Afterward, as I reached out to cuddle him, he got up from the bed and said he needed to get ready to go into the office. I grabbed his white dressing gown and walked down to the kitchen. As I waited for the coffee, I searched the drawers for paracetamol for my throbbing head, but couldn't find any. I made two cups and took them up to the top floor, where Laurence was dressing.

"Thanks," he said, as he took a cup from me. I noticed he couldn't meet my eye. Was he the kind of man who was embarrassed to admit he enjoyed sex? Did such men still exist? Perhaps they did—after all, he was the kind of chap who carried a handkerchief in his jacket pocket.

"That was great," I said, hoping to reassure him.

"Yeah," he replied. "Listen, last night was wonderful—it really was. And I think you're a lovely-looking woman. But . . ." His voice trailed off while he tried to find the right words. "I think it's best if we just leave it there, if you know what I mean."

"But I thought that you—"

"I'm not great at doing this—talking like this—but I want you to realize that I had a fantastic time. And I hope you did too. Normally I only have one or two drinks, but I had way, *way* too much last night. Things got out of hand. I probably shouldn't have kissed you in the taxi. I know that was wrong of me."

"It wasn't wrong, Laurence. There was nothing wrong about it. It was bloody sexy."

"Well, I'm pleased you didn't think it was a step too far on my part. As you know, I find you an extremely attractive woman. It's just that . . ."

As I waited for him to finish the end of his sentence I saw the dream life I had created for myself begin to collapse. There would be no "us." He would not be "the one." Instead, he'd just be another man who fucked me and then fucked off.

"I thought we had something, Laurence," I said. "I thought we might have been able to see one another again?"

"We did have something special—yes, very special—but it's just that I'm not ready for that kind of relationship at the moment."

Please don't say it, please don't say, "it's not you, it's me." If he did that I would have to stop myself from throwing my coffee cup at him, or something worse. Of course, he went ahead and said those words. The most excruciating fucking words in the English language.

Laurence continued to talk, but I stopped listening as I put on my clothes. I didn't tell him what I was really feeling. Instead, as I left, I turned to him and told him that I understood; we were both adults, I could deal with it.

"But can you do me a favor?" I asked. "I think it would be best if we kept this between ourselves, don't you? I'd hate it if Jen found out. I think she was quite taken with you."

"Was she?" he said, his bloodshot eyes lighting up. "Don't worry, I won't tell."

Two weeks later I got an excited call from Jen to say that Laurence had been in touch and that they'd been out for a drink. She told me they got on like a house on fire. At the end of the evening they'd taken a cab back to his place. The sex had been the best she'd had in years, she said. I thought that would be the end of it, that Laurence would tell her just what he'd told me—that he wasn't up for anything long-term. But they continued seeing one another, even after she had told him about the nature of her column—he admitted that he'd never read it—and about how she might have to mention that she'd met someone new. But she could change his name, so he needn't worry about being identified. He was fine with that, she said. Jen kept me, and her readers, up to date with every aspect of the burgeoning relationship. They seemed like the perfect match. In fact, I couldn't have chosen a better man for her if I'd tried. The sex continued to be amazing, she said. He made her laugh. His house was so neat and tidy. No wet towels on the floor, no dirty socks strewn across the bed. She loved his work. He seemed to adore her quirky sense of humor. Her unpredictability. The fact that she wasn't like all the other women he'd met. By the end of six months Laurence—or James, as he was known in her column—asked her to move out of her rented flat and into his big house in Tufnell Park.

And they had lived there happily together until . . . well, until that awful night.

The voice of the Uber driver telling me that we had reached our destination brings me back to the here and now. I thank him, get out of the car, and look for Jen. I can't see her. I walk up and down the street, check again that she gave me the right address, but there's no sign of her. I call her phone. But it goes straight to voicemail.

She's gone.

15

JEN

I can still feel someone watching me. I turn my head but can't see anyone. I look through the windows of one of the houses. I'm sure I see a sliver of something, someone, move away from the open shutters. Were they standing there, studying me?

I think about going back into Jamie's house. But I could tell Alex didn't want me to hang around. And they might regard me not as a professional but as a madwoman. I look at my phone. I don't want to stand on the street, waiting for Bex to arrive, and so I start to walk. I quicken my pace, feeling sweat on my forehead, under my arms. It's February, for God's sake—why is it so warm? I make my way down the street, along past a terrace of canary yellow, baby blue, and candy pink houses.

I can't get the image of that video out of my mind. Laurence—the jogger trying to hide his face in that black hoodie. What was he doing on the Heath that day? Had he followed me up there? And why didn't he stop? Why didn't he come forward and make himself known to the police? Was he hiding something? And this morning, when I saw him at Gospel Oak, what was he doing? I think about the tweets from @WatchingYouJen-Hunter. A wave of nausea hits me and I have to stop. I reach out and steady myself by a parked car. Surely that can't be him . . . can it?

I try to think it through. How else can I settle this once and for all? I know it's probably unwise, but I can't see any other way. And so I take a few deep breaths. As I look up I notice that I'm standing outside the purple-colored house that bears an English Heritage ceramic blue plaque in honor of Sylvia Plath. It's not the house where she killed herself—that one is in Fitzroy Road, around the corner—but it is the one where she lived with Ted Hughes between 1960 and 1961.

I'd been mad on Plath as a teenager and young woman. I couldn't get enough of the confessional mode of her writing—the blood jet of poetry—and although I know I'm not in the same league, I'm sure that reading her shaped my decision to become a professional oversharer. Sylvia's suicide was a tragic end to the story, but I suppose Plath and Hughes had always lived at such an intense pace. One only had to think of their extraordinary first meeting. The way he ravished her with such force her silver earrings fell to the floor. How she bit him hard on the cheek, drawing blood.

Had that scene played some part in what happened that night, the night Laurence and I broke up? I try to push the memory out of my mind as I walk on. It's too painful to think about. At the time Laurence had told me that he never wanted to see me again. And I had agreed that that would be for the best. But recently I was sure things had been getting better between us. There had been the friendly emails and sweet texts, and then the real breakthrough, the agreement that we should meet up. But now I knew he was the jogger, that he had been there the other day. That changed things. How could I trust him? I had to find out what the fuck was going on. I had a right to know. And I was doing my job. I was a journalist following a lead for my story.

I pace ahead, but as I turn a corner onto Regent's Park Road, I feel the heel of my shoe slip underneath me on a pile of wet, rotting leaves. Luckily, I manage to right myself before I fall. I take a moment to swap my heels for the trainers I've been carrying in my bag. I see a 393 drive past and run for it, managing to flag it down just in time. On the bus I think about what to say to Laurence, but every opening gambit sounds mad.

It was you. I know it was you. That day. Jogging past.

I know you're the mystery jogger. Why didn't you say anything?

What were you doing up there, on Parliament Hill Fields? Are you @WatchingYouJenHunter?

Have you been spying on me? What do you want from me? Do you still love me?

I take some deeper breaths and I nearly convince myself that this is a bad idea. But I'm determined to find out the truth.

I take out my phone. There are some missed calls from Bex, and a text, asking me what is going on. Shit. She'd arrived in Primrose Hill and found me gone. I can't tell her what I'm about to do—she would be furious with me—and so I message back to say I'm sorry. I'd had another panic attack in the street. I'm safe now. I've gone back to Penelope's. I will call her later.

I get off the bus at the stop before Tufnell Park station and walk through the network of streets toward Laurence's house. How do I know he'll even be in? Won't he just take one look at me and slam the door in my face? I push the doubts away and carry on regardless until I'm standing outside his house. I ring his bell. Nothing. I ring it again, leave my finger on the button, until I hear footsteps coming from the top of the house.

"All right," he shouts. "I'm coming."

I prepare myself for the encounter. I haven't seen him since that awful weekend when everything went wrong. I have to stop myself from just melting into grateful submissiveness. I need to remain strong. He opens the door, his face drops as he sees me. He looks awful, like he hasn't slept, and dark circles shadow his eyes. Has he been grieving for me? Does he miss me that much?

"Jen—what are you doing here?"

"I need to ask you something."

"I thought we were going to meet up next week?"

"I couldn't wait until then. I want to ask you about what happened on the Heath."

"You know I was sorry to hear about that—are you okay?" He takes another look at me—he can see how upset I am. "Look, you'd better come in."

He stands back as I enter the house and touches his left arm, a fleshy spot just below his elbow. I push memories of the last night I was here from my mind, but the sensation of coming home is almost too much to bear. The familiar smell of beeswax lingers in the air. The colored parallelograms of light cast by the stained glass in the front door, squares of ruby red, ochre yellow, and sapphire blue shimmering on the wooden floor. He leads me into the huge kitchen and I see cups and glasses I used to drink from. I notice the big salad bowl I bought for him from Heal's. The enormous Vitra glass vase he gave me for Christmas is gathering dust on the shelf. It stands empty. When I left I didn't want anything from him or the house.

The memories of our time together—happy times, mostly—insist on flooding back and I have to do everything in my power to keep myself from falling apart.

"So what's wrong?" he asks. "Sorry, stupid question. I mean, how have you been?"

"Okay, and thanks for sending that email," I say. "It means a lot."

It's difficult for him to get the words out. "It must have been . . . awful for you to witness something like that."

I pause as I feel the anger building inside me. I bite my lip, almost tasting blood.

"But I wasn't the only person to witness it," I say.

"Yes, I saw—that MP, what's her name? And so brave of that guy to try to intervene. Is he okay now?"

"Just minor injuries to his hands, nothing more, but perhaps the whole thing could have been different had he had some extra help."

He can't meet my eye. He turns from me as he walks toward the worktop. "Fancy a coffee?"

"No, thanks. You know, there was one thing that never made sense to me—about the attack, I mean."

"What's that?" he says, as he feeds a coffee pod into the machine and then puts an espresso cup underneath.

"There was a jogger up there that day and when Jamie pleaded with him to stop, to try to help, he just carried on running."

Laurence remains silent, pretending to be preoccupied with making the coffee.

"I think if Jamie had had some support he really could have taken down Daniel Oliver," I say. "And Victoria Da Silva might still be alive."

The kitchen fills with the sound of the coffee machine.

"I mean what kind of man would come across something like that—an attack like that—and refuse to help?"

Laurence waits for the last drips of coffee to come through.

"I suppose he must be a coward, that can be the only explanation," I say. "I even tried to confront Daniel. He still had a broken champagne bottle in his hand. He was waving it around in the air, threatening to cut up anyone who came near him. Do you know that? When I tried to get Victoria away I got kicked in the stomach. I didn't think of it at the time, but I could have been stabbed to death."

Finally Laurence turns to me, his face drained of color.

"But I don't suppose you care whether I live or die," I say. "After all, you more or less said as much to my face."

"Look, Jen, if we're going to get into all of that then I'm going to have to ask you to leave." He speaks in the measured voice of the supremely logical man he is, a patronizing tone that I have learned to loathe.

"Just cut out the crap, Laurence," I snap.

"Okay, I've tried to be sympathetic, about what you've just been through, but I don't see how—"

"I know it was you, Laurence. I've seen a film."

"I don't know what you're talking about." He raises the cup to his lips and takes a sip. "I don't know whether the therapy isn't working, but—"

"Shut the fuck up. Don't you dare give me that."

"What? It's not my fault that you've got . . . issues."

"This is not about me!" I scream. "It's about you. About what you did—or didn't do. You were there, on the Heath, on Thursday. You were jogging up past the viewing point when it happened. Jamie called out for you to stop, to help, but you just ran past us, leaving us . . . leaving that poor girl to die."

"Honestly, this is ridiculous," he says, slamming his cup down onto the work surface. "I've just about had enough. Is there anyone I can call? Your doctor? Therapist? What about Bex?"

I refuse to let myself be sidetracked. "Jamie's boyfriend, Alex, was taking photos that day," I say. "And his phone turned itself into video mode. Without knowing it he took a film. It's shaky, not great quality, but it clearly shows you. You may have been trying to hide from me, but you couldn't hide from the camera."

"Jen—I don't know what you've seen. But I was at work on Thursday. I've got colleagues who—"

"I don't doubt it," I say. I'd always had my suspicions that he was attracted to Zoe, a sexy thing with a fondness for high heels who works with him at his practice. I knew he had been seeing someone new, perhaps it was her. "But what do they say? The camera never lies."

"Jesus fucking Christ, this is unbelievable," he says, taking out his mobile phone.

"Who are you calling?" I ask, pushing my hand into my pocket for my own phone.

"Someone who can help you," he says. "It's obvious you aren't well. You must realize I still care about you, I still worry about you. It's me you're talking to, Jen. I know all about the problems you've had. But you know what needs to happen when you get like this."

My fingers shake as I open WhatsApp and find the message from Alex. "Before you call anyone, I suggest you take a look at this."

"What is this?"

"It's the video that Alex took of the crime."

"I'm not watching that," he says, pushing the phone away from me.

I grab his phone. I look at the screen. He was about to call Bex.

"What the fuck are you doing, Jen?"

"I want you to watch the film. I'll give you back your phone when you've seen it."

"For God's sake, is this really necessary?"

"Just watch it," I say. "And then we can talk."

I open the file, click on the arrow to play the video, and hold the phone in front of his face. Laurence blinks in protest, and he winces as the noise of the screaming fills up his kitchen. He tries to look away, but I tell him he has to continue watching until the end. I wait for the telltale signs of guilt, a hardening of the eyes or a blush of the cheeks.

"So what do you have to say for yourself?" I ask.

"I don't follow," he says.

"What were you doing there? Why didn't you tell me you were there? And why didn't you stop?"

"Really, Jen, I know how much stress you've been under, and it must have been a terrible thing to witness," he says, passing the phone back to me. "I can see why you think that jogger was me. There's a superficial resemblance, I suppose. But I promise you, it wasn't me."

I feel my throat beginning to close up. The familiar signs of panic are invading my body once more.

"How can you stand there and say that?" I ask, my voice rising. "I know it was you. You were there."

"You said if I watched the film I could have my phone back," he says, holding out his hand.

I slam his phone into his palm. He immediately calls Bex. "What are you doing?"

"I'm calling someone who can help you," he says. "It's either Bex or . . . and I'm sure you don't want to go through that again."

The memory of that night fills me with shame. I see myself, but not as myself, more as a stranger, throwing things, swearing. I have a vague memory of biting something, someone. I feel hands on my shoulders, something being pushed into my mouth. "Okay, call Bex, and I'm sure that when she sees the video she'll tell me what I already know—that the jogger up there on the Heath last week was you."

Laurence presses a button and waits for Bex to pick up. I try to listen to her voice, but can't make out what she's saying. "Yes, I'm pleased you feel the same way," he says. "I'm worried too. Okay, see you soon."

He cuts the connection and looks at me as if I'm a sick dog that should be put down. "She's on her way," he says. "She was actually coming here, because—"

I try to speak, but he shouts me down.

"She was worried, Jen, don't you see that?" he says. "You said you were in Primrose Hill, but when she arrived there was no sign of you. And so she thought you might try to call in on me. Thank God she's only five minutes away."

"She's nearly here?"

"Yes, she's walking down St. George's Avenue now."

"Good," I say. I clutch the phone nearer to me so he can't take it. "She'll put a stop to this. Once she sees this she and everyone else will know the truth. Just you wait."

We fall into silence. Laurence sighs and turns his back on me. I start to play the video again. Once it finishes, I press play again. I see his shoulders tense, watch as his hands grip the edge of the work surface.

"For fuck's sake, Jen, can't you give it a rest!" He swivels around, anger making his face ugly. He storms toward me. "Can't you see it's not me! I know you probably want it to be me, for some reason of your own. You know what the sad thing is? I actually thought we might stand a chance of getting back together. Laughable, isn't it?"

Suddenly, I wish I'd never come to his house. I want to wipe the last few minutes from my personal history. Why did I fuck up everything?

"We could still—"

"Are you joking? Do you think we've got any kind of future together? After you come around here and start to accuse me of—"

"I know I probably shouldn't have just sprung this on you like this. But if we could just talk about it."

"Get it into your head—that . . . that jogger is, was, not me!" He moves toward me to try to do something—I don't know what, take the phone from me, or perhaps even threaten me. As he lunges toward me my throat constricts and my insides turn liquid. What is he really capable of? Just then the bell goes. He freezes and then takes a step back.

"That will be Bex," he says. He gives me a warning stare and then goes to answer the door.

I hear some whispering and then the sound of running footsteps.

"Jen? Oh my God, Jen, are you okay?" calls Bex as she rushes down the hallway.

"Sorry, I know I should have told you I was going to come here, but—"

"Let's not talk about that," she says. "The main thing is that you're safe." She turns to Laurence. "What's wrong?"

I hold out my phone. "This—look—I've got proof," I say. I press play and hand the phone to her.

Bex forces herself to watch the horror. If she'd been on time that day she would have seen it all for real. She presses play again, this time moving the phone closer to her face to get a better view of Laurence. She watches it for a third time, squints, and then compares the image with the man standing in front of her.

"So what do you think?" I ask. "It's him, isn't it?"

Bex takes hold of my hand and smiles sympathetically. "I can see why you might think it was him, but—"

"Don't give me that, Bex. You know it's him."

I grab the phone from her and press play again. "Look," I say, waiting for the moment when the jogger turns toward the camera and his hoodie falls back. "See here," I say, pausing the video and jabbing my finger at the screen. "It's him!"

"It does look a lot like Laurence," she says, softly. "But I'm afraid I don't think it's him. Oh my darling, I'm so sorry."

16

BEX

I lead Jen out of Laurence's house, holding her by the hand like a lost child. For a moment back then, when I told her I didn't think the jogger in the video was Laurence, I thought Jen would collapse. But instead of falling to the floor Jen went into some kind of shock. We left without a scene and Laurence asked me to keep him informed on Jen's progress. Even after their relationship had broken down, Laurence said he still cared for Jen's well-being and I was only too happy to keep a close eye on her and report back to him. Eventually, I told him the truth about how Jen had lost her column, and the lies she had written about her parents. He was shocked, said that she was even more messed up than he realized, and, although he didn't confess it to me, I'm sure that he was relieved that they were no longer living together.

Jen didn't seem to mind that I remained on friendly terms with him, as I think she liked to keep up-to-date with what was happening in his life. I thought it would be for the best if I still kept from her the fact that Laurence and I had had a one-night stand. I didn't want to alienate Laurence, and so, one day when Jen had left us alone together, I reassured him that I didn't bear him any ill feelings. We'd had a fun night together, we were both drunk, and there was no point in ruining what each of us had with Jen because of that. And, truth be told, if I was a bloke I'd much rather go out with Jen than with me. That had made him laugh and had put to rest any concerns he might have had. From that moment, we became friends of sorts. Even after he and Jen had split up, we'd meet up for the occasional drink or coffee, and sometimes he'd ask me to check on his house when he was away on work trips or on holiday. I often remember the happy times when Jen lived there with Laurence. She had seemed so happy then, so carefree, her voice ringing around the house like a familiar melody.

But now, as we stand on the pavement outside the house, Jen is mute. Even though my flat is only ten minutes' walk from here, I don't think she could make it. She has all the energy of a rag doll. And so I order another Uber. The radio's on in the car and suddenly "Nothing Compares 2 U" by Sinéad O'Connor blasts through the speakers. I listen to the haunting lyrics, but I can't allow myself to be dragged back into the past and so force the memory out of my mind. I snap at the driver and ask him to turn off the radio and we sit in silence until we pull into my street. I open the main door, lead Jen up the flight of shared stairs to the attic space, and guide her into an armchair. I kneel down by her feet and take her hands. She looks hollow and drawn.

"Jen, you were right," I whisper. "It was him, Laurence. He was the jogger."

Life begins to stir in her eyes again. "What?"

"I didn't want to say anything in front of him, in case . . ." I say. "I could see that he was angry, and I didn't want to make it worse. I didn't want him to become violent."

"Do you think he would have . . . hurt me?"

"I don't know what he's capable of."

"But you . . . you *believe* me?" She says the words as if I'm confirming a miracle.

"Of course I believe you," I say.

"Oh my God, for a while, I was convinced I was going mad again," she says. She tries to laugh, but instead of laughter tears stream down her face.

"Don't cry," I say. I pass her a tissue and wait for the crying to stop.

"What should we do now?"

"I suppose you should tell the police," I say.

"The police?" She pronounces the words as if they have the potential to do her real harm. "But won't there be a risk that it will all come out—about what happened between me and Laurence? And then they'll learn about my sacking, about . . ." Her voice cracks and she can't say any more.

I look at her, the poor frightened girl. "Don't worry—I'm sure we can work something out," I say.

"I suppose you're right, somehow we'll have to tell the police." She sounds resigned to the pain that will cause her. "But what do you think he was doing up there, on the Heath? I mean, besides jogging."

"I don't know," I say. "Maybe he's got a perfectly innocent explanation."

"Such as what?"

"That he was out running, he saw what was happening, and decided to flee the scene of the crime."

"Do you think he was following me?" she asks. There is a note of hope in her voice, as if she wishes this could be true. It's sad that she still loves him because it's obvious to me that Laurence has moved on.

"Maybe," I say.

We sit in silence again and then I go into the kitchen to make her a cup of tea. As I wait for the kettle to boil I wonder what to do next. Perhaps there is another way.

17

JEN

What would I do without Bex? I can't believe that I doubted her belief in me. But when I was standing in Laurence's kitchen and she told me that she didn't think the mystery jogger was Laurence I felt like I was losing myself. It's an odd sensation, almost as if everything is melting away, like being trapped in one of those surreal paintings by Salvador Dalí.

At that moment I was back in Laurence's kitchen's again, but it was summer. The bifold doors were open to the garden, and a warm breeze drifted inside. Laurence had cooked something from Ottolenghi, laid the table, lit a candle, opened a bottle of rosé. It should have been the setting for a perfect romantic evening. But it was far from that. It was a Saturday, the day after I'd been sacked. I'd confessed everything to Bex, but had said nothing to Laurence.

"Come and sit down," he said, as I stepped into the kitchen. "Supper's nearly ready. I've got some wine, but you may not want any after last night."

"Or it might be just the thing I need to perk me up," I said, pouring myself a large glass and flashing him a false smile. "How was your lunch?"

He talked about his friends from the practice—Chris, Peter, Zoe—and how they'd enjoyed the food at Trullo and then an exhibition about the Bauhaus. His mates were going to really miss him, he said, when he left to start up the new office. But Basel was only an hour or so away by plane, he'd be back and forth to London all the time. He had found us a nice Airbnb, but was looking forward to flat hunting with me.

I didn't really listen. I kept rehearsing how best to tell Laurence about my job. About what I had done. But I couldn't form the words. I had managed, eventually, to confess to Bex. But what would Laurence think of me when I told him the truth?

"How much did you drink last night?" he said, as he forked a piece of black bream into his mouth.

"Too much," I said, gulping down some more rosé.

"Perhaps you should take it easy on the wine," he said. "Actually, I was thinking we should both probably go on a detox for a while. What do you think?"

Laurence was an exercise nut, which meant that although he enjoyed the odd glass of wine, he wasn't in the habit of drinking to excess. He had to be up early to go to the gym or stay in shape to do his regular evening run on the Heath. Nothing could interfere with that. If we opened a bottle, he would have a glass, and I would finish off the rest. So what he was really saying here was *you* need to stop drinking for a while, not me. I'd written about my fondness for alcohol in "Being Jen Hunter." And under normal circumstances, this little row we were about to have would have made the perfect material. But now I no longer had a column.

"I hope now that we're moving to Switzerland you're not going to go dull on me," I said.

Laurence didn't respond, just cleared the plates. I hadn't eaten much of the meal. The stuffing of paprika-flavored pine nuts and rice that oozed out of the fish looked like something I'd seen splattered across the pavement outside our local lock-in. I reached for the bottle of rosé and emptied it into my glass. I knocked back the wine and went to the rack in the understairs cupboard.

"What are you doing?" he said, when he heard the rattle of the bottles.

"Just opening a nice red," I said. "You said you'd bought some cheese, right?"

He didn't respond. He laid the cheese from Neal's Yard and some charcoal biscuits on a wooden board. As I went to pour him some wine, he put his hand over the top of the glass. I don't know what possessed me—perhaps it was his sanctimonious expression that annoyed me—but instead of stopping, I continued to pour. The red liquid covered the top of his hand and cascaded down the side of his glass onto the walnut table, a table I knew he had bought from Matthew Hilton.

"What the fuck are you playing at, Jen?" he said, pulling his hand away. He jumped up to fetch a cloth to wipe himself. I suppose he must have thought I'd done it by accident, but when he turned back to face me he realized that I was still pouring the wine. A red puddle sat on the table, working its way into the expensive wood and dripping down onto the floor.

"Jen—have you gone insane?"

He reached for my hand to stop me. But I managed to outmaneuver him and continued to pour from the bottle until every last drop had been emptied out.

"What's wrong with you?" he shouted. "What the fuck is wrong with you?"

"Have you thought whether I want to move to Switzerland?" Despite writing in my column about my enthusiasm for a new life, I'd started to have some doubts about it.

"I thought we'd talked about that," he said, as he began to mop up the red wine. "You said it would be good for your column. A change of scene. A new culture to write about and all that."

He studied me and the empty bottle of wine that I was holding forth like some kind of ersatz trophy, trying to make sense of what had just happened.

"But if that's the case, if you didn't want to move to Basel, what's all *this* about?" he asked, squeezing the wine-saturated cloth over a bucket. His hands were stained red now. "Talk to me, for God's sake. You're supposed to be the queen of the confessional column. Nothing's 'off limits.' You go where 'no columnist has ever dared go before.' And there you sit, so pissed you're barely able to talk."

I knew that most of the time Laurence was an easygoing, good-natured man. But even he had his point of no return. And now he had reached it. I had pushed him toward it.

"If we're talking about feelings, have you ever given a moment's thought to how I might feel?" he continued. "After I've read about one of our conversations repeated verbatim in your column? Has that ever crossed your mind?"

I reached out for my own glass of wine, unable to meet his eye.

"No, I guess it hasn't, because you're so self-involved, always on the lookout for a way to sell yourself and your life, always ready to betray a confidence for the sake of your tawdry column." The words came quickly and easily, as if he'd been waiting for an opportunity to express them. "No wonder you haven't got any friends left. Well, let me tell you, if you carry on like this, you'll find yourself without anyone at all."

I finally roused myself to speak. "What do you mean?"

"Isn't it obvious what I mean?" he asked. "Do I really have to spell it out to you?"

"You said you didn't mind me writing about you."

"I didn't, to begin with," he said. "In fact, I found it flattering at first. But then it became embarrassing."

"But I changed your name."

"All my friends and colleagues knew James was me," he said. "Why else do you think I put myself forward to lead the Basel office?"

I felt sick in my stomach.

"I became a laughingstock in London," he continued. "A fucking joke. And all thanks to you and that stupid fucking column of yours, which was supposed to give readers a sense of the real you. Well, if this is what 'Being Jen Hunter' looks like, I think I'll take a pass, if it's all very well with you."

"Laurence, don't talk like that, you don't mean that."

"Like what? You're the one who has just ruined a table that cost the best part of four grand."

"So it's about money, is that it? You could never deal with the fact that I've always earned just a tiny bit more than you." I still couldn't bring myself to tell him that my only source of income had disappeared.

"Jesus Christ, can't you hear yourself?" he said.

We fell silent, the air poisonous with rage, as Laurence continued to clean up my mess. After mopping up the wine, he started to try to get the stain out of the table, but as he did so some of the red liquid splattered onto his crisp white shirt.

"For fuck's sake!" he shouted. He threw the cloth down onto the table and faced me, his eyes full of anger. "And don't even think about writing about this. Don't you fucking dare." He started to run through some of the things I had described in my column. "That time we had a row in an Italian restaurant because I accused you of flirting with the waiter. Oh yes, that was just great, to read about myself being portrayed as some kind of Neanderthal. I also really appreciated the one in which you talked about the feelings I had toward my mother and how I never forgave her for leaving my father. Yes, I know both my parents were dead at that point, but there was still a lot of explaining to do when it came to my two sisters. But my favorite—the column where you really excelled yourself—was when you described, in minute detail, my penis. Yes, that was a real classic. All my friends loved that one. And real, groundbreaking journalism, I must say." His voice was rich with sarcasm. "You must be very proud of yourself."

It was this last line that broke me.

18

BEX

Jen's eyes light up when I tell her about how I'm going to deal with Laurence.

"Would you really do that for me?" she asks.

"Of course I would," I say. "Laurence knows not to mess with me. I'll tell him that I know all about his dirty little secret. I'll threaten to expose him as the sender of those weird Twitter messages. I will say that if he doesn't go to the police himself and confess that he was the jogger, then someone might just tip them off. By the way, will you send me the video that Alex took? It might prove useful."

"I'll do it now," she says, taking out her phone.

A moment or so later I hear the familiar ping of the WhatsApp message.

"After all, the police won't realize that you had a relationship as you gave him a false name in your column. And if he so much as breathes a word about what happened, how you were sacked, then I will make his life hell."

She looks at me with admiration. "I'd never want to cross you," she says.

"Well, make sure you never do," I say, holding up a finger and wagging it at her.

The comment lightens the mood and we both laugh. She tells me again how she can't imagine life without me. Apart from the year when I was away traveling the world, she's been by my side. We talk again about that first day we met, back in university, and how we've changed over time. She wonders about what will happen during the next twenty-odd years.

"Perhaps we'll end up as old spinsters, living in the same old people's home," she says. "I can really imagine that. Just like going back to how it all started, living in rooms next to each other. Wouldn't that be hilarious?"

"I can think of worse ways to end up," I say.

She begins to talk about Laurence again. She looks out of the window, over the rooftops of Kentish Town, and gazes northward, toward Tufnell Park.

"I know it sounds mad, but . . . but do you think it's too late for us—Laurence and me?"

"Are you kidding?" I say. "After all that's happened?"

"I know it sounds strange, but hear me out."

I guess my shocked expression must be obvious because Jen adds, "And don't look at me like that. Let me explain."

I sigh and cross my arms. "Go on then," I say. "God knows what case you can make for you two getting back together. But I'm listening."

She takes a deep breath. "What if Laurence was up there on the Heath, jogging, that day. Put yourself in his shoes."

"Okay," I say skeptically.

"Just as Daniel starts to attack Victoria, Laurence sees me standing there. He panics. He runs. He can't bring himself to come forward and make himself known to the police in case it looks as though he was following me."

"Maybe, but then why would he then start to send you creepy messages?"

"How do we know those tweets are from him?" she asks.

"Who else could they be from?"

"I don't know, but—"

"Don't you think it's too much of a coincidence that you got those tweets just after you witnessed that murder-suicide? And that a man who fled the scene of the crime turned out to be your ex-boyfriend?"

"Let's suppose you're right and that those tweets did come from Laurence. What if he didn't send them to frighten me . . . but to get my attention?"

"What are you trying to say?"

"Ignore me, I'm just thinking out loud."

"No, spit it out."

As she continues to gaze out of the window her eyes take on a dreamy quality. "What if Laurence . . . What if he still has feelings for me?"

"Please—you can't be serious. You saw how angry he was back there, in his house. When I arrived it looked as though he wanted to hit you."

"But you can be angry with someone and still love them, right?"

I pause for dramatic effect. "You know what?" I say. "I think you're the most fucked-up person I've ever met."

19

JEN

How could I even think that Laurence wants anything more to do with me? As soon as I say it out loud, I realize how ridiculous it sounds.

Although Bex is joking, I know that I am fucked-up. No wonder men don't want anything to do with me. First Chris, who jilted me if not at the altar then as near as dammit. After that I thought I was washed up, that I'd never find another man again. I couldn't believe it when Laurence had come along, someone I thought I'd be with forever. And so when he told me that he never wanted to see me again after I poured that bottle of wine over his precious kitchen table and . . . I hate to admit what I did. But my therapist tells me that admitting to my behavior is the first step on the road to recovery.

My mind goes back to that night again. I've poured the wine on the table. I've sat and listened to Laurence's big speech. About how he felt he had to leave London and make plans to open the Basel office because of the embarrassment my column has caused him. But then he said that sarcastic comment about my "groundbreaking" journalism, and how I must be so proud of myself.

I felt something snap, like a broken muscle or tendon, only it was in my head. My therapist says I probably did what I did because I felt I couldn't tell Laurence the truth.

The voices telling me that I would never amount to anything, that I would be a failure, that I should never try to get above my station, crowded in my mind. Everything had been leading up to this moment, I thought. And Laurence was just telling me what I already knew. What the editor of the *News* had told me. What Janice, the managing editor, had told me. I was a disgrace. Worthless. A little piece of nothing.

Laurence was saying something, but I couldn't make out what. I felt deaf to the outside world. An image of Mum's face came to me. She was on her deathbed. Cancer had left her looking like a skeleton. She opened her mouth to say something—that she loved me, despite everything. But then another memory—no, it wasn't a memory—came to me. Mum at the wheel of a car. Her head smashed into the steering wheel. With Dad by her side, his skull cracked open.

"No, it's not true," I said.

"What—that your 'work' doesn't make you proud?" asked Laurence. "That's something, I suppose. You've finally got a bit of self-awareness."

"I'm sorry, Mum, I didn't mean to lie," I said.

Laurence fell silent as he realized something was wrong, something much more serious was unfolding before him than a nasty row with a drunk girlfriend.

"Oh my God, Jen, I think I need to get you some help," he said.

As he reached out to comfort me, I smashed his hand away. He must have rung Bex then, I think, and told her to come. "It's all my fault," I shouted. "I've ruined everything. I want to die."

"What's wrong?" he asked. "Has something happened?"

"Nothing happened. That's the problem." I started to lash out, sending the glasses, cheese plates, knives, a pot of fig chutney, onto the floor.

He tried to take me in his arms, to restrain me. At that moment, as his left arm circled around behind my head, I bared my teeth and, feeling like an animal in a trap, I bit deep into his arm. He tried to push my head away, but my teeth remained locked into his skin.

He screamed, and hit me around the face. But still my jaw refused to dislodge itself. I felt someone wrench open my mouth and something soft being forced into it. I bit down hard until I wanted to choke.

The sensation brought me back to the awful reality. What the fuck had I done?

"Oh my God," I whispered, feeling sick at the taste of blood in my mouth. I wanted him to hit me again. I didn't deserve to live. "Just kill me," I said. "Put me out of my misery."

20
BEX

I'm not entirely joking when I tell Jen that she is one of the most fucked-up people I've ever met. It makes her laugh, which is good. But thank goodness I know how to handle her. She talks about that night, the night of her breakup from Laurence. I remember getting a panicked phone call from him, asking me to rush over. Jen had gone absolutely mental, he said.

I threw some clothes over my pajamas—it was a hot night so I didn't need a coat—and I ran up Lady Margaret Road toward his house. I'd been worried about Jen, about how she would tell Laurence the truth about her sacking. His voice sounded frightened, I hoped she wasn't going to hurt herself—or him.

By the time I reached Laurence's house I was out of breath. I rang the bell, kept my finger on it until the door opened. I couldn't take in the figure standing before me—Laurence, his white shirt soaked through with blood, pressing a tea towel to his arm.

"What's happened?" I asked.

"It's Jen—she's having some kind of breakdown."

"What did she do to you?" I said.

He didn't answer, but led me into the kitchen. Smashed glasses and plates littered the floor. There was a huge red stain on the table. Jen was crouched in a corner of the room, a handkerchief clamped in her mouth, her hands pressed onto her head with such pressure it looked as though she was trying to squeeze out her brains.

"Jen?" I asked softly.

I gently removed the handkerchief from her mouth before stepping back. She took in a series of deep breaths as if she had just emerged from a long spell under water. It took her awhile to know what was going on, but when her eyes focused on me she started to howl like a wild animal.

"Oh my darling, it's okay," I said. I crouched down beside her and tentatively held her.

"I'd watch out if I were you," said Laurence, taking the tea towel away from his arm. "When I tried to calm her down she did this."

"What?"

Laurence took me through the rough sequence of events and how the argument had culminated in her biting him on the arm.

"And did she tell you?" I asked. "About the fact that she lost her column?"

Laurence looked dumbfounded.

"She was sacked—yesterday," I added.

"Shit," he said. "Those miserable bastards and their fucking cuts."

I thought it was not up to me to tell Laurence the truth just yet. And so I left it there, for the time being, and helped Jen to her feet.

21

JEN

"So let's get this straight," says Penelope. "The man who was up there, on the Heath, the mystery jogger, he was Laurence, your ex-boyfriend?"

I tell her that's right and I show her the film again. Nothing shocks Penelope—she has seen and done everything. She has witnessed horrific violence and observed at close quarters how human beings can inflict hurt and harm and pain, sometimes for the most idealistic of motives.

"And you think he may be the one who is sending you these odd tweets?" she asks.

I outline my theory, but she rejects it straight away.

"It doesn't sound like the kind of thing a man like Laurence would do," she says. "From the little you've told me about him he seems to be a chap who would just come out with it straight. If he still has feelings for you, as you believe, would he not ask if he could have another chance?"

"Perhaps," I say. "Before all this happened we were supposed to be meeting up for lunch." I haven't told Penelope the whole story about that awful night and how I tried to take a chunk out of his arm. No doubt if I did she would be less likely to believe me. Why would a man want anything more to do with a woman who had done such a terrible thing?

Penelope begins to reminisce about some of her lovers. There had been the famous war correspondent, married with children, whom she had met in Vietnam. He was on the point of leaving his wife and family for her when he was shot and killed. She thought she would never recover, but then one day in London she had met a handsome man in publishing at a boozy party in Notting Hill. Six months later they were married. They'd had two children, had bought this house in Hampstead when the area was full of bohemian types, not the awful moneyed people you get today. Bankers had a lot to answer for, she said. "And talking of bankers, do you know any more about the one behind the attack, Daniel Oliver?"

"Not much more," I say.

"I think it's about time we paid a visit to see his family, or the family of Victoria Da Silva, don't you think?"

"What do you mean?"

"Well, we're not going to solve this if we just wait for answers to come to us."

"So . . . you want to help me?"

"I'm sure you're more than capable of getting to the bottom of this by yourself, but there's nothing like a little sisterly solidarity," she says, her eyes twinkling at the prospect. "I know your friend Bex probably has your best interests at heart, but she's never been a journalist. What does she know of the thrill of the chase?"

Penelope talks about some of her past adventures, when she roamed the world with a blank checkbook or a suitcase of cash.

"I feel sorry for young journalists today, I really do," she says. "Always chained to a desk and limited by the law and the boundaries of good taste. So much you read in the papers today is so goddamn boring."

"So what do you think I—we—should do?" I ask. "Don't you think it's too early to contact the families?"

"It may be," she says, batting her huge eyelashes, "but we'll never find out unless we ask. That's always been my first rule: it's always worth asking the question."

I realize that I could learn a lot from Penelope. She has the personality—the "I'm not taking no for an answer" attitude—and the experience, not to mention her contacts. I wouldn't be surprised if she knew some dodgy private detectives and bent coppers. But I would have to be careful that she didn't suggest doing anything illegal. I didn't want to end up being hauled in front of the Press Complaints Commission. Then everything about my past might come out.

"Don't look so worried," she says, touching my arm. "I know what you're feeling anxious about."

"You do?" I say nervously.

"Before we go any further, I want you to know that this is still your story," she says. "I'm not going to steal it from you. But it's not every day something like this drops into your lap. It could earn you a good deal of money. And I wouldn't dream of sharing any of the proceeds." She raises her hand. "I'm not going to argue. I know you've been a little down on your luck after losing your job. Oh, Jen, I can see I've shocked you a little, I can tell by your expression. I know I may sound a little cynical, mercenary even, but you'll just have to get used to these little remarks of mine."

"No, I find it refreshing," I say. "I think I've been so caught up writing about myself—all that personal confession stuff—that I've lost a little of that journalistic spark I used to have. I'd love it if you could give me some advice and help." I think over what's happened since last Thursday. "So you really think there's a bigger story here?"

"It certainly looks like it," she says. "Especially the possibility that Daniel didn't kill his girlfriend. Obviously, all the evidence and the witness statements point against it. Your own eyes—what you saw that day up on Kite Hill—tell you this can't be right. That message you received sounds absolutely unbelievable. It could well be the work of some crank. But we won't know unless we do a bit of digging. But that's what makes it so delicious, don't you think?"

I'm not quite sure I would use that word. "Yes, I suppose so," I say. "So what do we do next?"

22

BEX

After Jen had bitten him, Laurence said he didn't want to involve the police. He did, however, go to the Whittington Hospital, up the road in Archway, where he told the A&E staff that a stray dog had attacked him. He got his stitches, a tetanus jab, and was home by 3 A.M.

I took Jen back to my flat. She was distressed, remorseful, still in a panic. I was worried that if I called a doctor there was a risk that she would be sectioned, and so I decided to look after her myself. I was certain that she wouldn't try to hurt me. I made her comfortable in my bed, gave her a couple of sleeping pills, and told her not to think about what had happened. It would all be fine in the morning, I said, not believing my own words. I held her hand as she drifted off to sleep and whispered to myself, "What are we going to do with you, Jen Hunter?"

The next morning I was awoken by a howl. I ran from the sitting room to find Jen sitting up in bed, her head in her hands. Clearly, she had just remembered some of what she'd done the night before. She looked awful, with dark shadows under her eyes, her skin all swollen and puffy.

"Tell me it was just a bad dream," she wailed.

"Oh babe," I said, going to sit by her.

"Fuck—what happened? I remember some things, but a lot of it's in a haze."

Quietly, and with as much tact and sensitivity as possible, I explained what Laurence had told me and what I had witnessed.

"Fuck, did I really do . . . *that*?"

"I think it was all too much for you—hearing the news about your job and then—"

"Jesus—and I hadn't taken any drugs," she joked. "Shit, the sad thing is, if I still had my column this would make for confessional gold."

"It sure would have been one hell of a column," I said, smiling.

She fell silent for a moment before another thought occurred to her. "I can't remember—did I tell him about my job? I mean, about why . . . why I lost the column?"

"No, all Laurence knows is that the newspaper let you go, but he thinks it was because of budget cuts," I said. "And I didn't tell him anything different."

"Thank God for that," she said. "I'd rather be known as a cannibal than a liar." I could tell she was putting a brave face on things, but the comment made both of us laugh.

"But seriously, Jen, I do think you need some help," I said.

"You're not going to send me away, though, are you?" she said, sounding like a little girl.

"No, you're not going anywhere," I said.

"Promise?"

"Yes, I promise."

I watched as the tears spilled down her cheeks. I held her tight as she thanked me for being the best friend in the world. Over the course of the following few weeks I barely left her side. I told my boss at Camden Council that I had suffered a bereavement in the family. I also had some holiday owing. I took her to the GP, waited for her when she went in to see her therapist, stood by her to make sure she swallowed her medication, cooked her meals, and made sure she got plenty of exercise—walking on the Heath was her favorite. She really cut down her drinking too, which really impressed me. She was desperate to try to see Laurence again, if only to try to explain, but I advised her against it. I did allow her to send him a card and some flowers. She was hurt when she heard nothing back from him, but I told her that it would take time for him to forgive her.

By the autumn she was showing progress. By the new year she was like a different woman altogether. She went into February with a renewed sense of optimism and purpose. She wanted to get her life back. She moved out of my flat and into a rented room at Penelope's. Her future looked bright. But then she got back in touch with Laurence, and soon after witnessed that horrific incident on Parliament Hill Fields. That's when everything changed.

23

JEN

I'm standing outside the enormous house, or rather mansion, belonging to Mr. and Mrs. Da Silva on The Bishops Avenue wondering what to say. It's exactly a week since the murder-suicide, and the sight of the house intimidates me. It is one of those buildings that appears Edwardian, with its grand proportions, twin turrets, and mellow brickwork, but actually dates from only five or so years back. It's set behind tall security gates, equipped with video entry, and no doubt a whole host of other features all built as the estate agent would say "without regard to cost and expense." Inside is a grieving couple, mourning the loss of their daughter.

Penelope persuaded me to write a letter to the Da Silvas. We found their address on the electoral roll and I wrote to them telling them that I had witnessed the attack. I was honest and told them that I was a journalist, and included the link to the news story I had written. But I assured them that I didn't want to interview them. Rather, I thought it might be helpful for them if they met someone who had been there at the scene of the crime. Perhaps they had some questions that they could put to me that the police had not been able to answer. Within a day I received a response—Pedro Da Silva sent me an email—and we made an appointment at the house.

Despite the assurances I had given them in the letter, I still feel nervous and more than a bit of a fraud. I have to tell myself that I'm here not so much as a journalist but more as a concerned citizen. The message about Daniel Oliver not being the real killer of Victoria Da Silva has to be investigated, if only for it to be dismissed. And so I try to channel my inner Penelope, take a deep breath, and press the buzzer on the intercom. I feel a camera watching me. But what does it see? A smart, not-that-bad-looking blonde woman, wearing an expensive, dark navy Paul Smith wool suit—although I had never bothered to invest in property, I used my salary to purchase a nice collection of clothes over the years. Yes, I look good on the surface. But, of course, the camera is not able to pick up on what's underneath—all the mental scars and well-buried miseries.

A few seconds later I am buzzed in. I walk across the gravel path, past an extravagant fountain of dolphins spouting water from their mouths, and to the front entrance. The door is opened by a sad-eyed old lady, who introduces herself as the family's housekeeper, and then ushers me into a marble and gold hallway. She tells me that Mr. and Mrs. Da Silva are in the sitting room and she guides me past an elaborate staircase, through an atrium with a reproduction mosaic floor that looks as though it could have been copied from a Roman villa, and to a room that overlooks the expanse of the neat back gardens. Mr. Da Silva gets up from his place on the white leather sofa, but his wife remains seated. There is a gigantic chandelier that casts its light into every corner of the space, but there's something dark about the room. Grief casts its shadow here, and no amount of artificial light can banish that.

"Miss Hunter, so very pleased to meet you," says Mr. Da Silva, stretching out his hand. He realizes his tone is a little too upbeat and, after a quick but worried glance back at his wife, says more solemnly, "Thank you for coming to see us." He is a small man with a bald head and a carefully manicured beard. "Please, sit down."

I sit across from Mrs. Da Silva and smile sympathetically, but she continues to stare down at her lap. She seems empty. The loss of her daughter has hollowed her out.

"Thank you for seeing me," I say. "I didn't know whether it would be appropriate. But I . . ."

"It's very kind of you, Miss Hunter," says Mr. Da Silva.

I tell him he can call me Jen. He bows his head in acknowledgment and he presses a buzzer for the housekeeper to bring us tea.

"Now, before we go any further, I just want you to assure us that what we say won't be repeated or printed in any newspaper or go online or whatever," he says. He talks now like the successful businessman he is. His words are not a question, but a statement of fact.

"Yes, of course," I say, choosing my own words carefully. "As I outlined in my letter, although I'm a journalist and I wrote a news piece about the . . . incident, I've no intention of including anything you say in any article I write."

He nods his head again. "You know, Vicky . . . Victoria—at one point, before she got into interior design, she thought about training as a journalist," he says. "In fact, I think she was even a fan of yours, isn't that right, Ana?"

His wife does not respond, and continues to stare down at her hands.

"Sorry, I'm afraid my wife is . . . well, it's all hit her rather hard, quite understandably so," he says. "But Vicky had the world at her feet. She could have done anything with her life."

"She seems like quite a remarkable young woman," I say. "And I'm pleased to hear that she liked what I wrote. Not that you'd describe what I did as real journalism."

"Why is that?"

"I wrote a column, about my life, confessional stuff, very light. Nothing that would change the world."

"I see—you talk about it in the past tense. Why is that?"

"I've moved on to pastures new, as they say."

After a little more small talk—about the house and the Da Silva business (a chain of successful restaurants, food imports, property)—Mr. Da Silva asks me about what I witnessed on Valentine's Day. I describe the events as best as I can, obviously leaving out anything too graphic or violent. The last thing I want is to upset him or his wife. Mr. Da Silva wants to know how quickly the police turned up. I tell him it seemed like an age, but it was only a matter of minutes after that first call. Did they do everything they could to save Victoria? I assure him that they had. Luckily, he doesn't ask for my opinion on whether his daughter had or had not suffered. I'm not sure I could have answered that question honestly.

"Here, have a cup of tea, it looks as though you need it," he says, as the housekeeper returns with a tray. "Ana, will you have some too?"

The housekeeper pours tea for the three of us, but the teacup sits untouched on the table by Mrs. Da Silva.

"It must have been a dreadful thing for you to witness," says Mr. Da Silva. "And the police told me about what you did to try to stop . . . stop it. I'm grateful you did everything in your power to help. You and that other man—what was his name?"

"Jamie Blackwood," I say.

"Yes, him, he was very brave too. But what of the other men at the scene? The police told us that there was a jogger who ran away—and then there was a teenager who fled too? Who were they, do you know?"

I don't want to lie to Mr. Da Silva, but I can hardly tell him about what I know about Laurence. "I think the police are still looking for them," I say, feeling uncomfortable.

"Cowards," he says under his breath. "If they had helped, all this could . . . well, it could have turned out very differently, don't you think?"

I agree with him and I'm about to ask him a question when Mr. Da Silva begins to talk about his daughter: what she'd been like as a child, how funny and clever she was, how talented—she was a wonderful flautist, he said, and a fabulous artist. She had some lovely friends, both from school (she had gone to City of London School for Girls) and university (Durham).

"And Daniel, what was—"

Mr. Da Silva holds up his hands and cuts me off. "I refuse to have his name mentioned in this house," he says. "I'm sorry, Jen, but it just causes too much pain for me, and for Ana too."

"I understand," I say, looking over at Mrs. Da Silva. I suppose she must be on some kind of medication or sedative. I can't imagine what she must be going through. My natural instinct is to thank the Da Silvas for their time, stand up, and say goodbye, but then I think of Penelope and what she will say to me when I get back to her house. I had to toughen up, she had told me. I had to forget about myself and my own opinions. I had to get to the rotten heart of the story.

At the root of this particular story was a mystery, she added. It was not only a case of *why*: what was the motive behind the killing; was it, as the police maintained, driven by jealousy, or was it something else? But it was also a case of *who*: namely, who was responsible for the crime? Could there be any truth in the suggestion that Daniel Oliver didn't kill Victoria Da Silva? And even if that allegation turned out to be baseless, why would someone else want to try to shift the blame away from Daniel?

But my immediate concern as I'm sitting here across from Mr. and Mrs. Da Silva is what to do next. What do I say to this grieving father and mother?

"I can't imagine how you must be feeling," I say. "I know it's not the same, but I lost both my parents when I was fourteen. They died in a car crash."

As soon as the words are out I immediately want to swallow them back down. I think of Bex and how angry she would be with me. I think of the expression of disappointment on the face of my therapist. I think of my poor mum and dad. I stand up to leave.

"Please don't go," says Mr. Da Silva. "Please, stay a little longer."

I do as he says, feeling a blush creep across my cheeks. "That must have been awful for you, to lose your parents at such a young age," he says, before turning to his wife. "Imagine that, Ana." But still there is no response and so he faces me again. "There's a natural order of things—parents aren't supposed to bury their children. And to be taken from us in such a way. By someone who said that they loved her."

I clear my throat and ask gently, "Did Victoria think she would marry ... him?"

"At one time I think she planned to," he says, softening now. "I admired his energy. His ambition. But Ana here, she wasn't so keen. She was suspicious of his good looks. She always said a woman should avoid marrying a handsome man, because in the end they will betray you. And, well, he," he says, still refusing to use Daniel's name, "he was as handsome as they come. Victoria was infatuated."

"And how did they meet?" I ask.

"I don't know—it could have been through her friend, Caro—is that right, Ana?"

His wife looks like she is about to say something, but the effort proves too much for her.

"Caro Elliott," he continues. "Lovely girl. A friend from university. Works in public relations, I believe."

I make a mental note to look her up later.

"She's devastated by the . . . by what happened," he says. "She was in tears when she phoned here . . ." His voice trails off and he stares into the vast garden. "Vicky always said she wanted to be married here, in the back garden. We'll never have that now, will we? No, the only party we'll have for her here will be her wake."

Tears come into Mr. Da Silva's dark eyes. He takes a handkerchief out of his pocket.

"I'm sorry I disturbed you today," I say.

"You haven't disturbed us at all, my dear," he replies. "And please do come and see us again."

I thank him and stand to leave. I say goodbye to Mrs. Da Silva, and he walks me across the room. But just as we are about to pass into the atrium I hear a weak voice. I turn back. It's Mrs. Da Silva. Her posture doesn't change and her gaze is still fixed straight ahead.

"Vicky was going to have a baby," she says, almost as if she is choking on the words. "She was pregnant when . . . when she died."

24

BEX

I watch him watching her. Jen is sitting on a bench at the front of Kenwood House. He is standing behind her, pretending to check his phone. Although I'm not certain, I think I know who he is. He's the teenage boy who ran away from the scene of the murder.

I didn't notice him at first. Why should I? He must have been mingling amongst the crowd of tourists, young mothers with their children, and retired Hampstead types. He stood out because he wasn't moving—he was just standing there, uncertain about what to do next—and because he kept glancing over at Jen, quick, furtive squints to begin with, and then longer, more intense looks. My first instinct was to go over and confront him, but I stopped myself. By watching him I knew I had the advantage. I had the chance to study him.

I walk over toward him, but I'm careful not to let him see me in case he recognizes me; he may have followed Jen during the times we were together. I take shelter behind a tree and notice every little thing about him. He's wearing a pair of sandy-colored chinos, a blue Oxford shirt, and a tweed jacket. He's not sporting the latest trainers, but a pair of brown brogues. I wonder whether he dresses like this all the time or whether he's in disguise.

Jen gets up from the bench and begins to walk along the path. The boy follows at a safe distance. I begin to shadow him. I consider messaging or calling Jen to tell her what's happening, but I worry about her reaction. That maybe she'll panic or cause a scene.

I quicken my pace, hoping that the boy doesn't look around. I also hope that Jen doesn't turn her head. We move away from the track, away from the crowds, and onto a stretch of pathway shielded by a long line of trees. The temperature drops a few degrees. There is a strange hush, as if the birds in this shaded spot have flown away and deserted us. If I can't see anyone apart from Jen and the boy it probably means no one else can see us either. We are two women, alone on the Heath, and one of those women, a particularly vulnerable one, is being followed. I refuse to let the images I've seen in the newspapers and on television over the last few weeks—boys and girls, men and women stabbed to death at an alarming rate—get to me. But at the same time I have to be prepared to protect Jen.

What if he has a knife?

As I step forward I feel an obstacle in my path. My foot is stuck on a gnarled tree root and, before I know it, I'm falling. I swallow the pain as my palms make contact with the stony ground. I squeeze my eyes shut in the naive, childish belief that if I do so nobody will see me. I look up, half expecting to see the teenage boy standing before me, but he's gone. I strain my neck and can see no sign of Jen. I push myself upward, wince as I clear the cluster of small stones and twigs from my stinging palms, and run.

25

JEN

I hear the sound of someone behind me. I tell myself it's nothing to worry about, it's my overactive imagination at work again. It will be someone and their dog, a mother with their toddler. But when I glance behind, I see him. He's dressed differently than the time I saw him on Parliament Hill Fields, but I know it's him. The boy who ran away from the crime scene.

My first instinct is to get the hell out of here. I quicken my pace and take a path that I think leads away from the wooded section and into a more exposed space. I don't want to look around, but I know he's still on my trail. What does he want? Why is he here? And how did he find me? But instead of opening into an expanse of greenery, the path only takes me deeper into the wood. I hear the snap of a twig, the shuffle of some decaying leaves. I take a deep breath and slowly turn around.

Standing by a tree is the boy. He begins to walk toward me. I look around for signs of other people, but there's no one here. Just as I open my mouth to scream he puts up his hand to try to stop me.

"I just want to talk," he says.

Although my throat feels like it's beginning to seize up, I manage to rasp out a couple of words. "What about?"

"About what happened—last week," he says. "With that bloke and his girlfriend. I read your piece in the newspaper."

"How did you find me?"

"I saw you, at the place where it happened, and then I followed you back to where you live," he says. It's obvious he is not proud of this fact. "I didn't know how else to get hold of you."

I think of those Twitter messages.

"What's your name?"

He hesitates slightly before he says, "Steven. Steven Walker."

He takes another step forward, at which point I take a step backward, steadying myself by a tree.

"I'm not here to hurt you or to cause any trouble," he says.

"How do I know you're telling the truth? How do I know I can trust you?"

The questions seem to confuse him because he doesn't answer. And so I ask a third question.

"Have you got something to hide?"

"No, what makes you say that?" he says defensively.

"I'm just wondering why you fled the scene of the crime. When the police arrived."

He runs his hand over his smooth, closely cropped head. "I guess I was frightened," he says. "You might not have noticed it, but black kids haven't had an easy time with it when it comes to the police, especially when a knife is involved."

The thought that he may have a knife hadn't occurred to me, but the mention of one immediately makes me more fearful. But I realize that the person who I've been searching for is now standing in front of me. There are things I need to ask him.

"Look, as I said, I'm not here to hurt you," he insists. "I just want to talk." He begins to walk toward me with an expression of desperation in his eyes. "I didn't do anything wrong, you've got to believe me," he insists.

"Why do you think you might have done something wrong?" I ask.

He continues to move toward me. He's only a few feet away now. He doesn't seem like the violent type. If anything, there's an air of sensitivity, indeed delicacy, about him.

An expression of disgust fills his eyes as he begins to recall what happened that day. "I shouldn't have been up there, on the Heath," he says. "I shouldn't have seen that happen. I should have been at school, William Ellis. I belong to the chess club which meets each Thursday lunchtime. But that day I'd had . . . well, I'd had a difficult morning."

"None of us should have seen what we saw," I say. "Tell me what you remember."

"I walked up to the top of the hill. I go there when I'm feeling stressed, when it's all been too much, y'know? I like the view of the city. I don't know, it makes me feel like I might achieve something one day. That my life isn't completely useless."

I smile and encourage him to continue.

"You see, I live with my mum. She's ill. Mental illness. Started soon after my dad left. Anyway, that morning she had really kicked off. Started saying things she didn't mean. Smashed some pots in the kitchen. I know when she's like this that it's not really her. Sometimes she misses her medication, right? I was supposed to have chess club, like I said, but I got these texts from her all morning. I was worried about her. And I know I should have gone to check on her. But I couldn't face it. And so I came to the hill to get some air and clear my head."

He thinks for a moment while he assesses me. "You're not going to write all this down, are you?"

"Well, I am a journalist, that is my job." The response is more of an expression of wish fulfilment than anything else.

"But you won't print anything I tell you." An aggressiveness has crept into his voice now. "You won't write those things I said about my mum."

"Don't worry, Steven," I say. "I won't write anything unless I clear it with you first. And no, I won't write about your mother."

"I can trust you?"

I think it's odd that only a few minutes before I was asking him the same question. I still don't know the answer to that. After all, he's admitted to following me, to watching me. How do I know he isn't the one sending those creepy messages?

"Yes, you can trust me," I say. "Why don't we go and grab a coffee somewhere?"

He nods and smiles. Just as we turn to make our way out of the wooded area I hear the sound of running and someone calling my name.

"Jen? Jen—are you there?"

It's Bex's voice. What is she doing here? A moment or so later I see her coming toward us at top speed. Her face is flushed and there's panic—and anger—in her eyes.

"Get away from her!" she screams.

Steven doesn't know what to do. He looks confused, scared, and his head turns from side to side as he tries to process what's going on. "What?"

"Don't you dare touch her!" she exclaims. "Get away from her!"

"It's fine, Bex, it's only Steven, he was another witness—he's trying to help," I shout back.

But it's too late. Steven takes one look at the fury descending toward him and he bolts with the speed of a frightened deer. I call out his name, try to explain, but it's no use.

"Oh my God, Jen, are you all right?" asks Bex.

"How did you know I was here?"

"I knew something like this was about to happen," she says. "Thank God I was nearby. Did he hurt you?"

"No, not at all, and he was about to tell me something important—about what happened that day."

"Was he following you?"

"Yes, but I'm sure he's not dangerous."

"How can you possibly know such a thing? Why was he stalking you?"

"Obviously, he wasn't the only one." My fingers fly up to my lips, almost in an effort to push the words back into my mouth.

I see the amazement and then the distress in Bex's face. She looks as hurt as if I'd just slapped her across the cheek.

"Sorry, in the future I'll just let you get cut up into little pieces by the next madman who follows you into a dark wood."

"Bex, I didn't mean it like that, really I didn't."

There is a hardness in her eyes. Bex hardly ever gets cross or angry, well, at least not with me, and to see her like this is frightening.

"Do you know what, Jen? How about you try to take care of yourself for a change?"

"What do you mean?"

"Just that. It's obvious that you've found my attentions a bit too much."

"It's not that—it's since witnessing the attack I've lost sight of—"

"How many times have I watched your back?" she asks. "How many times have I got you out of trouble?"

"I know—and I'm grateful, really I am."

"And with all that business over losing your column and then Laurence . . ."

"You've been so kind—the best friend anyone could want." I reach out to touch her, but she takes a step back.

Her expression is harsh and cold, like she's turned a light off inside of her. The effect almost winds me.

"I suggest if you want a best friend you start hanging out with your new favorite person—go and ask Penelope for some support. And, by the way, good luck with that."

I can't believe this is happening. She turns from me and starts to walk away. I keep expecting her to spin around, her face full of laughter as she shouts, "Gotcha!" But she doesn't. She just carries on walking, past the trees and out of the wood into the sunlight, while I'm left standing alone and in the dark.

26

BEX

It's good for her to see if she can manage by herself, I tell myself, as I walk off across the Heath. What do they say—sometimes you have to be cruel to be kind? Jen really had it coming to her though. What a fucking cheek she had to accuse me of stalking her when I was only doing my best to protect her. Who knows what could have happened in that isolated woodland if I hadn't turned up when I did? Jen believed that the boy—what was he called? Steven?—was harmless, but who knows? I left her knowing that she wasn't in any real danger—I had seen him run off. But it was important to teach her a lesson.

As I walk I realize that perhaps it's time to get on with my own life. I'm due back at work at Camden Council soon. I've my own friends and interests that have nothing to do with Jen. But as soon as I start to make plans I feel a terrible sense of sadness and guilt. I'm so bound up with Jen that we're like sisters. And, like sisters, although we have our occasional rows and nasty spats, we will always return to each other.

I take out my phone to see if she's sent a message or a text, but there's nothing. I'm not going to ring her, I tell myself. Let her sweat. Then she'll learn to appreciate me and everything I've done for her.

I replay the scene on the Heath in my head, hardly noticing the route I take toward Kentish Town. At the flat, I try to fall back into my normal routine—I had some washing to do, some work emails to check, a spot of cleaning—but I can't get Jen out of my mind. She haunts me like a ghost, a shimmering mirage just out of reach. I go for a walk, but she's still there, temporarily inhabiting the bodies of passing strangers. She's around every corner, at the bottom of each street, glimpsed in windows, on passing buses, her blonde hair a beacon of light in a gray, lifeless world.

At night, I take a couple of pills and wash them down with some white wine. But as I gulp down the cold, golden liquid, even that reminds me of her. I sleep fitfully, my dreams saturated by distorted images of her. Jen on the Heath, desperate and lost, her clothes torn, her arms scratched by brambles. She is calling my name. She says she can't live without me. She walks down to the ponds and looks into the water, her reflection beckoning her in. She steps forward and disappears into the murky depths. But this then morphs into a vision of Jen at university, seeing her for the first time that day in halls. The awkward little thing desperate for someone to take her under their wing. She looks terrible. Her skin is a mass of acne. Her hair is a lank mess. Her breath smells. *Help me*, she says. *I need you.*

She begins to tell me how she's suffered. She talks about the tragic death of her parents in that car accident. I see her in the car with them, but she's driving. She's smiling as she presses her foot on the accelerator, a mad look on her face. Her mum and dad are screaming at her to slow down, but as the car speeds through a network of deserted country lanes Jen laughs like someone unhinged. There is a manic look in her eyes. She wants them to die. As the car turns a bend she takes her hands off the steering wheel and the vehicle crashes into a tree. Her parents are catapulted through the windscreen—the glass tears their skin into shreds, the force of the collision bends their heads backward, almost decapitating them—but Jen just sits there, serene and unhurt, a smile of accomplishment on her face. It wasn't an accident, I realize. She had it all planned. She wanted them dead.

I wake up sweating. I get up to go to the bathroom, switch the light on, and splash some cold water on my face. I look at myself in the mirror. I don't have brown hair, but blonde. The shape of my nose is not right, the contours of my cheeks are different. My eyes are not my eyes. For a moment, I see not my face but Jen's staring back at me. I gasp in fear—this can't be happening to me, I think—but the noise in my throat wakes me up. I'm still in bed, still clammy with sweat, still dreaming of Jen.

27

JEN

'm no longer crying by the time I reach Penelope's house, only furious with myself. Bex has been the one good, constant thing in my life, and I've gone and pushed her away. I think about a future without her. Everything seems so bleak. What can I do to make it up to her? To show her that I didn't mean what I said? I will ring her later and apologize. Even though I haven't got any money, I'll suggest taking her out for a meal or a spa day at a fancy hotel.

I turn the key in the lock of the front door and immediately hear Penelope's voice.

"Darling, is that you?" she calls out.

"Yes, only me," I reply.

I never stopped to think that Bex would ever feel jealous about my new friendship with Penelope. What is there to envy? Yes, I admire Penelope a great deal from a professional point of view. She is feisty and full of anecdotes. She has lived a good life. She makes me laugh. And yes, she inspires me. But I can't compare our superficial acquaintance with the depth of the friendship I enjoy with Bex. When I speak to Bex next I will tell her this, and more.

I walk into the kitchen where Penelope is sitting at the long wooden table reading the papers and listening to Radio 4. When she sees me she raises her head and asks, "Now, tell me, how did you get on? I want to hear each single detail, from the very beginning, as soon as you stepped into the Da Silvas' home until you left. Leave nothing out, no matter how insignificant." Over a cup of tea I tell her everything. At the news of Victoria Da Silva's pregnancy her eyes light up and she claps her hands like a small child at a birthday party. The instinct for news, however unsavory or tragic, has not left her. I think about that quote—now, whoever said it?—about how writers have a splinter of ice in the heart. I go on to tell her about the encounter with Steven Walker, but I say nothing about my argument with Bex.

"But this is simply wonderful," says Penelope, fluttering her eyelashes. "You're making real progress. Victoria's pregnancy could be the key to the whole thing. But what a shame the young boy ran away before he had the chance to tell you what he knew. Cold feet, I suppose?"

"Yes, I guess that must have been it," I lie.

"But never mind, now that you know where he goes to school you can just wait for him outside the school gates. That's if he ever turns up for class. He seems like he's got his hands full trying to deal with the situation at home. And, of course, you must follow up the other good lead about Victoria's best friend, what did you say her name was?"

"Caro Elliott," I reply.

"Have you heard from Julia Jones again? Or that young doctor?"

"Not yet," I tell her. "I need to chase them."

"Yes, you do," she says. She's about to ask another question when she stops herself and looks at me. I feel her eyes burning into me. "Jen—are you sure everything's all right?"

"What do you mean?" I ask, turning my head away from her so she can't see my expression.

"I don't know, I feel there's something you're holding back."

"I think I've told you everything," I say. If I explain about what happened with Bex I'm afraid I will burst into tears again. "Thanks for the tea," I add, standing up. "I'd better go and send a few emails."

Penelope clears her throat, pushes herself up from her chair, and says she has something to say to me. There is something about the tone of

her voice—something like that of a headmistress at an expensive girls"
school—that strikes fear into my heart.

"Yes, what is it?"

"You mustn't look like a rabbit caught in the headlights," she says. "It's
nothing serious. Just that since you've been out I've been doing a little
research myself."

"What did you find out? Anything interesting?"

"It has potential," she says, mysteriously. "You see, one of the advantages
of being an old, decrepit specimen such as myself—particularly if you're an
elderly *woman*—is that no one seems to notice you. You become invisible.
You, my dear, are still an attractive young thing—"

I try to tell her that by definition I'm middle-aged, but Penelope holds
up her hand, a signal that she will not be interrupted. "You are still an
attractive young woman," she continues, "and so you won't understand
this. Why would you? When I was your age, well . . . I could tell you a
few stories." She smiles to herself, no doubt amused by some of her past
adventures. "But I mustn't digress. The point is that as an old crone one is
able to slip past certain people unnoticed."

I begin to feel anxious at what she is about to tell me. "Penelope, what
are you talking about? I hope you haven't done anything—"

"I've told you before, you don't find anything out by just waiting for
things to happen," she says, crossly. "You need to show more—what is that
unfortunate word used by Americans?—spunk."

I smile and let her continue.

"Don't stand in judgment on me, but I thought it was about time we
found out a little more about the killer, Daniel Oliver," she says. "And so
I paid a visit to see his mother."

"Tell me you're making this up."

"I went to see his mother—what's wrong with that?"

I try to control myself. "Oh, Penelope, I wish you hadn't."

"But why?"

"Just that I was trying to do this on my own terms, with sensitivity
and—"

"Sensitive is my middle name," she responds.

"I know, but—"

"So what's the problem?"

I don't know what to say, so I sigh deeply. I regret ever involving Penelope.

"And I suppose you don't want to hear what she told me then?"

She takes up an opened bottle of red wine and pours a glass. She passes it to me with a wicked glint in her eye. It's impossible to remain angry with Penelope for long, and even though I try my best to continue to look cross with her, I feel my mouth relaxing into a smirk. I take a sip of wine as she pours another glass for herself.

"I haven't lost my touch, I can tell you," she says. "The house was being staked out by a couple of the tabloids. They were so obvious. Young men sitting in cheap cars, dressed in even cheaper suits. They kept their eyes out for their counterparts, but what they hadn't reckoned on was an old lady. Even though I doubt they would have recognized me, I did go out of my way to disguise myself a little. I put on a pair of thick spectacles and an unflattering hat. And of course, I went entirely without makeup, which as you know is very unlike me."

She's not wrong there. I have never seen Penelope without her trademark pink lipstick, flawless and evenly applied foundation, and extravagant eyelashes.

"I felt so awful without my warpaint that as soon as I came in I made myself up," she says. "Anyway, what was I saying? Oh yes, I was hobbling down the pavement, doing my best old lady act—do you know that I actually had an audition at RADA when I was young? I would have gone onto the stage if it hadn't have been for—"

"Penelope—tell me what happened!"

"Yes, of course, my dear," she says, laughing at my impatience.

"I was hobbling down the pavement when I passed the house. Number 57. I'd found the address of Mrs. Oliver beforehand, obviously. I simply pretended to feel a bit dizzy, like I was going to faint. One of the spotty-faced young lads, from the *Mirror*, I believe, jumped out of his car and came to my rescue. He offered me some water, but I told him that I wanted to use the loo—quite urgently. You should have seen the look on his face! He was scared that I was going to shit myself."

"Penelope!" I exclaim.

"Don't pretend to be shocked."

"I'm not pretending—I am shocked. Not by your language, but by the fact you would use such tactics to get into someone's house."

"This is tame stuff compared to some of the stunts I've pulled in the past. Before Leveson and all that crap spoilt everything. One day I'll tell you about the time I used a wooden leg and a blonde wig."

"No doubt you will," I say. "But back to earlier today."

"The lad from the *Mirror* escorted me up the driveway and rang the bell of Number 57. Mrs. Oliver thought he was asking for yet another interview, but when he explained that he'd come across an old dear who had nearly collapsed outside on the street, asking to use the nearest toilet, she promptly ushered me into the house. She was the salt of the earth type, a decent working-class woman who would never dream of turning away someone in need."

"Did you not tell her what you were really there for?"

She looked startled by my suggestion. "Of course not! What do you take me for—some kind of beginner?"

I am about to tell her that what she had done was probably against the law, when she launches into her account of her encounter with Mrs. Oliver.

"She couldn't have been kinder," she says. "She showed me to the loo, where I ran my hands under the taps. I came out and thanked her, told her that she was a lifesaver. I said that I was on the way to visit my daughter's grave in the local cemetery—"

"You told her *what?*"

"That I was going to clean my daughter's grave and I had taken a turn for the worse. The grief was still fresh. I knew she'd understand."

"You can't say that."

"Well I did, and I'm pleased to tell you—"

"But Penelope, you must realize that the things you've done and said in the past—well, you can't do and say them today."

"Perhaps not, if you're happy to be the average kind of reporter. I like to think that I've always operated on a different plane." The audacity of her behavior takes my breath away. "And luckily, the tactic worked," she continues. "She invited me for a cup of tea, over which she told me about the incident with her son. Of course, she never mentioned the words "murder" or "suicide." Mrs. Oliver—Karen—said that Daniel had been under a lot of pressure at work. He had a good job, a well-paying job, in the city. She was so proud of him. He'd done so well, not like his sister, Tina, a waitress who is now living in Australia. I got the impression mother and daughter are no longer in touch.

"Karen started crying when she related what happened next, about how Dan had done what he'd done on Hampstead Heath. She was still trying to come to terms with it, she said. She didn't understand it. I didn't need to ask any questions. I just listened while she poured out her heart to me. There had been some trouble when he was a teenager, an infatuation with an older woman. But with the arrival of Vicky on the scene she thought he was on the straight and narrow. She thought he'd put his problems behind him.

"Mrs. Oliver talked about what a lovely girl Vicky was. Well, she thought that to begin with. But then Dan had started to lose his temper with her, his mother that is. He'd fly off the handle over any little thing. Karen knew there was something wrong. You can't fool a mother's instinct, she said. He became moody, depressed. He began to drink more. She suspected other substances were involved, too, perhaps cocaine. She knew that the men in the city liked to work hard and play hard. But one day, when Dan was visiting her alone, Karen asked him if he was happy. He normally played the hard guy, you know the type, she said. But on that occasion his face just crumpled and he fell to pieces. She cradled his head in her arms, just like she'd done when he was a little boy. But now, she said, she'd never be able to do that again."

Penelope pauses as she sips from her glass of wine.

"Mrs. Oliver told me that nothing would excuse her son's behavior. She would always be angry with him for what he had done, for killing himself as much as doing what he did to Vicky. Looking back, they probably should never have got together. He should, she said, have stuck to his own type of person. He should never have tried to aim out of his league. The problem, of course, was the fact that he was handsome. And posh girls did seem to like him. It was then that I asked my one and only question: why had Dan been so upset that day when he came to see her? She told me that Dan thought Vicky was having an affair. That day he said that if he found out that this was true he would kill her. But Mrs. Oliver thought it was just a figure of speech. She never believed he would do that. Never in a million years."

28

BEX

I wake up, drowning in a sea of guilt. I look at my phone. It's 6:15 A.M., too early to call or message. I lie there, thinking of Jen. I type out a line or two on WhatsApp, include a funny emoji, but then delete it. I try to put myself in her position. If I was feeling paranoid and had received some weird messages on Twitter I would be feeling jittery too. I might very well lash out. Despite my flare-up of anger that had exploded inside my head when Jen accused me of stalking her, I am ready to forgive her. I tell myself that I will make everything better today.

I get up and put on my running gear, grabbing a water bottle as I leave. A long run always helps to recharge me. In a matter of minutes I'm out on the streets, taking in the cold, early-morning air.

I take the longer route to the Heath, across the bridge over the railway line and through Dartmouth Park. I jog past Julia Jones's house, a warm glow coming from one of the windows inside. As I run I enjoy the feeling of energy being expended, the rush of blood to my head, the sound of my breath as I inhale and exhale. At Parliament Hill Fields I choose the pathway that leads to the viewing point. The cordon is still there, a marker that something terrible happened here.

I pause for breath and take in the view. The city is shrouded in low-lying cloud, the sun casting its delicate rays onto the enormous glass skyscrapers.

I start to run again, across the Heath and down to the ponds. I do a circuit, tracing the line of the water, entranced by the reflections of the ever-changing sky. Then, as I pass by the entrance to the men's pond, I see a figure in the distance. It's Laurence. He's coming toward me. I jog on the spot for a moment to make my turn less noticeable and then start running, slowly, away from him. I take a left and continue to jog on the spot, in the hope that he will run straight ahead; if he comes in my direction I will start off again in an effort not to be seen. I watch as he jogs ahead. I follow him, allowing a few other runners to occupy the space between us.

I think about the recent conversation I had with Jen about Laurence. I remember how he hurt her. I recall, once again, the horrific scene that night in his kitchen when Jen went to pieces. I wonder whether that relationship could ever have really worked. They are such different people, after all.

Laurence glances at his wrist, most likely his Fitbit, and bursts into a sprint. I increase my pace, hearing my breathing quicken. As I run I begin to think about what might happen to him. A series of images flash into my mind. He's being pushed in front of an oncoming tube train, his body mangled. I see him bludgeoned over the head, blood spilling from his temples. I imagine him running across the Heath, on such a morning as this. There are lots of isolated spots where it could happen. He's passing through a stretch of woodland, he's got his buds pushed deep into his ears, just as he has today. He's unaware of the woman running up behind him. She has a knife. She plunges it deep into his neck, severing his carotid artery. There is a spurt of blood and he falls to the floor. He opens his mouth to talk, but nobody can hear him. He dies a lonely and a painful death.

Whatever happens I'll make sure of one thing: he's going to suffer.

29

JEN

I couldn't sleep last night. Now it's early in the morning—too early—and I'm on my phone. I can't believe what I'm reading on MailOnline. I'm finding it difficult to catch my breath, as if the words themselves have the power to choke me.

VALENTINE'S DAY MURDER VICTIM
WAS PREGNANT

I reread the headline, thinking that there must be some mistake or that it's about another woman, a different case. But as my eyes scroll down through the short news report, and I see the accompanying photograph of Victoria, I feel as though I am going to be sick.

> Victoria Da Silva, the daughter of multimillionaire businessman Pedro Da Silva, who was murdered by her boyfriend, Daniel Oliver, was pregnant.
> The beautiful 26-year-old was brutally stabbed on 14 February—Valentine's Day—at a well-known viewing point on Parliament Hill Fields, north London.
> Oliver, 28, a city trader, then stabbed himself to death.

A source close to the investigation says, "Not only did Daniel kill Victoria, but that day he also murdered Victoria's unborn child." The source, who did not want to be named, did not know how long Victoria had been pregnant, or whether her family or friends knew whether she was pregnant at all, but suggests that this could have been a factor in the killing. "We've all been wondering why Daniel did such a cruel and terrible thing—it all seems so senseless, somehow—but there's been talk that perhaps the baby wasn't his," says the source. "If he discovered this then it might have been enough to send him over the edge. Even so, of course what he did was completely indefensible. Victoria was like a beacon of light. She was such a lovely person."

The Metropolitan Police refused to confirm or deny Victoria Da Silva's pregnancy. They told MailOnline that there would be an inquest held in due course. Mr. and Mrs. Da Silva, who live on The Bishops Avenue, refused to comment.

Shit. I take a couple of deep breaths and throw down my phone in disgust.

"Penelope!" I shout, opening the door of my bedroom.

"Yes, darling, what's wrong?" she calls up from the kitchen. "I'm down here."

I storm down the stairs, hardly bothering to use the bannister that snakes down through the space. As I run I think how easy it would be to fall; one false step and I could plummet down the hard, marble steps.

"Normally, I wouldn't be up at such an ungodly hour, but today I have to—"

"What the hell do you think you're playing at?" I interrupt, my voice rasping.

She glances up from her breakfast of smoked salmon on toast and asks, "Excuse me?"

"I know it was you."

"Me? Please tell me what I'm supposed to have done."

She has an amused expression in her eyes that infuriates me.

"You gave a tip-off to MailOnline, didn't you?" I say.

"I don't know what you're talking about," she replies as she continues to eat her breakfast.

"About Victoria's pregnancy. Who else could it have been?"

"I'm sure it could have been one of many people," she says, refusing to meet my gaze. "One of her friends, perhaps? What's the name of that PR you told me about? Caroline?"

"Caro, Caro Elliott," I say. "And I doubt she would have done something as low as that. And besides, you've got contacts there."

"Oh come on, Jen," she says, placing her knife back down on her plate. "Let's get a few things straight." She shifts in her seat, turns to me, her eyes blazing. "One: I am not a liar. If I'm asked a direct question by a friend I tend to tell the truth. Two: I wouldn't dream of getting in touch with MailOnline. If I wanted to tip someone off it would at least be one of the top editors at the paper, not some hack on the digital division. And three: I know this is your story, and I told you I would help, but I wouldn't interfere."

"What, like when you went to pay Daniel Oliver's mother a surprise visit without informing me? That's not interfering?"

"Oh, come on, you know that visit netted a valuable piece of information."

I could feel my face burning red now. "It may have done, but by doing it you went behind my back."

"Well, I don't have to help," she says. "I can always let you get on with this in your own rather pathetic and half-hearted manner."

"I think I'd appreciate that," I reply.

"And to think I thought you had something," she murmurs to herself under her breath.

"Sorry? What was that you said?"

"Oh, nothing." She bites into a piece of toast and crunches it, the sound seeming to amplify around my head.

"If you've . . . if you've got something to say . . ." I can feel my voice breaking, the words splitting apart. "I'd like you to tell me."

"Well, if you'd like to hear some home truths, let's start with this," she says, taking up a white napkin and running it across her lips. As she puts it back in her lap, I notice there's a trace of her pink lipstick. "You've got a nice way with words, you can tell a good story, but I think the years working as—what do people say now?—a confessional columnist have rather corrupted your journalistic instinct. In my day none of my contemporaries would dream of talking about, well, about some of the intimate aspects of one's life. And if they did, it would never be classified as journalism, rather something more appropriate to what you'd see scrawled on the door of a public lavatory."

I am so shocked I can't respond. So that's what she really thinks of columns such as mine.

"My advice would be to abandon this story altogether—it's clear you haven't got what it takes to pursue it, to do it justice," she adds. "Yes, I see now that your friend Bex was right. No wonder she was so worried about you. You're not ready for this. Perhaps you never will be."

The mention of Bex's name makes me want to cry. I want to call my friend and apologize. I want to hear her voice. If only we could have a glass of wine together. I feel for my phone in the pockets of my jeans, but realize I've left it upstairs. Penelope continues to talk—about the need for toughness, for objectivity, for distance—but I can't stand listening to her a moment longer. I don't want to humiliate myself by weeping in front of her. And so, without a word of explanation, I turn from her and make for the door.

30

BEX

I let Laurence jog away, confident he hasn't seen me. I'm good at hiding, making myself invisible. I always have been, ever since I was a child.

I suppose it started at home when I had to make myself invisible out of necessity. Dad would come home, invariably wanting a fight. Mum, after too much wine, would say something inoffensive, but Dad would twist it into something else, and accuse her of nagging or criticizing him. Their voices would rise, and soon I would hear the noise of Dad's fist smashing into Mum's face. I can still remember the sound of something cracking. The splatter of Mum's vomit as it hit the lino in the kitchen. The clatter of a couple of her teeth dropping into the sink. Once, I tried to intervene. I ran into the hallway to try to pull Dad off her, but he brushed me aside with such force that I fell into the stairs, bruising the side of my face. Since then I learned how to pass into a room unnoticed, and just stand there, unobserved, like a ghost watching the living. The skill has come in useful over the years, both at work and when I've been keeping track of Jen, watching out for her, making sure she is safe.

Jen. I say her name to myself. I can't continue being angry with her, and so I take out my phone and I'm about to ring her when I feel as if I'm being watched. The idea someone might be studying me from a distance, spying on my every move, unsettles me. I look up, half thinking Laurence has spotted me. But I can't see him—or anyone else suspicious. I glance at the time on my phone. It's still quite early—I don't want to wake Jen—and so I text her instead. I hold the phone, hoping that by looking at it I can will some kind of immediate response from her, but there's nothing.

I see the back of someone I vaguely recognize. I quicken my pace. Yes, I'm sure it's the teenage boy I saw yesterday with Jen. What was his name? Steven. Is it him who's been watching me? I follow him at a distance, running on the spot when I sense that there's a risk he might turn around. What's he doing here this early in the morning? I don't trust him. I didn't like the way he was looking at Jen yesterday. And why was he following her, shadowing her, like that? Jen accused me of stalking her, but I was doing it out of a need to protect her, not like him. And why did he run off? He's got something to hide, I'm sure.

The realization of what is happening stops me in my tracks. How could I have been so stupid? Steven is walking in the direction of Hampstead. And Jen.

31

JEN

I still can't believe what Penelope said to me. What a bitch. I'm so furious I forget to pick up a jacket or coat, and I'm freezing. But I don't want to risk going back inside. God knows what I would do to her. Perhaps I should think about moving out, getting another place. But where would I go? I run through my list of friends. My stupid column had brought about the breakdown of most of my relationships. There was only Bex left.

I walk as quickly as I can, both in an effort to keep warm and to dispel the hot ball of anger and frustration that burns within me. I hardly notice anything around me, and a few minutes later I realize I'm on the Heath. Perhaps I can pop over to Bex's flat in Kentish Town. But no doubt she's still cross with me after what I said to her. I reach into my pocket for my phone, but remember I left it in my room. Fuck. Could I just surprise her? If I turned up on her doorstep with something—flowers, some chocolates, a bottle of wine for later?—then she would have to forgive me, wouldn't she? I start to make my way across the network of paths that lead across the Heath. Myriad thoughts cloud my head. My whole life has been a mess. At one point I thought I was so successful. It looked as though I had everything. An amazing wardrobe of designer clothes. I had a string of handsome and clever boyfriends, culminating in Laurence. I had a voice: millions of people read what I had to say. And yet it was all a facade. My swish clothes served to disguise my inner demons. I drove those boyfriends away, and Laurence ended up hating me. Even my name, which I'd changed by deed poll, wasn't real. And my column? It served no purpose but to give a quick hit of *Schadenfreude* to the readers—they may have crap lives, but at least they're not as batshit crazy as that Jen Hunter.

Thanks to my therapy, I realize that I had become addicted to writing about my life, but also addicted to seeking out dysfunctional situations that made for better copy. And although I know I should look upon losing my column as an opportunity to start again, I still found the withdrawal process painful. "Think of it like giving up alcohol or drugs," my therapist had told me. "It's not going to be an easy process, but you'll be a happier person at the end of it."

Easier said than done.

I thought following the story of Victoria Da Silva and Daniel Oliver might help. It would take my mind off myself, for one thing. On a practical note, I might actually be able to use it to relaunch my journalistic career. But after what Penelope said to me, I doubt my abilities. Perhaps it is better if I put it to one side. But then what would I do with myself? How would I earn a living?

A vision of myself comes to me. I'm not that old, perhaps in my late forties. I'm living in a dump of a council flat somewhere, not even in London. All of my designer clothes have been sold off, and I'm sitting in a formless gray tracksuit. My face is free of makeup and I look pale and unhealthy. I'm on benefits and on medication, a toxic combination. I don't have anything to live for. I have no job or friends. Even Bex has deserted me. A pile of yellowing paper sits in the corner of the room—my old columns, which I read and reread as a form of both escape and punishment. What is the point of carrying on? I've been stockpiling pills ready for the time when I end it all. I see myself as a corpse, lying on a cheap, stained mattress, a body that goes undiscovered for weeks on end until the neighbors begin to complain about the smell.

The cry of a bird overhead brings me back to the present. I'm standing at the tumulus, a mound that I've heard described as an ancient burial site—some say it's Boadicea's grave—or an old battleground. It's a deserted spot today, and the trees that surround it whisper an unknowable message in the wind. I go and sit on one of the benches and close my eyes for a second. If only I had had more sleep last night. I can feel myself drifting off, my consciousness fading. I'm vaguely aware of something rustling in the bushes behind me, but I assume it's a bird or a rat. It all goes quiet, apart from the wind. But then I hear it again, but this time it sounds like footsteps. I open my eyes, but just as I do so I catch a glimpse of a figure in a mask. It's a Guy Fawkes mask, used at demos like the Occupy movement. Everything happens so quickly. I open my mouth to scream, but something hits my head. I hear a crack and I'm falling to the ground.

32

BEX

"Oh my God, Jen," I scream. "Jen, wake up!"

I'm not sure whether I should move her or not and so I bend down and check to see if she's breathing. I feel a faint flow of air coming out of her nose. She's not dead. I run my fingers through her smooth blonde hair and when I withdraw them I see that they're covered in blood. I look around me. I can't see anyone.

"Jen, oh please, wake up," I say again. I gently nudge her shoulder. "I'm so sorry for everything. You know how much you mean to me."

I see her eyelids begin to stir. She emits a low groan. I watch as she tries to focus. She brings her hand to her head and scowls as the pain hits her. Her face crumples like a toddler who has just hurt herself but doesn't understand why.

"Do you know what happened? Did someone do this to you?"

She can't speak. She tries to sit up, but the effort is too much for her.

"Shall I call the police?" I ask, but there's no answer.

I hold her head as she retches into the grass. Again, I look around for signs of people, but all I can see in the distance are a couple of mums pushing prams, and an elderly man walking his dog. When she's finished being sick I give her a sip from my water bottle. I help her onto the bench and examine the wound on her head. It's not too deep, but still Jen will develop a nasty lump. There's also the risk of concussion.

"I think we need to get you checked out," I say.

"Is it bad?" she asks in a weak voice.

"I'm not sure, but you're bleeding," I say. "What do you remember?"

She blinks as she tries to recall what happened to her. "I was sitting here—I remember I had my eyes closed. I was feeling so tired. And then I saw someone wearing one of those funny plastic masks, you know the Guy Fawkes one that people wear when they're protesting."

"Oh fuck," I say.

"And then I just blacked out. I suppose they must have hit me with something."

"Did you get any sense of who it was? Any other details—what he was wearing? How tall was he?"

"No, sorry," she says, looking as though she has failed me.

"Don't worry." I hesitate as I think how best to express what I have to tell her. "I don't want to alarm you, but there's something you need to know."

"What is it?" she asks. She screws up her eyes as another wave of pain consumes her.

"I was out for an early-morning run when I came across that boy who followed you yesterday—what's his name? Steven."

"Steven was here? On the Heath?"

"Yes, I saw him walking from the Dartmouth Park side of the Heath toward Hampstead. In your direction."

"Did you see him do this to me?"

"No, because at one point he started running—I'm not sure whether he thought he was being followed or not. And although I thought I was quite a good runner, I'm nothing compared to a teenage boy."

"I don't understand it—why would Steven want to hurt me?"

"I'm not sure, but that's not all," I say. I take her hand as I prepare myself to break the news. "There's someone else I saw on the Heath earlier."

"Who?" she whispers in a way that sounds as though she doesn't want to hear the answer.

"Laurence."

33
JEN

The name reverberates through my mind. I remember the moment when I saw the video taken by Alex at the scene of the murder-suicide.

"It's not possible," I say. I'm conscious of shaking my head as if I'm trying to get rid of what I've just heard. I tell myself that Laurence would never do anything to hurt me, not like this. "It must be a coincidence."

"Perhaps," says Bex.

"No, it's not him," I say. "He wouldn't do this to me."

"What if . . . ?" But she stops herself.

"What?" I ask.

"No, it's too ridiculous for words," she says. "But what if Laurence is the one behind all of this?"

"In what way?"

"No, just forget I ever said anything," she says.

"For fuck's sake, Bex, just tell me!" I shout.

She looks slightly taken aback and so I repeat the question in a more reasonable manner. But instead of saying anything, Bex takes out her phone and tells me that we should phone the police. Her fingers linger over the screen, but as she's about to dial 999 I take the phone from her.

"No, not if it's Laurence," I say.

"What do you mean?"

"If there's a chance it is Laurence who's done this then it will all come out about what I did to him," I say.

"So?"

"I just can't bear it," I say. "I've got enough shit going on at the moment without all that being dragged up."

"You can't be serious?" Bex looks incredulously at me. "Somebody nearly brained you, Jen—can't you see that? And what if it wasn't Laurence? What if it was Steven? Or someone else entirely? Someone you don't know."

I lower my head and say nothing.

"Jen—what aren't you telling me?" asks Bex.

I start to talk, too quickly. "Did you see the MailOnline this morning?"

"No, why would I? I never read that shit."

"There was a report that Victoria Da Silva was pregnant," I say.

"Oh my God, the poor girl—but what has that got to do with you?"

"I went to see the Da Silvas and when I was on the point of leaving, Mrs. Da Silva told me that her daughter was pregnant. I told Penelope the news. God, I wish I hadn't. I had a horrible row with her this morning. I accused her of leaking it. She denied it, of course, but you should have heard her, Bex, she said some truly awful things to me. Really cruel."

"Well, I never liked her, you know that," she says.

I smile, even though I'm in pain. "I'm sorry, Bex, for what I said yesterday. I didn't know what I was—"

"Ssh," she says, squeezing my hand. "It's all forgotten. The main thing is that we're friends. Friends forever."

"Thank you," I say, my eyes filling with tears. I cough, clear my throat, and try to resume my earlier train of thought. "So I'm wondering whether the person who did this to me is neither Steven nor Laurence, but someone who believes it was me who betrayed Mr. and Mrs. Da Silva. I can't say I blame them. After all, although they knew I was a journalist, I did promise them not to reveal anything about their daughter's pregnancy."

"Do you think they would go so far as to send someone out to attack you like this? And would they be able to organize something so quickly?"

"The story has been online for hours, since late last night I think. The Da Silvas seemed like such nice people, but I suppose you never know."

"But if you're suspicious, then you really do need to go to the police," orders Bex.

"I'm not sure," I reply.

I can feel the strength of Bex's harsh gaze on me. "I understand you've had a horrible shock," she says. "And even though I think you're mad, I can understand why you may not want to involve the police. But what if L—this man tries again? What if next time he hits you harder? Jen, listen to me, you need to report this to the police, and you need to do it now. Okay?"

I know she's right. "They might be able to extract some DNA, or whatever it is those CSI people do, from the surface of your scalp," she says, a comment that makes me smile. "I won't leave your side, I promise, and after that we're going to Penelope's and you're going to pack a bag."

I begin to protest, but she shouts me down.

"Don't worry, I'll deal with that bitch if she gives you any trouble," says Bex. "And then you're going to move back in with me, until all this has blown over."

I feel my eyes light up with joy, as if Bex has given me the best present ever.

"You mean it?" I ask.

"I mean it. Now let's get you to the police station."

At Kentish Town police station I tell them that I've been attacked. I'm taken in a car to the Whittington Hospital. In the back of the car a policewoman asks me a series of questions. I tell her about the man in the mask. Did I know if anyone had a reason to attack me? I shake my head. The police are bound to know about the fact that I was a witness to the murder of Victoria Da Silva, and so I tell her that perhaps it is linked to that. But that was a straightforward murder-suicide. The person who killed Victoria is dead. I inform them that I wrote a brief news story about the incident, but don't say any more about what I've discovered since then. Neither do I tell them about Laurence. And I don't want to point the detectives in the direction of Steven Walker or the Da Silva family because I need to carry on with the investigation myself. I'm given some advice on personal safety, and they wait for me while I go in to see a doctor.

I grip the edge of the examination table as a young medic gives me something for the pain and patches me up. As the doctor treats me I close my eyes and think back to the attack.

I am sitting on the bench. There is a noise behind me. I open my eyes. A man in a mask, wearing a hat. He's also gone so far as to cover his neck with a scarf and his hands with gloves to make sure no hair or skin is showing. How tall is he? It's difficult to say, as I only caught a glimpse of him. It could have been anyone, perhaps a thug employed by Mr. Da Silva. But Bex mentioned that she had seen both Steven and Laurence.

I know it's time I let go of Laurence completely. Thinking of him is driving me insane. I tell myself—yet again—that I have to acknowledge that he has no feelings for me. Or rather, that his feelings for me are far from loving ones. If anything it seems as though he might actually hate me. Who was I trying to kid? To think that I believed we had another chance. I'm pathetic, I realize that. I must ask Bex whether she managed to have a word with him about being on the Heath that day. Perhaps she did, and this was his idea of a response. Nice. I think about the video that Alex took that day. I'm certain that Laurence was the mystery jogger. But what would make him want to attack me? Was it some kind of revenge for what I had done to him? Or was it a warning of some kind? A message to leave the case alone? To put me off the scent? But what did he have to do with Victoria Da Silva and Daniel Oliver? I'd never heard him mention either of them. But again, apart from the texts and emails and that brief meeting at his house, I'd had no contact with him since that awful night.

And then it comes to me. I feel faint and nauseous. "Do you need some more pain relief?" asks the doctor.

I don't answer. I think about what Bex said on the Heath: the possibility that Laurence was behind all of this. I knew Victoria Da Silva had been having an affair.

But what if the man she had been seeing was Laurence?

34

BEX

'Ve prepared myself for a stand-up row with Penelope and so I'm disappointed that when Jen opens the door we find that she's not there.
To make sure, Jen climbs the marble stairs, calling her name, but after
exploring the upper floors she shouts down to tell me she's out. There's no
note of explanation of where she's gone or when she will be back. Although
I'm sure Jen is relieved, I'm angry. It would have been good to get a few
things off my chest.

As Jen is upstairs packing her bag I take the opportunity to look around
the house. My first thought is, what does one person do with all this space?
In Penelope's case she fills it with clutter: paintings, many in gilt frames,
books—shelves upon shelves packed with them—antique vases, candle-
sticks, display cases full of glasses, sideboards crammed with ceramic bowls,
desks crowded with postcards and paperweights. I spot a laptop and slowly
open it. When it asks for a password I try "PENELOPE," then "Penelope,"
and finally "penelope," but give up after the third attempt. Next to the
laptop is an A4 pad, full of scribbles. A couple of names jump out at me:
Victoria Da Silva, Daniel Oliver, followed by the facts of the case. There
are some notes in shorthand, which I can't read, and a few newspapers.

I walk over to her drinks cabinet, a glittering altarpiece of glass and
steel, sporting every liqueur and spirit you could name. I take two heavy

crystal glasses and pour a couple of decent measures of expensive cognac. I'll have a drink ready for Jen for when she comes down with her bag. We can toast her escape.

Driving in the car over here from the hospital Jen had told me some of the things Penelope had said to her during their argument. While some of them might have been true—I agreed with Penelope that Jen wasn't in a fit state of mind to investigate the story of the murder-suicide—there were other things that she had said that were just plain cruel. All that stuff about the meaningless nature of Jen's column, about how it was like something you'd read on the inside of a toilet door. Why did she have to go and say that to her?

The bitch better watch out.

35

JEN

Back at her flat Bex makes sure I'm comfortable. She takes out a pile of lovely blankets and cushions and arranges them around me on the sofa. She even rustles up some hot chocolate for us and tops it off with frothy cream. She knows that's what I like.

"You're spoiling me rotten," I say when she hands it to me.

"Well, you've had a shock. And I'm still feeling guilty for storming off like I did and leaving you on the Heath."

I pat the sofa and she comes and sits next to me like an obedient dog.

"Woof!" she barks, which makes me laugh.

She says it's lovely to see me like this—here, once again living with her, and nearly back to my old self, even if I have suffered a minor head injury. "So you're sure the doctor says that you'll be fine?" she asks.

"Apparently so," I reply. "There's no concussion, and I just have to take it easy for a while." I study her closely. "But how are you?"

"Me? You know me, I'm always fine!" There's a certain brittle, artificial quality to her words. She takes a sip of the hot chocolate.

"Are you sure?"

"Of course—it's you we need to worry about. You need to get some rest. Put everything that's happened to the back of your mind. Try to forget about that awful thing you saw on the Heath."

"But that's just it," I say. "I can't forget about it." I shift my position and look directly at her. "Don't you think it's odd that I'm attacked just as I start to delve deeper into this thing? It can't be a coincidence, surely? That must mean one thing—I'm getting closer to the truth."

I'm sure Bex doesn't mean to snigger, but she says she can't help it. "Sorry, Jen, but you should hear yourself, you sound . . . I don't know. Weird."

"I know it might sound absurd, but what other reason could there be?" I say, putting down my hot chocolate. "I witness a terrible murder and then a suicide on Parliament Hill Fields on Valentine's Day. One of the people there, who runs away from the scene just as it unfolds, turns out to be my ex-boyfriend, Laurence. I start to get a series of creepy messages from an account called @WatchingYouJenHunter. I begin to look into the crime, in order to investigate whether there could be any truth in the idea, suggested to me by this @WatchingYouJenHunter, that Daniel Oliver didn't kill his girlfriend, Victoria Da Silva. Then, soon after I learn that she was having an affair and that she was pregnant, I get attacked by some man in a mask."

"Yes, when you put it like that it does seem odd, but the truth is I'm worried about you. I don't want to see you get hurt. Have you had any more of those weird messages?"

"No, not for a while, so maybe that's the end of it," I tell her.

"Let's hope so." She pauses. "But in a way that makes me even more worried."

"What?"

"I just wonder what he has planned."

I can hardly get the words out. "Do you think I'm in danger?"

"Not with me around to look after you. You feel safe here though, right?"

"Yes, of course I do."

"You know you can stay as long as you like. I know it's not as fancy as Penelope's house—I'm afraid I don't have a garden as big as a tennis court—but I want it to feel like home."

"Thanks, Bex, for everything," I say. "I don't know what I'd do without you." I fall silent for a moment before I continue. "Can I ask you about Laurence?"

"Oh yes, that fucker. What about him?"

"Don't take this the wrong way, but I wondered what you said to him?"

"I told him not to mess with you or he'd have me to answer to."

"Seriously, I want you to tell me what you said to him and what he said back. Just in case it was him who attacked me, I need to know everything."

"Okay, but what about another hot chocolate?" she asks as she stands up.

I shake my head.

"Something stronger?" she asks.

"No, I'm fine at the moment. So—what happened?"

"I went round to Laurence's house and of course he denied once again that he was the jogger," she tells me as she comes and sits down again. "He's such a lying bastard."

"What did he say?"

"I played him the video that you sent me, over and over again, until he finally admitted that it was him. He had no choice."

"Really?"

"I know. However, he did deny the fact that he ever sent you any messages on Twitter or that he had set up any fake account. By the end of the conversation, I persuaded him to go to the police and give a statement about being on the Heath on Valentine's Day. He said that he was scared, that's why he ran away, but that he has nothing to hide."

"And do you believe him?"

"To be honest, I'm not sure I believe a word that comes out of his lying mouth."

"But why didn't he tell the truth to begin with—about the fact that he was on the Heath that day?"

"He came out with all this stuff about not wanting to get dragged into a police investigation. Said it wouldn't look good for his reputation and his practice, crap like that."

"Did you ask him whether he knew Victoria Da Silva?"

"No—should I have done?"

I tell her my suspicions: that Laurence might have been having an affair with the dead girl, that I believe there's a chance that Victoria was pregnant with his baby.

"Fuck, so let me get this right—you think that Daniel found out about his girlfriend's affair and her pregnancy? And do you think, that day on the Heath, that he recognized Laurence as her lover?"

"There's every chance," I say. "Perhaps seeing Laurence there on Parliament Hill Fields was the final straw. Daniel might have thought that Laurence was taunting him. And so he took the ultimate revenge—he killed Victoria, along with the child she was carrying. And that would also explain why Laurence didn't want to acknowledge the fact he was there on the Heath that day."

"Obviously there's the video, but do you have any other proof? That Laurence was Victoria's lover or that he was the one who got her pregnant?"

"No, not yet," I reply. "But I intend to get it."

36

BEX

I tell her that I will help her—but only if she wants me to. I know it's something I discouraged her from doing, that I was worried about whether she was strong enough, but now I can see that she is going to investigate this crime no matter what. She's got that look in her eye that means she's determined to see something through, despite or maybe even because people have warned her against it.

"What's the saying—if you can't beat 'em, join 'em?" I quip. Jen flings her arms around me.

"Easy, tiger," I say and we both laugh.

Before I know what's happening she's jumped up to fetch her bag. She pulls out a pile of papers, a couple of notebooks, and her phone and starts to talk about the case at top speed. The words come tumbling out: Victoria Da Silva. Daniel Oliver. Champagne bottle. Stabbing. Blood. Affair. Secret pregnancy. Stalking. @WatchingYouJenHunter. Witnesses. Julia Jones. Jamie Blackwood. Ayesha Ahmed. Steven Walker. Parliament Hill Fields. Mystery jogger. The video. The attack on the Heath. The man in the mask. Laurence. Laurence. Laurence.

"Slow down," I tell her. "If we're going to do this properly we need to approach it in an ordered and logical manner."

She talks to me about everything she knows, takes me through the interviews she's done. I start to make some notes of my own and begin to plot everything out so I have it clear in my head. I want to make this work.

"So although it can't be denied that Daniel Oliver killed his girlfriend and her unborn child, what you're suggesting is that there was someone else involved? Is that it?" I ask. "You think that there's someone in the shadows who was manipulating all of this?"

"Yes, that's exactly it," she says, her eyes lighting up with energy. "What we need to do now is find out who that was."

"But Jen, what if it's . . . dangerous," I say, hearing my voice break. "I don't want you—or us—to get involved in something that puts us at risk. I mean look at what someone did to you."

"I know, and I've thought about that," she says, her hand rising automatically to her head. "But this means that I'm onto something. Of course, I could step away from it and go back to my failure of a life trying to eke out a living from the occasional freelance piece. Or I could take the easy option out and give up journalism completely. All the signs are there telling me I should. I've been sacked as a columnist for making stuff up. Nobody is in a rush to commission me. I suppose I should be thankful the industry doesn't know about why I was given the push. But what else is there for me?"

She falls silent and tears come into her eyes. "You know up there, on the Heath, before . . . before someone came up and attacked me, I was actually thinking about the possibility of ending it all."

"Oh, Jen—" I say, reaching out to her.

But she interrupts me and carries on, brushing the tears from her cheeks. "Don't worry, I wasn't actually thinking of . . . doing it. But I had a vision of myself in the not too distant future, living alone, drinking too much, my mind destroyed by mental illness, living on benefits and just . . . fading away. Becoming nothing. The hardest part wasn't dying, but recognizing that no one really noticed that I'd gone."

"Don't say that—look, you know you'll always have me," I say, squeezing her hand. "If you ever left me I don't know what I'd do."

"Thanks—for a moment on the Heath, after I said, well, after I'd stupidly accused you of stalking me, I thought I'd never see you again."

"Well, just don't push your luck," I say in a mock-aggressive fashion. "Now, tell me, what do you want me to do?"

37
JEN

I was expecting the call. It's Mr. Da Silva. I answer and raise the phone to my ear, preparing myself for a mouthful of abuse. But instead there's a quiet, broken voice, full of grief.

"We . . . we told you in confidence," he says.

"I'm so, so sorry, Mr. Da Silva, but you've got to believe me when I tell you that it wasn't me."

He carries on as if he hasn't heard me. "My wife, she trusted you. She said that you had a kind face. That you wouldn't betray us. And now the papers are full of . . ."

His voice trails off and I picture him crying, standing in the grand hallway of his opulent, expensive home.

"I know it may be hard to believe, but it wasn't me who leaked the news," I say.

"How can I believe a word you say? You're a journalist. I was a fool to trust you in the first place."

"Look—I know nothing I say will convince you. All I can do is give you my word—for what it's worth."

The line goes quiet before I hear the sound of him sniffing. "If you didn't tell them . . . then who did? I'm not sure who else knew."

I blush as I think about Penelope. "What about the friend you mentioned, Caro? Caro Elliott?"

"Caro would never betray us like that," he says. "Anyway, I just wanted you to know that you and your colleagues have taken whatever dignity we had from us. Goodbye, and good luck in your career, Miss Hunter. I hope you feel satisfied with what you've done."

"But Mr. Da Silva—"

The line goes dead, the words leaving a nasty sting. They remind me of what Laurence said to me the night we broke up: "You must be very proud of yourself."

I consider ringing Mr. Da Silva back, pleading with him to understand that I hadn't betrayed his confidence, but what's the point? I have to take responsibility. It was me who told Penelope about Victoria's pregnancy. I feel another surge of anger rising up, directed toward her. How could she have done it? However, I have to acknowledge that I knew what she was like. She lives for news, for the thrill of the chase. What a fool I had been to ever trust Penelope. I had left without a note or forwarding address. I hoped I would never see her again.

I find Caro Elliott's details online and write an email to her, explaining that I was a witness to the attack and that I'd like to speak to her. I don't say anything about the fact that I'm a journalist. I just hope that Mr. Da Silva hasn't already warned her that I might try to contact her.

I go into the kitchen and make myself a cup of tea. Bex is out at the shops, getting some food—and drink—for later. Although this flat is small and hasn't any of the fancy furniture or aesthetic flourishes of Penelope's, I realize how much more at home I feel here. I can relax in this cramped attic flat in a way I never could at Penelope's. I take a couple of deep breaths. But I know that, for all of Bex's kindness and protestations that I can stay here for as long as I like, that I should treat it as though it were my permanent home, I still have to forge a future for myself.

As I sip the tea and look out over the rooftops of Kentish Town I feel a sense of purpose. Despite the attack on me and the unpleasant phone call from Mr. Da Silva, I tell myself that I am going to do something with my life. Perhaps getting to the bottom of what really happened between Victoria Da Silva and Daniel Oliver is the first step.

I can do this.

Now that I have Bex's support I don't need to rely on Penelope. I've got someone who believes in me—my oldest friend, someone I know will never let me down.

I take my tea over to my laptop and write to Julia Jones again. I send another email to the junior doctor, Ayesha Ahmed, asking for her to get in touch, and begin to do an internet search for Steven Walker. I work quickly and efficiently, buoyed along by a wave of adrenaline. Just then an email pings into my inbox. It's from Caro Elliott. I scan it quickly, reading it for words such as "sorry," "I'm afraid," and "impossible," but instead she talks about how awful it must have been for me and what a shock I must have suffered. Of course she will agree to see me. Just name a day and a time and she'll be there.

38

BEX

I tell Jen I'll be her shadow, that I won't let her out of my sight. She doesn't need to feel afraid when she's got me by her side. And, true to my word, I'm sitting at the next table to her in the café at the National Gallery. I have my phone and a book, which I'm pretending to read. I try to keep my head down and look inconspicuous, but I listen to every word.

Caro Elliott is of a type you often see around London: tall, leggy, blonde, glamorous. If I had to make a judgment about her based on her looks I would write her off as silly and superficial. But as she talks I get the sense that she is far from that. She begins by asking Jen about how she is coping. She doesn't want to hear about the incident itself—she read Jen's account in the news, she says, and that's enough—but she is keen to talk about Victoria. She wants to remember her for all the good she did in the world. For her beauty, her intelligence, her sense of life, her loyalty. She doesn't mind if Jen wants to use any of what she says for a piece. She says she knows Jen from her column, of course. She is a fan.

"But I haven't seen it for a while—are you having a break?" asks Caro.

"I've been laid off—budget cuts," Jen replies, looking down at her notebook.

I have to admire Jen's technique. She's gentle, lets Caro lead the con-versation, and listens carefully with an empathetic manner, only speaking when she needs to, and even then she keeps her questions short and to the point. She tries to maintain eye contact, even as she writes down the odd note. But I know what's coming and I'm waiting for it.

In the meantime, they continue to talk about how the two women met—at university—and I can't help but think back to my own first encounter with Jen.

"And Vicky was happy—with Daniel?" asks Jen.

Caro doesn't answer immediately. I look over and I can see the uncertainty in her eyes. She casts me a look, and I shrink back into invisible anonymity.

"I suppose they must have been," continues Jen. "After all, I heard there was talk they were going to get married."

Caro leans forward and lowers her voice. I have to really concentrate in order to hear what she's saying.

"Promise you won't . . . you won't include this in anything you write," she says.

Jen nods her head. "Of course," she says. "It can be off the record."

"You sure?"

"Yes, look—I won't write anything down." Caro stares at Jen as she decides whether to trust her. "You probably know, there was that awful story in the MailOnline, but Vicky was thinking of leaving Dan."

"Oh, I see," says Jen. "She was serious about that? About leaving him?"

"Yes—she'd met someone else. She wasn't quite sure how her new man felt about her though. Whether he was serious." Tears come into Caro's eyes and she rustles through her handbag to find a tissue. "I still can't believe she's not here," she says, dabbing her eyes. "That she's not coming back. God, why did that bastard do that to her? I wish now she'd told him to fuck off months back."

"Do you regret introducing them?"

"I'm sorry?"

"Dan and Victoria—I thought you were the one who introduced them?"

"No, that wasn't me. Don't know who it was actually."

"Okay . . . And did you want her to leave Dan?"

"Too right I did. He was a bully. Not that I saw him hit her or anything. If I had, I would have reported him to the police. But . . . I was afraid how Dan would react if he ever found out about . . . It's right what the MailOnline said. Vicky was two months pregnant, you see. She couldn't be sure, but she suspected that the baby wasn't Dan's."

"Why?"

"I'm not sure how often they . . . how often they made love."

"I see."

"And I suppose somehow Dan must have discovered that she was pregnant. If only Vicky had come to stay with me. Or gone to live with her parents. God, she really was the sweetest, nicest girl you're ever likely to meet. And I'd hate you to think that Vicky was the kind of woman who was . . . well, who was promiscuous. Not that there's anything wrong with that, of course. But she wasn't into one-night stands or flings."

"Did you ever meet him?" asks Jen. "Her new boyfriend?"

"No, but she told me a lot about him. Tall, older than her, but nice looking still."

"Do you know what he did for a living?"

There's another pause. But I know what's coming. "Architect, I think."

I close my eyes. I can't bear to look over at Jen's face. But I imagine her trying to keep a stoic expression as inside she falls apart.

"Did she . . . did she tell you his name?" Jen asks in a low, barely audible voice.

"Yes, she did. Let's see if I can remember," answers Caro.

I know what she's going to say.

"I never knew his surname, but his Christian name was . . . No, it wasn't Luke . . . That's it, yes, it was Laurence. Not with a 'w,' but with a 'u'—I remember her telling me that. She also said she'd met the love of her life. But, as I said, she was worried that he didn't feel the same toward her."

"Did you ever . . . ever see a photo of him?"

"Yes, I think she did show me one once."

Jen, her hands trembling, takes out her phone and swipes a finger across the screen.

39

JEN

It seems I have all the evidence I need. I feel nothing but numbness, a sense that everything inside me is dying. I try to give Caro a reassuring smile, but I'm afraid it's more of a scowl than anything.

"Are you all right?" she asks.

"Yes, yes, I'm fine," I manage to say.

I look over at Bex at the next table, she has her head down and is playing with her phone, but I know she must have heard what Caro just told me. My instinct is to jump up and seek out comfort from Bex—a hug, a reassuring word—but I have to continue to sit here opposite Caro, pretending my world hasn't just fallen apart.

Of course, I had no right to determine who Laurence should or should not date—after all, although we had been due to meet up, we hadn't been seeing one another since the previous summer. But I still feel jealous, jealous of a dead woman. For a moment, I understand how Daniel must have felt when he found out about the affair. I imagine myself holding a knife, pressing it to Laurence's throat. But then I stop myself. What am I thinking? The revelation has unsteadied me, I tell myself, and it's threatening to warp my perception. I have to be careful, I know that. I take a sip of sparkling water and do what my therapist says I must do if I find reality slipping away from me: I have to "return to the moment."

But suddenly an awful thought occurs to me. "How long had this man . . . Laurence . . . how long had he been seeing Victoria?" I ask.

"I'm not sure," says Caro. "Anyway, I'd rather not dwell on that, if you don't mind. As I said to you, I want to make sure that Vicky's positive side comes across. You do promise me nothing of this, what I've just told you, will come out?"

"Don't worry, I promise," I tell her.

She asks me why I have an image of Victoria's lover on my phone. I tell her that he was a friend of mine and I try to smile as I say something banal about life's strange coincidences.

"Anyway, I really must be going," she says, clearly unsettled by my odd behavior.

I tell her that I will settle the bill. It's the least I can do. She stands up, checks her phone, says goodbye. I watch her walk across the room, waiting, waiting for her to disappear around the corner, before I burst into tears. The release is immense. Bex rushes from her table to sit next to me.

I can't get the words out, but there's no need. She tells me she heard everything.

"Oh, Jen," she says, putting her arm around me. "What a shit. But at least you know now."

I take a deep breath and manage to spit out the words, "But what—what I don't know—is how long?"

"You think that they were together when you were . . . ?"

I can't speak. The thought of that turns my stomach. It's not so much the possible infidelity, but that's bad enough. It's the idea that Laurence could have been lying to me, about this, and so much else. I think of that email he sent me just after the murder-suicide. It seemed so caring, so nice of him. But in it he neglected to mention that he even knew Victoria, never mind that they were, or had been, lovers. What else was he hiding? He was there that day, at the top of Kite Hill. He must have known that his girlfriend was about to be attacked. And yet he ran away.

He left her to be butchered. Was it cowardice that compelled him to act as he did, or something else, something more sinister? Images, thoughts, past conversations swirl through my head. I feel weak.

"Let's get you back to the flat," says Bex. She takes out her purse and leaves cash for both our tables.

She helps me out of the café and calls an Uber. Mercifully, the traffic up Charing Cross Road and Tottenham Court Road isn't too bad, and we get back to the flat within half an hour. She leads me to the sofa like a member of the living dead.

"Don't think about it," says Bex, plumping up a cushion. "I'm sure Laurence wasn't seeing Vicky then, back when you were together."

"But how do we know?" I mumble. "That could have been the reason why . . ." I don't complete the sentence as I search my memory for possible signs of his infidelity.

There was that weekend he said he was going to a conference in Berlin. I know he went there, I saw some of the restaurant and bar receipts, but could that have been with Vicky? Then there were countless evenings when he said he had to work late. I never complained, of course, as I understood the pressures of his job.

I begin to wonder too about my own behavior. Had this unconscious knowledge—the vague but formless sense that Laurence was seeing someone else—shaped the way I reacted during that awful scene at dinner? Since having therapy I have learned to try to understand the invisible factors that influence me. I had suffered one rejection—the loss of my job in particularly humiliating circumstances—but was I afraid of another? The desertion by Laurence? Was that why I wrecked his kitchen and bit into his arm?

Of course, it was all too late for Laurence and me. I know I could never get him back. Stupid of me to fantasize about ever reviving our relationship. But perhaps it isn't too late for something else—it isn't too late for revenge.

40

BEX

I'm worried about Jen. Since arriving back at the flat she hasn't said a word apart from the sentence, "But how do we know?" She's fixated on the idea that Laurence and Vicky were seeing each other while she and Laurence were still together. I go into the kitchen and think of what to do next. Jen is no good to anyone when she's like this, least of all herself. And she was doing so well. The investigation had really given her some purpose. I have to focus her energies once more. I return with two large glasses of brandy.

"Here, take this," I say. "It will help with the shock."

She holds out her hand, but it has all the vitality of a dead fish. Her eyes look lifeless too.

"Take a sip," I tell her, but she simply puts the glass on the table next to her.

"Oh for God's sake!" I snap. Before I know it my hands grab her around the shoulders. I force her to stand up, like a rag doll controlled by a sadistic puppeteer. I slap her around the face. I hear the crack of my palm on her cheek. Her eyes stretch wider, as if she is being woken from a deep dream. Her fingers travel up to her burning cheek. She can't believe what's just happened.

"What . . . ?" she says.

"You need to fucking snap out of it, Jen," I say.

I know this is not how a trained mental health professional would deal with Jen. But I had lost patience with her. I needed her to act, not sit around wallowing, drowning, in a sea of self-pity.

She starts to cry and I let her. At least she is having a reaction, feeling *something*. I pass her some tissues. After a few minutes she stops sobbing. She looks at the glass of brandy with an expression of surprise—as if to say *Who put this here?*—and gulps it down. Gradually, I see life begin to seep back into her. Her eyes light up and there's a flush to her cheeks, a rush of blood not caused just by the slap I've given her. She looks around the room with a renewed animation.

"I'm sorry, Jen, but I did it for your own good," I say. "If you give into this thing you'll let Laurence win. You told me that you wanted a purpose to your life. You need to direct that hatred, use it. That sense of anger and frustration can be channeled. I'm not going to allow you to be beaten by this. So what if Laurence was sleeping with Vicky behind your back?" She winces at this. "You knew he was a coward—he ran away and left his lover to die. Now you know he's a prick too, right? Do you really want to be with a man like that?"

She looks at me and smiles. There's something calculating about the smile, though. Like a cat that has a mouse in its sights. She's coming back to me.

"That's my girl," I say.

41

JEN

I don't want to tell my therapist, Annabelle, everything I'm thinking, everything I'm feeling, but I do talk about what it was like to witness the murder of Victoria Da Silva and the suicide of Daniel Oliver. I take her through it, the whole ghastly business. As I relate what I saw I can tell she is shocked and appalled, not just about what happened—the murder of a young woman, the suicide of her boyfriend—but its implications for me.

"I'm worried that this will bring up all sorts of issues for you," says Annabelle. "It could well trigger some unpleasant memories, causing you to relive some trauma from your past." I don't say anything. The silence lingers, heavy in the bland, characterless room at the back of an Edwardian house between Archway and Highgate. I'm comfortable with the silence, though, and I let it embrace me like a shroud.

Annabelle has talked to me in the past about the roots of what she calls my compulsion for oversharing. She has been keen for me to explore what she regards as the split between myself as subject and myself as object. It sounds like jargon, but she says I created a false self—myself as object—through which I could channel all sorts of emotions, feelings, fears, and desires. It is this object self, which I gave an alternative name, that of Hunter, that I've used over the years as a basis for my confessional journalism. I had to feed it like a ravenous dog. It was insatiable, as was my readers' fascination with it. I became addicted to giving it more material—tidbits from my life—knowing that to keep my readers' attention I had to supply a steady stream of confessions, the more sensational and extreme the better.

The relationship between my readers and myself fit into a classic codependent model, she said. Those anonymous people out there, who gobbled up my column, acted as enablers, encouraging me to continue a dysfunctional existence. And it was hardly a surprise that I had turned to fictionalizing my own experience. It was, said Annabelle, the logical conclusion in a cycle of abuse. On a positive light, she assured me, my lies resulted in the loss of that column, which in turn functioned as an escape from the damaging situation. I may be out of a job, but at least I'm still alive. If I had carried on writing about myself in this way there was every chance I would have taken up other forms of addictive behavior: greater dependence on alcohol (my intake was already highly dangerous, said Annabelle), the use of other drugs, or a descent into paranoid or schizoid behavior, possibly even self-harm, and ultimately suicide.

"By bringing about the loss of your column you effectively killed off your false self of Jen Hunter," said Annabelle. "Your unconscious protected you by highlighting the fiction of yourself. You should thank it—it saved you. And perhaps you should start to think about using your real name again, Jennifer Hesmondalgh."

The sound of my old name, with its ugly, clumsy mouthful of consonants, disturbs me. It reminds me of everything I tried to escape from.

We lapse into silence before Annabelle asks me if there's anything else I want to share with her. I decide not to tell her anything of Laurence and his role in all of this, about his presence on the Heath and why he chose to lie about it. I do, however, talk to Annabelle about my arguments with Bex and Penelope. Initially, she does not interpret my actions, choosing to let herself serve as a sounding board for my experiences. I can feel her eyes on me, however, and as I speak I can sense a heightened level of concern.

Finally, she takes a sip of water and says, "So you're intending to write about . . . about the incident?"

"Oh yes," I tell her. "I've written a news story already and think that a larger piece might work well. It could also help me get out of the work rut I've been in."

"So you're reporting on an event that you witnessed?"

"Yes, and there might even be a book in it," I reply. I tell her about the weird messages from @WatchingYouJenHunter, and the claim that another person could be involved. "So you see it may not be a straightforward case of Daniel Oliver killing his girlfriend. Victoria Da Silva was pregnant when she was killed, probably by another man." Again, I say nothing about Laurence. "I'm going to interview the other witnesses again and follow up . . . some other leads."

"Do you think that's wise?" she asks. "I mean, Jen, you really do need to think about this. You know you haven't been well. Witnessing a murder and then a suicide is bad enough. But reporting on it is another thing entirely. I would have thought you'd need some sense of objectivity, and even then, doing such a thing could have serious consequences for your mental health." She pauses. "You know I don't make a habit of telling you what to do, but on this occasion I must advise you that I think you should stop, and stop right away."

I want to ask her how else does she expect me to pay for these fucking therapy sessions, but I rephrase it as, "But what do you expect me to do? I need to earn a living."

"Have you thought about getting another kind of job, one that's nothing to do with journalism? After all, you told me yourself that journalism, or print journalism at least, is on the way out. You said there's no future in it."

"I'm not fit for anything else," I say. "Really, I don't know what else to do."

"You've got a good degree. Lots of experience. You're personable, you get on with people. You could retrain as . . ."

"As what?" The words come out rather more sharply than I want. "I'm sorry, but I've thought about it, and nothing suggests itself to me as a natural way forward. I can't think of a way out." I tell her about the horrible vision of myself I had, living alone in a strange town, without friends, surviving on benefits, dying without being found, a bloated corpse on a dirty mattress. By the end of it I have tears streaming down my face.

"It's a very powerful symbol of all your fears," she says, softly, passing me a tissue. "But that's all it is. It's not your reality. And it won't become your reality. It needn't be your future. You're a strong woman, Jen. A survivor. And you'll survive this—as long as you don't continue down the route of reporting on this crime. You know we talked about the false self? Well, I think this could bring about the resurgence of that artificial identity."

She doesn't say the words, but I know what she's thinking: *that way madness lies.*

42
BEX

I don't trust Penelope. In fact, I've never trusted her, even since before I first set eyes on her. All that crap she spouted about journalism being the first draft of history. She's nothing but a parasite, feeding off the misery of others.

I'm pleased that Jen has fallen out with her, but I'm still worried that the old bitch may have some hold over my friend. I can't be too careful. That's why I'm standing outside her house in Hampstead, waiting for her to go out. The joy of it is I don't need to break in. I'm holding the key that Jen took with her when she moved out, which I found inside her bag.

I've been waiting just over half an hour. Fortunately, I have plenty of time on my hands. I've told my bosses that I won't be back at work until the end of March: Camden Council are very understanding about the unpredictable state of my mental health.

I'm standing on the same side of the deserted street as Penelope's house so she can't see me from her windows. And to anyone else, the occasional passerby, I'm just a normal-looking woman in her early forties. What could be threatening about that? Finally, just after noon, a car pulls up outside. I step behind a tall yew hedge and watch as the driver makes a call, presumably to tell her that he is outside. A few minutes later, Penelope appears at her door, carrying a laptop bag. Today, she is dressed in a black suit and high heels. She locks the door and totters down the pathway to the car. There is a brief interchange about where she is going—yes, that's right, she says, to the RAC on Pall Mall. She's the guest of honor at a lunch. The driver says she must be famous and she laughs in a sickeningly affected manner. Then the door is closed, she puts on her seat belt, and they drive away.

I give it a few minutes before I take the key out of my pocket and walk up to the house. I don't check to see whether anyone is looking because this will only make me appear suspicious. So I open the door in a slightly bored manner, as if I've done this a thousand times before. And I step inside.

The air carries a trace of Penelope's perfume—I can smell rose, jasmine, vanilla, and sandalwood. Is it Chanel No. 5? I walk through to the kitchen. There is a pile of newspapers on the table and a dirty coffee cup, its rim stained with Penelope's pink lipstick.

Even though I've been to the house a few times I'm still astounded by how much space there is—and all for one person. I think about some of the men and women I've met at the food bank and how little room they have, not only for themselves but for their children too. Penelope is a symbol of everything that is wrong in Britain today: rich, privileged, entitled, blinkered, narrow-minded, and self-serving. A bubble of anger and hatred for her seeps up from deep within me. Instead of swallowing it down I give vent to my feelings. "Fuck you, Penelope," I say. "Fuck you and everything you stand for." I climb the flight of stone stairs to the first story and go into what was Jen's room. I sit on the bed and touch her pillow. There's a long, blonde hair, one of hers. She's at her therapy session now, no doubt talking of the trauma of witnessing the murder-suicide on Kite Hill. When she gets back she'll probably be feeling a bit low. I'll make sure to try to cheer her up somehow. But I won't tell her about my little visit to Penelope's.

I make my way up the stairs again to the very top of the house and into Penelope's large study, carpeted in jute matting. There's an enormous mahogany desk that sits by a window overlooking the garden. The room is full of shelves of books. In the corner of the room there's a filing cabinet. I pull it open and search through files: bank statements, insurance certificates, old papers relating to mortgage payments. There are letters from readers, fans, former colleagues, postcards from friends sent from various destinations around the world. Yet, no matter how hard I look, I can't find anything relating to either the murder-suicide or to Jen herself. Perhaps Penelope was carrying the material in her laptop bag.

I walk back over to the desk. It's free of papers, apart from a letter asking her to renew her membership of the Conservative Party. There's nothing here of use to me, but then I spot something that is in plain sight: a large rectangular pad of blotting paper, an antique affair edged in a brass frame. There's something written in ink in one corner, but it's in reverse. I look around the room for a mirror, but there isn't one. I take the blotting pad into Penelope's bedroom. It's a vision—or rather, a nightmare—in pink, as if she's taken interior design inspiration from the color of her lipstick. I move over to her dressing table and see myself reflected in the triptych of mirrors.

I lift the blotting paper up to the mirror. The reverse image, a quick squiggle of ink written using a fountain pen, comes to life. *Bex, full name: Rebecca Shaw.*

And next to this there's a question mark.

43

JEN

I go through the motions of setting up and carrying out interviews, even though all I can think about is Laurence and what he's done. Bex accompanies me as I travel around London, waiting for me while I go and see Julia Jones again, who is nice enough but who doesn't tell me anything I don't already know. I do notice, however, that during our early evening meeting one Friday night, she knocks back the best part of two bottles of white wine, while to my amazement I only have one glass.

With bloodshot eyes she talks about the stress of Brexit and the tortuous progress of the Withdrawal Bill through Parliament. She likens Brexit to a cancer eating up the country from the inside, a festering mass of tumors that will ultimately end up destroying the body politic. By the end of our time together she is slurring her words as she talks about her dead son, Harry. She's never talked about him in public before—luckily the papers here never reported news about his death and she asks that what she says remains confidential. She tells me how, late at night, she locks herself in her study and looks at old photos of him. Sometimes she still can't believe he's gone. It will be his birthday in a couple of weeks' time, she says, a day she always dreads. She imagines what his life would be like had he not died: he was always looking out for the underdog even as a young boy, she says, and it's likely that he would have gone on to work for a charity, or perhaps in development in Africa or South America. He'd be married by now, too, with a growing family; he told her he always wanted children. She wipes her tears away, apologizes for being sentimental, but I tell her I understand.

"It's strange how the grief has got so much worse since . . . since I saw what happened on the Heath," she says, as she stands up to show me to the door. "I can't explain it. It's like what I saw is somehow pulling me back into the past. God, listen to me going on about myself!" she says, as she wipes another tear from her cheek and tries to smile. "I should be worrying about the family of that poor girl, instead of thinking about my own problems."

I'm tempted to tell her something about my difficulties, but Julia's daughter Louisa comes bounding down the stairs on the way to the kitchen and the moment is lost.

"Darling, you remember Jen—Jennifer Hunter—don't you? Let me introduce you again." As she says this she stretches out her arm to gesture for her daughter to come to us, but the movement unsteadies her. "Oops, nearly."

"Mum—how much have you had to drink?" asks Louisa.

"Only a couple of glasses."

"Sorry," mouths Louisa to me, and then whispers something sharp to her mother.

"I'd better be off," I say. "I'll see myself out."

I don't take any pleasure in noticing the signs of alcohol dependency, but as someone who has an ongoing battle with drink I can certainly empathize with what Julia is going through.

Just as I'm walking down the steps from the house I hear the door open. It's Louisa.

"God, I'm sorry," she says again.

"It's been a difficult time—for all of us, since the incident on the Heath. I guess it's her way of coping."

"Listen—I know you're a journalist. But you won't write about any of this? About Mum's . . . problems, will you?"

Oh God, she thinks I'm that kind of journalist. "Don't worry. I give you my word." I feel what I'm saying sounds hollow, empty. I think back to the promise I made to Mr. and Mrs. Da Silva. Even though it wasn't me who leaked the story of Vicky's pregnancy, I still feel guilty. "It must be difficult for her. What with the pressures of her job and the stuff going on in Parliament. And now all of this."

"It does seem to have hit her hard," says Louisa. "I wonder how it has affected you—and the other witnesses?"

I'm not sure where to start. "It's an interesting question, but I suppose it's making its presence felt in different ways—for all of us, I mean."

"The thing is with Mum, she seems like a tough old bird. You know the kind of woman to give the PM a good blasting when she feels he needs it. A veneer as hard as stone and all that. But underneath she's, well, she's vulnerable and insecure. Anyway, thanks for being so understanding. I'd hate it if anything came out to make the situation even more difficult for her." She smiles and says goodbye.

On the way to meet Bex I mull over the brief conversation I had with Louisa about the effect of the murder-suicide on those who had witnessed it. I'm convinced that this should be the real focus of the feature. I take out my phone and write myself a short note as a reminder. As I finish, an email from Ayesha Ahmed drops into my inbox. The junior doctor who tried to save the lives of Victoria Da Silva and Daniel Oliver says that she will see me—she's free the next day—but on condition that I don't use her name or report anything that she says. She doesn't want to get into trouble with the health trust.

We arrange to meet outside Tate Modern, and again I travel with Bex, who blends into the crowd.

I spot Ayesha sitting on a bench, a small and lonely figure surrounded by swarms of tourists and middle-class Londoners with their children. There's a frightened quality to her and she winces and starts at every noise or sudden movement near her. She smiles shyly when she sees me and I go over and sit by her.

"Thanks for agreeing to see me," I say.

"I wonder whether I'll ever be able to sit on another bench again . . . without thinking about what happened that day," she replies, as she nervously runs her tiny hands over her well-cut navy blue trousers.

She asks me again about what I hope to gain by seeing her. She has nothing to say. She insists again that I can't use her name. I tell her that I'm hoping to understand the motivation and background to the crime. She starts to talk about how tired she had felt that day, how she had been up all night. If only she hadn't had her eyes closed or her headphones on she might have been able to intervene sooner, she might have been able to save Victoria's life. I tell her she did everything to help. She should be commended for her bravery and her sense of public duty. I get out my phone and play the video that Alex sent me.

"Do you recognize this man? The jogger?" She shakes her head. "He was there, that day on the Heath," I tell her. "He ran past the scene of the crime, but didn't stop, even though people asked him to, even though it could have made a difference."

Ayesha looks at me with her scared rabbit eyes again. "Are you sure you didn't see him that day?"

"No, why—is this important?"

"It could be," I say. "And what about the name Steven Walker—does that mean anything to you?"

"No," she replies. "Who is he?"

"He's the teenager who was there, who ran away, just as the police were approaching."

"I see," she says, swallowing. She pauses and continues, her voice full of sadness. "I read that there are some reports that Victoria was pregnant. That her unborn child died that day too."

"Yes, I think she was," I tell her. "There's one theory that Daniel suspected he wasn't the father of the child."

"I see," she says blankly. There's a certain intensity in her eyes though, as if she knows something, and she's keen to keep that something back.

"Would you mind going through what you saw, what you heard, again?"

The idea sickens her, I can tell, but she is gracious and polite enough to agree. She takes me through the scene, step by step. I've heard it all before, but I'm listening for inconsistencies, gaps, small details that might make a difference. But, like with Julia Jones, there's nothing new. I don't know what I think I'll gain from going over old ground, but I have an instinct that there's something I have yet to learn that might help. I'm about to thank her for her time and say goodbye when I ask her to tell me about those final moments, when Victoria and Daniel were both on the ground, their lives slipping away from them.

She looks at me as though I'm a sick bitch, but I try to smile sympathetically and encourage her to continue. I hate myself as I do this, as I know what I'm doing will cause Ayesha psychological pain. Perhaps I should drop the whole investigation. Perhaps I should listen to Annabelle. After all, it's doing nothing but upsetting those who witnessed the terrible crime. I'm about to tell Ayesha to forget it, let's pass over that question, but she begins to talk.

"The knife cut into both carotid arteries, the arteries that run up the sides of the neck, which supply blood to the brain. You see if they are cut there is a tremendous amount of blood loss. If they hadn't been cut, but the trachea had been, then there is a greater chance of survival. It's still a traumatic injury as the blood ends up flowing down into the lungs, and there is a chance of drowning in one's own blood. If the paramedics arrive in time there is a possibility that they can still do something to save a person's life. But the severance of the carotid arteries cuts off the supply of blood to the brain and a person lapses into unconsciousness in less than a minute, soon followed by a heart attack and . . . death."

Her description is so clinical that it takes me aback slightly. "And did both—both Victoria and Daniel—die like this?"

"Yes, it seems so," she replies. "Obviously, it's up to the coroner to make his or her judgment on the matter, but that's what I believe."

"And you'll be giving evidence at the inquest?"

She nods her head, obviously distressed at the idea of having to do so.

"I suppose all of us who were there will be called, to give our testimonies about what happened."

I wonder again what I should do about Laurence. If I go to the police with the video then he would be forced to appear. He would have to explain, on the record, about what he was doing on the Heath that day and why he ran away. I question whether I could endure the public scrutiny that would inevitably come when he confesses that he once had a relationship with one of the other witnesses—me. And whether he would talk about why our love affair broke down. Perhaps Bex is right, and we can deal with him ourselves.

"You may as well know now because I'm going to talk about it at the inquest," says Ayesha.

"Sorry, I was just thinking about . . . about that day," I lie. "What did you say?"

"Just that I may as well tell you now, about what Daniel Oliver whispered to me as he was dying."

I feel as though I am being injected in the arm with a shot of adrenaline. My heartbeat races and I feel my eyes widening. "I don't know if it makes any difference or what it means really," she continues. "I'd done what I could to save both their lives, but as I knelt down by Daniel I could hear that he was trying to say something. I leaned toward him and . . . it was obvious he didn't have much time left. I asked if he wanted to tell me something. He tried to nod, but he couldn't. I leaned further in, with my ear almost pressed onto his mouth. He didn't say anything for a moment or two and I'd thought he'd gone. But then he said, in a voice so slight and weak it was hardly even a whisper, he said . . ."

She goes quiet.

"Ayesha, what did he tell you?"

"He said, 'That . . . that was *him.*'"

"Did he give you a name?"

Ayesha shakes her head. "No, no he didn't . . . and then, well you know what happened. That bastard died."

44

BEX

I'm sitting with Jen in the ground-floor café of Tate Modern. Through the line of silver birches I can see the dome of St. Paul's across the river, imprisoned by a square of brutal architecture. One of the baristas is talking loudly about how the coffee is roasted by hand in a Second World War Nissen Hut within the grounds of Tate Britain. A woman at the next table is telling her friends about how Brexit has ruined the property market in London—she hoped to sell this year, but instead she's resigned herself to building a glass box on the back of her property. I'm hearing all of this as I pretend to listen to Jen, who is telling me in great detail about what Ayesha has just told her.

I'm trying to support Jen, I really am, but at times I have to acknowledge that sometimes it's a pretense; all the details about the murder-suicide get a bit too much for me and, for the sake of my own sanity, occasionally I have to switch off and zone out. I take out my phone and check it.

She must notice my attention is drifting away from her because she says, with a note of irritation in her voice, "I'm sorry, you must be sick of this."

"That awful woman at the next table—she's got such a loud voice," I say. "Shall we go on somewhere else so I can hear what you're saying?"

"Good idea," she says. Just as she stands up her phone pings. She takes it out of her pocket, and, as she presses her finger down on the home button, her face freezes.

"What's wrong?" I ask.

"It's him again," she says. Her eyes scan the café, darting from face to face with the desperation of a woman hunted.

"What?"

"I've just got another message—look."

She passes her phone to me as she continues to look around her. It's from @WatchingYouJenHunter.

Love the blue blouse. Sexy.

I know already what Jen is wearing, but still I find myself focusing on her blue blouse. I also know it's from Zara, as we were together when she bought it. A moment later another message comes through.

What did the doc tell you?

"There's another one too," I say, as I pass the phone back to Jen.

"Fuck," she says. "He's here."

"I thought he'd stopped messaging you."

She doesn't reply. Instead, she storms out of the café, nearly knocking over her coffee in the process, and begins to run around the front of the building, weaving in and out of the silver birches, checking the faces of the people sitting on benches. She approaches one man who from the back has something of the look of Laurence about him, and reaches out to touch him on the shoulder. He turns around, startled and appalled.

"Sorry," mumbles Jen, holding her hands up as she backs away. "I know he's here, somewhere. He's watching me."

"Let's go," I say, as I try to take hold of her arm.

"No!" she shouts, brushing me away. "I'm going to find that fucker and tell him to leave me alone."

She starts to sprint along the front of the embankment, in the direction of the National Theatre, banging into tourists. I try to follow her and apologize in her wake.

"Help me, Bex—help me find him," she says, between breaths. "He's got to be here somewhere."

"I can't see him," I say. "Perhaps if we wait in one place then—"

But she's off again, changing direction as she runs along the embankment and up onto the wobbly bridge. There's some maintenance work going on, and signs restricting the flow of pedestrians have narrowed the access. Everyone is walking in single file in both directions, but Jen runs through the lines, banging straight into a woman carrying a baby in a sling.

"Sorry, so sorry," I say, as I try to pass through the crowds.

I continue to apologize as I try to catch up with her.

Finally, I reach her and force her to stand still. "Jen, you've got to listen to me," I say. "Whoever sent these, they've gone now. You need to calm down. Take some deep breaths. You know, you nearly knocked over a woman with her baby back there."

"I . . . I don't care, I need to find him."

Her phone pings again. It's another message.

You shouldn't get so worked up. It doesn't suit you.

Her head swivels from side to side as she studies the faces of the pedestrians on the bridge. She starts to run toward the St. Paul's side of the river, before she lurches back toward the South Bank. Again, she bumps into a pedestrian, this time an old woman with a walking stick.

Again, I apologize for the behavior of my friend. "Stop," I say, grabbing Jen's shoulders in a desperate effort to make her keep still. I'm seriously thinking of having to slap her around the face again. "Jen, listen to me. If he's here, we'll find him together. I'll help you. Honestly, I will. But you need to pull yourself together. Can't you see he wants you to fall apart. He's getting off on this."

I don't know what she's thinking, but it seems as though the message is beginning to sink in. She stands by the railings of the bridge, the east side that looks down toward the skyscrapers of Canary Wharf. She takes a couple of deep breaths. Her head stops moving in such a manic fashion.

"That's right," I say. "A few more deep breaths."

Her eyes begin to relax a little. I take hold of her shaking hand.

"Don't give him the satisfaction of knowing he's upset you," I tell her. "You can get your own revenge."

She turns to me, a glint in her eye. I can tell the idea intrigues her. Her phone beeps again. She holds it out to me.

You look hysterical. Deranged.

And then a moment later, there's another.

No wonder nobody loves you. You drive everyone away.

Now she has the look not so much of the hunted as the hunter. I think of her surname. I'd never considered Jen as a predator before. In fact, for many years she had played the part of the victim. But now I realize she could be dangerous.

45

JEN

We are standing outside Laurence's house. It's already dark even though it's only just after four in the afternoon. After the scene down by Tate Modern and on the bridge, Bex managed to calm me down, but only just. Wherever I looked I seemed to see Laurence's face staring back at me. I would spot him among the crowds, convinced he was *there*. I'd rush forward, almost feel as though I could smell him, reach out and touch him, only to be met by the shocked face of a stranger. Each encounter was like a little death, a small stab in the heart.

Bex had led me away, back across the Thames to St. Paul's. She bought me some water and made me sit on the steps of the cathedral. She kept telling me to take deep breaths, that she would help me, that she would be by my side no matter what. I tried to talk about the messages, repeating fragments from them, wondering how Laurence could be so cruel. What was he trying to do? Drive me insane? I've read numerous thrillers and watched countless films in which a man tries to gaslight his wife or girl-friend. This was not happening to me, I told myself, it couldn't be hap-pening to me.

"What the fuck is Laurence playing at?" I said.

Bex went silent before she said, "Are you sure it's him? I mean—"

"What are you even saying?" I interrupted. "Of course it's him, who else could it be?"

"I know, I know, but just listen," she said.

"You're kidding me, aren't you?" I stood up in a small act of protest, as if I intended to storm off, even though I had no intention of doing so.

"Just sit down and let me explain," she said, taking hold of my hand and pulling me back down. "I know it seems as though Laurence is behind all of this, but you said yourself we need some kind of proof."

"What kind of proof?"

"Just something that links him to this. Something on his phone or in his house."

"And how do you expect to get that? I doubt turning up on his doorstep and asking him to surrender his phone would work somehow. I don't know if you've noticed, but I'm not his favorite person at the moment."

There was a mischievous glint in Bex's eyes that I recognized as a sign of trouble. She reached into her pocket and took out a key.

"I may not have mentioned that I have . . . this—the key to Laurence's house," she said, holding it up as a kind of miniature trophy.

"Bex—where the hell did you get that?"

"Let's just say that I don't always give things back."

"I thought he'd changed the locks after I moved out."

"He did . . . but I managed to get hold of a new one."

"How?"

"Once when he was away on a work trip he asked me to check on the house. I kept one of the spare keys, thinking one day it might come in useful."

"So what do you think we should do?"

"We should go and have a look around, just to make sure that it is Laurence who is messing with you."

"Don't you think we should go to the police?" I asked.

"You could do, but what would that solve? I mean, all they will do is give him a caution, at the most. And he'll be there, free to walk the streets, free to spy on you from a distance. You never know how it might escalate or what he might be capable of."

I stared at Bex, certain that she could see the uncertainty in my face.

"Don't look so worried, nothing bad is going to happen to you. I'll be there."

"You promise?"

"Of course—I'm hardly going to send you into Laurence's house by yourself, am I? And this way we may be able to find some kind of evidence that we can take to the police."

I had dozens of doubts—the phrase *inadmissible evidence* came into my mind—but Bex told me that it wouldn't be like a burglary, because I had once lived there and, if I was stopped by one of his neighbors, I could tell them that I was picking something up I had left in the house. An old laptop. A box of CDs from the '90s. Something sad like that.

And so that's why we are here, watching and waiting. My heart is beating fast, too fast, and my mouth tastes like sawdust. We've been here for the best part of forty minutes, and no one has put any lights on even though it's gone dark. Bex whispers to say she's confident that Laurence is not at home. And that we should go in. I start to explain why I think this is a bad idea, but then she goes ahead, walks down the street and into the front garden. She looks at me as if to ask whether I'm coming with her. She's right, I tell myself. It's the only way to know for certain.

I try to think through the action of that day again, who was where, when, and doing what. Daniel must have planned something, as he had taken a knife with him. He knew about Laurence, as it seemed he recognized him. But why was Laurence there? Yes, he liked jogging, and Parliament Hill Fields was a regular spot for him, but more often in the evening after he'd finished work. Had he been following Victoria? Was he jealous of her relationship with Daniel? Did Laurence know that Victoria was pregnant? Perhaps some of these answers lie inside the house and so I take a deep breath and follow Bex toward the front door.

She rings the bell, just to be on the safe side, and when no one answers she opens the door and walks inside. I hesitate for a moment because the sensation is like stepping back in time for me. I feel a little disconnected—I've learned to recognize the signs of what my therapist calls dissociation—and I try to do the exercises that help me bring me back to myself.

"You'd better shut the door," says Bex. I blink and do as she says.

"We may not have much time. Now you know the house better than me, so where should we start?"

I think for a moment. "I suppose we could start with his office, upstairs. There's a computer there."

"Great," she says.

As we climb the stairs I inhale the smell of the beeswax. I see myself, the first morning after I had slept with Laurence here. I'm radiant with happiness. My skin is glowing. Everything seems sharper, brighter, more defined. I go into the kitchen and try to make a coffee for Laurence, who is upstairs, but I realize that his machine is beyond me. After five minutes of trying to make it work I'm considering searching for instant when Laurence comes into the kitchen. He sees the state of the coffee machine and the mess I'm in and laughs. He takes hold of me and leads me back to bed.

All that's gone now, I know that. But how could that sense of a love so deep it felt like a kind of hunger, how could that have turned into this?

I show Bex the office. She starts to look through a filing cabinet while I switch on the Mac. Of course, it's password protected. I tap in the password that Laurence used when we were together, a combination of the word "Bauhaus" and the year of his birth, 1972. The icon shakes its little head in refusal. I try using a lowercase "b," but again I'm refused. I put the year first, the word second, but this doesn't work. I try a series of other possibilities—the name of his mother, his first dogs, RexWhistler (yes, really), and then, saddest of all, my own name. But nothing works.

"How are you getting on?" asks Bex.

"It's not letting me in," I reply. "What about you—have you found anything?"

"Nothing but work stuff," she says. "But I do have to commend him for his filing system. Talk about ordered."

"That's Laurence for you. He always was. Used to drive me mad sometimes."

I remember the time we had a blazing row because I had put a wine glass down on one of his blueprints. There was no stain—I'd already learned that I had to be a bit careful around his things—but Laurence worried about the possibility of one. And of course, this conversation mutated into an argument about my general slovenliness versus what I called, during the heat of the screaming match, his anal retentiveness. He warned me not to put the incident into my column, but of course it ended up in there, related line by line. Laurence had stopped reading my pieces, but perhaps he heard about it from someone at work because the day after it appeared he made some snarky comment about it over dinner. I didn't want another row and so I ignored it.

"Let's check the bedroom, shall we?" suggests Bex.

The thought of walking into that space where we had spent so much time, where we had made love, makes me feel sick. "Do you want to look in there? It's just that . . ." I can't finish the sentence.

"I'll go ahead," she says. "Why don't you go and check out, I don't know . . . where would Laurence keep something he didn't want anyone else to find?"

"As you know he's not a big one for personal possessions." Suddenly something occurs to me that makes me look at the house in a totally new light. My voice drops to a whisper. "Bex, do you think there's anything belonging to Victoria in here?"

"Oh my God, of course!" she says. "There's bound to be. There might be something of hers that could help. Why don't you look in the bathroom and I'll check the bedroom."

I hear her open one of the drawers by the bed. I dread to think what she might find there and so I leave her and walk into the bathroom. It's a gorgeous big room at the back of the house, with an enormous freestanding bath in the middle. Part of me doesn't want to find any trace of Victoria in the house. The thought of coming across something like an old packet of contraceptives or an item of underwear, even one of her lipsticks, makes me want to retch. I can't seem to control my breathing. I feel like running out of the room, down the stairs, and into the road. I catch a glimpse of myself in the bathroom mirror. There's a nasty yellow and purple bruise on my forehead. My blonde hair is lank. I have shadows under my eyes.

No wonder Laurence doesn't love me. Perhaps he never loved me. Was he always waiting for the moment when he could finish it all? Did my bad behavior give him the perfect excuse he was looking for? I wonder again how long he had been seeing Victoria.

"Found anything?" calls Bex from the other room.

"N-no, not yet," I answer.

My eyes are drawn to the cupboard below the sink. As I reach out for the handle, I notice my fingers are trembling. I close my eyes for a moment, take a deep breath, and tell myself that I need to just do this. I pull the handle toward me.

The first thing I see is a bottle of Penhaligon's aftershave I bought Laurence for one of his birthdays. Behind this there's a pair of tweezers and an expensive pot of moisturizer. I twist open the top of the jar and see, in the top of the cream, the faint impression left by a slender finger. I imagine Victoria standing here, in front of the mirror, massaging the potion into her face. I can't let this distract me. I have to search the rest of the house. We don't know how long we have before Laurence returns. But just before I go to close the cupboard I notice something stashed away at the back, behind the bottles of cleaning products. I push my hand past the bottles and feel something with a sharp plastic edge. I wrench it forward, not caring whether I knock anything over. I can't believe what I'm holding.

It's the Guy Fawkes mask that I last saw on the person who attacked me.

46

BEX

So she's found it.

"Bex! Bex!" I hear her scream.

I run to find her slumped on the bathroom floor, holding something.

"What's wrong? What is it?"

She holds up the mask. "It's what he—what Laurence was wearing when he attacked me."

"Oh my God," I say. I go over and take her in my arms. She is sobbing and I can feel her tears on my skin. "So . . . it was him."

"Of course it was him," she says. "Who else could it be?"

"The fucker. He must have stashed it there after attacking you."

"I don't understand why he hates me so much."

"He's twisted in the head, that's why." I pull my phone out from my pocket. "But the fact that he's kept it means you're not safe. He's used it once, which means he may intend to use it again."

"You think so?" She sounds, and looks, terrified. "What are you doing?"

"What do you think I'm doing? I'm calling the police."

She falls silent as I go through the motions of dialing 999. "But . . . let's just think this through," I say. "What if we call the police, and after they leave, they come to the house and find nothing. It's our word against his. And we can hardly take this mask with us, can we? Laurence could turn around and say we've just gone and bought a Guy Fawkes mask ourselves. No, we need to be clever about this."

"Clever?"

"Yes, we need to think one step ahead of him."

She looks at me in the same way she's looked at me ever since the first day I met her. As if I'm her savior. It's a look that believes I can save her from other people, perhaps even herself.

"So what should we do?"

"Take a photograph of it, just in case. And then put the mask back where you found it."

"What? But it's proof—it's evidence that, that he attacked me."

"Don't worry, we'll make sure he pays for it."

47

JEN

After taking a photograph of the mask I put everything back where I found it and we make our way out of the house. Before we open the front door Bex tells me to step out as if it's the most normal thing in the world. People can sense guilt, she says, even from afar. And you never know who might be watching.

I try my best to do as she says, but I keep picturing Laurence as he walks down the path in the front garden, meeting us as we close the door behind us. What will we say to him if he sees us? I know this is illogical—it's him who should worry, he's the one in trouble—still I can't help but feel I've got something to hide. But, of course, we walk away without meeting a soul, apart from a couple of young mothers and their new babies.

As we make our way back to the flat I want to talk with Bex about what happens next—I've got a few ideas of my own—but I'm conscious someone might overhear us. We stop at Sainsbury's to pick up a few things and, while Bex is paying, I go outside and check my phone. There's been a missed call from Penelope and an email from her too. She wants me to ring her or drop by, she says, because she has something important she needs to talk to me about. I remember the things she said to me during our last conversation. I suppose she wants to apologize. Bex was right about Penelope. I should have listened to her.

I can't believe I almost drove Bex away. Those cruel words, accusing her of behaving like a stalker, the way I snapped at her on the Heath like that, nearly destroyed our friendship. She's only ever had my best interests at heart. Only someone like her would have the sense, and the sensitivity, to suggest that perhaps it wasn't the right decision to call the police. But she's keen to punish Laurence. And I'm definitely up for that. Various scenarios run through my mind. What kind of revenge would be most effective? They say it's a dish best served cold. So it would be good to do something when he is least expecting it. But I can't wait that long. I'd like him to suffer like I've suffered. I'd like him to experience the acrid taste of fear, the visceral panic that sets in, knowing someone is watching you, following you.

I picture him walking down a dark street. He hears footsteps behind him. He feels the hairs on the back of his neck rise. His heartbeat quickens. He increases his pace, takes a turn down an unfamiliar side street in an effort to outwit his pursuer. But the shadowy presence continues to follow him. Finally, he takes a deep breath and turns his head to see . . . me. What does he feel? Certainly not fear. I'm a woman, after all. And what kind of man is afraid of the opposite sex? Not Laurence, that's for sure. I can hear his cruel laughter echoing down the street, a horrible, mocking sound. He tells me that he pities me, that I am pathetic. He pushes past me and disappears into the night.

No, if I want to get back at Laurence I need to do something more elaborate, more baroque. What would hit him the hardest? I could trash his house, throw paint around the walls, smash bottles of wine everywhere. Or I could do something more subtle, like use the key to sneak into the house and hide prawns in a hundred secret places so the whole place stinks to high heaven.

The thing he cares most about is his job, his reputation. What about some kind of plan to bring about his ruin? But just as I begin to try to think up ways to smear him, another idea occurs to me, one that stops me in my tracks. What if . . . what if Laurence was angry with me because he thought that I was the one who had told Daniel about his affair with Victoria? After all, he would have seen me on the Heath that day, standing near the couple, and soon after this Daniel stabbed his girlfriend. Did he blame me for Vicky's death, for the death of his unborn child?

Suddenly, I don't know what to do. I'm struck by a paralysis of doubt. I realize Laurence's true feelings are completely unknown to me. Is it worth trying to talk to him? To tell him that I had never seen, met, or talked to either Daniel or Victoria before that day? But then the image of that mask, hidden away in the bathroom cupboard, comes back to me. If he's got so much anger against me—if he really does blame me for the murders—then how far will he go? Does he actually want . . . to kill me?

The thought makes the idea of my murder a reality. I try to dismiss it. Laurence would never do anything like that, I tell myself. Although the messages were distressing, they were a way of venting his anger, I understand that. If he'd really wanted to kill me he could have done it. He could have carried on smashing the stone into my head until my skull was reduced to fragments and my brains spilled out over the earth. But he didn't. He stopped himself.

However, I know from my therapist how the process of normalization begins, how each of us rehearses things in our heads or acts out various minor versions of fantasies and finally, over time, those small acts repeated often enough can mutate into unacceptable, transgressive, or even criminal behavior.

Is Laurence capable of murder? And if so, what can I do to protect myself?

48

BEX

'm navigating the narrow aisles of the Sainsbury's Local, browsing for comfort food, when I spot a pack of doughnuts, their insides oozing raspberry jam. As I add them to my basket I'm taken back to the moment on the Heath when Jen was sitting on that bench. I checked to make sure the mask was in place, running the fingers of my left hand around its sharp edges. I took a step toward her as Jen's head turned to me. I saw the look of shock and horror in her eyes. The rock was in my right hand and I smashed it down onto her head. I was careful to apply the right amount of force, just enough to knock her out, but not enough to seriously injure her. The sound of the rock hitting her head pleased me in a way that was immensely satisfying, like hearing the familiar chorus of a favorite pop song I haven't heard for years. I struck again. She gasped and fell onto the ground. I stood and watched her quietly for a moment, then I walked quickly away, taking the rock with me. As I passed the ponds I threw it into the water. A sense of achievement washed over me as I watched the ripples spread across the surface.

All this runs through my mind as I pick up some milk, some teabags, crisps, chocolate, loo roll, and a bottle of wine. As I leave to pay, I picture Jen taking a doughnut, biting into it, the jam squirting out and smearing her lips, the color of blood.

"Here, I got these for you," I say, as I pass the doughnuts to Jen.

"Great—so you've got a secret mission?" she asks.

I feel myself begin to panic. "What?"

"To make me pile on the pounds," she says, laughing. Jen digs into the packet and pulls out one of the doughnuts. "I'm only kidding. Honestly—it's exactly what I need. And anyway, haven't you heard, revenge is hungry work." She bites into the deep-fried dough and catches some jam with her hand.

It's the first time I've heard her say it, and it sounds good. "Revenge?"

"Oh, yes, revenge. Revenge, big time."

"On . . . Laurence?"

"Who else?"

"What do you have planned?"

"I'm not sure yet, but I'm not going to let him fuck with me."

He's not the one fucking with you, I think.

"What's so funny?" she asks.

"Just you tucking into that doughnut, that's all." She hands me the packet. "Want one?"

I shake my head. "Maybe later."

"I just got a message and a call from Penelope," says Jen, wiping some jam from her lips.

"What does she want?"

"She says she wants me to get in touch with her as soon as possible. I suppose she wants to apologize."

"What are you going to do?" I ask.

"Ignore her—at least for the time being."

The mirror image of my name on that blotting pad comes back to me. I don't like the idea of Penelope snooping around. As we start to walk I feel Jen look at me, in a way that I know prefigures a difficult or awkward question.

"What is it?" I ask. "You may as well spit it out."

"How do you know I want to ask you something?"

"Just something weird you do with your head. You sort of tilt it in an odd fashion."

"I do not!"

"You know you do," I say. "Anyway, go ahead."

"Well, I was just wondering whether you wanted your own space back. I know you said I could stay as long as I want, but I don't want to be a burden."

"Don't be stupid—you can stay as long as you like. I know it's not super comfortable. But you'll have the flat to yourself, during the day at least, as I'm due back at work on Monday."

"Are you sure?"

I tell her that of course I'm sure. She doesn't know the truth: I'm not due back at work until the end of March.

Inside the flat, Jen begins to tell me about some of her revenge fantasies. Clichés about prawns hidden in airing cupboards, suits cut up and thrown out of the window, attempts to smear Laurence's reputation at work. I listen and nod my encouragement, all the while having a plan of my own.

49

JEN

'm sitting in the flat, alone. Bex has gone back to her desk at Camden Council. Hard though it is I force myself to stop thinking about Laurence and what terrible things I might do to him. I need to focus on work. I'm conscious that I need to move the story forward. I'm also really short of cash. I dismiss what my therapist advised and concentrate on what I know and what I need to find out.

Obviously, I can't go back to Mr. and Mrs. Da Silva because they still blame me for leaking the news of Victoria's pregnancy. I doubt whether Caro Elliott has anything else to add. I think about what Julia Jones said to me about how she's been affected by witnessing the murder-suicide and how it's revived the painful memory of losing her son, Harry. I'm not sure whether I can even make the feature work or whether any of the group would want to help me, but nevertheless I tap out an email to Nick, the editor at the *Mail*, asking whether he'd be interested in a feature about the trauma of being a bystander at such a horrific event. Conscious that it needs some kind of catchy headline, I remember Julia's words, tinged with black humor, when we first met—"Witnesses for the Execution." I type this into the subject box and press the send button before I can change my mind.

As I wait for a reply I think about how I can use my time. I've interviewed everyone who witnessed the crime apart from Steven Walker. He

194

seemed keen to talk to me, that is until Bex ran toward him like something demented and scared him away. It's worth a try, I think.

I arrive at the gates of Steven's school just before lunchtime. I could easily be a parent who has turned up to give their child the packed lunch they forgot to pick up earlier, or the money they need for an after-school club. I watch the stream of faces that pass me, every shade, every ethnic origin, pleased that I live in such a thriving and dynamic multicultural city.

Just then my phone pings. A message. It's from @WatchingYouJenHunter.

Taking to hanging around the school gates now, have we? Classy.

I look around me, but all I can see is a sea of teenage faces. I walk up and down Highgate Road, peering into parked cars. Then, on the other side of the road, I see him. Laurence. He's standing by the bus stop with his back to me. I step out, but there's a blast of a horn from my right. The car brakes suddenly and I get a mouthful from a man, telling me that I'm a stupid fucking bitch and I need to watch what I'm doing. I stumble back onto the sidewalk, my nerves shredded. Passersby look me up and down as if I'm deranged. And as another message zings its way into my phone—

You better be careful. We wouldn't want you to have a nasty accident now, would we?

I feel as though my mind is shattering.

"Laurence, what the fuck do you want?" I shout, but a lorry thunders past me, drowning out my cries.

"Just stop it—what the hell is wrong with you?" I scream with such a force it feels as though my lungs are burning.

A slow-moving bus interrupts my sight line across the road. By the time the bus clears I half expect Laurence to have disappeared, but he's still there, haunting me.

I check the traffic and dodge the cars, running up to the bus stop.

"What the fuck do you think you're doing?" I shout again. I reach out and tap him on the shoulder, perhaps with a little too much force.

He spins around. There's a look of astonishment and fear on the man's face, a face that doesn't belong to Laurence.

"What . . . ?" I say.

The man steps back, clearly anxious I'm about to do something to him.

"I'm s-sorry," I manage to say. "I thought—I thought you were someone else."

I back away, wanting to turn myself inward. I'm ashamed by my actions. I actually scared a stranger. A nice, middle-aged man who was minding his own business.

Now that wasn't a very nice thing to do.

Fired up by adrenaline I have a new idea. Perhaps it's not Laurence sending me the messages? I look up and down the busy road, scanning everyone who has a mobile phone. There's a young girl with headphones, ready for a jog, no doubt selecting music for her run. Back near the school there is a host of boys all armed with phones, their faces slack, their eyes glazed and empty. Is Steven there? Could it be him? I run back over to the other side of the street and push my way through a mass of bodies.

And then I see him. Steven. He's coming out of the gates, talking to a friend, laughing and joking. I spring forward as if I'm an animal and I've caught sight of my prey. The sudden movement alerts him. He's scared and he bolts.

"Steven—wait. Stop!" I shout. "I just want to ask you some questions. Listen—"

But he runs, as quick as a leopard, down Highgate Road toward Kentish Town. I take off after him, already knowing there's little hope of catching him. I feel my lungs filling up with pollution and, as I stop to catch my breath, I see him disappear into one of the streets toward Gospel Oak. I fall back against some black railings. I grasp the top of the railings, holding them for support to prevent myself from falling to the ground, my fingers curled around the sharp points.

Then my phone vibrates once more. My hands are shaking now, from fear, from shock. I bring the phone toward my face, not at all certain I want to read what it says.

Careful of those railings. We wouldn't want you to come to any harm.

Fuck. I'm not sure if I can carry on. It's—he's—driving me insane. That's it. I've had enough. I go into the profile page of @WatchingYou-JenHunter and click on the icon. My fingers hover over the block option. I press it. It's done. There won't be any more messages. I can get on with my life. Why didn't I do that before? I suppose I believed it might lead to something, some information to help me understand the true motivation behind the murder-suicide on the Heath. I close my eyes, take some deep breaths. It's over.

I push myself away from the railings and try to assume the pose of a normal middle-aged woman in north London. I smile to myself—I know it's forced—but I hope by doing so I can trick myself into thinking that I'm fine.

My phone pings again. Perhaps it's Bex, messaging from work to check that I'm okay. I freeze when I see the words. It's from a new Twitter account, @WatchingYouJenHunter2.

I'm still here.

50

BEX

I am standing in the upstairs of the Bull & Last, a pub opposite William Ellis school, watching Jen have a complete meltdown. It was all so easy to arrange. I knew at some point that Jen would want to speak to Steven Walker. I also knew that although she did not have his home address, she did know where he goes to school. It was only a matter of time before she sought him out. I followed her as she left the flat and made her way up Highgate Road to the school.

The next piece of the puzzle fell into my lap like a dream. Over the course of the last year I had been dealing with the planning application of the Bull & Last, whose owners wanted to convert the top two floors of the building into space for six guest bedrooms. I was on friendly terms with the architect, and an informal site visit could easily be arranged. I knew too that the scaffolded facade was covered by a layer of plastic sheeting that prevented dust and dirt from spewing out onto the street.

From one of the rooms on the first floor, overlooking Highgate Road, it's easy to open the window and make a small tear in the sheeting. I can see out toward the gates of the school, but no one can see me.

I watch as Jen walks into the frame. She's looking quite pretty today in a floral print Zara dress, black boots, and a denim jacket. I can tell that she's on edge. She plays nervously with her hair and she moves as if she's drunk too much coffee or taken speed. I take out my other phone—the one that Jen knows nothing about—and tap out a message. The anticipation, the thrill of waiting to see how she is going to react, is a delicious sensation, like the best kind of drug. It's annoying that I'm standing too far away from her to see the expression in her eyes, but I imagine her pupils dilating. I can't hear her breathing quicken either, but I'm sure that's exactly what is happening.

She starts to walk up and down Highgate Road, peering into parked cars. Then she steps out into the road without looking. Fuck! A car nearly hits her. She's okay, thank God. I wouldn't want to see her die, because I have plans for her, like a cat has plans for the mouse it has captured.

I think back to Jen's cat, Henry, or Henrietta. It was a stupid old thing, but there's no doubt that she loved it. She'd taken it in as a favor for a neighbor, an old hippy called Lou, who was going traveling in Asia for three months. But Lou had changed her plans—she'd fallen in love with an Australian man and had no intention of coming back to London for at least a year. Would Jen be cool looking after Henry? After all, Lou knew how much Jen liked the old bagpuss. Jen thought she had no choice—what other option did Henry have, apart from confinement in somewhere like Battersea?—and so she agreed. Although Laurence only endured its presence in the house, she was besotted with the creature.

To begin with Jen thought Henry had gone walkabout. There was nothing unusual in this, as the cat occasionally spent a night away from home. After two days she began to worry, but still tried to convince herself that it was having a nice relaxing mini-break away from her. But then on the morning of the third day, a Saturday, she rang me to tell me she felt sick with anxiety. Laurence was still away on a work trip and Henry had not returned home. I tried my best to convince her everything was okay, but she said she felt something was wrong. I listened to her cry as she told me that she feared that Henry might be dead. I offered to pop over—we could go and ask the neighbors if they'd heard or seen anything—and half an hour later I was there.

"I'm so grateful," she said as she kissed me on the cheek and ushered me into the house.

"What else am I going to do with my Saturday morning?" I said, smiling. "Anyway, it's a good excuse to get out of Pilates." She made me a coffee, after which we searched the length of the expansive garden at the back of the house. We checked the shed once more—no sign—and then went around the neighbors on her side of the street. We checked outbuildings, bike sheds, old lean-tos, and summer houses, but there was no trace. Finally, as she was about to give up, I suggested going to talk to the people who backed onto the garden. Laurence knew them—an elderly couple, Phillip and Harriet—better than her, but she had waved to them on the odd occasion. We walked around the block, located their house, and rang the bell. After a little small talk Jen explained about Henry and wondered if they had seen her in their back garden. No, but we were very welcome to check their old shed. They ushered us in and, with a look of embarrassment, led us through to their rather overgrown garden.

We pushed past a giant hedge under a vine-heavy pergola, and emerged into an expanse of waist-high grass and weeds. At the end of the garden we could see the shed that backed onto the old fence that divided the two properties. As we came closer we saw that the door was hanging off its hinges. Jen started to whistle and call Henry's name, while I pushed open the door. The first thing I saw was a drop of blood on the floor.

"Let me go and have a look in here," I said. "You stay back."

"Why—what have you seen?" she asked in a panicked voice.

She followed my gaze to the ground and immediately pushed past me. "Henry! Henry—are you there?"

We were hit by a smell of something rank and rotten. Jen covered her mouth as she tried to make her way into the shed, which was piled high with old boxes and a rusty electric lawn mower.

"Henry . . . Henry?" she whispered as she tried to move some of the equipment that blocked her way. She froze when she saw a lifeless lump of fur in the corner. Her arm stretched out to touch it, but shot back when she came in contact with the blood.

"Come away from there," I told her. "You shouldn't see that." She tried to get rid of the stain of blood from her fingers by rubbing them repeatedly on her jeans. A line from *Macbeth* came back to me.

"Oh no, you poor thing," I said. "Let me deal with it."

"Do you think there's any chance?" she asked in a small and pathetic voice. "That—that Henry might still be . . . ?"

"I'll have a look," I told her. "You sit here."

I used the sleeve of my cardigan in order to pretend to cover my mouth and stepped into the shed. I knew exactly what I would find—an animal that had bled to death—but I had to feign surprise and horror and all those other emotions expected of you in such a situation. I think I even managed a few tears too.

"I'm afraid there's no hope," I told her. "Henry's gone."

"What—what . . . how did she . . . ?"

"I think it looks like a fox or something."

"Do you think she . . . ?"

"No, she won't have suffered."

I wasn't telling the truth. Of course it had suffered. I had put on some heavy duty gardening gloves and held it down as I stabbed it with some kitchen scissors in Jen's back garden, when she had popped out to get some more wine. It scratched and spat and struggled, but I managed to hold it firm. I let it go when I knew I'd inflicted enough deep wounds that would kill it, and pushed it through a gap in the fence. I watched it as it made its way into the neighbors', where it died.

Now, I'm watching Jen suffer. She's going really mental, walking up to strangers on the street and accosting them. Then she starts bothering the schoolboys outside William Ellis. Really, she should be locked up. She's a danger to herself and to other people. I see her looking at something, someone. I try to follow her gaze. There's a sea of teenage faces. Then she calls out, "Steven!" Fuck, so she has found him.

She tells him she wants him to wait. She has some questions for him. But the guy panics. He splits away from his friends and sprints down the road. Jen chases after him, dodging the children and their parents. I lose sight of her from the window and so I run down the stairs and out onto Highgate Road.

She must have lost Steven as she's slumped back against some black railings. She's messing with her phone and there's a crazed expression in her eyes. I go to Jen's Twitter account and discover that she has blocked @WatchingYouJenHunter. So, she's finally showing a little spirit. Good for her. Actually, I was wondering how long it would be before she did that. But I have it all worked out. I quickly create another account, similar to the last one, and send another message.

I'm still here.

And I'm not going anywhere.

51

JEN

can't stand this anymore. I need to stop it. I tighten my grip around my phone, willing for it to smash in my hand.

I try to take a deep breath. I have to think. I look around, conscious that someone must be watching my every move. I can't see Laurence anywhere. But could he have employed someone to spy on me and send me those Twitter messages? It doesn't seem like the kind of thing he would do, but then again none of this—the way he had acted on the Heath, his denial of his whereabouts—sounds like reasonable behavior. Although I feel like I am going insane, is he the one with the real mental health problems? I think of the day on the Heath again. Flashes of images burn through my mind. The bottle of champagne glinting in the sunlight. The blood streaming from Vicky's mouth. Her fingers grasping onto the edge of the bench in pain. Jamie pleading with the jogger to stop, but the guy in the hoodie, whose face I can't see, runs by. Then the horror of what happens next.

What was Laurence doing there? It seemed too much of a coincidence that he just happened to be on Parliament Hill Fields at the very moment his lover, Vicky, was murdered, and the attack was witnessed by his ex-girlfriend: me. Had Laurence been following her—or me? If Laurence was the one behind the Twitter stalking, then why would he want to alert me to the fact that the murder-suicide wasn't what it seemed?

I need some answers. I check my phone: it's 1:30 P.M. I walk back to the flat and change into some of Bex's clothes. I open her wardrobe, which is full of sensible, if not downright dull, work suits, skirts, blouses, and fleeces. Whereas, in the past at least, I had the money to shop for designer pieces, jackets, and dresses from Chloé, Acne, Prada, and Bottega Veneta, Bex buys clothes from the Gap, M&S, Primark, and Uniqlo.

I think back to the time when we first met, when I was the one that dressed like a country bumpkin and she looked like a cool, urban sophisticate. She had taught me so much. How to shop, what to do with my hair, how to look after my skin, what to eat. However, soon after she got that job at Camden Council, after returning from traveling, she began to dress in a way that made her look as if she didn't care about her appearance, almost as if she wanted to erase herself. When I dared to try to talk to her about this, hinted that she could make an effort to dress nicely, she closed me down and said that there were more important things in life than clothes and surface appearances. She made me feel shallow and superficial, guilty for caring how I looked. People were starving out there, she said. And I couldn't argue with that. I select a pair of supermarket jeans, a baggy beige blouse, a gray fleece, and an old blue jacket that's clearly seen better days. I stand in front of the mirror and catch a glimpse of an odd hybrid, a strange mixture of myself and Bex. The effect is unsettling and I feel as if my perspective is shifting on its axis. Despite my fuller figure and the creases around my mouth and forehead, the image reminds me of how I used to look, before I met Bex. The reflection fills me with distaste and I turn away. I suppose I don't have a choice—it's a good disguise, one I hope will throw Laurence off my track. I find an old gray woollen hat, put on a pair of my own trainers, and go downstairs and into the outside world.

I check to see if Laurence is on the street. He's not. I walk up to Tufnell Park, toward his house, a route I know so well it's hardwired into my brain. As I do so, I look over my shoulder to see if he's following me. The thought that he could run up behind me and push me in front of a bus or a lorry fills me with fear. I stop and take a sudden right turning, just in case. I feel my breath quicken. I look around me again, so quickly that my head begins to spin. I grab hold of a nearby wall and steady myself, all the time thinking that he is nearby, watching me. And yet I still can't see him.

Outside his house, I call his number. It goes to voicemail. I take a deep breath and knock on his door. No answer. I walk to the Tube and catch the underground north. At Archway I get off, walk down the platform, and get back on the same train. When I reach Highgate I get a train south, back down to King's Cross. I merge into a mass of people. If Laurence has been following me I'm pretty certain I've lost him by now. I cross the busy Euston Road and into the complex of streets leading up to Argyle Square.

When Laurence and his partners chose this location for their office fifteen years ago many of their clients thought that they were mad. A place for drug addicts, prostitutes, and cheapskate tourists, one of them had said at the time. And although it's true that some of the buildings look less than salubrious, there's a sense that the area has changed. The gothic St. Pancras station designed by Gilbert Scott is already a five-star hotel, and the brutalist structure that was once Camden Council offices is now being transformed into the London outpost of the swanky Standard hotel chain.

I check my phone again. No new messages. I look around me. Still no sign of Laurence. I power ahead through the streets until I see the glass-fronted office of Robertson + Galbraith Partners. Without much thought about what I'm going to say I press the intercom on the door and wait to go inside. A second later I'm buzzed in. I approach a young woman on reception, luckily one I've never met before, and tell her that I'm here to see Laurence Robertson. She looks at me suspiciously, no doubt because of the way I'm dressed. Do I have an appointment? No, I don't, I tell her. I'm a friend, I say, and give a fictitious name: Gemma. I just hope that my gamble pays off and that Laurence is out of the office. God knows what I would say to him if he actually walked into reception.

She rings through to someone, most likely Laurence's secretary. I scan the spiral staircase behind her, hoping none of the staff such as Zoe, Tom, or Peter come down and see me.

"I'm sorry, but Laurence isn't in at the moment," she replies, as she places down the phone.

I can tell by the way she looks at me that she isn't lying. "Do you know what time he'll be back?"

If I were a client she would get back on the phone and ask Laurence's secretary.

"Not sure, sorry," she says. "Do you have his mobile?"

"Yes, of course," I say. "I'll try that."

Just then I see a pair of red high heels descending the spiral staircase. I'm sure they must belong to Zoe. I hear her voice shouting back up the stairs to someone. Yes, it's her.

"Or you could always leave a message if—" asks the receptionist.

I cut her off. "Don't worry, I'll catch up with him later."

I hold my breath and turn away from reception just as I hear Zoe's voice getting louder. I hope she doesn't recognize me from the back. As soon as I'm outside I breathe a massive sigh of relief, and it takes me a couple minutes to work out what to do next. I walk down the street before I double back on myself, find a coffee shop that has a full view of the front of the office, and take a seat next to the window. Laurence is a workaholic and I guess that at some point he'll return. I pull out my phone and check my messages. There's an email from Nick at the *Mail*. I read it as I try to keep an eye on the entrance of Robertson + Galbraith Partners.

Nick is really keen for me to pursue the feature about what it's like being a witness to such a traumatic event. In addition to my own personal testimony, he wants me to speak to as many people as possible who saw the murder-suicide, particularly Julia Jones. He has an idea that might work: what about bringing all the witnesses together? "It might make for some really powerful stories," he says. Ideally, he'd also like me to organize a photo shoot for all the witnesses on the spot where the murder-suicide happened on Parliament Hill Fields. "And I love your headline, WITNESSES FOR THE EXECUTION," he adds. "All the editors here think it's great too. So if we could have 2,000 words we can give it a good spread in a Saturday edition. There's no immediate deadline, but it would be great to get it into the can just as soon as. How does that sound?" Nick says he knows it's a lot of work, and the fee would reflect that. He suggests £2,500.

That's a lot of cash, and it's money I desperately need. The last time I looked I was more than £5,000 over my limit at the bank. I tap out a quick email back to Nick.

"Great—can't wait to do this. Will let you know details for shoot and the mobile numbers of people willing to be photographed. Should make for a good piece. Thanks—Jen." As soon as I press send I begin to panic. What happens if everyone says they'd rather not take part? That they want to get on with their lives in peace? That they don't want to be featured in a national newspaper?

I have to make this work. I think back to the positive reception I had from both Jamie Blackwood and Julia Jones. If I can get them onboard then there's a chance that the others might follow suit. Steven Walker might prove difficult, as he is underage, as might Ayesha Ahmed, the junior doctor, but she said herself that she would give evidence at the inquest. I compose a few carefully worded emails and send them out.

I order another pot of tea and continue my watch. As I wait, I think over my time with Laurence. Is he one of those people who walks through the world, presenting themselves as a nice person when in fact they are the very opposite? I know they exist; I've even met one or two.

Just then I see him enter the office. I have to restrain myself from bolting over and asking him what the fuck is going on. Instead, I take a sip of boiling hot tea, letting the liquid burn the inside of my mouth. The pain is enjoyable, something to be savored.

I imagine Laurence suffering an agony that consumes his whole body, a torment afflicting every single nerve ending and cell. I picture him screaming like he's being tortured, his eyes stretched wide with terror. I see a knife scoring the soft skin on the side of his neck, drawing blood.

Stop it.

I can't let myself think like this. It's wrong, dangerous.

But then I ask myself why I should feel so guilty. After all, Laurence is the one who's been fucking with me. He's the one who sent me those messages. He's the one stalking me. He's the one who hit me over the head with a rock for God's sake. I continue to sit there, sipping my tea, waiting. At 5:30 the office begins to empty. I watch as the receptionist leaves, followed by the rest of the staff, including Tom and Peter. Finally, Zoe steps out, soon followed by Laurence. I watch as they flirt with each other. I know she fancies him by her body language. I wonder how much she knows about Laurence's connection to what happened on the Heath. That he was the mystery jogger who let his lover be knifed to death. How would she react when she learned the truth about him?

I bet she wouldn't be so friendly with him then.

Zoe smiles again and takes a step away. Laurence nods his head. They are saying goodbye. She turns away from him, he moves in the opposite direction, but after about five seconds Laurence swivels around to steal a glance at her. In that look there is lust, but is there also an expression of greed and possession? It goes beyond simple desire, more than the urge to fuck her. It's more proprietorial, a sense that he knows he's in control and can do anything he wants to her. Is that how he viewed Vicky? Was she nothing but a plaything? Is that why he doesn't appear to feel any sense of loss for a woman who was his lover?

Suddenly, I feel an overwhelming sense of relief that I managed to get away from him when I did. What would have happened to me if I'd stayed with him? Would he have made it his mission to destroy me too?

I quickly take out my purse and leave ten pounds on the table. I step outside and begin to follow Laurence down the street, keeping a safe distance, as he goes down into the Tube. The mass of people threatens to swallow him, and at times I fear I've lost him, but I spot him as he makes his way through the station to catch the Northern Line. At the barriers I have to hold back in case he turns his head and sees me. But when he's through the gates I push myself forward.

I stand about six people behind him on the escalator. I study the back of his head, thinking about the fragility of his skull. At the bottom of the escalator the crowd builds and there's a bottleneck as the commuters try to squeeze their way onto the platform. The temperature change, from chilly winter evening to humid hothouse enclosure, is too much for many and I see sweat begin to form on foreheads and faces begin to flush. Laurence turns left and slowly makes his way down the platform, but then, as he realizes the space is even more congested, he turns back in my direction. I quickly turn around and do the same, melting into the crowd. Luckily, there's a group of American children I can hide behind. He stops short of where I'm standing and looks up at the arrivals display. A train in three minutes.

I think of everything the bastard's put me through. The lies. The stalking. The intimidation. The attack. I feel my blood pulsating through my veins. He moves a little farther toward the edge of the platform. *What the hell was he doing on the Heath that day?* I feel the stirring of hot, dirty air as it blows down the tunnel. *Why did he run away?* I take a step farther toward him. *What kind of sick thrill did he get from sending me those messages, from watching me?* The noise from the approaching train roars toward us. *Why did he take a rock and smash it over my head?*

I ease forward so I'm standing right behind him now. I savor the moment as I watch his hair part with the force of the wind. The American kids move en masse toward me, unsteadying me, and I have to reach out and grip the shoulder of a besuited businessman. I smile by way of apology, but he doesn't smile back. Laurence stands tall as he overlooks the tracks. The whine of the approaching train hits us at the same time as the gale-force dry mistral of the wind. The doors open and Laurence steps inside, soon followed by the other passengers. After the doors close and the train departs I see Laurence pressed up against the glass. He looks out and squints in my direction. Does an expression of puzzlement and disbelief cross his face, or is it my imagination? The train speeds into the dark tunnel. I stumble down the corridor, fight my way against the next wave of commuters, and up an escalator.

I emerge, gasping for air, feeling sick, afraid of the reasons why I'd followed him down there.

52

BEX

I'm sitting there in the flat when the door opens. A woman I don't recognize stands before me. My instinct is to jump up and ask what the fuck this stranger is doing in my flat, before I realize it's Jen. And she's dressed in my clothes.

"Oh my God, Jen, you gave me one hell of a fright," I say.

"Sorry, I should have rung. But I . . ."

She can't finish the sentence and, as I get up to go to her, I know there's something wrong. She has a mad look in her eyes.

"What's happened?"

"I don't know what's come over me. I followed him and . . ."

"What are you talking about?"

"Laurence."

I have to keep my voice steady and pretend not to know what she's talking about. "What about him?"

"I went to his office. Sorry—I borrowed some of your clothes so he wouldn't recognize me. To put him off the scent. With those messages, you see. He sent me more. I went to look for Steven. At the school. And he must have been watching me. I don't know how or from where. But he was watching my every move. I felt like I was going mad." Tears come into her eyes as she collapses on the sofa.

"Let me get you a drink." In the kitchen I take a couple of deep breaths and try to rearrange my features so I look surprised by what Jen might say. I return with two glasses of white wine. "Tell me what happened. Don't worry, you know I won't judge you. After all, Laurence deserves everything coming to him."

She takes a gulp of wine and tells me more about how she followed him down to the Tube at King's Cross.

"I don't know what I was thinking. It was like I was in some kind of trance. I wanted to give him a taste of his own medicine, I suppose. For the stalking. Those awful messages. The attack on me on the Heath." She looks at me, full of guilt. "But I'm not sure whether he even noticed he was being followed."

I deliver the next comment as if it's a joke. "You should have finished him off while you had the chance. You should have pushed the bastard under the train."

She laughs, but as I stand up to fetch the bottle of wine I can tell that my words have resonated with her.

"But the sick thing is that it would've been *you* who would've gone to prison," I say as I refill her glass. Now is the time for the next revelation. "Listen, there's something you should know. Something I've just found out."

"What is it?"

I go and get my work bag from my bedroom and return with it to the sitting room.

"I wasn't sure whether to tell you. I wasn't sure how you'd react."

"Just tell me, Bex. What is it?"

"It's about Laurence." I reach into my bag and pull out an A4 brown envelope. I hand it over to her. "I went back to his house and found this."

Jen takes the envelope and, with shaking fingers, opens it. She pulls out the documents. I watch as her face creases in confusion.

"What are they?"

"I thought Laurence was hiding something, and I was right," I say.

"But what was he doing with my parents' death certificates?"

I wait for the inevitable realization, which comes a second or so later.

"Fuck. No. It was him? He was the one?"

"It seems like it."

"He's the one who wrote into the *News*? That I'd . . . lied about the car crash."

"Oh, Jen. I'm so sorry."

"And all that time he was planning on doing this? On exposing me? Getting me sacked?"

Tears start to well up in her eyes and fall down her face. She wants to continue talking, but she's finding it difficult to breathe. "Why does he . . . hate me so much?" she sobs. "I don't understand what I did to him."

"I don't know," I reply as I take her hands in mine.

Fat tears spill onto the death certificates, staining the green paper.

"I didn't know whether I should tell you. I knew that the truth would hurt you, but . . ."

"No, you did the right thing. Don't blame yourself, Bex."

I stand up to get her a tissue and pass it to her. All the pain she's stored up since the sacking, since the split from Laurence, since the cyberstalking, since her attack, comes to the surface. Her eyes, bright with tears, look like they are burning. She is on fire with anger.

"You never told him the truth about your parents?" I ask.

Jen shakes her head.

"Then I suppose he must have found out somehow." I don't tell her that it was me who provided him with the information. "Perhaps it was the fact that you kept that from him that made him do what he did. That you didn't tell him the truth."

"That can't be the reason. If he wanted to end it with me why couldn't he have done it like a normal bloke? You know, the whole, 'It's not you, it's me,' routine.'

The night I spent with Laurence comes back to me. I feel my face begin to sting.

"He's a shit," I say.

"More like a bloody psycho," Jen replies. She wipes away her tears and blows her nose. "I can't get it straight in my head. Okay, he hated me. Really hated me. Hated me in secret. But at the same time he was planning a move to Switzerland with me to start a new life."

Just hearing the name of the country makes me feel sick.

"But instead of just telling me he wanted to end it, he went out of his way to dig out some proof about how my parents really died, and then he sent the death certificates to my editor at the paper."

"I suppose he must be really fucking twisted."

"Understatement of the year," she says.

As she blinks I catch her looking at me like she's seeing me for the first time. Like she's stripped away the facade of my personality and is really glimpsing the truth of what I am. I begin to panic. Has she discovered something about me? What did she say about Penelope wanting to get in touch with her? Has the old bitch dug something up about me?

But then, a moment later, she's back to her normal self. Crying. Questioning. Trusting me. Asking for my advice. What should she do? What should *we* do?

53

JEN

Bex has gone to bed. I'm on the sofa and can't sleep. I'm staring at the death certificates of my parents. The truth is here in black and white: my mum, Gillian Hesmondalgh, died on 6 September 1997, from cancer, and my dad, Kenneth Hesmondalgh, died of myocardial infarction, a heart attack, on 3 June 1998. Ironically, seeing the details of their deaths set out so starkly like this makes them feel even more like strangers.

In many ways they became figures of fantasy to me ever since I told that stupid lie about them on that first day of college back in 1995. By creating an alternative history for them, a tragic one that I could tell again and again, I reinvented them in my own mind. Their deaths in that car crash were a bit more exotic than the run-of-the-mill illnesses of old age. Their end was much more dramatic than a slow lingering death from terminal illness or a sudden pain in the chest. A car crash was associated with a dash of danger, glamour even.

At the bottom of each certificate is the date when the copy was requested: 2 July 2018, just before the split from Laurence. I try to think back to that time. I'm convinced that we were fine. Despite five years together, the passion was still there. We got on well, made each other laugh, had fun together.

I wonder what made him suspect that I'd been lying about my parents, that they hadn't died in a car crash as I said? Had someone tipped him off? But who would that have been? I'd changed my name from Hesmondalgh to Hunter years back. There was no one in my close family still alive.

It feels too late to ask Laurence. He had the opportunity to talk to me about his feelings toward me, no matter how negative they were. But instead he chose to go down a different route: intimidation, stalking, violence. I recall the terror I felt on finding that mask in his bathroom. A cold tendril of fear snakes its way through my body. I look at the door. As Bex said to me tonight, who knows what he might do next?

◆

I still can't sleep. My stomach burns full of acid. My breathing is shallow. I jump at each bang of the communal door downstairs. I reach out for my phone. As I register the time—3.31 A.M.—I see that I've got a few notifications from Twitter. My finger hovers over the icon. I tell myself that they'll be friendly comments from random followers about a few of my past posts, or funny videos about cats with moustaches. I'd muted @WatchingYouJenHunter2, so I've nothing to worry about. There's no way I'm going to go back to sleep and so I open the app.

@ImStillWatchingYouJenHunter Can't sleep. Poor baby.

I look around me. I push the duvet off the sofa and pace the flat. The screen on my phone flashes. Another message.

@ImStillWatchingYouJenHunter You know I'll never leave you alone, don't you?

I rush over to the window, brush aside the curtains, and strain my neck to look out onto the street. There's a shadow cast by the bin shed. Is that him? Is he outside? I try to push open the window as slowly as possible so as not to make a noise, but the frame rattles and squeaks. I lean out, holding onto the ledge. I squint into the darkness, but I can't see anything.

@ImStillWatchingYouJenHunter Careful now. We wouldn't want you to fall, would we?

Fuck. I tighten my grip on the ledge and I scan the street for a sign of him. I try to peer inside the cars and the windows of the flats opposite. There are a few lights on, but the curtains and blinds are drawn. A black cab lurches its way up the street, carrying a young couple, but it continues on its almost funereal journey. Then it comes to me. He must be standing right beneath me, hiding in plain sight below the flat. I push myself further out. The cold March wind whips my face. Tears smart in my eyes, blurring my vision. The edge of the window ledge digs into the front of my thighs. I can't stand much more of this.

"Laurence?" I shout. "Is that you? What the—"

I feel somebody touch my shoulder. The shock of it forces me forward and I nearly lose my grip. I see the ground spinning below me, a vortex swallowing me up, before a hand wrenches me back.

"What the fuck are you doing, Jen?" It's Bex.

"I—I—" The words don't come out. "I got—more messages. From him. From Laurence."

I pass her my phone. "I thought he must be outside, watching me."

"Fuck," she says as she reads.

She goes to the window and looks out. She stands there for a minute, before slamming the window shut and pulling the curtains closed.

"I can't see him. He must have gone." She comes to stand by me. "Jen, you're shaking. And it's freezing in here. Let's get you back to bed."

She leads me to the sofa. I'm too nervous, too afraid, too angry, to sleep. I drape the duvet around my body, while Bex fetches me a glass of rum.

"Here, drink this," she says, pushing a tumbler into my shaking hands.

I know what the next step is, something I hardly dare acknowledge. My fear is so deep it seeps into my marrow. Earlier tonight, Bex asked whether

I wanted to go to the police and show them what we'd found. But I dismissed it out of hand. I knew what would happen if I did that: precisely nothing. Perhaps they'd drop by and question Laurence, ask him about the mask and the attack on me on the Heath. But he'd have some clever way of getting out of it. *Why had these two women—one of whom was his ex-girlfriend—broken into his house? Had they hidden the so-called evidence in his home? It was clear that I had mental health issues,* he'd say, and the police could check with my doctor and therapist. It would be, when it came down to it, a case of my word against his. And his would win. Men like Laurence always came out on top.

Not anymore. Not with me.

54

BEX

'm pretending to Jen that I have doubts about our plan. It's early Tuesday morning and we're having coffee at the flat. Neither of us slept much as we were up half the night talking. Jen's skin is porcelain pale and there are dark shadows under her eyes.

"But last night you said that we could give him a fright, that we'd do it together," she says.

"I know what I said. And it was probably the drink talking."

She is silent for a moment. "Remember all those times you told me that you'd do anything for me?"

"I know—but Jen, I was talking about helping you through normal life shit. Work problems. Relationship issues. Things you wrote about in your column." I drop my voice to a whisper. "I wasn't thinking about . . ."

I don't say anything more for a few moments.

"If you don't help me, I'll do it anyway, without your help," she says.

"What?"

"I'll go ahead and take the risk. I don't care if Laurence turns around and attacks me, or that I'm caught and sent to prison. I'm doing it, Bex."

"Just calm down. Let's talk this through."

"I've had enough of talking. You don't know what it's like. Waking up each day thinking someone's watching you. Looking at your phone and seeing those messages."

"Have you had any more?"

"Not since last night."

"Do you think Laurence saw you—when you followed him down onto the Tube platform?"

"I don't think so, but perhaps he could have caught a glimpse of me when the train pulled out of the station."

"Maybe that freaked him out, that's why he sent those messages last night."

Now it's her turn to go quiet. She gets up from the table and goes to make some more coffee. I hear her bang around the kitchen, noisily slamming things around the small space. "Look, I know you're angry," I shout, as I push my cup away and get up to follow her. "I get that."

"Do you?" A little color blooms in her face as she spits out the words, "Do you really?"

"Of course I do. Laurence is a horrible, violent man. And it's frightening to wonder what he's capable of, what he might do next."

"So—you'll help me?"

"Okay and—"

Her eyes light up. "You will?"

"Don't get too excited, but I think I know how we can get away with it." I go to my bag and pull out a map. "Over the course of the last few months the council has been in discussions with the Corporation of London about a possible expansion of security on the Heath. I've got a map showing every single CCTV camera. So we could—"

She finishes my sentence for me. "Follow him when he is out jogging."

"Exactly. And the beauty of it would be that if we choose the right area, the incident wouldn't be recorded by security cameras."

Although she doesn't respond, I can tell she likes the plan. "We'll show him he can't fuck with you any longer," I continue. "When we're finished with him he's going to regret he ever treated you like this."

The stovetop coffeemaker bubbles in readiness, hissing in angry agreement. "But we're only going to scare him," I state. "Nothing more. Okay?"

Jen nods her head, but something stirs inside her. Hopefully I've planted the seed of an idea in her head.

55

JEN

Bex says it's important to carry on as normal, and so I'm trying to work. I've followed up my emails to some of the witnesses, and it looks as though there's a chance that the feature might actually get off the ground. Jamie Blackwood says he is happy to take part, and Julia Jones is interested too. She is a patron of a mental health charity and suggests that my piece might help raise awareness of the effects of trauma and how talking about it is vital for recovery. She has one condition, however: the charity desperately needs funding and she hopes that the *Mail* could make a substantial donation. I write an email to Nick and outline how this might be the way to get everyone involved.

After lunch I pocket the map of the Heath with Bex's annotations and make my way up there. As I snake my way along the paths, I look out for the cameras on the tall, specially manufactured posts. Most of them are visible, but there are a few that Bex marked down that are difficult to spot. I draw some crosses on the map, noting areas that are safe and ones that are not. When I come to follow Laurence I won't know exactly which way he will turn—he could easily venture off down a path or across the grass to a different part of the Heath altogether—and I need to be able to act quickly. Obviously, I have to be able to do it when nobody is looking. Fortunately, Laurence often runs in the evening, sometimes when it's getting dark.

On my way back toward Dartmouth Park I realize I'm walking on the pathway that leads up to Kite Hill. It's a gray, overcast day but there are still a handful of people up here gazing at the spectacle of London's skyline. Today no one is bothering to look at the pile of rotting flowers placed there to commemorate the life of Victoria Da Silva. If I hadn't witnessed it myself or hadn't read the news reports I would never know what had happened here nearly three weeks ago. Tentatively, I go and stand by the spot where I was that day. I close my eyes, let the cold wind whip across my face, and try to remember the exact location of the other witnesses: there was Jamie Blackwood and his boyfriend, Alex, playing with their dog, Julia Jones running past, Steven Walker studying the plan of the city, and Ayesha Ahmed, who sprang to her feet from the bench when Vicky's blood hit her. And then there was Laurence, his face obscured in that hoodie.

Just then my phone rings. It's Penelope. As I see her name flash up on my screen I feel a pang of guilt that I've ignored her. She did speak out of turn, I won't forget what she said, but I'm no longer angry with her.

"Hello?"

"Jen, darling—how are you?"

She doesn't let me reply.

"Listen—I'm so sorry for those things I said to you the other day. You were quite right to storm out."

"I—"

She interrupts me. "I'm a stupid old woman. I know that. A stupid old woman with a big mouth, who wants to apologize." She takes a deep, dramatic breath. "Will you accept my humble apology?"

"I shouldn't have gone off in that huff like I did. And you were right, completely right, about me being a crap journalist."

"I never put it like that!"

"I know, but I could see where you were coming from," I say, laughing.

"Listen, darling—where are you staying? I've been so worried about you."

"At Bex's."

She goes quiet.

"It's been fine. I'm on her sofa, but it's comfortable. It's not like your big house, obviously, but it's a place to rest my head."

"It would be lovely to see you. And we can talk about . . . well, about a few things."

She sounds vague. I just hope she hasn't been trying to dig up anything more about the Daniel Oliver–Victoria Da Silva case.

"You haven't been stalking vulnerable, bereaved parents, have you?" I ask.

This makes her snort with laughter. "Of course not! What do you take me for? Anyway, you're probably too busy to pop over for a cup of tea."

"I'm not actually." I don't tell her I'm on the Heath.

"Really. How wonderful. Well, just come over when you're ready."

"That would be lovely," I say and ring off.

I spend the next hour or so retracing my tracks around the Heath. I check and recheck the areas with cameras and refer to the annotated map again and again until I'm convinced I have committed the plan to memory. I reason that if CCTV picks up images of me, and if I were to be questioned later about my movements, then I would say that I was out enjoying a walk. Surely, I'd say, there's no crime in that.

Once I'm finished I push the map deep into the pocket of my coat and make my way over toward Hampstead. When I arrive at her house Penelope's in her front garden, wearing gardening gloves and pulling up some weeds. I watch her unobserved for a moment, noting the determined look in her eyes even when doing something as ordinary as weeding. She's slim and trim, and it's clear she's still quite strong too. As I watch her I realize that I've missed her. She pulls the roots of something from the ground with a grunt and catches sight of me out of the corner of her eye.

"How long have you been standing there?" she asks.

"I've just arrived," I lie.

"Indeed," she says, not believing me. "Anyway, you've caught me all sweaty and dirty. I won't hug you as you can see what kind of state I'm in." She raises her dirty gardening gloves in the air and threatens to rub them into my face, a gesture that makes us both laugh. "I don't know about you, but I could do with a cup of tea."

She leads me into the house and takes my coat. As she talks it's as if we've never quarreled. That is all in the past now, I suspect. She won't refer to it ever again. After making the tea, we sit at her vast kitchen table.

"Now tell me, how have you been?" she asks.

"Fine, mostly," I reply. "I'm making progress on the story. The *Mail* have asked me to do a big piece about the effects of the murder-suicide on those who witnessed it. After all, none of us asked to be there that day, on the Heath. But we've all been affected by it in one way or another. Anyway, they want two thousand words. And the fee isn't bad."

"Brilliant!" she exclaims, clapping her hands together.

Doubt begins to shadow the good news. "Listen—you didn't put in a good word for me, did you? I mean, I'm grateful if you did, but I'd like to think that—"

"No, not at all. Obviously, I know all the editors at the paper, but no, this is the first thing I've heard about it."

I smile to myself and take a sip of tea. "Although Jamie Blackwood has agreed to take part, I'm still waiting on the rest. Julia Jones is interested in principle as long as the *Mail* makes a big donation to a mental health charity. I still need to persuade the doctor, Ayesha Ahmed, and the teenager Steven Walker. And of course, as he's at school I need to get the permission of his mother too."

"Yes, I can see that might be difficult." She drums her pink fingernails on the table as she thinks.

"But, listen, I don't want you going out there and trying to talk to him." I don't tell her about how I tried to do the same, how I frightened the poor boy, how he ran away from me. "You know that's against the law."

She waves a hand in the air as if that's of no consequence. She leans in and stares at me as if she's trying to see into my soul.

"Are you all right?"

"Yes, a bit tired. Didn't sleep that well last night."

She blinks, a sign that she doesn't quite believe what she's being told, and her extravagant false eyelashes flutter like black butterflies. "Are you sure that's all?"

And then she pauses, waiting for me to say something. God, she must have been a brilliant interviewer.

"I was kept awake worrying about whether I could pull off this feature. Just that it's a lot to ask to bring the witnesses together—and then there's the issue about where to do the interviews."

"Well, if that's what's making you anxious you can always do them here." Her hand falls back, gesturing to the series of big empty rooms that lie outside the scope of the kitchen. "I don't know if you've noticed, but I do have an awful lot of space. One may as well put it to good use."

"Do you mean it?"

"Of course I mean it! When have you ever heard me say something I don't mean?"

"Fair point. Well, yes, that would be great."

"Just let me know when you'd like to do it. And I can always help with interviews."

The idea of Penelope asking them questions makes me bristle. Although she managed to get useful material from Karen Oliver, her style of investigation left me feeling nervous.

I don't want to upset her, as the house would prove to be incredibly useful, but I don't want to commit either. "Perhaps; let's see if it works out."

"Of course," she says. "I wouldn't want to intrude in any way." She shifts in her chair and gives me another of her penetrating stares. "There's something else though, isn't there?"

I feel my heart begin to race. Has she somehow guessed about what I've got planned?

"Yes, you're right," I say. I take a deep breath. "It's not just the piece that's stressing me out. It's money, debts."

"Well, why didn't you tell me? You know I can help you out. How much do you need?"

"Oh God, Penelope, that's so kind of you. But I couldn't possibly take anything."

"Don't be so proud. I mean, do I look like a poor person to you? I've got more than I can possibly spend in my lifetime. It's always been my policy to give to my friends in times of need. Now, tell me. How much?"

"Listen, Penelope. You've already done so much for me. Letting me stay here when—"

"And you know you can move straight back in as soon as you like."

"Again, that's so kind. But I've got to learn to be independent again. Honestly, I'll be fine once the piece is written and I'm paid."

"Are you sure?"

"Completely," I lie. "The fee will more than cover my debts."

"Now, would you like some more tea?"

"No thanks, I'd better be going. Anyway, I've drunk so much tea I'm going to be pissing like a horse."

I know that this kind of rough language amuses her and as she claps her hands the delight lights up the laughter lines in her face.

"Actually, can I use your loo?" I ask.

"You know where it is," she says.

I close the door to the loo and breathe a sigh of relief. I've managed to put Penelope off the scent. Not by lying—she could sniff that out in a second—but by telling a different truth.

56

BEX

If you tell someone not to do something it's obvious they'll want do it all the more. I remember I learned this for myself when I was young. I don't know how old I was, probably only seven or eight. I recall it in a series of fragments, not like a normal narrative of beginning, middle, and end. The reasoning of cause and effect came later as my brain began the desperate task of piecing it all together.

It was a Sunday afternoon. Dad was in one of his black moods. Mum had been drinking from the bottle in the fridge and was looking out of the front windows. She had gone quiet but whenever she did manage to say anything she slurred her words and her eyes looked all dull and glassy. I wanted to get outside. A new family had moved into the house across the close and they had a little girl who had smiled at me the other day, and I wanted to play with her.

"Mum, can I go outside and play?" I asked.

She looked down at me as she tried to focus. "O-of course you can . . . but don't . . ."

I knew what she meant: don't go too far from the house.

"I won't," I promised.

Dad cast me a sour look. "Don't you be going anywhere near that new family."

I didn't understand. "Why?"

Dad struggled to find the words. "They're . . . he . . . they can't be trusted," he said as he cast a glance toward Mum.

"Just pl-play on your bike," Mum managed to say, stumbling her way toward the armchair. "I'll just have a little rest. Sunday lunch always . . ."

Dad looked cross at Mum, like he wanted to hurt her. I made for the door.

"And Becky, remember what I said," snarled Dad. "Stay away from that family."

I skipped outside, pleased to be out in the fresh air, and jumped on my bike, which was sitting on the drive. I pedaled up and down the cul-de-sac, letting the wind blow through my hair, imagining that I was flying through the clouds. I looked down on the little box-like houses, the tiny patches of gardens. I was escaping for a big adventure. I was going to a place where I didn't feel the necklace of fear tightening its grip around my throat. I cycled faster and faster, faster than I had ever done before, my feet spinning around the wheels like pistons. It was then that I saw Bella, the sweet little West Highland White Terrier belonging to Mr. and Mrs. Hastings. Had it got out again? I looked over to see if I could spot its owners—I didn't want it to run away again—but in that split second, in that moment when I glanced over, I took my eyes off the handlebars. I felt the bike drop beneath me, heard a terrible grinding sound, and then I knew I was flying through the air for real. I stretched out my hands to break the fall, but came crashing down onto the sidewalk. The shock of it all winded me into silence. It was only when I looked up to see a girl standing above me that I started to cry.

"It's okay," she said. "Don't cry."

She bent down and reached out to comfort me. I blinked through my tears and realized it was the girl who had just moved into the street.

"Are you hurt?"

The palms of my hands were stinging. My knees were bleeding a little. My mouth was wetter than normal and tasted funny.

She pulled out a tissue from her pocket and gave it to me. Instead of wiping away my tears, I used it to mop up the blood on my knees, clamping my mouth shut in an effort to control the pain. There was something about the color of the blood, standing so bright against the white of the tissue, that fascinated me. I watched as the blood seeped through until it had stained the whole tissue red.

"You were going really fast," she said. "The fastest I've ever seen, faster than any boy. What's your name?"

"Becky," I said.

"I'm Alice. Alice Jarvis. I've just moved in. This is my house here." She pointed to a house that looked exactly like ours. "Do you want to come inside? My mum could put a plaster on your knees."

I nodded and she helped me get up. Suddenly I felt sick, but didn't want Alice to see. I stumbled away from her, toward the curb. My bike was lying at an awkward angle, its front wheel twisted, its frame scratched. I opened my mouth to vomit, but nothing came out apart from spit and blood—I realized I must have bitten my tongue.

"Sorry," I mumbled.

"It's all right, I'll make you a nice cold drink and you'll feel better in no time," said Alice, in what sounded like an imitation of what her mum would say to her. "Come on."

She picked up my bike and, after making sure that the Westie was okay, I trailed behind her into her house. Although it looked the same from the outside, as soon as I stepped inside I realized that everything about Alice's home was different than mine. It was neater, cleaner, calmer. Even though I'd just fallen off my bike and my hands and knees still smarted, I felt happier here. Alice called for her mum and told her what had happened. The first thing I noticed as the lady swooped down on me with a first aid kit was that she smelt nice, like fresh flowers. She got a bowl of warm water and some soap and bathed my wounds. She had a kind smile and a nice, soothing voice.

"What's your name?" she asked as she applied a plaster to my knee.

"She's called Becky," answered Alice for me.

"Do you live on the close?"

I nodded.

"Which number?"

I didn't want to tell her because for the first time, and without quite knowing why, I felt ashamed of where I lived.

"What's your dad do?" asked Alice.

"He paints people's houses."

"My dad works in an office!" she boasted. "Mum, can Becky stay for tea? I could show her my room and my toys. And then there's Digby, she'd love Digby."

"He's the family guinea pig," explained Becky's mum.

"Can she, Mum? She can, can't she?"

"Of course, just as long as Becky's mum and dad are okay with that."

Dad. I remembered what he said, what he warned me against. But the family seemed lovely.

"I can ask them, but I'm sure they'd think that was fine," I lied.

Alice could hardly contain herself and started to talk quickly about how pleased she was that she'd found a new friend, how worried she'd been about moving, how much she'd loved her old house, how hard Digby had found it all. I told them that I'd go and ask Mum and Dad and be right back. I walked over to my house, but I knew I wasn't going to go inside. I peered through the window. Mum was still sitting in her chair, asleep. Dad was drinking from a can and watching the telly. I counted to ten once, twice, three times. Then I ran back to Alice's house. There, I lost myself in a daze of happiness: playing with dolls, making a den, talking to the long-haired guinea pig, trying to squeal like Digby, eating cake and drinking lemonade. It was nearly four o'clock when the front door opened and a tall man with dark wavy hair walked into the house. I felt my tummy jump. I didn't think that I had ever seen anyone more handsome.

"Daddy!" shouted Alice, running into his arms.

He was all smiles and cuddles as Alice tried to explain the presence of a new girl in the house. Becky was simply her best friend in the world. She nearly died when she fell off her bike, but she made a miraculous recovery after Mummy tended to her injuries. And she was going to stay for tea. Just then there was a knock at the door. I felt something die inside me, which I later realized was hope. Again the knock, louder, more violent.

"I wonder who that could be?" asked Alice's mum, as she came in from the kitchen.

I knew who it was. I didn't want a scene. I would do anything to stop him from . . . "I think it might be my . . ." I said, jumping up to try to answer the door.

"I'll get it," said Alice's dad, Mr. Jarvis. "Don't worry. There's nothing to be scared about."

For a moment I really believed him. But then as he opened the door my fear returned. It was Dad. His face was red and full of fury.

"So there you are," he bellowed as he pushed his way into the house.

"Excuse me?" said Mr. Jarvis. "I don't know—"

"Get out of my fucking way."

I felt his fat hand grab the skin on the back of my neck. He pushed me toward him and told me he was taking me home.

Mr. Jarvis started to speak, "I don't think that's called for—"

But he was cut off by Dad. "I think you should stay away from me and my family, don't you?" He looked down at me. "It looks like you've done enough damage already."

Now it was Alice's mum's turn to try to calm down Dad. "But Becky fell off her bike. She said she'd checked with you and that it was okay to have her tea here."

I started to blush. Alice began to cry. "Did she now?"

Dad grabbed my arm so tightly it hurt. But I knew better than to say anything.

"Look—you're upsetting everyone here," said Mr. Jarvis. "My daughter, your daughter. I don't think it's the best way to—"

Dad took a step toward the man and squared up to him. "Best way to do what?"

Mr. Jarvis raised his hands toward his face in a gesture of defeat. "Mate, listen, I'm just—"

Dad's eyes were like two ball bearings, hard and steely.

"Why don't we all try to stay calm?" said Mrs. Jarvis. "I'm sure we don't want to cause any trouble, do we Alan?" She looked at her husband and then my dad.

The men continued to stare at one another, before Dad mumbled something under his breath and pushed me toward the door. Before I left I cast one last look at Alice, whose face was wet with tears. Outside, I bent down to grab my bike and ran with it back to the house. I heard the slam of the door, the anger in my dad's voice. I smelled fear in the air.

I knew what was coming next.

57

JEN

I take a sip of water and breathe deeply. The witnesses are due to start arriving at Penelope's house, all apart from Julia Jones who has sent me a message to say she's running a bit late, signing off with, "Who'd go into politics, eh?"

Nick at the *Mail* had agreed with the editor that the paper would make a donation of £5,000 to Julia's mental health charity. It had been this grand gesture that had finally forced everyone—even the reluctant Ayesha Ahmed—to take part. Although I didn't want to know how Penelope had found it, she had unearthed the address for Steven Walker's mother and she had written to her seeking her permission for her son to take part, outlining not only the donation to charity but the promise of a sizeable fee, which Penelope said she would pay out of her own pocket. The next post had brought a faded envelope containing a scrappy sheet of paper bearing a shaky signature from Leonora Walker.

We'd spent the morning getting the house ready, and Penelope suggested that her large study on the top floor might be the best place for the one-to-one chats. Toward the end of the week a photographer would take some individual and group shots on Kite Hill. It wouldn't be easy for the witnesses to go through with this, to rake through the painful memories and to return to the place where the horrific attack occurred, but the fee to the mental health charity would mean that hopefully something good might come out of it.

Jamie Blackwood is the first to arrive, with his Weimaraner. "I know you said you didn't mind if I brought Freddie," he says.

I look behind him, expecting to see Alex.

"Alex? Oh, he's not coming, I'll tell you everything. Big drama."

I take him through to the kitchen and introduce him to Penelope. She adores his dog, makes a real fuss over him and settles him into a sunny spot by the French windows. Over tea, Penelope and Jamie get on so well that I practically have to drag Jamie up the stairs and into the study.

"God, I love that woman," he says. "If I'm ever reincarnated, I want to come back as Penelope Frasier."

"I know what you mean. She really is something." I'm conscious of time and so I get down to business. I turn on the tape recorder, which sits on a small table between us. "So, it's a shame about Alex."

"Yes, it is, it was," he replies. "You're probably not surprised to learn that he wasn't a big fan of me doing this . . . talking to you."

"I'm sorry if this feature has caused trouble. I hope—"

He cuts me off. "Don't worry, we were having problems before that." He runs a hand through his auburn hair, now shining gold in the morning sun. "Anyway, Alex has moved out. It's over."

I wait for him to continue.

"We went out the other night, we'd had a few drinks. We came back to the house and started an argument about . . . well, about us doing this. Although I told you that he was up for it, he wasn't that keen. In fact, he was dead set against it. I was adamant that it was a good idea and I tried to persuade him. He accused me of not listening to him, bulldozing away his opinions, his feelings. I'd been doing a lot of thinking since it all happened, since we saw what we saw on the Heath. They might be clichés, but they're true. About how we only have one life. How we have to make sure it matters. That we can't let ourselves live a lie. God only knows, I did enough lying to myself when I was younger." He clears his throat. "Anyway, witnessing the incident on the Heath, and then also thinking of talking to you, really forced me to address a few things, things I'd been trying to hide from."

"Such as what?"

"I wasn't in love with Alex. I fancied him, God yeah, but that wasn't the same as love. And I think he knew that. During the argument he kept going on about how, despite the promise of marriage, I found it difficult to commit. How I didn't look at him the right kind of way. How I didn't allow myself to be loved. He wondered whether it was something to do with the amount of drugs I had taken at one point. He even asked whether I am still using. I told him that I'm not, which was the truth, but perhaps I should have led him to believe that. That might have spared his feelings. It might have been easier to bear. He said he wanted to hear the truth, but when I told him . . . well, I wondered whether he was robust enough to deal with it. He fell to pieces. He was broken. He talked about how much he'd been looking forward to a future with me. With Freddie. Perhaps with kids."

"And what is the truth? What did you tell him?"

"I'm still in love with Sam . . . in love with a dead man." The irony of the situation is not lost on him and he emits a half-laugh, half-cry. "I suppose I've always known I was. And perhaps I'm just in love with an idea of him. No doubt if he'd lived I might feel differently. But I suppose Alex felt there was no way he could compete with someone who wasn't even here. Anyway, I don't know how much of this you want to put in your piece. I'm fine with it all, obviously. But I think Alex would rather you left his name out of it."

"Of course," I say.

He gives me a sympathetic smile. "How have you been? How's it affected you? Sorry—I know you're supposed to be asking the questions."

I wonder how much I should tell him. "No, don't worry. I don't mind. It's been hard. Nightmares. Anxiety. I . . . I wasn't in a good place to begin with. I'd lost my job. I'd had a relationship breakdown. And a few other problems too. So no, it's not been the best time for me either." I try to get the interview back on track. I ask about the wounds to his hands, his business, his sleeping habits, his dreams. I ask about whether he thinks about Victoria Da Silva and her murderer, Daniel Oliver. He tells me about how he used money as a way to protect himself, as a substitute for love. He doubts whether he'll ever love another person again the way he loved Sam. But he'll be fine, he says. He has his dog, Freddie, and his friends. He ends by talking about the man he saw jogging that day.

"I do wonder if it would have made any difference if that guy had stopped to help," he says. "But then, of course, Alex refused to step forward. Perhaps that changed my view of him. If more of us had laid into him, into Daniel, then Vicky might have survived. I still see her, lying there, on the ground: covered in blood, gasping for breath, that desperate expression in her eyes. That's the thing that keeps me awake at night. How things might have turned out if the jogger had stopped to help. Do you know: did the police ever get hold of him?"

"No, I don't think they have, not yet," I say.

58

BEX

It was just another typical Friday afternoon. I'd come home from secondary school and taken refuge in my bedroom. I tried putting my hands over my ears, squashing the pillow around my head, but I could still hear Mum and Dad arguing so loudly their voices seemed to echo through my brain. When it got like this we had complaints from the neighbors—people would bang on the walls, ring the telephone, stand outside and threaten to phone the police—but Dad would just tell them to fuck off and mind their own business. There were some well-meaning women on the close who tried to help, offered to put Mum in touch with organizations that specialized in domestic violence, but she told them that she didn't need their help. Brian never laid a finger on her, she said.

Although I tried not to hear, odd words broke through. Fucking bitch. Slut. Dad had got it into his head that Mum had taken a fancy to Alice's dad, Mr. Jarvis. Looking back, it all made sense. Why Dad had told me not to play with Alice, why he'd behaved so strangely that day when I'd gone over to her house against his wishes, why he'd banned me from stepping inside her home ever again. Alice's father was a handsome man. Even I could see that. Perhaps Mum thought so too. But I'd certainly never seen her show any interest in him. Dad was convinced she had what he called "the hots" for him. And he was determined to punish her for it. When he came back from work he questioned her about her movements: where she'd been, who she'd talked to, even whether she'd stepped outside the front door.

Dad was convinced he could smell Alan. He said the house stank of sex. Of course, I knew about sex, well, I'd read about it, talked about it at school, but I didn't want to hear my parents discussing it at home. It made me feel sick. The thought of *them* doing it was repulsive enough, but Mum and Alice's dad? Although my dad was convinced, I didn't believe it. He went around the house searching for evidence. Pulling back the duvet to examine the bedsheets. Checking Mum's pockets. Looking in the bathroom. Pulling out old tissues from the bin and sniffing them.

If Mum told him he was mad—that there was nothing to it, all she'd ever done was say "hello" to the man in the street, nod and smile as she walked past him—he'd get mad and hit her. That sound, the thud of his fist against the bone of her cheek, would make me want to scratch his eyes out. But I knew better. Once, in the middle of a horrible row, I tried to hit him on his back, but he turned to me, eyes blazing with crazy anger, grabbed me around the neck, and nearly squeezed the life out of me. I think it was only when he believed there was a risk that I was in danger of passing out that he let me go, falling choking and coughing onto the carpet. As I gasped for air I vowed to myself that I wouldn't let him get away with this.

That day I remembered the sound of glass breaking. Mum never screamed—she didn't want to make Dad angrier than he already was—but I heard her call out my name. I jumped out from the bed and, with hands that trembled, opened the door. Another wave of noise hit me like a brick around the head. I stood at the top of the stairs, digging my nails into the bannister to prevent myself from running down to attack him.

"Becky!"

"There's no point calling for her—anyway, she's just as much a slut as you."

"Don't you say that. Don't you say another word about my daughter."

"I've seen the way she looks at boys, at men. She got that from you."

"Leave her alone."

"She's a slag. A slag like you."

"I said don't you talk about her like that."

"What—she's your little darling now, is she?" Mum didn't say anything. Dad's tone was sneering, sarcastic. "Your little precious one?"

There was an uncertainty to Mum's voice. "She—she's always been precious."

"Are you sure about that?" Again, nothing from her.

"I said, are you sure about that?"

"Y-yes."

"It's just that I seem to remember once you weren't that keen on the idea of having a little Becky around."

"No, please no, she might hear. She's upstairs."

"Shall I refresh your memory?"

"Brian, I'm begging you. I'll do anything—anything you want, but please not—"

"Not what? That you never wanted her." He shouted up the stairs, making certain I could hear, spelling everything out so that there was no doubt to the meaning. "Never wanted a baby at all. It wasn't the right moment, you said. You wanted to try and qualify as a teacher. Not that it would ever have happened, not with someone as stupid as you. A pipe dream, that's all that was. And you tried to keep it from me, do you remember? Tried to keep it a secret."

What? I didn't understand what he was saying, like he was gabbling something in a foreign language.

"Brian, no. No more."

"In fact, you were so desperate not to have a child that you tried to get rid of it."

Mum's unintelligible cry split the air.

"That's how much you loved your little Becky." Dad sounded triumphant. "You loved her so much you wanted to abort her. You loved her so much you wanted to kill her."

59

JEN

Steven Walker is the next to arrive. He's nervous, jumpy, and his eyes don't dare settle on any one spot. It's obvious he'd rather be anywhere else but here. I thank him for agreeing to come here and stress once again the importance of the work of Julia Jones's mental health charity. I tell him that he can have quote approval: anything he says to me I'll read back to him, and I reassure him that it's okay if he wants me to leave anything out or rephrase something. I briefly introduce him to Jamie and Penelope, and he thanks her for the fee she has agreed to pay to his mother. It will be a great help, he says. He accepts a glass of Diet Coke from the fridge and we go upstairs. Before we start, I talk to him about his school, his taste in music, his friends. Twenty minutes later he's finally a bit more relaxed, and he's happy for me to switch on my tape recorder and start asking real questions.

"I know you've told me something of that day—the day of the attack on the Heath—but could you bear to go through it all again?"

He takes me through his morning, his time at school, and his mum's mental illness. He shows me some of the texts that she'd sent him—a string of paranoid, accusatory messages—and tells me how he felt so upset and angry that he bailed out of chess club to walk on the Heath.

"I know I should have gone home to check on Mum, but I just couldn't face it," he says. "I couldn't face her." Suddenly, he checks himself. "You won't put that in, will you?"

I reassure him I won't.

"I just needed a bit of fresh air to clear my head," he says, falteringly. "And so I started to walk up the path that leads to the viewing point. I saw all these couples holding hands and getting all friendly with one another, yeah it was Valentine's Day." He tries to smirk at the memory, but it's a half-hearted attempt. "I carried on up the hill and stopped to look at the plan of the skyline. It was a beautiful day, not a cloud in the sky. Standing there, looking across London, I actually managed to kid myself I could have a future. Do something with my life. Pathetic, I know."

"Not at all, I'm sure you'll have a bright future—you can do whatever you want." As soon as I say them I realize my words sound false and hollow.

"Really? I don't know about that. Anyway, I was standing there thinking about what I might do with my life, feeling the prospect of something good about to happen, when it all kicked off. I heard the sound of a man's voice, raised, a woman pleading with him to stop. Then the smash of a bottle. I turned around to see. It was horrible, really horrible. The way he forced the broken bottle into her face, I'll never forget it. People tried to stop it—the man, Jamie, you. There was a lot of shouting about calling the police, for an ambulance. I thought the worst of it had happened. I couldn't imagine it could . . ." He breaks off and his voice drops to a whisper. "Then the knife came out. The posh-sounding, older lady—"

"Julia Jones, the MP."

"Yes, she tried to talk the man, Dan, out of it. I remember he asked her whether she was the fucking, sorry, whether she was the Queen. Dan then stroked his girlfriend's hair. I think he even kissed her. Said something to her in her ear so that no one could hear. And then he took his knife and slashed her across the throat. There was so much blood. The young woman who said she was a doctor tried to help save her life. I was worried that Dan was going to attack her, to kill her, and so I warned everyone. I didn't want anyone else to get hurt. Then I heard the police arrive, the sound of the sirens, and . . ."

I don't ask the natural next question; instead I wait for him to answer it himself.

"And yeah, I ran away. Back across the Heath, not knowing where I was going. I just ran, as fast as I could away from it all. Away from the blood. Away from the scene."

"Was it the police? Did they scare you?"

"I suppose so, yeah."

"Have you been in trouble with them before?" He falls silent.

"I mean, it would be totally understandable. If I was in your shoes I would have done the same. I mean, they hardly give kids like you the easiest of times." He looks down at his shoes and starts to fidget nervously. "Steven?"

He takes a deep breath. "I suppose you may as well know. You're the kind of person who would find out anyway. It's probably better coming from me . . . I ran away because I . . . because I was a witness at another killing. Lloyd Williams." The 2018 case was famous: a twelve-year-old boy in his school uniform had been stabbed to death in the stairwell of his council block.

"The boy who got knifed to death in Camden?"

He nods his head.

"It was a gang thing," he continues. "Not that I'm in a gang. I'm not like that. I just happened to be there that day. My friend Lucas, he lived in the same block. We were just coming home from school, walking up the stairwell, when we heard this noise, people running. We came up to the next level and saw a group of boys. I recognized a few of their faces, knew about their reputation. They had this poor kid cornered. He was doing everything to try to escape. He looked over the edge of the railings, perhaps he thought about trying to jump down to the street, even though it was three stories up. But there was no time for him to do that. One of the lads produced this . . ." His voice breaks. He clears his throat. "This huge samurai sword, another a machete, the rest of them had knives. There was a moment when everything seemed to go quiet. I heard a bird singing in a tree. But then the guy with the machete stepped forward and sliced into the front of the boy. Lloyd put his hands over his stomach, but . . . but . . ."

He didn't need to complete the rest of the sentence. I'd read in the papers what had happened next: his guts had spilled out onto the floor. "Oh, Steven, that's so awful. I'm so sorry."

"Lucas and I took one look at each other and ran. A couple of the gang members chased after us, and they nearly ran us down, but Lucas knew the streets around there really well and we managed to get away. We rang the police as soon as we could, but of course it was too late to save Lloyd. But that wasn't the worst of it. The police assumed that we'd had something to do with it. That we were in on it. That we knew something. We were both questioned separately for hours. It was really awful. My mum couldn't deal with it. Even she thought I'd been involved with Lloyd's death. It sent her . . . well, let's just say it didn't help her condition. We weren't charged or arrested or anything, but it seemed to drag on and on. I had a really great solicitor, this young woman, who finally made the police understand the truth. Lucas and I ended up serving as witnesses and helped with the prosecution. The police gave us protection and said that we wouldn't come to any harm. It was as scary as fuck. Sorry."

"Swear all you like. I can understand how traumatic that must have been."

"Although the gang members were charged and arrested and put in prison, of course there are other members out there. So you can understand now why . . . why that day on the Heath. Why I ran away. I thought the police would think I had something to do with it. I'd be taken in for questioning again. That, or I'd be identified in some way, and the gangs would find out my name, come looking for me. I just couldn't take it and that's why I ran."

He suddenly realizes what he's told me. "You won't—"

"Don't worry, I won't identify you as a witness to that particular crime. I'm sure it might be against the law for me to do that."

He still looks worried. "And you mentioned something about a photograph?"

"I'll make sure your face is pixelated out. So no one can see it's you." I give him a comforting smile, but inside I feel like screaming. Is there anything of the interview I can use? How am I going to explain this to my editor at the *Mail*?

"And how have you been since the incident?"

"Up and down. I have dreams . . . well, nightmares really. It's like the two killings have somehow been blended together. Sometimes I see Daniel Oliver standing there with a machete and cutting into Lloyd. Then it's Vicky Da Silva who's on the landing of the council block, surrounded by a circle of gang members."

"Have you been able to talk to anyone about it?"

"Not really. There's a counselor at school, well, the Spanish teacher who likes to think she's good at that sort of thing, but it's not for me. I guess it's best to try to get on with life."

We talk a little more about his ambitions—he wants to become a pilot, he says, or do something to do with airplanes, but he's worried he won't get the grades. I tell him it's best to aim high.

"And whenever I go out I have to look over my shoulder. I think someone's following me. Although the kids who killed Lloyd have all been locked up in prison, I still think there's one of them out there, waiting with a knife to finish me off. Or there's someone from the police keen to fit me up for the crime. That's why I freaked out when I saw you the other day at the school, why I ran off like I did."

"I'm sorry, it was wrong of me to turn up at your school like that."

"I've noticed I can't deal with sudden movements, loud noises, even normal things like exhausts going off," he says, as if remembering my earlier question. "Anything like that freaks me out. Stupid, I know."

"Not at all."

"Like the other day when your friend turned up on the Heath, near Kenwood, and surprised me."

"Yes, I'm sorry about that—that was Bex being overprotective."

"I suppose that's what she was doing that day, the day of the murder-suicide. Looking out for you."

"Looking out for me? No, it's just that we'd arranged to meet there—at Parliament Hill Fields. We were going to grab a coffee and then get the bus into town."

Steven doesn't say anything for a moment. He looks puzzled, like he's thinking something over.

"Is there something wrong?" I ask.

"I don't know," he replies. "You say your friend's name is Bex? The one who scared me away the other day?"

"Yes, that's right."

"It's just that I recognized her. I'd seen her before. I knew I had, but I didn't realize where for ages."

"What do you mean—recognized her? You've probably seen us around together. We spend a lot of time hanging out with each other. I've moved back into her flat, you see."

"No, it's not that. It's from that day, the day of the murder-suicide."

"Yeah, like I said, we'd arranged to meet."

He goes quiet again.

"Steven?"

"I saw her earlier, talking to someone on the Heath. The man you said the police were looking for, who ran away—you called him 'the mystery jogger.' I saw your friend talking to him."

60

BEX

So Mum never wanted me. She planned on aborting me. Flushing me down the toilet like a dirty tampon, like a piece of shit.

She knew that I knew, that I'd heard the row between her and Dad. The next day I couldn't meet her eye and whenever she tried to reach out to touch my shoulder or give me a cuddle I pulled away like she disgusted me. She tried sitting me down and talking about it, but I said I didn't want to hear. I told her I couldn't listen to her empty words. She begged me, really, properly begged me, asked me to try to understand what had been going on with her at the time, how she felt she needed more from life, how she didn't want to be trapped, how she thought she might have a different kind of future. But I met her pleas with a blank stare and cold eyes.

At night, in bed, I kept thinking about how she might have done it. Obviously, she hadn't gone to a clinic, but why had she tried to do it herself? I'd heard of women using knitting needles, gin, hot baths, even throwing themselves down the stairs. But that seemed like ancient history. How many times had she tried to rid herself of me? Had her heart leaped with joy every time she bled, hoping that this was the moment she'd start to lose the baby? Did she sit on the toilet, looking down into the bowl, willing the white ceramic to be streaked with blood? How old had I been when she had attempted to kill me? A few weeks, a few months? And how had she felt when she realized that she was going to have to keep it . . . keep me?

I studied the photographs of an embryo at differing stages of development in my biology textbook, tracing my fingers over the images: a mini *Alien* monster at four weeks, eyelids and ears forming at eight, two inches long at twelve, prints on toes and fingers at sixteen, sucking its thumb at twenty, and a good chance of survival if the baby had to be born prematurely at twenty-eight weeks. I felt tears sting my eyes when I thought of myself curled up inside her, feeling all safe and secure swimming around in the warm sac of amniotic fluid, until she tried to do everything in her power to dislodge me. What had made her want to do that? What lay behind her decision? Did she realize she didn't love the man she went on to marry, my dad?

All these questions and more fizzed through my head, until I was sickened by the thought that she might have hurt me in some way. I'd read about babies being born with various syndromes after their mothers had drunk too much or taken drugs. But could her attempt to abort me have left me . . . I don't know . . . damaged? I was good at school, so it obviously hadn't hurt my intelligence. And that's all that most people seemed to worry about: whether you could pass exams. Neither Mum nor Dad had done any education after leaving school. Mum had wanted to be a teacher, but had met Dad during her A levels. They'd started to go out, she'd gotten pregnant, tried to get rid of me, that didn't work, so they'd ended up getting married. End of story.

Except it wasn't. As I lay in bed, festering in the heat of a summer's night, I started to think of a different kind of life, a life away from them. I let the word "divorce" play around my mouth, imagining what it would be like if they split. They were clearly not suited to each other. And then they had their own problems. Dad with his violent temper, and Mum with her drinking. But did I really want to have to spend time with either of them? A father who would beat me at any opportunity, or an alcoholic mother who had tried to abort me? I realized that if I told anyone about what was happening at home—a teacher, say—the social services would get involved and I would be taken into care.

I started to imagine a number of different scenarios. Mum and Dad in our old banger of a car, fighting, the argument getting out of control, Dad lashing out, Mum hitting back and accidentally hitting the steering wheel so the vehicle careered off the road, smashing into a tree at top speed, causing the death of the two passengers. Mum contracting a devastating terminal illness—liver cancer, a result of her heavy drinking—and Dad dying of a heart attack. Mum committing suicide, tablets washed down by vodka or white wine, and Dad falling off a ladder while painting the guttering outside a house. Unfortunately, all these depended on chance or circumstance, or simply waiting to see if the passing of time resulted in their deaths. But what would happen if Mum died and I was left with Dad, or Dad passed away and I was trapped at home with Mum? If I did nothing, I could be stuck with them forever, or at least until I was eighteen and I could move out, go to university, which seemed like forever.

Was there another way? I knew Dad was a jealous bastard. He didn't trust Mum. He still believed that she'd been having an affair with Mr. Jarvis. Each night that sweltering summer I played a game in my head. *What would happen if . . . ?* I'd start the sentence and then see what happened next, moving around the figures of Mum and Dad and Mr. and Mrs. Jarvis ike pieces on a chessboard.

Occasionally, I'd stop myself, tell myself that the game wasn't a nice one, but then I'd be tempted by the delicious prospect of it and I'd start plotting again. *What would happen if . . . ? What would happen if . . . ? What would happen if . . . ?* My English teacher always said I had a wild imagination, that I should allow it to take flight.

Now here was my chance to shine.

61

JEN

I quickly draw the interview to a close and usher Steven down the stairs. He asks me whether there's something wrong, but I tell him not to worry. I thank him again for his time and his honesty. Downstairs I find that Ayesha Ahmed is already here. I go through the motions of greeting her, thanking her, introducing her to Steven, but my mind is elsewhere. I tell everyone I just need to make a quick phone call. I step into the back garden feeling as though there's not enough oxygen in the air. I quickly dial Bex's number. She doesn't pick up. I dial it again, but this time using WhatsApp. I hear a click.

"Jen?"

"What . . . what were you doing that day, on the Heath? The day of the murder-suicide."

"Erm—I was meeting you, remember?"

"I know—but before. Before you met me."

She goes quiet.

"I've just spoken to Steven, Steven Walker. And he told me that he saw you talking to Laurence before the attack."

I hear her take a deep breath and then exhale. "Jen, it's something I wanted to tell you, something I should have told you a while back."

I let her speak.

"It's not something you're going to like. But you'll understand why I didn't tell you, or at least I hope you will."

"Go on."

"I was walking up to meet you on the Heath when we bumped into one another, almost literally. I was coming round the corner, you know where the loos are, opposite the café? Laurence didn't see me and nearly ran into me. We talked for a while before he ran off, and that's why I was late to meet you."

"But why didn't you say anything?"

"I know, and I'm sorry. I was about to tell you, but . . ."

"But what?"

"Do you remember the first night we met Laurence? In the French House?"

The question takes me aback. Why is she talking about this now?

"Yes, of course, but I don't understand—"

"We'd all had plenty to drink. You went back to your flat in south London and Laurence and I shared a cab back north."

What's she going to say? I almost don't want her to tell me. I wish she'd stop, that she'd cut the connection.

"At the end of the journey he asked me into his house for another drink and—"

"What? You *slept* with him?"

I hear what sounds like crying.

"I had a drink, and after that I can't remember anything else. It's a blank. But . . . but I think . . . Jen, I think he . . . raped me."

I can't take in the enormity of what she's saying. I'm unable to speak, as if my tongue is paralyzed.

"I woke up in his bed. I could remember getting out of the cab, going into this house, saying what a nice place he had, and taking a sip of wine. After that . . . nothing."

I remember Laurence's bed. I recall the feel of the sheets, the smell of our two bodies together. "But you had sex?"

"I suppose so."

"Fuck! So he drugged you? Some kind of date-rape drug like Rohypnol?"

"I don't know."

I suddenly feel sick. I spent five years of my life with Laurence. A man who has not only stalked me, sent me creepy messages, attacked me on the Heath, but one who had raped my best friend. "Oh God, Bex, but why didn't you tell me?"

"I was going to, I really was, but I wasn't sure what had happened. Whether *anything* had happened. It would be my word against his. And then you started to date him. I thought it might fizzle out after a few weeks. I didn't think you'd be a . . . proper couple."

Hearing these words makes me want to scream. I turn to see the little group of strangers in the kitchen. Penelope. Steven. Ayesha. Jamie. His lovely dog lying in a spot of sunshine. The doors to the garden are closed, no one can hear my conversation, but Penelope stands up and stares at me through the glass with a concerned expression. I move away and walk down the lawn to stand under the magnolia tree. The white and pink flowers split open like something indecent. I hear the sound of a bird singing in a nearby tree. The peace and beauty of the moment sit in contrast to what I'm feeling inside. It's a kind of anger I've never felt before. A fury that goes beyond what's happened to me. A rage that desires revenge.

I try to keep my voice steady. I think back to the early days of my relationship with Laurence. Initially, I had picked up a certain coldness between Laurence and Bex, but I'd put it down to some kind of unconscious rivalry for my affections. "How could you still be friends with him? After what he'd done?"

"I suppose for y-you," she says, as sobs begin to fragment her voice.

"And what about that day? On the Heath?"

She sniffs and blows her nose. "He started to flirt with me. He said how well I was looking. He told me . . . he told me that he was just coming to the end of a relationship."

"With Vicky Da Silva?"

"He didn't mention a name."

"And then what?"

251

"He asked me out on a date."

"*What?*"

"I know, I know."

"What did you say?"

"I felt like punching him in the face, but of course I didn't. I told him to fuck off, in a jokey kind of way. Not that I should have tried to let him down gently."

"For God's sake, Bex. After what he did to you?"

62

BEX

I can't believe I managed to think so quickly. I had no idea that Steven Walker had seen me talking to Laurence on the day of the murder-suicide. When Jen told me, I felt as though everything was going to crash down around me. All my careful planning, everything I'd done, would turn to dust. The months of plotting, drawing people together, dropping hints and suggestions here, clues and questions there, gathering everything together in an elaborate dark tapestry, would start to unravel. But then I'd remembered that night with Laurence.

I'd hoped that our encounter would come in useful, and now was the time to take full advantage of it. I reasoned that if Jen were to confront him with the words, "Did you rape Bex the night we met?" he would deny it at first, but most probably during the conversation he would end up saying something like, "Of course I didn't rape her. Yes, I slept with her, but—" I was certain that Jen wouldn't hang around to hear the rest of the sentence. No other words would matter.

As I finish the call I picture Jen in Penelope's house. She had told me that she intended to interview all the witnesses there and that there'd be a photographic shoot on Parliament Hill Fields.

My main worry is the old bitch. I fantasize for a few minutes, imagining what it would be like if I managed to manipulate Jen into killing her—she could push the old lady down those hard marble stairs and it could easily be made to look like an accident—but I realize that this would be too difficult to orchestrate at such short notice. No, if I want to get rid of Penelope I will have to do it myself. But how much does she know about me? I think again of the reverse image of my name on her blotting pad. She'd obviously been doing some digging into my past. I doubted Penelope had uncovered anything significant about me—if she had, there's no way Jen would still be so friendly and trusting of me—unless, that is, she had made the decision not to share that information with her.

I realize that the only way of knowing is to see Penelope for myself. I text Jen and ask her if she wants to meet after the interviews are over. I tell her again that I'm sorry for what happened with Laurence. I'm feeling a bit weepy at the moment, I add, and could do with a bit of support. I could drop by the Hampstead house if that would be easier for her, I say. A few minutes later I get a reply, telling me to come over whenever I'm ready. She's pleased she finally knows the truth, she says.

I pull on a jacket and start walking. As I pass through the network of streets that lead onto the Heath I'm conscious that someone is watching me. I look around: there's nothing but a cluster of well-off mums with pushchairs and a couple of elderly men talking in the street. I carry on walking, cross Highgate Road, pass the tennis courts and café, and make my way up to the viewing point. As I stand there on Kite Hill, looking out over London, I get the sense again that I'm being watched. I turn my head quickly as if to catch whoever it is off guard, but it's just a group of Italian tourists. I wonder for a moment whether I'm becoming paranoid.

I spend the next hour or so walking around the Heath, noting again the sections of the park that are equipped with CCTV and those without. I know that Jen took my map of the Heath, which I had annotated with lines showing the areas covered by security cameras. I wonder if she thinks that I didn't notice her slip it into her pocket. But as I move along I still have a sense that I'm being observed. I stop, turn around, and walk in the opposite direction, take a different path, cross a stretch of grass. But it's still there, the sense of something hovering just out of sight. It's like a dirty smudge on the edge of my vision that disappears when I try to examine it at close quarters. And the sense of it near, this thing I know is there but cannot see, makes my skin crawl.

63
JEN

Penelope waits for me to finish the call. As soon as she sees me put the phone back in my pocket she dashes out toward me, lifting two fingers that flutter in the air, a sign that she wants to say something to me in private.

"Are you all right?" she asks as she glides over.

I tell her that everything is fine, but Bex would like to drop by once the interviews are over. She's just had some upsetting news, I add.

"That's absolutely fine, darling. I'd like to see her, as there's something I need to ask her . . . Now, as to the matter in hand—the interviews—I've just been talking to the young doctor, Ayesha, and, well to be honest, I've got a few concerns. She's so uptight and stressed. Of course, you can't blame the poor girl, after what she witnessed . . . I know she's only young, but even so . . . Jen? Are you listening?"

I'm finding it difficult to concentrate and I miss lots of what she's saying. I can't get the thought of Laurence out of my mind. I see him in his house, with Bex, after that night out at the French House. He's slipping something into her drink. She falls unconscious and he drags her upstairs to bed. He takes her clothes off and . . . The idea of what he did to her makes me feel sick.

"Anyway, if she proves difficult, monosyllabic, and uncooperative, ask her what she was doing the night before the murder-suicide."

"What do you mean?"

"Just ask her."

I'm almost past caring—there are other things on my mind—but I say, "I hope you haven't been interfering again." Penelope's eyes twinkle with a mischievous, girlish delight; there's almost a coquettish quality about her. "Penelope?"

"I have done a little research, yes, just in case. And in Ayesha's case it proved fruitful. I remember you telling me that Ayesha had told you that she was tired because she had been up all night. Well, yes, that's true, but only part of the truth. You assumed she had been working in the hospital, the Royal Free. But in fact, Ayesha had not been on duty that night. Instead, a friend tells me she was working somewhere else."

"What, another hospital? As a locum?"

"No, in a completely different field altogether." She pauses for effect. "Are you ready for this? Ayesha was working at an establishment that goes by the name of Pink Diamonds."

The name sounds familiar, but I can't place it. "I don't understand. What's that?"

"It's a lap-dancing club in Shoreditch."

"No—not Ayesha. She's not that kind of woman. She's not like that."

"She's got one hell of a good figure."

"But she's serious, studious. I mean, she's a *doctor*, for God's sake."

"A doctor who needs the money. My contact discovered that she has serious credit card debts, due to a compulsive shopping habit."

It's true that every time I saw her she had been wearing expensive-looking clothes.

"But Ayesha? In a lap-dancing club? Are you sure?"

Penelope nods her head. "It explains why she was so tired, why she fell asleep, and also why she was so reluctant to tell you the whole story. No wonder she wants to keep it a secret—imagine if the head of her NHS trust found out."

"Do you know what she does there?"

"She's not a dancer, apparently. I'm told she's a 'waitress.'"

"And when you say a little friend told you? You mean a private detective?"

"You know a good journalist never reveals her sources," she says, her eyes glinting. "Anyway, it's probably not necessary to tell the world about her little sideline, but you may want to use the information to get her to talk."

Under normal circumstances I would snap at Penelope, but I don't have the energy to be angry. I manage a weak smile and thank her.

"Are you sure you're okay?" she asks.

"Yes, fine. Just a bit tired, what with doing one interview after the next."

She doesn't look convinced. She slaps me on the shoulder and tells me to keep my pecker up. Despite everything, the comment makes me laugh: no one I know apart from Penelope would use such a quaint expression. I step inside, apologize to Ayesha for keeping her waiting, and lead her upstairs. As soon as she sits down to do the interview I know she hates being here. She shifts in her chair to signal her unease and looks at my tape recorder as if it's a poisonous spider.

I start by asking her to take me through her memories of that day again. Her answers are to the point, but without detail, color, or emotion. She tells me the facts and nothing else. As she speaks I study her in a way that I haven't before. She's wearing a black double-breasted pinstripe trouser suit that looks like it could be Saint Laurent. Her hair is pulled back off her face, which is mostly free of makeup. The effect is businesslike, professional, a touch severe. What does she look like when she really dolls herself up? I imagine her standing in front of the mirror, applying a light foundation, lipstick, eyeshadow, selecting clothes that show off her good figure and highlight the curve of her breasts, the promise of hidden flesh.

I move on to the second stage of the interview: what kind of impact did witnessing the murder-suicide have on her life? She tells me that it was horrific to watch, of course, and she wishes that she could have been able to save the lives of both Victoria Da Silva and Daniel Oliver. But she was following her medical training, and as a result she forced herself to remain as professionally distanced as possible.

"Now, if you'll excuse me, I've really got to go to work soon," she says as she gets up from the chair.

I have a choice: either I can thank her for her time and let her go or I can reveal to her that I know about her other job at Pink Diamonds. The latter option is what Penelope would do. But I don't have the guts. That, or maybe I don't have the right to take the moral high ground. And so I smile and shake her hand. Ayesha smiles back, relieved the interview is over, and thanks me. I don't kid myself that I'm a nice person.

Penelope is waiting for me at the bottom of the stairs. "Did you get her to tell you?" she hisses.

"I've got everything I need," I reply.

"Excellent," says Penelope, clapping her hands with glee. "But Julia's still not here. Can you believe it?"

64

BEX

started with small things. A card for the local Italian restaurant slipped down the back of Mum's chair. A spray of cheap aftershave that I bought from the market spritzed in their bedroom. A pair of white socks that I picked up from a pound shop thrown under their bed. I thought of them as little grenades that had the power to explode at any moment. I liked the unexpected nature of the game, the fact that no one, not even me, knew when their lives were about to change. I visualized what might happen next: Dad's face when he realized he'd found some actual evidence of Mum's affair; his rising voice as he accused her, once again, of fucking Mr. Jarvis behind his back; the vein in his neck that throbbed like a disturbed worm when he got angry; the sound of his hand hitting Mum across the face; her repeated denials, her threats, her pleas; and then the awful silence when everything was over.

Funnily enough, that's not how it played itself out. Instead of shouting and screaming, lashing out and punching, Dad went quiet, unnaturally so. Whenever he did speak his voice was thin, just above a whisper. He looked terrible: pale, shadows under bloodshot eyes, unshaven. He stopped eating and, when he wasn't working, he seemed to spend more time in bed. When Mum asked him what was wrong, he didn't reply. She suggested he go to the doctor, but he shook his head.

It was the week leading up to Valentine's Day, and everyone at school was talking about who would get a card. When Susan, one of my friends, asked me whether I was going to send any Valentines, I suddenly got the idea. Throughout the day I couldn't concentrate on my lessons: the thought of it burned itself through me with a delicious intensity.

After school, I went into town and bought a cheesy card with red roses on the front and some sickly rhyme inside that talked about everlasting love and shit like that. As I held the new black ballpoint pen, bought specially for the task, I felt short of breath, light-headed, almost drunk. I tore out a page from one of my exercise books and practiced in a different hand-writing. I wrote out the note over and over again until I felt ready. Finally, I opened the card and wrote, "Mandy, my one and only love. I can't wait until the day we can finally be together. All my love, Alan xxx." I enjoyed running my lips across the sticky edge of the envelope, letting the stream of my saliva mix with the taste of the glue. I wrote "Mandy" on the front of the envelope and put the card in my schoolbag.

When I arrived home there was no one in. I had the house to myself. I set about preparing the scene. I took out the aftershave, which I'd hidden in the cupboard in my bedroom, and gave a few generous sprays around the living room. I tried placing the Valentine's card in various locations. On Mum's dressing table, partly hidden under her makeup; inside her bedside drawer, secreted away inside an old Jackie Collins paperback; in the drawer where she kept her knickers and bras. I settled on a place I knew Dad often searched, an old shoebox at the bottom of her wardrobe where Mum kept sentimental mementoes such as old exam certificates and ticket stubs from the days before she met Dad.

Mum arrived home first and started to make the tea of sausage and mash. As she cooked she gulped back a couple of glasses of white wine and listened to the radio. Dad, still a ghost, drifted in twenty minutes later. The cloying smell of the cooking meat fat dominated the kitchen and so he didn't notice the aftershave straight away. It was only when he'd taken his overalls off and settled down in the sitting room that he started to pick up the traces of the heady, sweet musk that hung in the air. I sat on the sofa pretending to read as I watched his nostrils begin to open. He recognized the smell as the one he associated with Alan's presence. He continued to sit for a few minutes, but then he sprang up from his chair and stormed into the kitchen. Color flushed into his face, and his eyes were full of a manic energy. The dad I knew, the one I feared, was back. I followed him into the kitchen and watched the scene unfold.

"Mandy? He's been here again, hasn't he?"

"Not that again," she said wearily, not bothering to look up from the frying pan.

"Alan—I know he's been here. I can smell him."

"Brian, we've been through this. Mr. Jarvis has never stepped foot in this house."

"Why does the lounge smell of him then?"

"It's just your imagination. The tea'll be ready in five minutes. Becky—can you help set the table for me?"

"What did he do to you?" said Dad, his eyes bulging out of their sockets. "Did you do it over the settee? Did he bend you over the sofa and take you from behind?"

"Becky—go to your room. She doesn't have to listen to this."

"She can stay here. She can have a lesson about what happens to women when they turn into—"

"Brian, you should hear yourself. You're pathetic."

"Don't you give me that. I know he was here. I can sense him." He turned from her and bounded up the stairs. I heard him in their bedroom, pulling out drawers, throwing things on the floor.

Mum quietly sobbed as she continued to turn the sausages. "It's you I feel sorry for," she said. "I don't mind so much for myself. I've learned to live with it, with him. But you shouldn't have to."

A loud crash from upstairs shook the ceiling. The frying pan spat out a globule of hot fat onto Mum's wrist. She took in a sharp breath and rubbed her skin. I heard Dad bound down the stairs. He had something in his hands. The card.

"What do you call this?"

"I don't know, you tell me, Brian. What is it?"

"You know fucking very well what it is. It's a Valentine's card from him—Alan."

"I don't know what you're talking about."

"How you have the cheek to stand there and deny it—when I've got the evidence in front of me."

As he started to read from the card—'Mandy, my one and only love. I can't wait . . .'—the words I had written sent a thrill through me.

"Right, tea's ready," said Mum in a bored voice. I suppose it must have been her indifference, her refusal to engage, that pushed him over the edge.

With a quick movement he grabbed her left hand and forced it behind her back. She winced in pain.

"You're a fucking liar," he shouted. He squashed the card in his fist, brought it up to her face and, with a voice breaking with emotion, finished reading the message, ". . . until the day we can finally be together . . . All my love, Alan. Kiss. Kiss . . . Kiss."

Tears welled in his eyes, his whole body seemed to shake, and for a moment I thought he might break down. Mum kept repeating his name. She didn't know what he was talking about or where the card had come from. It had to be a mistake, she said. A hoax. Some kind of cruel trick. The tea was getting spoiled. The sausages were done.

"I knew you never loved me," he continued. "Not good enough for you, was I? You thought you could do better. Wanted to be a teacher. What did I do—drag you down? Well, if you think I'm going to stand by and let you go off into the night with that ponce opposite . . ." He tightened his grip on her arm and thrust it further behind her back.

"Brian, you're hurting me now. And the sausages, look—they're burning."

"I don't care about the fucking saus—" Before he finished the sentence he grabbed Mum's right hand, the one she had been using to push the sausages around the frying pan, and slammed it into the hot fat. Everything happened so fast after that. She screamed, temporarily drowning out the song on the radio, "Nothing Compares 2 U." She tried to struggle, but Dad held her hand down harder. The smell of burning skin and flesh filled the room. She called for me to help her, but I found that I was paralyzed on the spot. By fear. Fascination. Something I could only describe as pleasure.

"Becky!"

As she started to thrash about she managed to free the hand that Dad had pinned behind her back. It clawed its way across the worktop like a creature from the seabed until it settled on something. A knife. A second later she had it in her grip and, with a force I never expected, brought it up to Dad's neck.

There was a desperation in her eyes I'd never seen before, even during the worst beatings. I often wonder what went through her mind just then. Did she think about what she was about to do? Or was it something she didn't have to think about, something primeval, an overriding survival instinct? She gripped the knife so strongly her fingers turned white and she slashed across his throat, cutting deep into his neck. Blood spurted out over the cooker, onto the kitchen floor. Dad released his hold on Mum and, with an expression of disbelief, reached up to his neck. Mum, still holding the knife, fell down to the floor, the pain from the burns almost too much to bear.

After a minute she looked over at Dad, his body slumped on the floor in an ever-increasing pool of blood, as if she couldn't believe what had just happened. She focused on the ripped, bloodied fragments of the Valentine's card on the floor and then turned her head toward me. I don't know what she was thinking, but she shook her head as if to say—what? That she couldn't live with what she'd done? That she suspected me of something? That she wished I'd never been born? Then she raised the knife once more and, with eyes locked on mine, slashed her own throat.

65

JEN

'm still thinking about Laurence—what he did to Bex, what he's done to me—when Julia Jones arrives. She apologizes for being late—she says another bloody Brexit crisis meeting overran.

"I'm so grateful to you for taking part. I know the *Mail* isn't your favorite paper."

"No, you're right there, but at least you know where you stand with them," she replies. "And I'm grateful for their support for the charity. That kind of money will make a real difference." Penelope swoops into the room to greet her and, although she's written some vile things about the Labour Party during her career, with Julia she's all charm and smiles. The MP, in turn, is gracious and polite. She asks Penelope if she could use the bathroom—she got stuck in a traffic jam on the high street, she says, and so she decided to jump out of the taxi and run the last bit to the house.

Penelope announces lunch is served at the kitchen table—nothing fancy, she says, just poached salmon, new potatoes, with roasted vegetables—and asks if anyone would like a drink. Julia, stepping into the room again, is the first to say "yes." She knocks back the fizz and then holds her glass out for another. I tell Penelope I'll have a drink a little later, once I've finished the interview. We climb the steps to the top of the house and in the study we make a little more small talk about politics. She asks me about how

I've been coping, wants to know more about my friends, and I tell her a little about how Bex has been a huge help to me, not just over the course of the last few weeks but throughout the time I've known her. She quizzes me a little more—how I met Bex, what she's like—and I begin to wonder whether she would have made the better journalist. But then she takes another gulp of the champagne and, before I even ask a question, she starts to talk about that day on the Heath.

"And you mentioned that you've been having nightmares?"

"Yes, awful. Just terrible. All about Harry, my son who . . . who died." She takes another sip of her drink. "I'm with him, in India. We're trekking on the side of a mountain. He's laughing. He looks so young, so handsome. Sometimes he turns into a boy before my eyes, and I tell him that he seems to be getting more youthful by the minute. His eyes sparkle, his teeth are so white that when he smiles the light from his mouth almost blinds me. Then a shadow passes across his face. He takes a step back, reaches out to me, asks me to save him, but then the ground gives way underneath him and he falls, falls so far, and disappears. I wake up just when . . ."

She bites her lip as she tries to stop herself from crying. "I know it's twenty years now since I lost him, but . . . Anyway, yes if you're wondering whether there's a link between seeing the murder-suicide on the Heath and the resurgence of these kind of painful memories, I'd say the answer is yes. Obviously, the deaths were very different. We witnessed a terrible, shocking murder and then a suicide, while Harry's death was . . . an accident." There's something odd about the way she says this last word, as if she's not sure. "And of course, there's this too." She holds up an empty glass. "I've told myself that I'm going to cut back once Brexit is over. But will that ever happen?" She laughs hollowly. "Actually, I could do with a top-up."

I offer to go and fill her glass, but she refuses. She's more than happy to do it herself and she says she needs the loo anyway. I take the opportunity to check the tape has worked. I look through my notes and questions, check my phone and reply to a few emails. What's taking Julia so long? She should be back by now. I look out of the study window and spot Julia in the garden puffing on a cigarette. I didn't know she smoked. Penelope comes to fill up her glass and the two women start to talk. Shit. Penelope could be quizzing her for hours.

I look around the study and, after examining the bookshelves, I come to stand by the desk. On it there's a large pad of blotting paper, framed in brass, an object that strikes me as belonging to another, more antique, age. When was the last time I'd used blotting paper? Was it sometime at school? Something to do with chemistry? Yes, it involved dabbing some ink onto blotting paper with water and watching the black or blue separate into different colors. I remember the teacher telling us at the time to take note that things were often not what they always seemed on the surface. "The experiment goes to show that appearances can be deceptive," she said.

I run my fingers across the smooth surface of the pad, but there's something underneath. I lift the frame to find a green cardboard file. I bring it out and place it across the desk. For a moment, I freeze. This isn't mine, I tell myself. Put it back where you found it and pretend you never looked. But then my curiosity gets the better of me and I open it. At the top of an otherwise blank sheet of A4 paper is the name "Rebecca Shaw." Bex.

66

BEX

I stayed looking at the bodies for hours afterward. They held a beautiful fascination for me. I traced my fingers above and around the wounds, just letting them hover over the gaping flesh, the reddened lips. I stared into their lifeless eyes, intrigued by the idea that they were forever blind. I was careful to avoid the ever-increasing pool of blood that gathered around their bodies. I didn't want to get tainted.

I felt a deep sense of satisfaction, of a job well done. This was all my work, my doing, my creation. And yet none of it could be traced back to me. The injuries—the burn on Mum's hand, the wounds on their bodies—would speak for themselves. I picked up the fragments of the Valentine's Day card and washed them down the loo. I left the knife where it had fallen onto the floor, made sure there was nothing else that could be seen as, what was that word used by detectives on the telly?—incriminating, yes that was it—and then took myself off to bed. I reckoned that Dad's absence would be noticed first, followed by mine from school. And fair enough, the telephone started to ring, which I ignored, then loud and repeated knocking. Eventually, someone must have broken down the door because I looked up from my bed to see a policewoman staring back at me.

I was taken away to a nice, clean house, where a couple of women asked me questions. I told them about Mum's drinking and Dad's temper. Life at 22 Maplestead Close had been a living hell. That day, the day of the last row, I heard them arguing. I shut myself in my room and put on my music to drown out the noise. Finally I came down and saw the bodies on the floor. I realized I should have dialed 999, but I just froze. I didn't know what to do. I was sick in the loo upstairs. And I suppose I must have passed out on my bed, where I stayed until the police arrived.

They had to break the tragic news to me that my mum and dad were both dead. From the initial evidence it looked as though my dad had forced Mum's hand into the frying pan, after which she retaliated by stabbing him to death. Sadly, it seemed she then took her own life. I was being terribly brave, they said, but they told me I'd have to continue to be brave. There was a great deal I would have to endure. The funerals. The inquest. It was likely that the local newspaper would cover the story.

The policewomen outlined what would happen next. I would be placed with a nice foster family who would do their very best to look after me. I would be transferred to another school, and I wouldn't have to go back into education until I was ready. I would see a counselor, and social workers would continue to visit me at home. My welfare was what was important now, they said. I had to remain strong. Could I do that, they asked. I nodded and said that yes, I could.

After a year of being fostered, I was adopted by a Mr. and Mrs. Shaw in a lovely big house in the countryside just outside Colchester. She made her own bread and marmalade, and he was a lecturer in history at the university. Their house, which had a vast garden that backed onto farmland, was full of books—it was like the public library—and I think they were pleased that I spent a lot of time reading. My education wasn't interrupted by what had happened; if anything my marks improved at my new school.

The person I was assigned to talk to about the "trauma," a counselor called Louise Dean, also said that it was obvious I was intelligent. It was easy for me to tell her just what she wanted to hear. Of course, there were certain things I didn't talk to her about. The real reasons that lay behind my actions. How I hated my dad for his violent temper. How I loathed my mum for trying to get rid of me. How the fear of rejection ate away at me like a cancer. Neither did I tell her about the clues I'd hidden around the house, the occasional spritz of aftershave, and my masterstroke, that Valentine's card. And why, from that time onward, Valentine's Day always held a special place in my heart.

67

JEN

I hear Penelope call from the stairs. She's on her way up. There's no time to look through the papers inside the file, but it's clear that she's been doing some digging into Bex's background. I think about hiding the documents back where I'd found them, but I'm so angry with her. I'd put up with Penelope's meddling in the past, but this is a step too far, even for her. I grab the papers and wait for her at the top of the stairs. I'm in the mood to shout down the stairway so that the others can hear, but I force myself to stay silently fuming until I see her.

"What do you call this?" I ask, holding the file in the air.

"Oh, I'm pleased you've found that," she says as she eases herself up onto the final step and to the top landing. "It's something I want to talk to you about. It doesn't make for pleasant reading, I'm afraid. A chap I used—"

"You put a private detective on Bex? How could you?"

"Thank goodness I did. Now, I can see you're upset, but—"

"Upset? I think that's the understatement of the year."

"Jen, let's go into the study, where we can talk in private. You probably don't want all this to come out like this."

"What?" I lower my voice. "You don't want Ayesha to know what methods you used to find out about her job? By the way, I didn't mention what you told me. I didn't want to stoop to your level."

Penelope raises her eyebrows and lifts her hands in the air as if to say, "That's too bad—your loss." She takes a step closer to me. "Jen, at the risk of sounding melodramatic I'm afraid you may be in danger."

"Are you out of your mind?"

"Look—the other day when you were here, it was obvious there was something troubling you, even though you denied it. You told me it was the worry of doing the interviews, and although I know there's a certain level of stress involved, I knew there was something else going on."

"What are trying to tell me?"

"You may have a perfectly innocent explanation for what I found, but what are you doing with a map of the Heath, showing the areas covered and, most importantly, not covered by CCTV?"

The question hits me like a bullet to the stomach. "You went through my *pockets*?"

"It was only because I knew you weren't telling me the truth and—"

"Jesus, Penelope. You've really shown your true colors now."

"I know, I know, it sounds bad—it is bad. But thank goodness I did. Because there's something going on you're not telling me. And my guess is that it's got something to do with Bex. Listen, some of my best stories have come from nothing more than a hunch. And since you first introduced me to Bex I had an uncomfortable feeling that something wasn't right. And so I started to do a bit of a background check on her. If you'd only read the file, you'd see that—"

I push the file toward her so that she has no choice but to take it. The action forces Penelope to take a step back, nearer to the top of the marble stairs. She tries to grasp the file, but the movement unbalances her. A wrong step and she could lose her footing. Although I'm cross with her, I don't want her to hurt herself.

"Watch out!" I say and instinctively reach out to stop her from falling.

As I grab hold of her, she stretches out her right arm and steadies herself on the curve of the bannister. But as she does so she drops a couple of pages from the file, pages which flutter down the stairwell.

"Jesus Christ, Penelope. You had me worried for a second." Penelope ignores the fact that I saved her from a nasty fall. But instead of thanking me, she continues to carp on about Bex.

"How much do you really know about her?"

"Listen, I don't know what you think Bex has said or done, but I don't care. She's been the best of friends to me. And now is not the time to go and start accusing her of—"

"I need to warn you about something. You see—"

"I've just had enough of this, Penelope."

"And the CCTV map in your pocket?"

"What about it?"

"I don't know what's going on in your life right now, Jen. But I'm worried that Bex has something to do with it, that she's trying to control or manipulate you in some way. I know it sounds ridiculous, but it would fit the pattern. You see—"

Just then Julia walks up the top flight of stairs, face flushed, glass in hand. How much of the argument has she heard?

"Sorry, hope I'm not interrupting, Jen. It's just that I wondered if you wanted to finish the interview. I've just had a call—they need me back at my office soon."

"Yes, of course," I say. "And don't worry, you're not interrupting. Penelope was just about to go back downstairs to ask if anyone else needed any more food."

We stare at each other in a silent battle of wills. Finally, Penelope smiles and tells me that she will talk to me once the interview with Julia is over. She grips the file of documents close to her chest and nods as she passes Julia. In turn, Julia apologizes to me for taking so long. She tells me about her craving for cigarettes, a habit she thought she'd kicked years back, and we take our places in the study. I switch on the tape recorder again and we pick up where we left off. She tells me more about the nightmares, about Harry, about how much she misses him, about how the death of her son created an ocean of grief between her and her first husband, but as she talks I realize I'm not listening. All I can think about are Penelope's words of warning and the possible contents of that green file.

Once it's over, I lead Julia back downstairs. Everyone has breathed a collective sigh of relief: the interviews are over. The group, their spirits lifted by the champagne, discuss the seemingly never-ending drama of the current political situation, where things seem to change by the hour, but luckily the conversation doesn't descend into unpleasant Brexit bickering.

As Penelope glides around her large kitchen, offering coffee, I'm conscious of her watching me. I know she's just waiting for everyone to leave so she can talk to me again. But I'm not going to hang around.

I still can't forgive her for rifling through my coat pocket the other day. So what if she'd found that marked-up map of the Heath? It told her nothing. I could easily be writing a feature about the presence and absence of security in public places. And how could she say those things about Bex? There was no way I'd let my friend call here now. She's vulnerable enough as it is without an interrogation from Penelope Frasier. I take out my phone and text Bex to say that the interviews are overrunning and it'll be best if I meet her back at the flat.

I make an effort to go around and thank everyone in person—Jamie, Julia, Ayesha, Steven—and reassure them that what they've told me will be handled sensitively. People start to say their goodbyes. I don't want a scene with Penelope—it would be awful if any of the interviewees saw that—and so I move toward the door. I latch onto Julia and suggest we walk across the Heath together. She's going back to her office, she tells me, but I go through the motions of leaving with her just so I don't get drawn back into the house. But just as we near the front door Penelope calls out.

"Jennifer? I need to talk to you about something. Do you remember?"

"I'm just leaving with Julia."

"Don't worry about me," says Julia. "I'm going into town now. You're very welcome to a lift, but I thought you said you were going—"

"That's very kind of you, but I'm meeting a friend," I shout back in an overly polite manner so that Penelope can hear.

"It won't take a moment," says Penelope. "But it is important. It's some-thing to do with—"

There's actual distress if not an edge of panic in Penelope's voice now, but I say I'm sorry, that I'll call her, and I slip out of the door.

68

BEX

One of the things Louise, my counselor, was always banging on about was cause and effect. Just because I was the daughter of my parents it didn't mean that I was to blame for their deaths, she said. If only she knew.

I could have talked to her about how I really felt and the reasons why I did what I did. I kept silent not just because of the consequences—the truth would result in me being sent to prison or some kind of psychiatric ward—but also because there was something delicious about keeping it all to myself. At night, I would replay the lead-up to the events of that Valentine's Day over and over in my head. I would see everything in slow motion: the never-ending spritz of the aftershave, the droplets spreading slowly through the room, hiding those cards from the Italian restaurant, practicing the handwriting over and over again, and finally writing that card and placing it in that shoebox in the wardrobe. I remembered the thrill I felt while I was waiting for Dad to find the card, the chord of ecstasy that played up and down my spine as I counted down the minutes. The anticipation, as always, was just as thrilling as the actual event, the deaths that followed.

Of course, over the years I did ask myself what lay behind it all. And the answer was so simple even my counselor could have understood it if I'd told her. How would she have felt if she'd heard that her mother tried to abort her before she was born? That she'd never been wanted, never been loved? That she feared the specter of rejection with such a primal dread that she was prepared to do anything—she was even prepared to kill—rather than risk its approach? Sometimes, during these sessions I'd be talking about how hard I was finding it to fit in at school (a lie) and wondering whether I'd ever be happy (another lie) when inside I'd be conducting a different kind of confession. I'd play both roles—those of counselor and subject—myself, silently asking and then answering a series of questions.

Q: Do you think you're damaged?
A: Yes, I'm sure I am, but I don't care. In fact, I think I can use it to my advantage.

Q: What do you think was the source of that damage?
A: I don't know. Perhaps what my mum tried to do to me when I was in her womb. Was it something to do with that? I'll never know. Or was it living with them? Growing up in a violent home? Watching my mum being beaten. Seeing her turn herself invisible through the drinking. Knowing I wasn't loved?

Q: What do you think of your mother and father now?
A: I'm pleased they're both dead. They deserved it. If they didn't want to bring me into this world, why did they?

Q: How do you see your future?
A: As bright as the sun on a summer's day, almost impossible to look at.

Q: What did you feel when you were planning it all?
A: Alive. More alive than I've ever felt before.

Q: Did you hate them? Is that why you did it?
A: I suppose so, but it went deeper than hate.

Q: And why did you choose Valentine's Day?
A: All that hearts and flowers shit . . . It's all fake. I mean, I suppose it's about love, isn't it? Or the lack of it.

Q: Will you do it again in the future?
A: It depends.

Q: On what?
A: . . .

Q: On what?
A: If nobody wants me. If someone tells me they don't love me. If I feel I'm going to be cast aside.

69

JEN

'm sitting on a bench on Kite Hill, the place where it all began. But I'm not thinking about the attack now. Instead, I'm holding two sheets of paper, the ones I picked up from the landing on the first floor. I suppose when Penelope had gone down the stairs earlier she must not have seen them lying there. Or had Penelope deliberately left them there for me to find?

After the interview with Julia was over I had come downstairs and quickly bent down to sweep the papers up. I had said goodbye to Julia and, instead of going straight to the flat, I'd come back to the viewing point. After the day of interviews I needed some time to myself.

Words jump out at me like nasty little tacks, but I try to remain calm. Part of me wants to tear the sheets into the smallest pieces possible, so I never have to read their contents, but I realize I have no choice but to confront what's in front of me. The typed pages take the form of an interview transcript, presumably carried out by Penelope, with a woman whose name I don't know—it looks like I'm missing the beginning and end of the interview. It's only as I read that I begin to understand.

—and he was a lovely little boy. No trouble at all. Always was beautiful, even as a baby. But of course he grew up to be proper handsome. A real heartbreaker. The girls couldn't get enough of him and he got through plenty, especially when he was a teenager. Some of the scenes I had to witness, you wouldn't believe. Tears. Phone calls in the middle of the night. Oh, the drama of it all. He was a bright little thing too. Wanted to go places. Wanted more, much more, than what we could give him. And always good with money, even from when he was small. Such a little businessman he was, always trying to sell you something. Me and his dad used to joke about how he'd get his own market stall one day, but of course he went and did better, a lot better, than that. We were so proud of him. Of course, he had his problems, we knew that.

What kind of problems were they?

Like I told you before, the last time you came, it was drugs. Cocaine mostly. Helped him with his job, he said. Gave him an edge, or something like that. I told him it was bad for him. I could see it was making him worse. Nervous. Anxious. Paranoid. And his jealousy. Like I said, that was always a thing with him. Something you had to watch. Of course, it was endearing when he was a boy. A sign of his passionate nature. A sign that he cared. Do you know what I mean? When I was young and I was courting his father he could be just the same. I suppose that's where Dan got it from. That temperament. Having said that, I never expected that Dan would do . . . what he did.

[Sound of crying, sniffing.]

No, that was something completely out of the blue. I don't know what pushed him over the edge. I suppose Vicky wasn't right for him. Probably a cut above him, if you know what I mean. He probably would have felt happier with someone from his own background. But that was typical Dan, always wanting more. And what he did to Vicky was horrible. But I suppose it was his jealousy, like I said. He must have discovered that Vicky was having a relationship with another bloke.

Do you know who that was?

No, I never did find out. And now they're saying she was pregnant. No wonder Dan lost it. I mean, as I say that's no excuse for what he did. But you've got to put yourself in his shoes, haven't you? He was in love with her, with Vicky I mean. I know that. And to suspect that the love of his life might have been carrying another man's child. Well, that must have hit him hard. Like any red-blooded man. If Vicky told him that she wanted to leave him for this other man, this man might be the father of her child, that would have pushed him over the edge.

The last time I came to see you, you told me about Daniel's infatuation with an older woman. Can you tell me a little more about that?

Did I? I can't really remember. Oh you mean with—yes, of course. I do remember telling you now. Yes, Dan did get into a bit of trouble there. I suppose it was the other way round—the opposite of what Vicky did to him. He was the one who ended it all, or tried to end it.

And what happened?

Oh, there was such a scene. He'd had enough of her. I think he'd secretly taken up with another girl on his course. He was only at college, you see. Only 18 or so. And this woman—the one who caused all the trouble—she was older than him. I think she was a friend of Tina's—that's my daughter, the one who lives in Australia. But when he tried to break it off with her, she threatened all sorts of things. Said that she'd kill herself if he left her. He thought that she was just pretending, that they were empty gestures, but she did it—or nearly did it, I should say. They found her just in time I believe. He felt sorry for her, I think. Said that he wouldn't leave her. But of course, he'd fallen head over heels in love with this other girl. That didn't last neither.

Do you know what became of this woman?

What, the one he fell for at college?

No, the one you said was older. The one who attempted suicide?

I don't know. She moved away I think. Never liked her, though. Had cold eyes. Like she was always scheming.

[I take out the photo and show it to her.]

Is this her?

[She is shown the photo.]

Yes, that's her all right. *[Karen pauses.]* Anyway, what's this got to do with all that happened on Hampstead Heath? What's Becky got to do with—

Becky. The name was there in black and white, but this couldn't be my Becky. I knew that Bex had grown up in Essex, but this couldn't be her. No, not Bex.

I'm walking back to the flat when my phone pings. Another message. Before I even open it I look around me to check the street for any sign of him. I scan the faces around me. Nothing. I hear a scream. I jump and turn around only to see a gaggle of schoolgirls who've come out of La Sainte Union. I stop in the street and raise my phone.

@ImStillWatchingYouJenHunter It's nearly time.

With shaking fingers I follow the address and tap out a direct message.

@onlyoneJenHunter For what?

As I wait, I continue to look around me. The girls disperse, their screams fading away into the distance. A cyclist—male, balding, rake thin—speeds past. At the end of the street I see a jogger, a man. I squint past the cars, the other pedestrians. I take a couple of steps and feel the prick of a yew hedge on the back of my neck. He can't do anything here, I tell myself. It's daytime. There are people around. I edge toward the gate. Is there anyone inside the house? I strain my head to look up. The jogger is coming closer. I can only see his legs pounding along the pavement as the rest of him is obscured by a couple of mums pushing what seem like excessively large prams. My phone pings.

@ImStillWatchingYouJenHunter You know.
@onlyoneJenHunter WHAT??

And then the messages come thick and fast.

@ImStillWatchingYouJenHunter You saw what happened on the Heath.
@ImStillWatchingYouJenHunter You know how easy it is. How quick it is.

I feel all my strength seep out of me as if my blood has already been spilled. I sink back against the hedge and slip down on the ground. I hear the sound of running coming toward me.

@ImStillWatchingYouJenHunter I'm going to slaughter you like a pig.

I see myself walking down a dark street, fear coursing through my veins. I turn a corner and see him. Laurence. He holds up a knife. Its blade glints in the moonlight. There's a manic quality in his eyes. He no longer cares about the consequences of his actions. I try to make a run for it, but he's too quick. He grabs me and although I try to fight him off, he holds me tight. Once I adored his embrace—now it's like the touch of death itself.

I feel the cold blade on my neck, the edge of the knife beginning to slice into me.

I realize then, as I slump down onto the tarmac, that I don't want to die. Not like this.

My whole being is consumed by anger. How dare he think he can do this to me? I'm not going to spend the rest of my life being afraid of what he might do to me. I think back to how I've changed over the last few weeks since the murder-suicide on the Heath. If witnessing that wasn't bad enough, I've also had to endure humiliation after humiliation, assault after assault. I recall the feeling of being sacked, the utter sick-making shame of it. His actions resulted in the loss of my job and my home. I remember the moment I was sitting on that bench by the tumulus on the Heath. The shock of being hit over the head with a rock. And then the discovery of that mask in his bathroom. If that wasn't enough I'd then learned the horror of what he'd done to Bex. I pictured him on top of her unconscious body.

I whisper the word "No" to myself, repeating it as a mantra.

I'm not going to take this anymore.

I swallow a great gulp of air and push myself back up. I look around for something—anything. I search my pockets and my bag for a make-shift weapon. My fingers wrap themselves around my set of keys. I clasp my hand behind my back. It's not much, but I figure I could stab him in the eye.

@ImStillWatchingYouJenHunter By the time I've finished with you you'll be begging for me to kill you.

Just then as I dig the edge of a key into the palm of my hand, priming myself with pain, readying myself to strike, the sound of running intensifies. I focus, open my mouth to scream, but as the jogger speeds toward me I realize it's not Laurence: he's blond, younger by a good decade. He casts me an odd sideways look as he dashes past and disappears.

The tension in my body feels as though it could break me into a thousand pieces. I let out an almighty exhalation of breath. I can't carry on like this. I don't want to be a victim. It's time to fight back.

70

BEX

The door opens and Jen rushes into the room. It's obvious she's got the messages. She's raging. Her eyes have taken on a crazed look and her blonde hair is a mess, cascading down over her face.

She doesn't so much spit the words as spew them out. "If he thinks he can fuck with me . . . If he reckons for one second he can get away with this . . . I'm not going to stand back and let him do this to me anymore—not for one fucking second." Spittle forms in the corner of her mouth. "I can't stand this a moment longer . . . I am literally going—"

"Jen, Jen—you need to calm down. Come and sit down. Tell me what's happened."

She pushes her phone at me. "Read them—read what the fucker sent me. He wants . . . he says he's going to . . . slaughter me like a . . . like a pig."

I take her phone and scroll through the messages. "Jesus. This means we can go to the police now. This is a blatant threat. The police will be able—"

"No police. I'm not going down that route. If we do that then nothing will change. They'll give him a warning at best—that's if they can trace the messages to him. By which point he will have deleted his account. No, that might make it worse. That will . . ."

She looks at me as if seeing me for the first time.

"Fuck, Bex. How could I have been so unfeeling? You must think I'm a complete shit."

"Sorry?"

She envelops me in her arms. "I'm so wrapped up in all of this—the messages—I'm so full of anger for him that I haven't stopped to think about you. What he did to you."

I start to cry and tell her that I'm sorry, that I should have told her sooner, but that I didn't have the words.

"I know you liked him . . . I shouldn't have done it . . . I'm such a bad friend," I manage to rasp out between sobs.

"What are you talking about? He's the one who should be sorry. All you did was go into his house and accept a late-night drink. You shouldn't feel guilty for doing that." She stands back, holds my shoulders and looks into my tear-filled eyes. "If I'd known what he'd done to you, I would have killed him back then. You know that, don't you?"

"I suppose that's why I didn't tell you," I say, taking a tissue from my pocket to wipe my face. "I was frightened of what you might do—to him and to me."

"To you?" She sounds appalled at the idea. "Like I've said, you're not the one to blame here. Did you think about going to the police—after it happened?"

"I suppose so, but how would they have proved it? It would have been so messy. I was scared that the interrogation, the whole fucking process, might be more distressing than the . . . thing itself. Not that I can remember anything about it."

"So let me get this right, you got the taxi back with him, he invited you in, offered you a drink, and then . . . ?"

"Nothing. Apart from the next morning. It was obvious what had happened. I was in his bed. I had no clothes on."

"Did you say anything to him?"

"No, I just got my things and left. I felt so dirty, so ashamed. I thought about telling you, like I said I really did, but then you seemed so keen on him. I kept waiting for the right moment, but then I started to question whether it was the right thing to do. I'd had a lot to drink, we all had, that night. Was it just a blackout? I'd had them before after a heavy night—both of us have, haven't we, where we've drunk so much we can't fill in the gaps of what happened? I've beaten myself up about it ever since, not telling you. But the reason I didn't tell you was because I was . . . I was worried that I might lose you."

She hugs me closer to her again. "Don't be stupid."

"You're not mad at me then?"

"Not with you. Of course not. But with him? If you're asking whether I'm mad at him . . . I'm so fucking angry with him I could . . ."

"Could what?"

"You probably don't want to know."

"You still want to give him a fright, then?"

"Absolutely," she mumbles, turning away from me. She goes to the fridge, gets out a bottle of white wine and fills two glasses. "I'd actually like to—"

She cuts herself off, but I prompt her to continue. "Like to what?"

"It's best if you don't know." She runs a hand through her hair. "Let's talk about something else."

She starts to tell me about the interviews—she's pleased she's got everything she needs for the piece—but she never mentions Penelope. When I ask Jen about her, she clams up. However, it takes a little more prompting before she explodes once more. She's a nightmare, she says. She goes on to tell me about how Penelope enlisted the services of a private detective—something which is against the law—to find out that Ayesha Ahmed, the doctor, was heavily in debt and had a job at a lap-dancing club in the East End.

"Of course, I didn't use it against her—Ayesha's been through enough without that, and who cares if her shopping habit's got out of hand. We've all got things we'd rather keep to ourselves." She goes quiet, takes another sip of her drink. "And . . . I wasn't sure whether to tell you this, but it seems Penelope's taken it upon herself to try to find out stuff about you too."

"Me? Why would she want to go digging up anything about me? I mean, what's there to unearth? She can ask me anything to my face. I'm an open book."

"Exactly. She tried to make me read this file about you that—"

"You mean to say she's got a whole *file* on me?"

"That's what she reckons. She was asking all sorts of stupid questions about how much I really knew about you. Anyway, she's full of shit. Once this piece is over I don't want anything more to do with her."

I can feel my heart begin to race in my chest, but I keep my composure calm and my voice steady.

Jen digs her hand into her pocket and pulls out a couple of pieces of paper that she's folded into squares. She looks at me and then down at the paper as she unfolds it, her cheeks coloring as she reads something. I take a sip of wine. I don't know what she's about to say, but it's clear Jen has something. Something on me.

"I hate to ask you this, and I'm sure it's nothing, but—"

"No—ask away. Honestly. I don't mind." Even though I feel like I want to sink into a black pit, I try to make light of the situation. "If Penelope has dug up some dirt on me, I'd love to know what it is."

She clears her throat. "It's an interview that Penelope did with Karen Oliver, she's the mother of Daniel."

"Okay."

"And in it—honestly, it's stupid, I'll put it away," she says, folding the pages up. "Forget I ever said anything."

"Jen—it's fine. Please, just tell me what it is."

She opens the papers again and her eyes scan over the words. "Look—I'm just going to ask you. I know it sounds ridiculous. In the interview, Karen said that her son Daniel got involved with this older woman, a woman she said was called Becky. She didn't give a surname, but it's obvious that Penelope showed her a photograph of the woman. I have to ask: did you used to know Daniel Oliver—in the past, I mean?"

I know I'm a good liar, and I use every trick in the book, lowering my chin down to my neck and opening my eyes a little wider so that I look like an innocent child. "Him? No, why would I know him? The first I ever heard about Daniel Oliver was that day on the Heath."

"That's what I thought," she says quickly. "Sorry, I should never have asked you. It was stupid of me."

No, it wasn't stupid of her, it was stupid of Penelope for telling Jen that she had compiled a dossier about me. She may as well have signed her own death warrant.

71

JEN

I can't bring myself to ask Bex to help me deal with Laurence. This is something I'm going to have to do by myself. However, I'm pleased I did ask her about whether she knew Daniel Oliver. At least I can put that out of my mind now. But I'm still annoyed with myself for allowing Penelope to inveigle her way back into my life.

I should never have accepted the offer of her house as a base for the interviews. I was in danger of compromising myself. Not only are Penelope's methods seriously off the wall, but her suggestions about Bex make me wonder whether she's beginning to lose it. Since I left her house after the interview sessions she's sent me nearly twenty messages, all of which I've deleted without opening. As I begin to transcribe the interviews I let her calls go straight to voicemail. I can't be bothered to listen to the messages she leaves. When my phone rings I expect it to be her and I almost don't look, but it's Jamie Blackwood.

"Jen—can you talk?"

"Hi Jamie—is there something wrong?"

"Are you alone?"

It's late at night. Bex is at the twenty-four-hour gym. Exercise, she always says, is the best thing to get rid of stress, anxiety, and anger. As she left the flat, leggings and trainers paired with a big parka, she told me that she felt she needed to hit something. I'd joked about how a punchbag would have to serve as a substitute for Laurence.

"Yes, why?" I ask Jamie.

"Listen—this is going to sound a bit . . . weird. But Penelope's really worried about you and—"

"Don't talk to me about Penelope. You don't need to know the details, but she's proving to be a bit of a pain at the moment."

"She asked me to check on you just to make sure you're okay."

"Yes, I'm fine. Just a bit knackered, but apart from that—"

"She thinks you might be about to do . . . something."

"Such as what?"

"Something drastic. That's what she said. She's really worried about you. She says she's tried to call you, she's sent you some emails."

"Sorry that you had to get dragged into this, Jamie, but to be honest it's a load of shit."

There's a pause on the line and I can hear him breathing. "Jen, you may not like what I'm going to say, but Penelope has shared with me some of the information she's gathered—she didn't know what else to do—and there may be something in it."

"What?"

"Look—if you want an objective opinion, I think you should take her concerns seriously."

I can feel the rush of blood to my head, the sudden breathlessness that accompanies the onset of anger. "I don't know what she's told you, but—"

"It's about your friend, Rebecca—I think you call her Bex. I don't know the background, but Penelope showed me some stuff. And some of it . . . well, it's worrying. Just promise me one thing—if I send it over to you, will you take a look at it? That's all I'm asking. That's all that Penelope wants."

"Anything to shut her up," I say wearily. "But really, it will turn out to be nonsense."

We chat a little more about that day's interviews before we end the call. A few seconds later an email pings into my inbox. It's a scan of an old newspaper cutting from the *East Anglian Daily Times*, dated 28 April 1990.

VALENTINE'S DAY MURDER-SUICIDE

A Colchester woman in an abusive relationship killed her violent husband and then herself.

Amanda Paterson, 34, cut the throat of her husband, Brian, 38, before killing herself. The couple, who lived in Maplestead Close, Colchester, was found dead by the police on 15 February this year. It's thought the incident occurred the day before, on 14 February—Valentine's Day. The inquest in Colchester today heard evidence from pathologist Dr. Bruce Robinson, who said that mother-of-one, Amanda, suffered severe burns to her hand during the incident. A frying pan was found by the bodies, which were discovered in the kitchen at the couple's semi-detached home, and it was suggested that Brian Paterson held his wife's hand down in the hot fat for some time before Amanda could take no more. Police said that it's likely that this was the factor that drove Amanda to pick up a kitchen knife and murder her husband, a local painter and decorator. After slashing his throat, she then used the same knife to kill herself.

Neighbors submitted evidence to the inquest to say that they were worried that Amanda was a victim of domestic abuse. "It was difficult because although we suspected all was not well within the house, Mandy didn't want to alert the authorities," confessed one concerned neighbor who did not want to be named. "I wish now I'd said something—if I had, perhaps things would have turned out differently."

Neighbors say that the dead couple are survived by a young daughter, Rebecca, 13, who was at the house at the time of the incident, but was uninjured. She has since been placed with a foster family.

◆

The name, Rebecca, sears itself into my consciousness. That, and the fact that the murder-suicide occurred on Valentine's Day. I feel a wave of nausea work its way up from my stomach, but I force myself to swallow it down. The text begins to blur and swim across the screen. This can't be happening. I tell myself that it's the wrong surname. This is about a Mr. and Mrs. Paterson. Bex's last name is Shaw. But then I realize that she could have taken the name of the family she went on to live with. I look at the date of the newspaper—28 April 1990—and the age of the young daughter left behind, thirteen. If she was alive today that would make her forty-two—the same age as Bex.

72

BEX

'm standing outside the old lady's house, waiting for the darkness. Through the open curtains that frame the front I can see a weak light that looks like it's coming from the top floor. I wonder what she's doing. I picture her sitting at her mahogany desk, working her way through that file of documents she's compiled on me. I need to know what she's unearthed so I can understand how to deal with the situation, how to deal with *her*.

The feel of Penelope's key in my hand is comforting. I enjoy running my fingers up and down its indentations and ridges. My plan is balanced on a knife edge, I realize that. I'm not sure how much Penelope knows about me, how much she has shared with Jen. My assumption, based on Jen's recent behavior, is that she knows relatively little: only that a woman called Becky once knew Daniel Oliver, and that Steven Walker saw me talking to Laurence before the murder-suicide on Hampstead Heath.

I was pleased at how I managed not only to explain that but to spin it to my advantage. Jen had been primed in such a way I could hardly dare imagine. I'd laid the foundations of the scheme with the precision of an architect. I'd drawn Jen in by sending her those mysterious messages, suggesting that Daniel Oliver hadn't really killed Vicky Da Silva. I knew that her curiosity would get the better of her and that she wouldn't be able to resist investigating. I'd made the messages more threatening, so by the time of the attack on the Heath—and her discovery of that mask in Laurence's house—she was as malleable as a piece of wet clay in my hands. All it would take would be a few final turns of the wheel and it would all be over. I smile as I think about what is going to happen to Laurence, before I turn my attention back to the job in hand.

Penelope.

I need to find out what she's got on me, that's a given. But what else? Although it would be tempting to snuff out the old lady's life, I know enough about leaving traces of one's DNA at the scene of a crime, information I've picked up from watching too many thrillers on TV, that it would be unwise to do that. Despite this, I could still have a little fun.

The light at the top of the house goes out and I wait for another twenty minutes before I make a move. I walk down the path and listen at the front door. Nothing. I take the key and ease it into the lock. I slowly turn it and hear the lock click. I hesitate for a moment, before I push the door open. I step inside—the house is dark, quiet—and quickly close the door. The smell of cooking—something rich and meaty—lingers in the air. I slip my trainers off so I can move through the house as quietly as a ghost. I take out my torch and use it to guide me through the blackness. I go into the kitchen, straight to the long, wooden table, but despite there being a few papers, there's no sign of the file. I check a few drawers, but I only find what I'd expect: pots, pans, cutlery, and in the rest the detritus of living: Sellotape, old postcards, stamps, glue, playing cards, pens, string, discarded phone chargers. I move to the sitting room, scan the shelves, the side tables and sofas, but again nothing. I make my way back to the hallway and listen up the stairwell for any signs of life. It's quiet apart from the distant scream of a fox outside. With a delicate step I begin to climb the marble stairs.

I decide to bypass the first floor and head straight for the top. If the file is to be found anywhere it's most likely to be in her study or bedroom. When I reach the third story I stop on the landing. Although I'm fit, I can hear myself breathing. Of course, I've had to address what I would do if Penelope were to step out of her bedroom. There are a few scenarios I've dreamed up, most of which involve pushing her down the stairs. She's a frail old lady.

The steps are hard. She would hit her head. The chances of death would be high. When the forensic team came to do their DNA analysis they might find traces of me, but of course this could be explained by the fact that I had paid a number of visits to the house when Jen lived there. The main thing was to avoid her scratching me as I know I wouldn't be able to explain my DNA under her fingernails. Hopefully, it wouldn't come to that.

From the landing I move into her study. I use the torch to search her desk, its surface and drawers. There are papers relating to a future talk at a journalism college, a few books for review, along with notes from adoring commissioning editors, and a checkbook from Coutts. There are packets of staples, blank postcards, a ring punch, stacks of A4 paper, printer cartridges, and ink for a fountain pen. But there's no sign of anything relating to me. Gently I ease open the filing cabinet that sits in the corner. I've searched this cabinet before and I'm convinced there's nothing new in here. I scan the shelves and look under the printer. Her laptop is not here and neither is the bag that she carries it in. Fuck. The bitch must have taken everything to bed with her.

As silently and stealthily as I can, I inch my way forward to her bedroom. I wrap the torch inside the end of my sleeve so it only gives out the dimmest of lights. I stand outside the door, which I notice is slightly ajar. I steady myself before pushing the door forward a fraction. I'm relieved when it doesn't squeak. I press my foot against the door to ease it open a little more.

Through the gap I can see a double bed, at the far end of which lies the outline of a dark shape. Penelope. I step into the room and, as I move closer, I can hear the sound of gentle breathing with only the faintest hint of a snore. I come to stand by the bedside table. I lift the edge of my sleeve higher so that the torch can illuminate what's on the surface: a stack of hardback books, a pot of expensive-looking night cream, a copy of the *New Yorker.*

I move the light across the floor, but there's nothing I can see that looks like a file or that would contain a file. With small, silent steps I shuffle my way around the bottom of the bed to the side that is nearest the window. In the dim light I see Penelope's lined, unmade-up face, so different to the one she presents to the world. As I move the torch across the bed I see it. The file is there, on top of the duvet, enclosed by an arm.

I step forward and take another, closer look. Her hand is fixed like a claw around the file. Presumably she must have fallen asleep reading—but if so, why isn't the bedside light still on? It would be easy to wrench the file from her, dash down the stairs, and run out of the house. But in doing so I would wake her up and alert her. Even easing open the file to peer inside at its contents would be too much of a risk. I wait in the shadows, hoping that she will turn over and in doing so release her grip. But she does not move. I wonder for a moment whether she's asleep at all. Does she know that I'm here, watching her? Is she playing some kind of game with me? As I observe her, part of me thinks about taking a pillow, pressing it over her face, and squeezing the life out of her. But again, I know too much from TV: such a death could not be dismissed as the result of natural causes, and it would be investigated. Even though it's tempting—so tempting—I resist. Finally, with a heavy heart, I retreat. I slip out of the bedroom, casting one last look at the file on the bed. I will have to leave Penelope until later. She won't escape unscathed from this, I promise myself.

But just before I leave the bedroom I notice a pair of shoes that she must have kicked off before she got into bed. I pick up one of them—a little black number with a nice heel—and as I start to descend the stairs I place it in the middle of the second step down.

If she were to trip and fall to her death, whose fault would that be?

73

JEN

'm on the sofa pretending to sleep when Bex comes in. She doesn't put the light on, but I sense her moving around the room. Then she walks over to me. I can feel her looking down, studying me. I have to make an effort to keep my breathing steady and calm. I want to bolt upright and ask what the hell is going on. But I know I have to keep still. I feel like I'm choking, like something is blocking my throat, but I daren't even cough. I begin to count to ten, slowly, hoping that Bex will soon leave me alone.

One . . . *The words from the 1990 report still play around my mind. Valentine's Day. Murder-suicide. Neighbors say that the dead couple are survived by a young daughter, Rebecca, 13, who was at the house at the time of the incident, but was uninjured. She has since been placed with a foster family.*
Two . . . *Penelope's interview with Karen Oliver, in which she said that her son Daniel had had a relationship with an older woman called Becky.*
Three . . . *If Becky knew Daniel Oliver from way back did the murder-suicide on Parliament Hill Fields have anything to do with her?*

The thought of that is like a tight hand around my neck and I can't swallow.

> **Four** . . . *And what about everything that's happened to me since then?*
> **Five** . . . *The messages from @WatchingYouJenHunter.*

I can feel my breathing begin to quicken.

> **Six** . . . *The feeling of being constantly observed, stalked.*
> **Seven** . . . *The attack on the Heath, the man . . . the person in the mask.*

I can feel saliva pooling at the back of my throat.

> **Eight** . . . *Finding the mask in Laurence's house. My increasing hatred, my utter loathing, for him.*

I can't control my breathing any longer. The fear makes me take a great gulp of breath like a dying fish, a gasp that I try to cover up by coughing. I open my eyes and see her dark shadow standing over me.

"Don't worry—it's just me," she says.

"What are you doing?" I ask, clearing my throat again.

"Sorry, I was just looking for my charger."

Using the light from my phone I make a half-hearted effort to look under and around the sofa.

"Never mind. Perhaps it's in my room." She continues to stand there, looking at me.

The air is heavy with many things unsaid. I want to ask her question after question, but I remain silent.

"Is there something wrong, Jen?" she whispers.

"Just a bad dream. It's nothing. I'd better get back to sleep. I've got a big day tomorrow."

"Why?"

"Just that the editor wants me to file the piece early. He also wants me to go into the office to look at the layout to make sure I'm happy with it all."

It's dark. Bex can't see me. But will she still be able to tell I'm lying?

"Is that normal?"

"It's a bit odd, yeah." I try to keep my voice steady. "But Nick, my editor, said something about how because I was involved in the story—as a witness—I should be there to oversee its production. They want it to be handled as sensitively as possible."

Bex goes quiet again, before she switches a light on and comes to sit by me.

"You don't mind, do you?"

I can feel my heart racing now. "No, that's fine," I say, as I sit up properly and swing my legs off the sofa.

We've sat as close as this—closer—so many times, but tonight there's something wrong. It's like every cell in my body is screaming out to tell me to get as far away from her as possible. I sense her studying me, examining me for what—signs of guilt? Some kind of secret knowledge? A marker of betrayal?

"Have you got anything to tell me?"

"Tell you?"

"Yes—something's on your mind. You know I can sense when there's something wrong. Is it about Laurence? Have you changed your mind about . . ."

"No—I want to . . ."

"You want to give him a fright that he'll never forget?"

"Yes, yes I do. After hearing what he did to you, I want to see that fucker really suffer."

"So do I. So there's nothing else?"

"It's probably just the interviews. Listening to the other witnesses. It brought a lot of things up. Remembering the incident. All that blood. Those deaths."

"That must have been hard. So there's nothing else? Nothing about Penelope?"

"Penelope?"

She nods her head slowly. "Have you heard from her?"

"No—no I haven't."

I can feel the power of her gaze, stripping off the layers of deceit I've accumulated around myself like some kind of powerful acid.

"Are you sure?"

"Nothing but the usual rubbish. Some shit about you."

"What did she say—I mean, the exact words?"

"That she had this file, the one I told you about. There was the transcript of the interview she did with Daniel Oliver's mother. But I only saw the two pages that dropped out." I don't tell her about the question Penelope asked me about the map of the Heath and its CCTV coverage. I don't tell her about the emails and voice messages from Penelope. I don't tell her about the newspaper cutting I've seen, the report into that murder-suicide on Valentine's Day 1990. "She asked me . . . asked me how much I really knew about you."

"And what did you say?"

"You've always been there for me." The words sound empty, hollow. "That . . . that I'd trust you with my life."

74

BEX

'm up early and so, of course, is Jen. Despite the fact that she managed to lie to her readers for so long, she's always been bad at lying to me. I know at once when she's not telling the truth: she blinks too quickly and there's a shifty quality to her eyes. I was right not to trust her.

As I follow her out of the flat I wonder if she's on the way to the Royal Free. Did Penelope trip over that shoe I placed on the stairs and is she now in hospital? But it seems as though Jen's heading somewhere else. From the flat she walks to the Tube and she takes the Northern Line to King's Cross. If she was going to the office she would change onto the Circle Line to transport her west to High Street Kensington, but she travels east to emerge at Liverpool Street station.

I watch her from a safe distance as she buys her ticket from a machine. What's going on inside that pretty blonde head of hers? What has Penelope told her? Obviously, she knows much more than what she told me last night, otherwise she wouldn't be here, looking up at the display board that lists destinations that lie to the east of the capital: Cambridge, Norwich, Ipswich, Clacton-on-Sea, Harlow, and Colchester, my hometown. I know that's where she's headed—if she felt she had to lie to me, where else would she be going?—and, as she's queuing for a coffee, I buy myself a ticket.

I follow her onto the platform, keeping well back from her, and enter a carriage three down from hers. As the train begins to snake its way out of London, past supercool lofts and swish offices, I feel uneasy. It's a journey I haven't taken in years, a journey I hoped never to take again. The sensation is not as simple as feeling nauseated. It's more like there's something crawling under my skin, desperate to escape. I can't allow the feeling to overwhelm me. I need to think about Jen, not myself. I still don't know what I'm going to do if she does dig up stuff about my past.

Of course, I could kill her, but that would defeat the object. No, I've never wanted that. Rather it's the opposite: my goal is that she'll stay with me, forever. Perhaps I could injure her so that she would have no choice but to depend on me. A spinal injury. A terrible amputation. An awful disfigurement. Blindness? There are a few options that could be explored. But then, when I think about it, I can't imagine doing any of these things to her. I want to keep her just as she is.

Sitting on the train, with Jen just a few carriages away, reminds me of that time I followed her up north. She lied to me then too. I remember that it was in June 1998 that she phoned me to say that her aunt Kathleen had died and that she intended to go to her funeral in Preston. I asked her whether she wanted me to come with her, but she told me that she'd be fine going on her own. Unknown to her, I was with her every step of the way from the moment she took the Tube to Euston, to when she stepped on the train north, to the crematorium.

I'd taken a taxi from the station through streets of red brick terraced houses, passed soulless industrial estates, circled around endless roundabouts, until we came to the crematorium. As I sat in the car I spotted Jen, dressed in black. A woman, perhaps an elderly relative, embraced her. I waited for the small group of people to enter the building before getting out, asking the driver to stay behind for me.

I spotted a stern-faced undertaker and asked him if he could tell me the name of the deceased. He pulled a piece of paper from his pocket. Hesmondalgh, he said. Kenneth Hesmondalgh, who had died on 3 June.

It was the funeral not of Jen's aunt, but her father. I thanked him, got back into the car, and drove away. I was back in London ready for Jen's return.

Armed with this information, it was easy for me to send off for Kenneth Hesmondalgh's death certificate. Cause of death was not injuries suffered by a car crash, but myocardial infarction—a heart attack. Eventually, after a few further searches online, I managed to find a record of the death of Gillian Hesmondalgh, Jen's mother, who had passed away in September 1997, from cancer.

Initially I felt a sting of betrayal: one of the reasons I had felt so drawn to Jen was because I thought we had so much in common. We'd both lost our parents as teenagers. We were alone in the world. We'd both changed our surnames: me in my teenage years, Jen when she was an adult. And weren't we supposed to be best friends who told each other everything? Then I realized that there were certain things I had kept from her, aspects of my life I thought it was best not to share. That's one of the reasons why I'd been so paranoid about Jen naming me in that first piece she ever wrote in the student newspaper, and why I made her promise never to mention me in print again.

I also recognized that I felt a level of admiration for Jen's actions. She was more like me than I had thought. And now that I had this knowledge about her I felt I had a hold over her. The power of that thrilled me, more, much more than the pleasure I got from sex. A quick orgasm was nothing compared to the twisted knot of tight energy that grew inside me, the realization that I had power over Jen.

There were times, often when we were drunk, that I thought about telling her that I knew her secret. But no matter how close I got—it was on the very tip of my tongue, nearly slipping out of my mouth—I always reeled back at the last minute. Everyone else in my life had left me.

I wasn't going to let her go.

75

JEN

I press the button to open the doors of the train and step down onto the platform. As I walk toward the sign that says "Way Out" I notice a figure standing there. It can't be. I squint my eyes closer together. It must be someone who looks like her. With each step closer the fear I'd felt the night before takes repossession of my body. My skin feels cold. My chest begins to tighten. My breathing is shallow, like a hunted animal. She's followed me. She's here.

I'm about to turn to get back onto the train when the doors close and lock. I look around to see if there's anyone to help, but the commuters have long left for London. I bite the inside of my lip. I have no choice but to face her. Perhaps this is for the best, perhaps an honest conversation could end it all here. I just need to be brave. As I approach I realize there's something wrong with her. She's standing too near the edge of the platform. She's got her arms crossed and she's rocking back and forth. Her face is fixed on the tracks in front of her.

"Bex?"

She doesn't answer. It's almost as if she doesn't know I'm here. I say her name again and she turns her head slightly toward me.

"Are you okay?"

Her only response is to step a little closer to the platform edge. I look up at the display. There's nothing due for another ten minutes.

"What are you doing here?"

Big fat tears form in her eyes and begin to spill down her cheeks. The tracks on the line begin to crack and in the distance I can hear the rumble of a train approaching.

"Bex—talk to me. It's me, Jen."

The sound of my name seems to rouse her. "Jen?"

"That's right. I'm here."

She looks at me like a little girl. "Are you angry with me? Please don't be angry with me."

I am furious with her, of course, on many levels. More than furious. I can't tell where anger starts and fear begins. But now's not the time to tell her that.

"Why would I be angry with you?"

"I c-can't carry on."

"Why? What's happened?"

Again she falls quiet. She's fixated on the tracks, seemingly hypnotized by their hum.

I'm scared now. I look up at the display. An announcement flashes up to say that there's a fast, nonstop train that's due to speed through the station in a minute. "Bex. You need to snap out of this."

Her body is shaking now and she rasps out the words. "It's—too—late. I know I've h-hurt you. I didn't tell you the truth."

"What didn't you tell me?"

Panicking, I look around me to see if I can see anyone in a hi-vis jacket. But apart from a mother with three young kids, one in a pram, standing at the far end of the platform, there's no one around. I think about shouting down to her.

"Bex. You need to tell me what's going on."

The hum of the tracks rises to a rattle and is fast approaching a scream. The train is due any second. I don't want to frighten Bex into making any sudden movements and so I take a small, almost unnoticeable step toward her. If I had to, I'm confident I could launch myself toward her and grab her. I'm primed, watching her every movement, ready to save her. Even though I've got my suspicions about her—questions swarm around my head like a mass of trapped wasps—I can't let her do this.

"I promise I'm not angry with you."

Finally, she turns her head so her eyes—red, raw, sad eyes—meet mine.

"I thought you'd—"

Just then the train whooshes by at what seems like two hundred miles an hour, a violent, thundering machine that would have crushed Bex in its path. I can feel its shuddering impact vibrate through my body. The noise is terrible, all-consuming. My hair erupts into a mad frenzy, dancing above and around my head. The tunnel of wind forces Bex back and she collapses onto the platform. And then, once the train has passed, the station is left silent again apart from the sound of sobbing.

I bend down so I'm at her level and take her in my arms. I hold her for what seems like an eternity, until the sobs lessen. I tell her to take some deep breaths and finally she's able to look at me again. I help her up onto a nearby bench.

I find it hard to contain my anger now. "What were you thinking? Bex—talk to me!"

She wipes her nose on her sleeve and through yet more tears she begins to explain. Her confession comes in fragments, as if she's incapable of speaking fully formed sentences.

"He was a boyfriend—I knew him, Daniel, I mean—I know I should have told you. He was sweet back then—I was older, more experienced. He was the younger brother of a friend—she's in Australia now, a waitress, haven't heard from her in years. Dan was jealous back then, too, had a temper. We went out for a few months. But I couldn't bear him watching over me, always asking whether I'd seen another bloke, constantly on my back. I finished it. He was devastated. Had some kind of nervous break-down, I think. I had to do it for the sake of my own sanity. I wasn't sure about my safety. I had to move away. You see I had to be careful. I was . . . vulnerable, you see. After what happened to me. I couldn't tell you because—because it would risk bringing everything else up too."

I wonder if I can risk asking her a question. "About your parents?"

She nods and is silenced by another wave of crying.

"I've read about what happened, Bex. It's okay—you know you can tell me."

"You won't hate me?" I shake my head.

"My family—my birth family—was a mess, I mean a real mess. Mum drank. Dad was . . . violent. They say children don't know any different when they're young, they accept whatever goes on because they think it's normal, they've got nothing to compare it to. But not with me. I knew what went on wasn't . . . right. It all got so bad for Mum—the beatings and everything else—that one day in 1990, during a horrible row it all got so much worse. Dad pushed Mum's hand . . . He pushed her hand into a frying pan. I still remember the smell of that burning flesh."

She breaks off to cry some more. I squeeze her shoulder to show that I'm here for her. "If it's too much for you—"

But she cuts me off. She tries to smile, more for my benefit than her own, and she continues. "That was seared in my mind forever. Anyway, Mum reached out for something to stop him and she . . . she took hold of the closest thing to hand. A kitchen knife. She . . . stabbed him to death. And then . . . Mum used the same knife to kill herself. I tried to stop it all, but I couldn't. I was scared. I wasn't strong enough. I still feel it's all my fault."

76

BEX

It looks like it's worked. We're on the train back to London. We're not talking—well, at least not about what I told her on the platform. It was perhaps not the whole truth, but a version of it.

She's looking concerned and worried, as if at any moment I'm going to jump up and throw myself out of the train. She'll never leave me now, not when I'm on suicide watch. I wonder how long I can keep it up for. Of course, I can do the weeping at will, the appearance of being consumed by the black dog of depression, but I know I shouldn't overplay it. Subtlety is the key.

Inside, I smile to myself, knowing that I've prevented Jen's impromptu visit to my hometown. No doubt she was on her way to talk to Karen Oliver. I don't know exactly what Dan's mother would have said about me, but none of it would have been good. Luckily, both sets of my foster parents and adopted parents are dead now, so they can't tell tales. But it's possible Jen could dig up some of Daniel's old mates, even some of mine from school. Yes, I've bought myself a bit of time, but I know that it would be impossible to stop Jen from making future investigations. To prevent that I realize that I need to have some kind of hold over her.

Of course, the answer is staring me straight in the face: our plan to "scare" Laurence. I know I can't mention this on the train, and so, after repeated apologies about my silly, thoughtless, selfish behavior, I ask her more about her feature. In turn, she says that she's sorry for not telling me why she was on the way to Colchester. She insists that she does have to file the piece early and that she will have to drop by the office to look at the headlines and layout. We pass the rest of the journey staring out of the window with occasional glances at one another. At intervals, Jen's phone vibrates with a flurry of texts.

"Don't you want to answer those?" I ask.

"It'll just be Nick at the paper, hassling me again," she says.

"I don't mind—honestly. It's work. You should see what he wants. Get back to him."

"It'll wait—you're the priority here."

I study her jeans pocket and see the outline of her phone pushing through the denim.

"I insist—work's important to you. Especially now, especially this piece."

I fix her with my eyes and smile. She has no choice. She takes out the phone, looks at the screen and slips it back into her pocket.

"Yep, just as I thought—Nick asking where I've got to. But honestly, it doesn't matter. I can stay with you."

"Thanks."

As the train speeds through the Essex countryside, I catch her looking at me with what looks like suspicion, but then the suspicion turns to sympathy. I continue to watch her. Sometimes, a thought crosses her mind and she opens her mouth as if she's going to ask me something, before she thinks better of it and remains silent. That, or she questions me about my work, local planning applications, my colleagues at the council. To a fellow passenger we would appear to be two acquaintances, both perhaps a little pale from lack of sleep, who don't really know one another; women who've met by chance on a train and are passing the time of day with one another, catching up with one another's news, until their eventual arrival in London. They would not know the secrets we carry, both about ourselves and each other.

But then again, how much does Jen really know about me?

And how much do I know about her?

77

JEN

We're back at the flat. I've settled Bex on her bed, given her a couple of sleeping pills, and told her that she'll feel better after a rest. The relief I feel when I shut her bedroom door is immense. The mask I've been wearing since traveling back from Colchester slips away. I don't have to endure her looking at me, studying me, at least for the hour or so that she's asleep. I don't know what to think, what to feel.

The scene on the station platform plays itself over and over in my head. I don't know whether she believes the story about me having to go into the office. But it's all I could think of and I need an excuse to get away. On the sofa, I read through some of Penelope's messages, messages that I could only glance at when I saw them flash onto my screen on the train.

She's sorry for going through my coat pockets.

She needs to speak to me. She is insistent.

And the last text: she thinks I'm in danger.

78

BEX

Think, Bex, think. I'm pacing the room, working out what to do next. Different scenarios swirl around my mind like scenes from an imaginary play or film. Then it comes to me, an idea almost perfectly formed. I feel the thrill of adrenaline surging through my system.

I go and listen at the door of my bedroom. I can hear Jen talking to someone on the phone. She says the name Nick a couple of times. He's the editor working on her story. I wait until she finishes the call before I open the door and see her sitting on the sofa, still staring at the phone. She looks even paler than normal, like a ghost. She looks up, surprised, perhaps even frightened.

"Sorry, I didn't mean to scare you," I say.

"I t-thought you were asleep."

"I didn't take the pills. I've got too much to think about."

"You should try and get some rest."

I don't respond to this. Instead, I walk across the room and stand by the sofa, moving behind Jen like her shadow. I watch as she slips the phone back into her pocket. I sit down next to her. I smell the nervousness coming off her. I sit down next to her and she edges slightly away from me.

"Is it your editor? Is that the problem?"

"Nick? Yeah, he's still hassling me. I tried to put him off, but he still wants me to call in at some point."

She continues to talk about the people she interviewed, and about how each of them was haunted by that day on the Heath. I stop listening to her. It's time for me to make a confession—of sorts.

"You know I followed you this morning, don't you?" I interrupt. "To Colchester. I waited until you left the flat and then I trailed behind, watching you." It's obvious that she's not expecting this confession. She blinks and swallows hard. "You see, I thought you were about to . . ." I continue. "I don't know, I thought you might be on your way to do something to Laurence."

"What—what do you mean?"

"I know we'd talked about it—giving him a fright—but I thought you'd got it into your mind to go ahead with the plan by yourself. I wouldn't blame you at all, after what he did to you. I assumed that you were also so angry on my behalf—after what I'd told you—that you intended to harm him in some way. And I suppose I wanted to see it. Witness it."

"Witness it?"

"After what he'd done to me—the rape—I wanted to see him suffer. So I called in sick at work and followed you."

She continues to stare at me as if she can hardly comprehend what I'm saying. She remains silent as I speak.

"I couldn't help myself. It was like I was being hypnotized. I saw you board the Colchester train at Liverpool Street and that's when all the memories started to come back. By the time I got off the train I realized that I was trapped in some weird kind of prison. Sorry, I'm not explaining this very well."

"No, it's fine. I understand. Go on."

"I thought the only way to escape the past—the terrible thing that happened with my parents, what Laurence did—was to . . . end it all. Of course, I don't think I intended to do it. After all, it wasn't even a proper attempt, and I knew you were close by, ready to save me. I suppose it was a classic cry for help. I realize I must sound pathetic to you."

She takes my hand, but her skin has a cold, clammy quality.

"Don't be silly. You're not pathetic. You've been through a lot, suffered terribly. You've been incredibly brave."

I look her straight in the eyes. "I'm going to ask you something and you must answer me honestly. Okay?"

"Of course."

"I think I've found a way of helping us both. It involves . . . Laurence."

She repeats his name like a whispered incantation. "Laurence."

"I know we agreed to give him a shock, a scare. But what if we . . . if we went further?"

"What do you mean?"

"I bet you've often wished that you'd never met him, that . . . he'd never existed—after what he did to you, after what he still might do to you. After what he did to me. I could help you . . . I could help both of us."

"You'd be willing to . . . ?"

"Of course—you know how I've always been there for you."

"But m—"

She can't bring herself to say the word.

"You know that map of the Heath I showed you, the one I marked up showing the sections covered by CCTV? Like we said, we could attack him when he was out jogging, but instead of just frightening him, we'd finish him off. And the beauty of it is, we wouldn't be caught. Nobody would see us, we'd make sure of that—we'd do it in an area not covered by any security cameras. We'd make it look as though he'd been attacked by . . . I don't know . . . by a stranger, a teenage gang member, make it look as though it was a robbery gone wrong."

Her eyes widen in astonishment, expectation, excitement. She sits there silently, taking in the implications of what I've just said.

"But why would you want to help me?"

"As I was standing on the station platform earlier I realized just how much damage Laurence might do to other women. Look what he did to you, look what he did to me. I know it's sometime in the past, but the rape . . . I still can't—" I break off, pretending the word is choking me. "Seeing what he's done to you, remembering what he did to me, set off some kind of, I don't know what you'd call it, some kind of trigger or something." I run my hand through my hair. "I've gone mad—sorry. I'm talking nonsense. Ignore me." I stand up to go back to the bedroom. "Perhaps I do need that sleeping pill after all—"

She reaches out and grabs my wrist. If she pressed a little harder I'd start to feel a band of pain.

"No, it's not nonsense," she says. "Sit back down and talk me through it all. Tell me again what we need to do."

79

JEN

We've started out at a gentle pace, dressed in black running gear, jogging at a safe distance, watching the figure of Laurence in front. We've followed him from his house, through the streets of Tufnell Park and Dartmouth Park, to the edge of the Heath. The sun is just beginning to go down, covering the landscape in a delicate apricot light. There are a few other joggers and dog walkers around, but we always knew that there'd be other people out and about.

Bex had thought about that, she said she'd thought of everything. She'd talked me through the plan. Despite my assertion that I was familiar with the annotated map, marked up with arrows showing which areas were covered by CCTV, she made me memorize it again. She'd talked through Laurence's transgressions once more. His callousness. His cowardice. His cruelties. He was a misogynist, a monster. He'd drugged and raped her. He'd stalked and attacked me. We had to protect ourselves. It was a form of self-defense. After all, he'd said he wanted to slaughter me like a pig. And if nothing else, our actions would stop him from hurting other women. It was the right thing to do.

She spent the best part of the day instructing and schooling me. Bex had used gaffer tape to strap a sharp kitchen knife to the lower part of my left arm, which I then covered with my long-sleeved top. How did it feel? she asked as she finished binding it to my skin. Not too uncomfortable? Not at all, I'd said. In fact, it felt great. Like I was wearing a piece of armor that shielded me from harm. I had to be careful not to injure myself when I was running, she told me; also, it had to be secured in such a way that it wouldn't drop out. And so we practiced various movements in the flat—lunging, jogging on the spot, squat jumps—but the knife remained in place. Bex said that I had to be able to retrieve the knife from its casing quickly and so this was something she made me repeat until I'd got it right.

She told me that we might not be able to kill him that day as it would depend on the correct alignment of various circumstances—our proximity to Laurence, being in a CCTV-free zone, the absence of other witnesses. But if all these things came together I had to be prepared to act quickly and decisively. Could I do that? I said I could. She showed me where to strike to guarantee death: the two carotid arteries in the neck. She would distract him, stop and talk to him, and all I had to do was steal up behind him and cut his throat. I had to go in deep, though. There was no point in just cutting muscle and skin. I had to slice open the arteries that supplied oxygen to the brain. If I did that he would bleed out in a matter of minutes—just like Vicky and Daniel, I thought to myself.

Did I want to say something to Laurence before he died? She told me that, after leaving the scene, we'd soon run into an area covered by CCTV and it was important to appear as though we'd witnessed nothing suspicious. Our clothes would have to be free of blood and the knife would have to be taped back inside my arm, out of sight. In her backpack she would stash some tissues and some more tape, as well as a change of gear. We could dispose of the evidence later, she said, at our convenience.

I shouldn't be afraid, she added. She'd be proud of me once all this was over. Perhaps we could even go on a holiday to celebrate. It would be her treat. She reiterated the litany of Laurence's crimes again. He was a serial abuser. A rapist. A sadist. He'd gotten away with so much over the years that his instinct for ever-increasing forms of violence was becoming normalized. By the end of the afternoon I was possessed by a fury. Anger surged through my veins. Murder was not only on my mind, but in my body too. Every cell in my being wanted revenge. I'd never understood the term bloodlust before, but now I felt it. A rawness. A hunger. An appetite that could only be satiated by death.

◆

Bex's.

Earlier, while Bex was in the bathroom, I'd crushed a sleeping pill into a cup of tea and watched her as she drank it. I left a note to say I'd gone into the newspaper office and would be back soon. Just to be certain she wasn't trailing me I took a bus up to Archway, in the opposite direction to my destination. On the top deck of the 134 I replayed the conversation I'd had with Penelope when I was in the flat. She had asked me whether I was safe to talk and when I'd said I was in the flat she had instructed me to make up a name of a caller just in case Bex was listening.

As I pretended to talk to Nick, Penelope had outlined her fears. Bex had come into her house last night, when she was in bed. Penelope pretended to be asleep, but it was obvious Bex wanted to retrieve the file of information about her. At one point, she thought that Bex might try to smother her with a pillow or strangle her. And it took every effort to draw on her long-forgotten acting skills and days at RADA to remain there in bed, lying as still as a corpse, her hand not moving as she clutched the file. When Penelope heard Bex leave the house she got up and found that she'd placed one of her high heels on a step at the top of the stairs, no doubt hoping she'd trip and fall to her death.

But that wasn't all.

She wasn't sure exactly how it might manifest itself, but she was certain that I was in danger.

She went over what I already knew: the deaths of Bex's parents in a murder-suicide, the fact that Bex had had a relationship with Daniel Oliver when he was a teenager. If I was in any doubt about the veracity of any of this, she implored me to contact Karen Oliver. I didn't have time to travel back up to Colchester again, but I had her number. Outside Archway station I scanned the streets for signs of Bex. Nothing. I dialed Mrs. Oliver's number with fingers that trembled so much it took me three attempts before I got the right number. The call went straight to voicemail.

Next, I phoned Laurence. It was imperative I speak to him. He was the only one who could answer my questions. I dialed his mobile and he answered, but he told me he was in a meeting and that he'd call me back. As he cut the line dead I realized that my nerves were shot to pieces. My head was a mass of unanswered questions. The whole thing was a terrible gamble. Would he return the call? Even if he did talk to me, how would I know whether he was lying? After all, he'd denied being on the Heath that day, and yet I knew it had been him—he was the mystery jogger.

But why had he not owned up? What had he to hide? I'd already accused him of sending me a string of messages, which he denied. But I needed to ask him about the mask and the attack on me on the Heath. When I saw his name flash up on the screen of my phone I had to do everything in my power to keep my voice steady. He'd had enough of me being hysterical. The last thing he needed to hear was me shouting. I apologized, told him that I was sorry for the way I'd behaved. But it was important that I see him, if only for five minutes. I wasn't going to accuse him of anything. I was proud of myself for controlling my emotions and, despite his initial reluctance, punctuated by a chorus of sighs, he said that he could give me a few minutes of his time if I came down to his office. Twenty minutes later I was standing in Argyle Square. I rang his mobile and told him that I had arrived.

When he first caught a glimpse of me I saw the expression on his face change from mild irritation at having his afternoon interrupted to one of concern. "Oh my God, Jen, you look terrible," he said. "What's wrong?"

I took a deep breath. "I need to ask you some things. Some of the questions may sound . . . well, they may sound like the rantings of a mad woman. But bear with me."

He studied my serious expression, nodded his head and said, "Let's find somewhere to have a coffee."

He led me to the same café where I'd spent hours waiting for him. Memories of how I'd followed him down onto the Tube crowded my mind. We took a table at the back of the busy space and, once we'd ordered, I began by telling him that I had to talk to him about what happened that day on the Heath. He closed his eyes in discomfort as if he were being forced to endure an unpleasant dental examination.

"I know I shouldn't have stormed into your house like I did," I said. "Asking about what you were doing there, accusing you of all sorts, and you'd every right to be angry with me."

"No, I'm the one who should be apologizing to you," he said, opening his eyes. "I should have told you the truth. But after what had happened, I was scared you might use it, I don't know, in a piece for a newspaper or magazine. You remember how much flak I got from my friends whenever I—or 'James'—made an appearance in 'Being Jen Hunter.' I knew you'd lost your contract, but I could see how desperate you were getting and I . . . I didn't want my name splashed across the press."

"I'm sorry about Vicky. I know you and she were, or had been, together." The comment took him aback. "How did you find out?"

"I've been doing a bit of research and—"

"I said I didn't want you to write anything about me. Fuck, Jen. You don't change, do you?" He pushed his chair away from the table and stood up. "That's one of the reasons why . . . well, I'm not going to get into all of that with you now. I've got work to do."

"It's not for a piece—it's much more important than that," I said. I wasn't sure how much to reveal. "Please sit back down."

"What's it for then?" he asked as he resumed his place at the table.

I didn't answer him. "You've got to be honest with me. I know I asked you once before—but did you send me a series of Twitter messages from @WatchingYouJenHunter?"

"No, of course I didn't."

I took out my phone and scrolled through my photos. I hesitated a moment before I showed him the image.

"Have you ever seen this before?"

"No—what is it?"

"It's a picture of the mask worn by the person who attacked me on the Heath."

He looked shocked. "You were . . . attacked?"

I bent my head, parted my hair and showed him the scab on my scalp.

"Fuck, Jen—who would want to do that to you?"

He took my phone and used his thumb and finger to focus in on the image.

"Hang on—is this . . . ? No, you've got to be fucking kidding me. This is in my bathroom. What were you—"

"I know what it looks like—and I can explain."

"Jen—what the fuck is going on? What is this?"

"Bex has the key to your house and because we thought it was likely that it was you who attacked me we decided to—"

"You decided to break into my house."

"Yes—no. But I found this—the mask—in your bathroom cabinet."

He looked as if I'd told him we'd found an alien lurking behind his deodorant.

"You're kidding me, right?"

"No, I wish I was."

"Are you seriously asking me whether I—what?—that I attacked you on the Heath, wearing this mask, which I then stashed away in my bathroom?"

"Yes."

"Listen, Jen. I know we've had our differences. For a while I thought we could put them all behind us and start again. I really did. But if you think that I could be capable of . . ."

It was then that something clicked. There was a time, just a few weeks ago, when I thought Laurence and I might get back together. I remembered telling Bex how excited I was at the prospect. Perhaps there was a chance, I had told her, that Laurence would have me back, even after everything that had happened between us. He might actually forgive me. But that was not how it had played itself out. The day before Laurence and I were due to meet up I'd witnessed that terrible murder-suicide on Kite Hill.

"Are you okay?"

I couldn't open my mouth. Was I having some kind of attack?

"Jen—you're scaring me. What's wrong?"

Everything was wrong. The whole fucking thing. The events of the last few weeks played themselves out in my head again. The murder of Vicky, the suicide of Daniel. The string of creepy messages. My growing distrust of Laurence. The assault on me on the Heath. The discovery of that mask in Laurence's house. The map showing the CCTV coverage on the Heath. The revelation that Bex had been raped by Laurence. But I saw these things from a different viewpoint now, as if my perspective had suddenly been shifted on its side. The effect was unsettling, similar to the feeling of dissociation. I felt enveloped by an unreality that threatened to push me over the edge. But through it all I realized that everything had been leading up to one thing, the ultimate ending: my murder of Laurence.

I took a sip of coffee, but it made me feel sick.

"I need to ask you some more questions," I whispered.

He must have seen the shock drain the blood from my face. Perhaps he realized what I had to say was serious.

"Okay," he replied.

"Why were you on the Heath on the day of the murder-suicide?"

He hesitated before he began, perhaps surmising that as soon as he started to talk there was a chance that everything else would spill out. "You say you know about me and Vicky? Well, it had all got to be a mess. To be honest, I wanted to end it with her. We wanted different things. She realized she no longer loved Dan, and she got it into her head somehow that I was the one for her. She was convinced that I wanted children, that I wanted to marry her. I've no idea where she got that from."

I took a deep breath. "It was Bex."

"Bex?"

"And she introduced you, didn't she? To Vicky?"

"Yes, but—"

"And why did you go to the Heath that day?"

"Bex told me—"

Her name again.

"—that she would help me. You see, Vicky had told her that she was planning on ending it with Dan that day. On Valentine's Day, for fuck's sake! I'd told her that would be a huge mistake. I pleaded with her not to do it. She'd told me a bit about Dan's temper, his jealousy, but I never thought . . . Anyway, Bex convinced me that it would be best if we met on Parliament Hill Fields, just to make sure that Vicky was safe . . . She was a lovely girl, and I had been very fond of her—shit . . ." His voice broke. "Sorry—it's just that—that since it all happened I've been bottling lots of things up. Of course I liked Vicky, I just didn't see myself staying with her. But that didn't mean I wanted her . . . wanted . . ." He coughed into his hand and cleared tears from his eyes. "I didn't want that. When I jogged up to the top of the hill I saw what was happening and I . . . I couldn't deal with it. I ran. Ran as fast as I could away from it all. I didn't know what was going to happen, I didn't know that Vicky was pregnant. I only found out from the newspapers. I don't think it was mine, but . . . God, Jen, I feel so fucking guilty. I should never have got involved with her in the first place. It was only supposed to be a bit of fun after . . ."

He didn't need to complete his sentence. "After you," he was going to say. After the fuckup that was our relationship.

"I'm sorry, Laurence," I said. "And did Bex ever come to you and give you a warning? Told you that you should turn yourself in to the police? Identify yourself as the man who was seen jogging away from the scene?"

"No—no she didn't."

Yet another way that she had lied to me.

"But she did tell me . . ." He went quiet, uncertain about what to say next. "Jen. This is so—"

"What?"

"I wanted to tell you all this so badly when you came round to my house just after . . . It's bound to come out now anyway, so you may as well know, but she—"

"It's about that night at the French House, isn't it?"

His face froze. "How? . . . I thought . . . but she said . . ."

"It's okay, Laurence," I said. "Go on."

"Bex made it clear that it would be for the best if you didn't know exactly what had happened in the run-up to the murder-suicide. She said that if I told you anything of what I knew then she would have no choice but to tell you about that night. You see . . ."

"You know that she told me that you raped her."

"What?" said Laurence, rubbing a hand over his eyes and face in a way that looked like he wished he could wash my words from his skin.

"She said . . . she told me that after you'd gone back to your house you slipped something into her drink. And that you . . . that you raped her."

"For fuck's sake. And you believe her?" There was anger in his eyes. A black, dangerous anger I'd only seen on rare occasions, such as the night last summer when he ended it all. "Do you really think I could do that?"

"No—I don't. Listen—I don't believe her."

"What the fuck is she playing at? If I see her, I'll—"

"Just tell me what really happened. Honestly—I won't mind." That wasn't entirely true: I had to steel myself for what came next.

"We had some kind of drunken sex, but it . . . it didn't mean anything. I didn't rape her. I didn't slip anything into her drink. And the next day, the next morning, I told her that . . . that it had been nice, it'd been fun, but it would be best if we went our separate ways. I wasn't ready for a relationship. But then, when I got to know you a bit better . . . Well, that changed."

If only I'd been able to ask Laurence these questions a month ago. Everything would have been so different. I felt so unutterably sad, and yet I couldn't cry. I thought of all the things that might have been: the future we could have enjoyed together, the holidays, the lazy Sunday mornings in bed, the parties, the quiet, intimate chats, perhaps even a couple of kids. But none of those things had happened. None of those things would happen. We had once been due to start a new life together. Was that what this was all about?

80

BEX

We're running on the Heath, and I've never felt more alive. I suppose the afternoon nap must have helped. The air is clean and cold on my face and Jen is in the mood to kill. I can see it in her eyes. They are hard and precise, and she's possessed by a determination, and a courage, that I have to admire. The final strands of the plan have all come together with a simplicity that's so pleasing, as though fate's on my side.

In the flat we went through what needed to be done over and over again. When I instructed her in the technique of cutting the carotid arteries, her eyes began to shine with an eerie brightness, as if her whole being was energized at the prospect. She held the knife with the confidence of a professional. She was an ideal pupil, staying silent when she needed to listen, asking questions when necessary, uncomplaining when I bound the knife to the inside part of her left arm. I'm sure she must have felt some discomfort, but she bore it all like a perfect stoic.

As Jen took in my every word I could hardly believe this moment had actually come. This was what I've been working toward. It would serve as a fitting counterpart to the scene I'd directed on Parliament Hill Fields, between Daniel Oliver and Victoria Da Silva. I'd been watching it all from a distance, only frustrated I couldn't witness it unfold at closer quarters. Over the years I'd kept in touch with Dan, and I even made him believe that I'd forgiven him for finishing with me back when he was still in his late teens. That had hurt me hard at the time. But I was able to put on a good front. He considered me a good mate, someone he could confide in. And because I was close to him, I was able to prime him, able to lay out the foundations for the crime with a precision that impressed even me. I knew he was unnaturally jealous, I'd learned that during my own relationship with him. And when he'd finished with me I vowed to myself that one day I'd get my revenge on him. All it took was for me to befriend his new girlfriend, Vicky, and introduce her to Laurence.

I hoped that not only would Vicky, an interior designer, look up to Laurence, an architect, but that she would fancy him too. And boy did she fall for him. Hard. Laurence was looking for a bit of light relief after the breakdown of his five-year relationship with Jen. And Vicky, beautiful, in her twenties, stepped into that role.

As a "friend" to both of them, I served as a go-between, ferrying messages back and forth, arranging illicit meetings. I was privy to the intimate details of their relationship—in particular Vicky used me as a sounding board, asking my advice about her increasingly strong feelings toward Laurence. I told her that she should definitely pursue the relationship, that it was obvious he loved her, that he was looking for a long-term partner, and perhaps she could be the mother of his children. When she told me that she was pregnant I couldn't believe it. It was beyond my wildest dreams.

It didn't matter whether the baby was Dan's or another man's; the sheer unknowability of it was enough to drive Dan mad. To unsettle him further I used some of my old tricks. Cards from restaurants. Fake hotel bills. Handwritten notes. But then I also employed some of the fruits of new technology. Intimate texts sent from unknown mobiles. Emails disguised to look like they'd come from a new boyfriend. Head shots of Laurence. Blurred obscene photos that seemed to show a woman who looked very much like Vicky having oral sex with a man whose face could not be seen. And the beauty of it was that it worked like a dream. Their Valentine's Day turned into a bloodbath, a real-life horror film witnessed by none other than Jen, who I'd arranged to meet at the top of Parliament Hill Fields.

I'd also told Laurence that Vicky intended to end it all with Dan that day on the Heath. I appealed to Laurence's chivalrous nature—despite everything, I knew he wouldn't want her to get hurt. Of course, I didn't know precisely how Dan or Vicky would react when they saw Laurence, but I was hoping that Dan might recognize Laurence from some of the images I'd sent over. That, or Vicky might be prompted to tell Dan the truth about her affair with Laurence. The whole thing was choreographed like a deliciously dark ballet, one in which Jen played a leading role.

It had all been done for her benefit, even though she would never know it. I realized that she would have to be at the center of it, she would have to see it all. But she would be forced to question what unfolded. On the surface the attack seemed like a straightforward case of jealousy, but of course the layers underneath were more complex and sinister. The messages tempted her into investigating the truth of the matter, they drew her into a web she could not escape. She would never know, however, how my revenge on Daniel and my manipulation of her came together like two strands of a dark melody in that one moment on the Heath. It was a case of the most perfect, most beautiful counterpoint.

Earlier that afternoon I'd laid out the plan as simply as possible, but of course I left out a few things. While it was true that we would only go ahead with it if we could be certain no one could see us—I didn't want any people who would witness us, or CCTV to capture our actions—I intended to add one extra element to the scheme, something that would guarantee I'd be able to control what happened next. I didn't want Jen to walk out of my life like all those others.

What she didn't know was that, just as she was about to murder Laurence, I would take out my phone and record everything. The camera would show her plunging the knife into his neck, drawing it across his throat, slashing into the arteries. It would document her wiping the knife with the tissues before strapping the weapon back onto her arm.

Obviously, I wouldn't dream of sharing the footage with anyone, I would tell her. This would be our little secret. No one need ever know. It would bind us together in a very special way.

81

JEN

I t's the thought of revenge that keeps me going. With each step, each *thwack* of my foot on the ground, I'm closer to killing her. The knife strapped to my arm rubs against my skin, chafing it raw, but I endure the pain. I know it will all be worth it. As we run, I'm tempted to stop, take out the knife and plunge it into her, slashing her across the throat just as she's shown me. But I know I have to wait until the right moment, until we reach a section of the Heath not covered by CCTV.

As I run I think of the irony of the situation. I was supposed to be here for Laurence—he had been the original target. At the end of our talk in the café earlier I'd asked him whether he still ran. Yes, he said; in fact, he was going to go for a jog on the Heath as soon as he finished work. Of course, I didn't tell him anything of my plan. As I sat there opposite him I felt ashamed of the overwhelming sense of misdirected hatred that I'd had toward him. I realized too that, at one point, I would have done it. I would have killed him. I would have enjoyed plunging the knife into him in revenge for what I thought he'd done to me, what I thought he'd done to Bex. At the end of our chat I stood up and took him in my arms. He was a little taken aback, but when he realized that all I wanted was a hug, he let himself be enveloped. I'd missed the muskiness of his smell. I whispered in his ear a quiet thank you for telling me the truth. I told him again that I believed him. I said that he was a good and kind man. And I asked him whether we could be friends. I had to choke back tears when he replied that yes, he'd like that very much.

When he left, I sat back down and opened the internet on my phone. I tapped in my own name, followed by the words "Basel" and "Switzerland." As I waited for the page to load I fantasized about what life would have been like if we'd made the move—I pictured us living in a charming flat in the old town and walking hand in hand by the Rhine. But none of that had happened, of course. After the split, and my breakdown, I had remained in London under the care of Bex, while Laurence had suggested one of his colleagues start up the new office in Switzerland. I'd heard he couldn't face it.

A few seconds later the headline "BEING JEN HUNTER: AM I HEADING FOR PASTURES NEW?" flashed up on my screen and I read the opening paragraph.

> James popped a big question last week. No, not that one! (Even though, if you're reading this, James, the answer would be a big "yes.") He asked me whether I'd like to move with him to Switzerland. The land of ski chalets, fluffy snow, snazzy watches, bank vaults hidden under pavements, and endless bowls of melted cheese. How could a girl refuse? He wants to open a branch of his architectural practice in Basel. I thought long and hard about it for all of two seconds before I screamed, "Of course!" After all, who wouldn't want to swap tramping across Hampstead Heath for hiking on the Hausstock?

I cringed when I read the words. No wonder I used to get a bagful of hate mail after the appearance of each column if that's the kind of crap I churned out. But then I felt so stupid. I'd been too blind to see what had been literally staring me in the face. My own words from "Being Jen Hunter" in which I'd talked about the prospect of a move to Switzerland. It was all there in black and white.

The only thing I'm worried about is Henry, my cat. But I can't leave her behind. She's coming with me.

Of course, there are things I'll miss. Cocktails at The Connaught. The delights of Net-A-Porter. And my girlfriends. I'll miss them the most. But we can catch up on FaceTime. And Basel's not that far from London. I can imagine jumping on a flight on a Friday night and spending the weekend with one of my best friends. As soon as we see each other, we'll start chatting like nothing has changed.

Before the column had come out I remember feeling reluctant to talk to Bex about my possible move to Switzerland. I was nervous about her reaction and hadn't been sure how to broach the subject with her. Finally, on the day the column was published, I couldn't avoid it anymore. I called her and asked whether she'd read my latest. She told me that she hadn't. I hesitated for a moment before I plucked up courage and told her of the plan. She went quiet, and I thought the line had gone dead. I said her name and asked her how she felt. She replied in an upbeat tone, said that it seemed like a great idea and that she couldn't wait to visit me in Basel. "It sounds wonderful, like a whole new life," she said.

The week after that my cat, Henry, disappeared. Then Bex had led me to the place where she'd died.

82
BEX

We've got him in sight. I look at Jen and nod, a sign that now would be a good time. We're making our way down a deserted dirt path that is about to disappear into a tangle of woodland, an area that I know is not covered by CCTV. I ask if she's ready. I scan the landscape again for other people, but there's no one around.

"I couldn't be more ready," she answers between panting breaths. "I feel like I've been waiting for this moment forever."

We gradually quicken our pace and then sprint toward him. Jen's right hand traces the outline of the knife under her long-sleeved top. My fingers dip into my pocket and caress the edge of my phone. I worry that the sound of our trainers scuffing the ground will alert him, but then I notice he's got his earbuds in. Jen pushes back her sleeve to reveal the knife strapped to her arm. She pulls apart the tape, wrenching it away from her skin, and takes out the blade. A ray from the setting sun catches the metal.

I look at Jen and have never felt more proud of her in my life. It's obvious she is going to do it. Her fingers grip the handle of the knife with a strength, a power that can only come from a deep-seated sense of anger. Her face is flushed from running, but perhaps she's also feeling what I've felt before: the ecstasy of anticipation before a murder is committed. I certainly felt it watching my mother and father in the kitchen that day. And

I felt it again just before the murder-suicide of Vicky and Daniel on the Heath, even though I had to witness it from a distance. Now I hope Jen is experiencing it too. The deliciousness of it is addictive.

Assuming that Jen will be concentrating on the job in hand—the murder of a man she hates—I take out my phone and turn on video mode. Laurence is so close to us now that we can hear him breathing. I'm certain these will be his last breaths. Soon he will be lying on the earth, bleeding out, and he'll be dead by the time another jogger or walker finds him. I lift the phone into the air and focus it on Laurence's skull. But as I do so I notice that Jen has stopped running. I turn back to see her standing as still as a statue, like some sculpture of a Greek goddess I'd once seen in a museum.

"What are you doing?" I hiss, as Laurence continues to run from us deeper into the wood. "We don't want him to get away."

"I need to ask you something," she says.

"What—now? Can't it wait until later?"

There's an oddness about her, and her eyes are shining even brighter than before. I turn around to see Laurence a good twenty paces in front of us.

"We've got time to catch him up—but not much," I say. "As soon as he comes out of the woods he'll be back in a stretch covered by the cameras. Jen?"

She takes a step toward me. "Was it you?"

"What? What are you talking about?"

"Was it you who sent in those copies of my parents' death certificates to the newspaper? Was it you who got me sacked?"

"Look—I don't know what you're talking about."

"Don't lie to me."

"Jen—calm down. We've talked about this—about your delusions. Your illness. You know you haven't been well. You're having another one of your episodes."

"Stop fucking with me!" she spits as she steps even closer, pointing the knife in my face.

"Jen—you're scaring me now. I thought we'd got everything straight. It's Laurence who's done all of this. He's the one who sent those certificates to the paper."

"I don't believe you. It's been you all along, hasn't it?" She raises the knife up to my face. "From the very beginning. The messages. The attack on the Heath. The mask."

I open my mouth to deny it all when I feel the point of the blade press on my neck.

"For fuck's sake, Jen, you need to—"

"No! You need to tell me the truth. Or I'll slit your throat. You taught me how to do it, remember?"

I look around me. Laurence has gone now, but I think I can hear the sound of someone running in the distance. Perhaps if I hold out long enough a jogger might come to my aid.

I speak as gently as possible, almost as if I'm reading a lullaby to a baby. "I know you've been confused. You've been ill—you know that. If it hadn't been for me you would—you would have been locked up—sectioned. Don't you remember how I looked after you? After you lost your job? After Laurence left you? I was there for you."

She can't deny this isn't true and, for a moment, I think I've got through to her. She's looking dazed, as though she's being hypnotized.

"You know I'd never hurt you. We're best friends, we always have been. We always will be."

But then something changes in her eyes, as if she's pulled herself out of a trance. "And what about Henry?"

"Who?"

"Henrietta. My cat."

"What about her?"

"She didn't get killed by a fox, did she? It was you."

The blade presses down hard on my skin. Fuck. It's cutting into me, drawing blood.

"I just want the truth, Bex. That's all. Just tell me the truth."

Jen turns the knife on its side so it's ready to slash into my throat. One swipe and I'm dead. I don't know what to do, what to say. For once, I'm lost for words.

83
JEN

"Tell me!"

Bex is looking frightened now. And so she should be. Laurence has disappeared out of sight completely and we're standing on a stretch of the Heath not covered by security cameras. With one quick cut Bex would be dead. But before I do that I want some answers.

"Just fucking tell me!" I repeat.

"Okay . . . But listen, before you do anything . . . reckless, you have to know that it was all done in your best interests. She was old, past her prime."

I do everything in my power to stop myself from killing her there and then. I need more from her. But I know I don't have that much time. I feel the questions burning my mouth.

"And the death certificates?"

"Yes."

Her voice is so quiet I can barely hear it.

"What did you say?" I press the knife down and cut into her skin.

"It was me. I sent them in to the paper." Her voice rises in pitch as she begins to panic even more. "But it was because I knew you wouldn't be happy—you wouldn't be happy . . . in Switzerland."

So it was all to do with me leaving.

"Before you called me, I'd read your column. About your decision to move to Basel with James—I mean Laurence. I didn't want you to go. I couldn't imagine a life without you."

"So you thought the best thing for me was to get me sacked?"

"You were always complaining about the column, how you felt trapped by it. How it ruined your friendships. How it put pressure on your relationships. I thought you could do . . . better."

"Better?"

"You're such a brilliant writer, Jen. I thought you could use that time to write that novel you were always going on about."

"Didn't you think about how the loss of that job—and the way I lost that job—would affect me? I had a nervous fucking breakdown, if you don't remember."

"But I was there, wasn't I? It wasn't too bad, just the two of us. It was like the old days."

"For God's sake, Bex. Can't you hear what you're saying?"

"But we were happy then. And we'll be happy in the future. Laurence wasn't right for you. He never was. He didn't support you like I did. I know you thought that there was a hope of a second chance, but . . . I was doing you a favor."

"And Penelope?"

"What about her?"

"What were you going to do to her?"

She doesn't answer me. I look down at her shaking hands. She's still clutching her iPhone. It's recording everything. I wrench the phone from her.

"And what do you think you're doing with this?"

"Nothing. I guess it must have just switched itself on."

I don't believe her. My guess is that she's going to use it for something. What? Was she going to blackmail me into staying with her? What lengths would she go to in order to try to control me?

Images from our friendship flash through my mind. The first day in halls. How she took me under her wing. How she remolded me. How she said she wanted to protect me. I remember how angry she'd been when I wrote about her in that student newspaper all those years ago. At the time I mistook her reaction as a simple desire for privacy, but now I realize that she didn't want anyone to go digging into her past. I didn't question it at the time. How malleable I had been. Had she always sensed that I could be manipulated like this? What was wrong with me? How long had she been planning her sick form of mind control? How else could you describe it? I'd come so close to doing it—to killing Laurence. But what was going on in her fucked-up brain?

With my free hand, I switch off the video and open up her Twitter account, looking for any signs of @WatchingYouJenHunter and those other accounts. But there's nothing. I put the phone in my pocket, out of her reach, but continue to press the knife down hard on her neck.

"And the messages?" She doesn't respond. "The messages?" I push the knife deeper into her skin.

"That—that really hurts." She takes a quick breath. "I—I used a different phone to send them."

"So I'm guessing you did everything. You were the one wearing that mask when you attacked me on the Heath. And then you placed it in Laurence's bathroom cupboard so that I'd find it there. All because you—you wanted me to feel so much hatred of him that I'd kill him."

She can't speak now.

"And the murder-suicide on Kite Hill? I can hardly bear to ask you. You did all of this . . . for what? So that I'd still *like* you?"

"You—you don't understand," she says, panic in her voice.

"But . . . *this?*"

"What other option did I have?" She pronounces the words with a normality that only emphasizes her twisted reasoning, as if she's explaining why she bought a jar of instant because the shop had run out of ground coffee. "I couldn't let you go to Switzerland. I couldn't . . ."

"But didn't you have any feelings for that poor girl? For Vicky?"

"She was collateral damage."

"What?"

"It was Daniel I hated. Because he left me."

So she had lied about that too—she was the one who had been rejected. Her eyes are full of anger.

"People shouldn't leave me." She spits out the words as if there's poison in her mouth.

It was all beginning to make some kind of sense.

"I loved him, once. He was everything to me. But then he said he'd found somebody else. I had to deal with him. I pretended to be his friend. It was a long game. But all the time I hated him."

"And Laurence? He didn't rape you, did he?"

"He used me," she says, her accent taking on more of an Essex twang. "Fucked me and then wanted to get rid of me. But then he wanted to take you away, out of the country. I couldn't let him do that. Even after I thought he was out of the picture, after everything I'd done with the death certificates, after you'd lost your job, after you'd split up, there was the prospect that you'd get back together. You were going to have lunch together. You seemed excited at the idea of seeing him. I couldn't risk that. It was the natural thing to do. I could get rid of them all. So I could keep you close."

I look at her as if seeing her for the first time. Her proximity to me—the sight of her—disgusts me. I feel my mind splintering apart again as I'm forced to reassess everything I think I've known about her.

"And that scene at Colchester station—you staged that just for my benefit?"

She doesn't answer the question. "It's always been the same," she continues. "People wanting to leave me, get rid of me. First my mum. She tried to abort me. But I taught her—and Dad—a lesson, all right."

The confession about her mother turns my insides. I think about the newspaper cutting and wonder what part she had played in the deaths of her birth parents. Bile rises in my throat, but I swallow it down, the liquid burning the back of my throat, my stomach.

"Then Alice." She whispers the name so softly I can hardly hear her.

It means nothing to me. "What? Who's Alice?"

"The girl across the road from us. He wouldn't let me play with her. She could have been my friend. Dad dragged me away from her house. It could have been different."

She isn't making any sense now. I spool through what she's just told me in a bid to try to understand. There are so many fragments that it's difficult to assemble them in my mind, like trying to glue together the shards of a broken mirror.

"So you thought that by making me . . . making me kill Laurence, you'd what—have me with you forever?" The thought of it almost makes me gag. "The truth is, you make me sick."

"Don't say that, Jen. You don't mean it. We've always been close. We're like sis—"

"We're nothing like sisters. In fact, it would have been better if you'd never been born."

The fury that burns in her eyes frightens me, but I force myself to continue.

"In fact, your mother should have got rid of you. She should have—"

"Shut up!" she screams.

Just then I hear something—someone—nearby. I turn my head away from her and in that moment Bex takes advantage of the diversion.

She brings up her leg and knees me in the stomach.

I feel the air rush out of my lungs.

She grabs my hand and presses down on my wrist, twisting it out of shape.

I try to keep hold of the knife, but the pain is too much.

The bones in my hand feel like they're breaking.

I let the knife drop, and hear it smash onto the ground, but, just before Bex bends down to grab it, the sound of running echoes around me.

There's a witness coming to Bex's aid.

They'll see the scene in front of them—Bex's injuries—and assume that I'm the violent one. I'm the one who should be locked up. Bex will tell the police about my history of mental illness, all of which can be checked out. I will be sentenced, and Bex will be free to carry on, perhaps even fixing her sights on a series of new, unsuspecting victims.

As I stumble backward I see a woman in gray jogging gear rush between us. I know her, but I don't understand what she's doing here. I do a double take. It's Julia Jones. She snatches up the knife.

"Thank God you arrived when you did," gasps Bex, now kneeling on the earth. "Can you call the police? I was being attacked . . . you must have seen what she was doing."

Julia looks from Bex to me and back to Bex again. "What the fuck are you waiting for?" shouts Bex. "Can't you hear what I'm saying? Look at me—look at my neck." She gestures to the cuts I made, shows her the blood oozing out of the surface wounds. "Look at what she did to me!"

Julia adjusts her fingers around the knife and in a flash, before either Bex or I know what is happening, she's brought it down to Bex's level. She swipes it across her neck, cutting deep into her skin. Julia stands back as the blood spills out of her. Bex opens her mouth to scream, but she finds she can't make a sound. Her eyes stretch wide. I'm back where I started, witnessing Vicky's terrible death and Dan's suicide on Parliament Hill Fields.

I think I must be hallucinating. That Julia is a figment of my imagination, some kind of specter conjured by my subconscious as a way to protect myself and my sanity from what I've just done. I must have killed Bex myself and this . . . all this is a kind of living nightmare. I force myself to blink, take some deep breaths. I turn away from the scene, look across the empty Heath, focus and refocus on trees, grass, the sky, the clouds in the distance. But when I turn back Bex is dying, and Julia is watching her die.

I can't understand it. I can't take it in. I don't know what to do. Before I open my mouth to ask her the question—why?—she stops me with one word.

"Harry."

84

JEN

We're standing at the top of Kite Hill, our figures silhouetted in front of the London skyline. Me, Jamie Blackwood and his Weimaraner, Ayesha Ahmed, Steven Walker, and Julia Jones. Once strangers, we've returned to the spot on Parliament Hill Fields where we all met. Each of us has a particular memory of that day, and what we witnessed will shape us for the rest of our lives. Penelope is sitting on a bench reading a newspaper, waiting for the shoot to finish so she can take me out to lunch to apologize again. I'm waiting for the moment when she turns the page to read a short news item about the discovery of an unidentified woman's body on the Heath. I wonder what she'll think when she learns the news.

Rory, the photographer, shouts out various requests: could Jamie come to the front, with his dog? Yes, perhaps he could kneel in the middle of the group? Could Julia please turn her head so she's looking directly into the camera instead of gazing into the distance? And could Jen not look quite so nervous?

"Don't be so worried—it will all be over soon, I promise!" jokes Rory.

Of course, he can't guess what's going through my mind, or what Julia is thinking. He hasn't a clue about what happened two days ago. I imagine him studying us through his lens, examining our faces, our faults. He wants to get the best photo to accompany my piece, but the resulting image will only tell one story, and a superficial one at that.

From simply looking at us you'd never guess what lies beneath. Jamie appears as glossy as ever, but he's just broken up with the man he was going to marry, partly because he's in love with a ghost. Steven's youth, his vibrancy, serves as a protective sheen—no one would surmise that he'd witnessed three violent deaths. Ayesha, dressed in a suit that must have cost her between £1,000 and £2,000, looks every inch the professional doctor she is—and yet both Penelope and I know something about her that would ruin her reputation. And Julia? I remember her daughter's words to me about how Julia shielded herself by wearing a disguise of toughness; underneath that shell was insecurity, vulnerability, pain, and an increased dependency on alcohol. No one would know she had recently committed a murder.

The pain in my wrist is a tangible reminder of what happened. It didn't take long for Bex to die. But still, her death was a horrible one. Painful. Ugly. I thought I should have felt some sympathy for her as she lay on the ground, a hand reaching out to me, her lips mouthing my name in a silent goodbye. But I felt nothing for her.

I had considered trying to explain my actions to Julia—after all, she must have seen me press that knife to Bex's throat—but I knew I didn't have time. I was conscious that we needed to act fast before we were discovered by a random pedestrian or runner. Luckily, Bex—in her sick way—had thought of everything. From her backpack I took out a new top and changed into it, pushing the old one, covered with drops of Bex's blood, back into the bag. Julia pulled on the replacement top that Bex had stashed away for herself.

"Harry," Julia had said.

Her son. But what had he to do with Bex?

"She was the one who had gone on holiday with him—in India. I saw her that day—on the Heath. Do you remember that I was sick—on the grass? Everyone must have thought I was vomiting because of the shock—after witnessing the murder, the suicide. That hardly helped, of course. But really it was because I saw her. Soon after the police arrived, she came to help you, and I realized then that she was your friend. I recognized her from some of the photos that Harry had sent me. To begin with I tried to convince myself it couldn't be her. But I kept looking at the photos, and the more I looked at them the more I knew. It *was* her. She was older, naturally, and a little dowdier than she'd been in 2000 when . . ."

I remembered with a sickening realization that this was the year that Bex had traveled around the world. When she'd returned I'd always thought it odd that she never liked to talk about her experiences. She didn't have any photographs either—she'd told me that her camera and all her film had been stolen. "I suppose that's one of the reasons why I agreed to do the interview with you. I knew you were friends. I thought you might lead me to her. And you did. I started to follow her from her flat. I watched her as she walked or ran across the Heath. That was why I was late to do the interview at Penelope's house on Monday. On more than one occasion I did notice that . . . that it seemed as though she was shadowing you. I don't know what she had planned, but it seems—"

"I'll tell you everything later."

"You see, I suspected that she might be dangerous. And then I heard you and Penelope having that heated discussion about Bex. As you argued, one of you dropped a couple of sheets of paper, which I read on the way back up to the study. They—along with what Penelope said—confirmed my suspicions about Bex. Anyway, I followed you both here today. I don't know what I thought I'd do to her if I came across her. But when I saw you, when I saw that knife on the ground. I'm sure she would have picked it up and . . ."

"But what—what had she done to Harry to make you want to—"

"Harry wrote me a series of letters, some of which I only got . . ." Her voice cracked before she sniffed back the emotion and continued, ". . . after his death. He wanted to be a writer, you see, and thought that the writing of letters back home would be a good discipline. He talked to me about this girl who had joined him on his travels. I'm not sure how they met. In one of the hostels out there, I think. He was really keen on her at first, he said. In one of the letters he enclosed a photo—Rebecca, she was called.

Nice-looking young woman with dark hair, English graduate. I never knew her surname, so I was unable to find her. Of course, this was in the days before I was an MP—I was still in social work—so I had significantly less clout."

I wiped the knife clean on a couple of tissues before strapping it back under my top. I checked Julia again for any signs of blood, dabbed her face with another tissue, and put everything back in the bag, all of which I planned on disposing of later. As I worked, Julia continued to tell me about the past. "The letters seemed to get more desperate as they went on. He was at the end of his tether with this girl. He wanted to end it. He'd thought the relationship was just a bit of fun, a holiday romance. But she thought it had been much more serious. And she threatened to kill herself if he finished with her. I was desperately worried about him and, in our last telephone conversation, I told him to come home. But he didn't listen. I even said that I'd fly out there and bring him back. But . . . I was too late. I didn't hear from him. I rang the hostel, but they said that he'd left. They didn't know where he'd gone to. Then, one night, I got a call from the British High Commission in India to tell me that a body had been found at the bottom of a gorge. There had been a terrible accident. He'd been trekking in the Hampta Pass and it seems he must have slipped, fallen to his death. But then, a few weeks later, I got his last letter . . ."

I knew what she was going to say next. She swallowed hard as she remembered its contents.

"He wrote about how Rebecca's behavior was getting more and more unpredictable. He was worried about his own safety. She now said that she would kill him if he left her. She started to follow him everywhere, turning up at bars and different hostels. He told me that in order to try to get rid of her he was going to trek the Hampta Pass by himself. That's the last thing I heard from him."

"So you think . . . ?"

"Yes—it was her. I'm sure of it."

She looked down at the body and then at me. The reality of the situation suddenly hit her. She had actually killed someone. "What will happen now? To my job? My husband. My daughter. What will Louisa think of me? Shit. Will you call the police?"

I shook my head. A cold breeze was blowing in from the east and I could feel a light drizzle on my face.

"Let's start running, but in separate directions," I said. "You go home. I'll phone you. Don't say anything about this, about what happened—to anyone. Do you understand?"

"Okay, but—" Her tough facade crumbled and she was finding it hard to hold herself together.

"Don't worry," I added. "I won't tell a soul."

◆

On Kite Hill the shoot is coming to a close. After posing for what seems like the best part of an hour I'm exhausted from trying to appear normal. The group begins to split apart, but none of us move that far from the spot. We're all tied to the viewing point on Parliament Hill Fields, as if each of us understands that a part of us has died here, and we don't want to stray in case we lose something more of ourselves. But the fact of the matter is we're lost already. This place will continue to haunt our dreams, our nightmares. Especially for me, for Julia.

I've felt Julia's eyes on me throughout the photo shoot and I know she wants to talk to me. But now is not the time, not the place. We had a brief chat on the phone last night when I reassured her that she would not be linked to the crime. When the police put out a request for information, she was to contact her local force and tell them that she'd been out jogging nearby at that time, but she had not seen the victim; neither had she come across anything suspicious.

When the police come to question me in detail, as I'm sure they would, I would tell them how Bex and I had started our jog together, but as she was a much more experienced runner—a fact that could be verified—she had sprinted on ahead.

We'd been due to meet up at the flat after the run. When she hadn't returned by ten o'clock I'd repeatedly called her mobile (which I'd already destroyed by that point, along with all the other evidence) and then reported her missing. Bex's body had been discovered the next morning by a dog walker.

I'm struck by the irony of the situation: Bex had tried to manipulate a group of people from her past to come together on that bloody Valentine's Day. But it was the one person from her past, Julia—whom she never expected to be there on Hampstead Heath—who brought about her own downfall.

Penelope lifts a hand in the air and waves me over. She wants me to sit by her. As I approach I can see the newspaper is closed on her lap. She doesn't say anything, but I can tell she's read the story about the discovery of a body. She narrows her eyes ever so slightly as she looks at me. She *knows*.

The question is: will she ever tell?

ACKNOWLEDGMENTS

Writing a novel is a mostly a solitary activity, but the truth is that it couldn't be done without a whole team of people.

Thank you to everyone at Aitken Alexander and in particular my fabulous agent and friend, Clare Alexander. She took a chance on me more than twenty years ago and I'll be forever grateful to her. A huge thank you to Lesley Thorne, Lisa Baker, and everyone in the foreign rights department, Amy St Johnston, Jazz Adamson, and Cony and Joaquim Fernandes.

A big, big thank you to my editor and fellow author, Phoebe Morgan, for making this book so much better than it once was. You are such an inspiration! I'd also like to thank Charlotte Webb for copyediting, Claire Ward for design, assistant editor Sophie Churcher, and everyone at HarperCollins.

Thanks, too, must go to Lisa Cutts, the crime novelist and detective constable, who provided me with some expert information and advice about certain aspects of police procedure. I'd also like to thank Dr. Susan Shaw, consultant psychiatrist and friend, who read the book in manuscript form and provided some useful feedback.

Here's to everyone close to me: my parents, all my friends who have walked through the streets of north London and trudged across Hampstead Heath with me over the years, and to one in particular: Marcus Field.